For Gina

how to *murder* a man

CARLO GÉBLER

Little, Brown and Company

A *Little, Brown* Book

First published in Great Britain by Little, Brown and
Company 1998

A CIP catalogue record for this book is available from
the British Library.

ISBN 0 316 64389 0

Printed and bound in Great Britain by
Clays Ltd, St Ives plc

Little, Brown and Company (UK)
Brettenham House
Lancaster Place
London WC2E 7EN

how to *murder* a man

Also by Carlo Gébler

FICTION
The Eleventh Summer
August in July
Work and Play
Malachy and his Family
Life of a Drum
The Cure

NON-FICTION
Driving Through Cuba
The Glass Curtain

author's note

In 1851, the Marquess of Bath appointed William Steuart Trench as his agent in Ireland. Trench went to live on his employer's estate outside Carrickmacross, Co. Monaghan. Within months of his arrival a group of local tenants sentenced Trench to death. These men were all members of an agrarian secret society known as the Ribbonmen, and they made numerous attempts to kill the agent.

Trench described some of these experiences in his memoirs, *Realities of Irish Life*, and this work formed the starting point for this novel. I have incorporated some of the events that Trench described in my narrative, but I have also invented a great deal. This is a work of imagination, not a reworking of Trench's fascinating memoir.

I gratefully acknowledge the financial support of the Arts Council/An Chomhairle Ealaíon, and the Arts Council of Northern Ireland.

I would like to thank William Vaughan for his encyclopedic advice on the Ulster custom of tenant right, as well as Irish agriculture in the nineteenth century, and Gordon Johnson for sharing his knowledge of nineteenth-century firearms.

All mistakes, of course, are my own.

The condition of man . . . is a condition of war of everyone against everyone.

Leviathan, Thomas Hobbes

"Tenant right was really an immemorial custom prevailing in a great portion of Ireland, but unrecognised in courts of law, or statute books, under which the ordinary tenant at will has acquired the right of selling the succession to his holding."

From a speech by T. Hughes to the House of Commons, reported in the *Morning Star*, 13 March 1868

chapter one

All histories are really murder stories. Sometimes they are epic and there are generals, and battlefields, and regiments of cavalry and foot, and sometimes they are just small, domestic, and there are pairs of men and alleyways and pistols in the back pocket. Either way, measurement of victory is always the same: he who murders most, wins.

Micky Laffin sat in a car with his friend McGuinness, the publican. The driver, sitting up on the seat behind the pony with the reins firmly in his hands, was Joseph O'Duffy. Micky and his friend McGuinness had left the courthouse in Monaghan town an hour earlier. Now they were coming along a road which cut through a bog. It was evening.

The road dropped and passed along a level stretch. The cuttings here had been exhausted forty years earlier, since when a forest of alder trees had sprung up.

Between the trees there were bog holes and old turf workings and over time these had filled with rainwater. The water was black and stagnant and shone like tar. When an animal fell into one of these, as happened from time to time, it could never get out because the soft peaty edges were too steep and afforded no grip. These unlucky animals would swim for a while and then tire and then drown, and then their swollen furry bodies would float in the pools of dark water, buzzing with flies, crawling with lice, until finally the rotten flesh fell away and the skeleton floated down and settled, several feet below, in mud that was thick as treacle and sticky as glue.

Some years earlier two small children had drowned in a cutting – they were found after a couple of hours, and then two unhappy lovers had filled their pockets with stones, tied themselves wrist to wrist and flung themselves into a hole in the middle of the forest. They were not found for a week, by which time eels had eaten their faces.

After these deaths, rumours began to circulate. Travellers along the road at night reported seeing the spirits of the dead children flitting through the trees, small phosphorescent shapes that wailed and wept. There were also accounts of terrible cries coming from the spot where the lovers had killed themselves.

As a result local people stopped hunting in the forest and cutting trees for fuel; it was believed that to bring anything from this place into the home would bring bad luck on the householder. The area was more and more neglected until eventually even the proper name for the district fell into disuse, and it became known instead as simply "the Bad Place".

The car rattled on. Micky raised his gaze from the screen of alders that flashed past and the pools of black water that he could glimpse between them, to the hills behind where there was still plenty of good bog. This was where the local men with turbary rights cut their turf nowadays.

Micky saw several trenches in the distance. They were the colour of chocolate. Men cut turf from these trenches, laid out the clods to dry in the sun, and then piled the clods when they were dry into heaps, or stoops. Micky saw row upon row of these now. They reminded him of the piles of stones that sometimes marked ancient graves.

Micky scanned the distant hillsides expecting to see men at work. The evening was warm and dry, perfect for this type of labour, but to his surprise he could see no one.

Now he wondered, in an idle way, if perhaps everyone who had been cutting turf an hour or two earlier had been told to clear off. He could easily imagine this and the thought troubled him.

Micky turned round in his seat and looked ahead. The car came out of the forest and on to open road. There was treeless old bog on either side. Forty yards ahead, the road bent to the right at ninety degrees. Behind the bend there was a grey stone wall, beyond which rose a meadow. The road, after bending to the right, climbed upwards through this pasture-land to a narrow passage at the top. But before they got there they had to pass the wall. Suddenly, Micky had an intuition that something was wrong.

The car approached the corner. The driver, O'Duffy, pulled on the reins and called, "Whoa!" The pony slowed. It was a savage corner which had to be negotiated with care. Micky decided to tell O'Duffy to speed up as soon as the car reached the straighter road on the far side.

The car curled into the corner and a voice cried out from beyond the wall, "McGuinness." The publican heard his name and turned without thinking. At the same moment the muzzle of a brass blunderbuss appeared. It looked like the end of a trumpet. It was three feet away from the publican's head.

There was a puff of grey smoke and a dull, muted bang. In the open air a gun makes a quiet noise that suggests it is ineffectual and even harmless. Micky had noticed this before and he knew it was a lie. He knew guns were very effective, and very harmful.

"You were warned," the voice shouted.

The next second Micky heard McGuinness scream. He had not been hit by a ball but by a mixture of metals. Nails and screws, tangles of wire and pieces of tin, had cut every inch of his face. They had cut his nose, his eyelids, his chin. The nails had gone into his mouth, cut his tongue, his gums, his palate, scoring terrible gouges in the soft wet flesh. The screws had gone up his nose, sliced the septum and passed on into his sinuses and cheekbones. The pieces of wire had passed into his ears and ripped through the stretched eardrums. The tangles of tin had run through his hair like a steel comb and ripped the scalp away. There were needles in his eyes. Blood sprang out everywhere. McGuinness threw his hands to face.

"We told you this would happen but you didn't listen to the Lodge," the voice shouted behind the wall.

McGuinness cried, "My eyes, my eyes."

The driver, O'Duffy, screamed "Stop!" at the pony and pulled frantically on the reins. McGuinness fell backwards. Micky caught him on his lap.

Behind the car four men, one of them carrying the blunderbuss, had jumped over the wall and were running across the road. They all wore flour sacks over their faces, eye-holes and breathing-holes cut in the material.

Micky saw the men as he kicked open the door at the back. O'Duffy had jumped down from the seat at the front and run round.

O'Duffy grabbed the injured man by the shoulders and dragged him through the door. The heels of McGuinness's boots clattered on the road. O'Duffy lowered him down.

The assailants had crossed the road now. They leaped across a ditch and on to the old bog.

Micky leaped out of the car and knelt down. He pulled his handkerchief from his pocket and put it across the hurt man's face. The handkerchief was white and the blood came through the fabric. The blood was warm and thick.

The assailants ran along the far side of the ditch. They were heading for the forest of alders.

Micky stood and pulled a pistol from his pocket. He had loaded it that morning, compacting the charge into the breech with a ramrod, wrapping the ball in a kidskin patch, and pushing it home. Everything in the barrel was thumb tight. He cocked the hammer.

Micky ran down the road and jumped across the ditch. The

brown land on the other side was springy beneath his feet. There was a small path worn in the earth here. It was a brown, wiggling vein. He ran along the path through scrub and coarse grass and green fern. The rich smell of the fern was in the air.

After a few yards, Micky felt his jacket pinching him under his arms. He undid the buttons as he ran, pulled it off, and threw it down.

The men, the assailants, were nearing the edge of the alders. Three of them were running fast. The fourth man was lagging behind.

Micky was hurting at the top of his lungs; he was forty-five and it was painful to run like this. Beads of sweat had sprung up on his forehead and now one trickled down and ran into his right eye. The salt was stinging and he blinked. With his thumb he checked the hammer was in the firing position. One squeeze of the trigger would bring it down on the percussion cap; a spark would jump into the breech; the charge would explode and the ball would fly forward.

The three front runners reached the edge of the forest and disappeared. The last man, the one who ran with a very slight limp, was pulling at his neck. As he got to the edge of the trees, something came away in his hand and caught on a branch. Micky stopped, pointed the gun and pulled the trigger. The ball was wide and there was a tiny retort as it buried itself in a tree. The man heard the noise of the gun and looked back at Micky. The man shook his head. Because of the flour sack that he was wearing, Micky had the impression that it was a skull and not a man who was staring at him.

Now the man bowed towards Micky, bending from the waist and throwing his hand forward with excessive mock subservience. Micky considered throwing the gun at the man but he was never going to hit him at thirty yards. The man gave a farewell wave and vanished into the trees.

Micky went forward. At the edge of the forest he stopped and peered ahead. There were alder trees everywhere growing at weird angles from the spongy ground. Close to him, the trunks of the trees were white and grey, and the leaves were olive-green and silver. Further into the forest, the different colours became less distinguishable as there was less light. Further away again there was no colour, and everything in the forest was almost black.

He looked along the edge of the forest, searching for flattened undergrowth, or broken branches. He saw nothing. Now he listened for the sound of a branch snapping, or a human cry. All he heard was birdsong, the wind, and finally the rustle of his shirt and the sound of his own breathing as his chest flew up and down. The men had vanished. The forest had opened its mouth and swallowed them down.

He looked sideways and saw what had come off the neck of the last man. It hung on a branch. It was a blue, spotted neckerchief, popularly known as a belcher after the well-known English boxer. Micky took it down and smelt it. He got a whiff of tobacco and male sweat. It was the only sign that anyone had been there.

Micky turned and ran back to the car, collecting his jacket on the way. He found O'Duffy sitting on the wall, sniffling. His friend McGuinness lay on the ground, blood on the road around him.

McGuinness, he saw, was not moving. Nor was he breathing. He realised his friend McGuinness, the publican, was dead because he had taken over a pub that some other men had decided should be theirs. The other men were there first, they said, and they wanted their man in the premises, not McGuinness. The men warned McGuinness off but he would not budge. He began legal proceedings against the other party. This was why he had been in the courthouse in Monaghan that day. McGuinness had won too, not that it did him any good. They had killed him and now he would never take possession of old Molly Day's public house. It would go to the other man.

Micky walked to the place where the blunderbuss had appeared and looked over the wall. The grass on the other side was flat. The assailants had trampled it down while they had waited there. Mickey saw two white clay pipes on the ground.

CARLO GÉBLER

He climbed over and picked up the pipes. The bowls were still warm and he tapped them against the wall. A mixture of ash and tobacco shreds and a few red embers tumbled out. Micky took the neckerchief out of his pocket and carefully wrapped up the pipes in it.

It was not until Thomas French came six years later, that Micky saw there was something to learn from all of this.

chapter two

The Dublin street was quite silent. It felt like a stage at the moment just after the curtain parts and before the first actor speaks. Thomas French stopped at the gate and looked over the silver points of the railings at the semi-detached red-brick house behind; the house had a half basement, a ground floor and first floor, window frames painted with white paint that had cracked, and heavy drape curtains behind the glass. There was a smell of burnt potato coming from somewhere.

Thomas took the letter out of his pocket and checked the address at the top. Ivy House, he read. It was the same as the name on the brass plaque attached to the railings and this was puzzling: Thomas had expected something bigger, he had expected a house that stood in its own grounds. Also, there wasn't a single leaf of ivy in sight.

He went through the gate and began to cross the gravel towards the suburban house. The name, Ivy House, had been taken, Thomas assumed, because it was much better than being just a number on a street of other numbers.

Thomas climbed the granite steps. Silvery speckles flashed in the stone. His wife, Helena, believed that one day everyone would live in the city in a house with a number, instead of in the country in a house that either had a name, or was known by the name of the occupants. Thomas did not care for this future but he suspected Helena was right, as usual.

The door in front of him was black with a brass knocker in the middle. The knocker was in the shape of a dolphin; the tail was the hinge, and it was the head that produced the knock. He lifted the knocker and brought it down on the pad three times.

He turned and looked back into the street. On the far side stood a row of semi-detached red-brick houses identical to the houses on his side. A gigantic mirror, he thought, placed along the middle of the road would have produced an almost identical picture to what he was now seeing.

Through the door Thomas heard the sound of footsteps approaching. A moment later the door scraped back. He found himself looking at the maid. She was a young girl, about eighteen years old, he guessed, with a square face and prominent, very dark eyes that bulged out.

"Yes, good afternoon," she said.

Whenever he met a new person, Thomas would always ask himself the same question: if the person was an animal, what animal would they be? It had started as a game between Helena and himself during their honeymoon. Over the years, they had found that more often than not they would choose the same animal.

"I am Thomas French," he said. "I have an appointment with Mrs Beaton at four o'clock. I might be a little early."

The protruding eyes, the shape of her face. He didn't have to think. It was obvious. She was a seal.

"Come on in," she said. Her accent was northern, Ulster. She was from Beatonboro' he assumed, and no doubt, as was usually the case with servants from the home estate, she always praised her employer in front of visitors. She pulled the door back and he stepped into the hall.

"Mrs Beaton's in the drawing room," said the maid.

To his left was a hideous heavy wooden table, figures and fruits carved into the legs. Screwed on the wall above was a large gilt mirror, the glass spotted with freckles. He noticed a sewing basket on the floor with threadbare stockings and several shabby but unrecognisable oddments bundled up in it.

The maid was behind him still, closing the front door. He glanced slyly up the stairs. On the rounded edges of the steps the carpet was worn away and the sack-coloured backing showed through. The wallpaper was stained along a line that ran up the wall in parallel to the banister. One of the panes of glass in the window on the return was missing and cardboard was nailed up in its place.

"In here, Mr French," said the maid. She passed him and moved ahead to the door on his right.

While the maid knocked and waited, he glanced into the back hall. It was a gloomy place with a grandfather clock, dark brown wood the colour of sherry, two dangling brass weights and a swinging pendulum, and a white moon clock face by which he saw that he was a few minutes early. Yet the maid was opening the door, and quickly shifting from the hall to the doorway, he had a vague sense of Mrs Beaton, sitting in the room beyond. Employer was waiting for the employee. Mr Hazzard had warned it would be like this.

Thomas went through the door and found himself in a room with green wallpaper and a large black fireplace. Mrs Beaton sat on a low chair covered with red velvet. She stood and extended a hand.

"Mr French," she said.

The door closed behind him smartly.

"Won't you please sit down?"

She asked about his journey from Cork to Dublin, if it been easy to get from Kingsbridge station to her house, if the directions she had given him were helpful. He answered these questions politely and studied her face. Her skin was slightly golden. There was a net stretched over her hair at the back but some strands had come free and hung down on either side of her face. The woman's features were sharp but not unpleasant. So what animal was she, then? he wondered. None sprang immediately to mind, which was odd. After years of this, he usually had it in seconds.

There was a moment or two of silence; then suddenly he became aware that she was looking intently at him and was about to speak. He assumed that the informalities were over and the serious business of the interview was about to begin.

"Are you a good land agent?" she said.

He looked at her for a moment, puzzled. "Surely you've had the letters with the details of my record, haven't you?" He circled his hand in the air. This was perplexing. "There must be a letter from my current employer, Mr Hazzard, and another letter from my previous employer, Mr Williamson," he continued.

"Oh, yes," she said. She was leaning back in her chair, head against the rim, looking down her nose at him. "But are you, in your opinion, good, or just all right, or even bad?"

It occurred to him right then what animal she was; why had it taken so long? The point at the end of her chin, the shape of her eyes, the combination of languor and vitality — she was a vixen.

"Well," she continued, "surely you must have some idea?"

He realised he was biting the dead skin at the side of his right thumbnail. He lowered his hand slowly, laid it on his knee, laid the other hand on top of it. He reconsidered her question, coughed and spoke.

"I'm not anything, really," he said, playing for time.

"Oh, come on. Are you a good land agent or not?" she asked. "That's all, it's a simple question."

Perhaps someone had told her that he was vain or arrogant, and her question was designed to find out if this was true. Pondering this, however, he thought it was doubtful that either Mr Hazzard or Mr Williamson would have said anything as harsh. Both men, albeit reluctantly, had accepted

Thomas's explanation for his leaving them; he never stayed with an employer longer than five years, otherwise he grew stale. He got estates back on their feet – he was good at that – and then he went elsewhere.

However, it now occurred to him that perhaps that had irked only nothing had been said. Maybe they had thought his five years programme suggested someone with a very high opinion of himself.

Well, there was only one way out of this: he would have to brazen it out. She would just have to take him or leave him as she found him. And if she didn't like him – well, there would be plenty of other places to go. The country was crying out for agents.

"Yes," he said. "If you must know, then I am, I am a good agent," and as he heard the words, in his own voice, booming out of his mouth and filling the room, he was again struck by how bizarre Mrs Beaton's question was. Are you good? Yes, of course he was good. What other explanation was there for his being in continuous employment since leaving Trinity, twenty-eight years before?

"That's excellent because I need a good land agent," she said.

"Why?" he asked abruptly.

"What do you know about me?"

"Almost nothing."

"My husband has been dead for eight years."

"I know."

"So you knew that then?"

"Your husband was killed on a train," he said. He had read about it at the time. Her husband was travelling first class on the Ulster Railway from Belfast to Portadown. Looking through his window, Mr Beaton had noticed a man climbing out of the third-class carriage hitched behind his. The third-class carriage was open at the sides, had no roof and no seats. It was the climber's intention to get to the first-class carriage because there he knew he would find a seat and a roof. It had just started raining.

Mr Beaton put his head out of his window. He told the

man to go back or he would be killed. While watching the man climb back into his third-class carriage, Mr Beaton failed to see the bridge ahead towards which the train was moving rapidly. His head struck the brick corner of the bridge at twenty miles an hour. The blow split Mr Beaton's skull and he died instantly. It was the first recorded fatality on the line.

"I have a son," continued Mrs Beaton.

He nodded.

"So that is another thing you know," she said.

"Anthony."

"Yes, but he doesn't use that name," she said gently. "We call him Patrick."

"I only have the broadest outlines."

"He's at Trinity. I live here in Dublin with him. We go to Beatonboro' rarely."

Where was this leading? She intended to sell the estate and his job was to get it in order. She had grown to detest the country: it was hard work and there were few distractions. It happened to a good many landowners in his experience. They got the taste for Dublin or Bath, and then abandoned their estates. On the other hand there was Patrick. Surely, she would keep it for him?

"I hear yours is a very agreeable part of the country," he said. "I presume your son Patrick, one day, will want to live there."

Mrs Beaton waved a hand. "For the last five years your predecessor has collected no rent." She shook her head. "Well, that's not entirely true. Those tenants who wished to pay, paid, and those who didn't wish to pay, didn't. I failed to appreciate what was happening. I have some funds from my own family. We've been living on those."

"I understand," he said, and he had understood, very precisely. Mrs Beaton was living with her son in a small, semi-detached villa in Dublin, where there was never more than one fire in the evening and where there was never more than one lamp to a room. Mrs Beaton needed money. The estate was not a paying proposition and she wanted him to make it into a paying proposition. All she wanted out of this conversation was his guarantee that he would do this.

"Have you been to our part of the country?" Before he could answer he noticed her sniffing at her fingers. "I touched that just now," she said quickly, and pointed at the small, square, mahogany table beside her, "and it was polished only yesterday and the smell of the polish is on my fingers."

He said, "It's the turpentine and beeswax that's stuck to your skin, I should think."

"Are you an expert on polish as well as on land?" she asked.

"I'm guessing," he said.

She said, "Yes, I know you are." Then she continued, "And maybe my fingers don't smell of polish at all, and I just want to get us off the subject of the estate and on to something, anything, else." She smiled at him.

How did he explain this sudden lurch in the conversation? In one sense it was a compliment. She was speaking to him as if he were her equal rather than a possible future employee. Yet he recognised this was a ploy and what her true purpose was here . . .

For a few minutes, in this small room with green wallpaper, they would chat and banter. She would encourage him to speak. She would laugh at what he said. She might offer him tea. Eventually, the conversation would come to an end and he would know it was time to go. He would stand and she would let him know the job was his, although not in so many words, of course. He was going to work for Mrs Beaton on the usual terms, five per cent of all the rents collected, an estate house, turbary rights, a couple of milking cows, and so on. He would shake Mrs Beaton's hand, trip down the granite steps outside and walk rapidly to the railway station, only pausing to call at the post office on the way to send a telegram to Helena with the good news. Then, in a day or two, a letter would come from Mrs Beaton. The letter would confirm that the job was indeed his. Mrs Beaton, furthermore, would express great confidence in him in that letter.

Then he would start the job and everything would go

marvellously until, one day, there would be another letter from her. He had made a specific undertaking, the letter would say, that afternoon in her house in the room with the green wallpaper, and now she wanted satisfaction. Where was the money he had promised her?

This was no interview. He saw that now. She had decided to offer him the job before he arrived. What she wanted now was his pledge to use against him later.

"No, I don't know your part of the country," he said.

This was not true. He had taken the train to Cullaville the week before and then gone on by hired car to Beatonboro'. He did not tell anyone he was coming. He did not want to see anyone from the estate. He wanted to be anonymous. He walked through the town with the brim of his hat pulled down over his face. He said, "Good afternoon," a half-dozen times, if that, and nothing more. He did not call in at the estate office to introduce himself to any tenants. It was therefore inconceivable that she knew of his visit.

"It's very beautiful countryside," he said. "I know that much."

He spoke slowly, mechanically, while his thoughts raced. It was time for him to state his terms. He felt free, and he had not felt free until this moment. This had nothing to do with knowing that the job was his. What counted was understanding her strategy.

"I have certain things I'd like to say about how I'd like to work for you," he began.

"Oh, please." She smiled. She was continuing to treat him as an equal. That was good.

"I know about the difficulties on the estate," he said, "and about the failure to collect rents."

"Yes, didn't I just now tell you about that?" Her intonation was crisp as if she distrusted this new direction in the conversation.

"You did, but you also wrote to Mr Hazzard about it. You told him about your difficulties and he gave you my name."

Mrs Beaton nodded quickly.

"I don't want to make any evictions," he said, "not for non-payment of rent, at any rate. Evictions don't work."

He could see the skin twitching around her mouth. This really was not what she had expected and she didn't like it.

"If they don't pay, what else is the landlord to do?" she demanded. "Is the landlord supposed to say to the defaulting tenant, 'Oh, don't worry if you can't manage your rent. Pay me next year if you have any money then.' Or not?" She huffed. "There seems to be this extraordinary difference between landlords and everyone else when it comes to debtors in this country. We landowners have to leave our agricultural debtors as they are, because they apparently have some sacred right to their plot of land. However, if it's a sub-tenant on a tenant's land, or if it's a squatter on a commercial property in town, oh, well, that's quite different. Evict at once, they say, that's the proper course of action.

"Well, I'm sorry," she continued. "The land is mine. If they want it, then they pay for it. And if they can't afford it, then out they go." She looked at him. Her eyes were open and clear. She did not blink. She was trying to out-stare him. "Yes, the estate is a mess, I grant you that, and I am the one at fault," she went on. "I want you to sort out the mess, but you must understand, I need an income."

He considered what she said. He had two choices – to state his terms or try to refute her case. The first was the easier.

"I will only undertake to manage the estate on one condition. That I will not be asked to turn out any tenant, even for non-payment of rent, without being able to offer to pay his passage to America, giving him his stock, waiving his arrears, and allowing him to take everything he has away with him, providing . . ." and Thomas paused here ". . . providing the land comes back to us in return."

Mrs Beaton was staring at him with her mouth open. He noticed her top front teeth sloped inwards. She was a fox with a touch of snake. Now there was a rare animal.

"What about tenant right?" she asked. She said this in a slightly nasty way. "You haven't taken that into account, have you? Or don't you know about our peculiar local practice?"

Although this custom did not exist in the south of the country, where Thomas had spent his working life, it was not true that he hadn't taken it into account. It was also not true that he knew nothing about it. He did. Hadn't Thomas been at school in the north? Champion College, County Tyrone. Besides, as an agent, it was his business to know about variations in practice across the country.

Tenant right, although it had no standing in law, was an established custom in the north that almost all landlords and tenants accepted. When a tenant gave up a farm, the incoming tenant would pay the outgoing man a sum of money. This was a multiplication of the annual rent; it could be three, four, five, six, seven, ten, even twenty times the annual rent. The money was meant to compensate the outgoing tenant for improvements he had made to the property. It was rarely handed over directly, new tenant to old tenant, but usually lodged with the agent and then passed over when the farm changed hands.

"I have thought about tenant right," said Thomas, in his politest voice, "and I propose to include it in my negotiations."

"How?"

"I'll estimate the tenant right of a tenant with rent arrears as, say, five times the annual rent and I'll promise to pay him this sum to go, just in exactly the same way that a new incoming tenant would pay him. After all, I am in a sense the new tenant, since we're taking the land back, and I'll argue as such."

"So I am to pay my tenants for the privilege of going off and leaving me their arrears?" said Mrs Beaton.

"It might seem like that but no, not in practice you won't be."

She wanted to say something but he pressed on.

"You see, the way that it'll work is that in the case of your tenants who haven't paid for, say, five years, my estimate of their tenant right and the rent that they owe us, will, as it happens, come to the same."

Well, of course they would come to the same amount, wouldn't they? He smiled. It was sharp practice, of course, on his part; on the other hand, it did allow the tenant to escape his burden of debt. And surely that counted for something?

"So," he continued, "no money will actually change hands. We won't owe the tenants anything. What they owe us and what they'd expect to get from the new tenant – us – will cancel each other out."

She still wanted to speak but he went on.

"And if any of the tenants say, 'No! My tenant right is twenty times the annual rent. Pay up or I won't go!' then I'll say, 'All right. You owe five years' rent; I'm offering you tenant right based on the five years rental owing; it's a fair exchange. Now you can sell off whatever you own, your furniture, your implements, and whatever money you raise that way you can keep – I won't come chasing you for it; and finally, I will pay your and your family's passage to America. All I ask in return is that you return the lease. Otherwise I'm going to take you to court for non-payment of rent and you'll end up with less than nothing.' "

He took a breath. "It's an argument I can only win because those with bad debts won't have the will to fight me. They'll just take this very generous offer, return the leases and go. I'm sure of it."

"But your very generous offer," Mrs Beaton cried, "it's going to cost me. To do what you're suggesting, I might as well throw my money down a drain."

She was still stuck, he thought, on the same idea she had been stuck on when he started.

"No, it's not the same as throwing money away." He said this very slowly and quietly. "I think it's the only sensible, practical solution to your problems. If we use my method, the farms come back to the estate, we reorganise, reconsolidate. Then we re-lease them, or we farm them ourselves and, in either case, the return rises, plus, we have no sullen or resentful tenants, or worse, ex-tenants hanging around and stirring up trouble."

"That is as may be," she said, "but I still say it will cost us hugely. You'll just have to evict." She spoke firmly. Thomas's suggestion was not to her liking.

His thoughts began to race as he wondered what to say next. Now and then, as he would have been the first to admit, when a tenant was particularly obnoxious or dangerous or unpleasant, eviction was beneficial; however, on the Beatonboro' estate, after years of mismanagement and neglect, turning out the tenantry in large numbers was not going to work. It was better to buy them out, piecemeal, and tenants with bad arrears would have no difficulties with an arrangement that relieved them of their debts. In the short term his scheme would cost money, but in the longer term it would increase Mrs Beaton's return enormously. If she did what he suggested, she was going to get what she wanted, which was money. The question was, would she be able to grasp this?

"Listen," he said.

"I have listened."

"My proposition has another merit."

"What is that?"

"Others have followed this course, others who were in your position, and with my system they have put their properties back together and made them paying propositions."

"Do you mean Mr Hazzard?" she asked.

"Yes."

"And it has worked?"

"Oh, yes, as he's probably told you. That's why I'm moving on. He doesn't need me any more."

"Yes," she said, and fell silent.

Although Mr Hazzard hardly amounted to a large body of like-minded landowners, none the less Thomas could hear that her tone was softening. She hadn't agreed but at least she was listening, and no doubt it was reassuring to her – the knowledge that she was not striking out on a limb. In his experience, that was the key to the behaviour of human beings, whatever their class. So long as they knew they were following a path already followed by others, they were happy, even if progress was difficult. It was following a line nobody had followed before – that was when people baulked.

For the next few minutes he cited further examples and continued to make his case. His way meant no trouble, no grievance, and therefore no outrages, and there was enough friction as it was without evicting and giving tenants and their families a new cause to be angry.

"But I need the estate to work," Mrs Beaton said finally, and circled a hand in the air to signify, he guessed, her difficulties: her son Patrick was about to mature, he needed capital, perhaps he was soon to marry. Thomas repeated his position. There was another diffident remark from Mrs Beaton. He repeated himself once more, and then again for good measure. He remembered the advice a barrister had once given him: the best way to sway a judge and jury was to keep it simple and say it often.

Their conversation continued for some half an hour or longer. He put his case, Mrs Beaton demurred. He heard the clock strike five in the hall outside. He wondered how much longer this could go on and then a few minutes later he heard Mrs Beaton saying, "Yes, all right, I agree, as you think it's the best way to proceed, I agree."

Thomas made Mrs Beaton repeat herself so there would be no misunderstanding. Then he stood and said, "I am so happy we have come to this decision."

The meeting was over and he was calling it to a close. This was another sign of his authority.

"I hope I shan't regret it," said Mrs Beaton, also standing.

"You certainly won't."

"I wish you well, and I hope we prosper."

They shook hands.

There was a small bell on the sideboard. Mrs Beaton rang it smartly. The girl with the face of a seal appeared at the door.

"Goodbye," he said.

Thomas followed the maid to the hall outside. She passed him his hat and gloves.

"Thank you."

She watched him intently and he saw an expression that was a mixture of the trusting and fearful. Her employer's well-being and therefore her own well-being lay in his hands. Only if he made a success of the estate was her position as a maid secure. And now she was waiting for a signal that he would succeed and that she would be safe. One smile would do it.

"Are you from Beatonboro'?" He pulled on his gloves, and began to button them at the wrist.

"Yes, sir."

"Do you miss it?"

"I like to be out of it, sir."

"Oh, why?" he wondered.

"I like the city, sir. I like to see different people. I like big houses."

Behind her clumsy words he sensed a grievance towards the place from which she came.

"What about the noise and the dirt and the crowds here in Dublin?"

"Oh, but I like it here very much, sir," said the maid.

"What's your name?"

"Ellen."

"Ellen?"

"Marron."

"Ellen, will you ever go back, do you think? Go home. Marry, perhaps? Do you have any such plans?"

Her eyes bulged even more than before and her pleading expression gave way to a look of panic. She didn't want to answer these questions, she didn't want to give up the truth about herself. He knew that at once.

"Well, you keep your plans to yourself," he said gently. "It's none of my business."

Her look of panic gave way to relief. Her story was safe. He wasn't going to worm it out of her.

Then he smiled at her. "And everything's going to be fine on the estate. Don't let Mrs Beaton worry about it, do you hear?"

"No, sir, I won't," she said, smiling back but with eyes downcast. He could see the relief in her face.

She had a small mouth, her skin was white, slightly flaky, and there were a few freckles here and there on her cheeks and forehead. She probably didn't turn many heads in the street, he thought. She wasn't pretty or handsome. Yet he felt drawn, as he was to almost every young girl he met nowadays. It wasn't so much their appearance that interested him, at least that wasn't the case here, as their energy, their vigour, their youth. Proximity to the young in itself was more and more a pleasure to him, which he took to be an unmistakable sign that he was ageing.

"Goodbye," he said again at the door. Then he ran down the steps and walked smartly away along the suburban Dublin street. He went straight to a post office and sent Helena a telegram. His message was simple:

'Job secured. Your loving husband, Thomas.'

That evening, as Thomas was walking across Carlisle Bridge over the River Liffey, his eye focused on the statue of Nelson at the end of the broad street in front of him, his thoughts on where he was going to eat, he heard someone calling, "Sir."

The voice was plaintive, low, female.

There were other men moving along the pavement around him. Perhaps the voice was speaking to one of them.

"Sir," he heard again. He looked around and saw that the speaker was a girl. She was leaning against the balustrade to his left. It was hard to gauge her age. She was eighteen or nineteen, he thought. She sounded English; she was from the Potteries, he thought, or somewhere in the Midlands. Girls often came across from England to work the Dublin streets.

Now that she had secured his attention, the girl straightened up and took a step towards him.

"Are you looking?" she said.

As he didn't say anything, she took his silence as agreement and seized his arm with amazing alacrity. It was cheeky, really, because he was about to say, "I'm not," or something like that.

But because he hadn't been quick enough, she had attached herself to him and now, suddenly, they were walking across the bridge together.

Without thinking about it, Thomas scanned the street ahead. Had anyone seen her approach him? heard her ask, "Are you looking?", seen her take his arm? Thank goodness no one had, at least judging by the expressions of those around him. What had just happened, he believed, had miraculously gone unseen, as sometimes happened in the city. He could walk on and no one would pass comment. He was just an older man with a younger girl on his arm. She could be a cousin, or even a daughter. The appearance he presented was innocuous, blameless. So much so that he could take this girl to a hotel now if he wanted. But did he want to?

He had done this sort of thing once, he remembered; oh, this had been many years before, when he was a student at Trinity College. He would meet them in public houses. Then he remembered a particular public house with a black and white tiled floor and a girl sitting down and starting a conversation. She had been English too, from London, he thought. Perhaps he remembered this one particularly out of all the others because the girl on his arm was from over there as well.

She wore gloves, he remembered, the one back then. They were brown, leather, and as they walked out of the pub and along the street outside, he noticed that the stitching along the seam of the index finger was coming apart.

"Why don't you guess my name?" she said.

"It's easier if you tell me," he said.

"I'm called after a flower."

"Rosie?"

"No."

"Thistle?"

She laughed loudly, as if she found his quip genuinely funny. He assumed she was laughing to flatter him.

"That's not a flower," she said finally.

"All right. Give up," he said.

"I don't think you've made enough effort."

"Goodness! All right, daffodil."

"Iris," she said.

"Irish!"

"Ir–is," she said.

"Oh."

"It was my mother's name."

They went to a small hotel and he signed the ledger in the name of Mr and Mrs English, which was exactly the sort of half-joke an undergraduate would make. They went upstairs to the second floor. Their room was small. It smelt of mould and candle tallow. The wallpaper was green with white stripes. Every room in Dublin was decorated with green wallpaper at that time, at least that's how it seemed to him.

"My name is Iris," said the girl, apparently having forgotten she had already told him.

He said nothing but pulled out her hat-pin and laid it down on the marble wash-stand. Then he pulled off her hat and hung it on the hook on the back of the door. He undid the buttons on the back of her gloves and pulled them off. He undid the buttons of her woollen coat. She turned and he pulled the coat off her arms and shoulders. He sat down on the bed. Iris understood what she had to do and took off the rest of her clothes.

She was a pale-skinned girl with small breasts. All her body fat was concentrated around her legs and her bottom. She had two bruises the size as well as the colour of a plum, one on each thigh.

"Where did you get those?" he asked, and Iris laughed, and with one hand to her stomach, and the other hand up in the air, she began to waltz around the room, murmuring to herself as she danced with her invisible partner. The candle threw a great shadow on the wall and as Thomas looked at the shadow, then at Iris, he saw she was drunk, very, very drunk, and he wondered why he hadn't noticed this before.

He undressed and she got into the cold bed beside him. She was warm from her dancing and she pressed her warm body

24

against him. Her breath was warm as well and smelt of wine and ginger.

Iris lay back with her legs apart, her knees raised, and motioned to Thomas that she was ready for him to start. He remembered her glove coming apart at the seam, and this made him think she was poor, and then he remembered the warning he had recently had from a friend, a medical student at Trinity, regarding syphilis, and by the time he came to the end of this line of thought, he had decided against making love. He pushed her head towards his stomach and then he felt her sliding down his body.

Afterwards, her breath smelling of ginger and wine and now his own intimate smell, she asked, "Feeling better?" and before he could answer, she named her price.

Six months later, Thomas graduated and started work. At the same time he met and married Helena, and since then he had never slept with another prostitute. He had remained faithful to his wife, although it was also true that he had often thought about other women. He and Helena had four children. He and Helena had always been reasonably happy, and luckily, he thought, they still were reasonably happy . . .

As he had this thought, Thomas noticed that the hand under his arm was small, but the grip was tight. Then he realised that for a moment or two he had been out of time, first with Iris and then with Helena, but now he was back in the present. He was on Carlisle Bridge, a stranger clamped to his side. A horse-drawn car rattled past, its iron-bound wheels rumbling on the cobbles. Pedestrians hurried around him.

They crossed the road and began to walk up Sackville Street. Thomas looked down at the girl's hand. She wore no gloves. She wore a Claddagh ring on her left index finger. He wondered if she loved an Irish soldier whom she had met in England and followed back to Ireland. He thought about asking but decided against this.

"Aren't your hands cold?" he asked instead. It was winter.

"No," she said in her flat, Potteries accent.

"I'm afraid you've been mis-led," he said calmly.

He stopped to look in the window of a shop. At the same time he disengaged her arm from his, put his hand in his pocket and pulled out two shillings – all in one continuous movement.

"Here," he said. He slipped the coins into her hand and she closed her fingers around them straight away.

"I hope you can get something with that."

She said nothing.

"Go on," he said.

The girl from the Potteries turned and walked back down towards the bridge. He guessed she was going back to the very spot where she had accosted him.

Thomas went on up Sackville Street and turned into a small hotel. He took his supper in the dining room. He ate two kippers poached in milk and drank a pot of tea.

Thomas went home by train the next day and that night, as soon as the candle went out, he rolled on top of Helena. As they made love, the girl from the Potteries kept appearing before his inner eye and it was only by making an effort that he was able to keep her out of his thoughts. After it was over, and Helena began to squeeze his hand affectionately, he was glad that he hadn't thought about anybody else, even if it had been a struggle to keep them out.

chapter three

Sitting behind the counter, perched on a stool, the constable looked across the day room of Beatonboro' barracks and saw that the fire was getting low.

He slipped down, took a step, and felt something under his left boot scratching on the floor. It was a loose nail in the sole and he had put off doing anything about it all day.

He selected two pieces of turf from the box. They were brown twisted shapes with a sheen of purple. He looked at the puddle of red-hot embers in the grate, felt their heat on his face, then dropped the clods. They splashed into the mixture of clinker and ash, and sank.

When they were red hot, as they were now, the embers behaved like water, as he had often noticed before. Of course, this was an illusion. They were just mimicking their opposite element. It was a convincing illusion, none the less.

He watched the shower of sparks now swimming up the blackened back of the chimney. He'd have to mend his boot, he thought. He took the brass candle lamp from the mantelpiece and walked over to the little door at the back of the day room. He turned the handle and went in.

The lumber room had a sharp, acidic smell; this was the lime in the mortar. A full moon hung in the sky outside the back window. He saw half a dozen broken chairs piled in one corner, an old desk with no drawers, a cupboard stuffed with documents.

He moved forward. His shadow floated across the wooden ceiling overhead. The moon was very low and big. It filled the whole width of the window. He found a hammer and the cobbler's last; this was a black, cast-iron tool, with two legs and a prong over which the boot went. In one of the legs there was a cavity filled with nails, and as he carried the last out of the storeroom, he heard the nails jingling inside.

In the day room he moved back to the fire and sat down on a stool, took off his boot, fitted it snugly over the prong like a sock and pulled out the old nail. Then he took up the hammer, took a new nail and banged it in. That was a satisfying feeling. He put his foot back in his boot and tied the long leather lace. He picked up the last and the hammer and stood, intending to carry them back to the lumber room.

That was when he heard the front door of the barracks banging open. That would be the door from the street to the porch. He looked up.

A second later, the door from the porch to the day room swung back, a small woman came in, and the door closed behind her. He judged she was in her fifties. She had grey eyes and curly hair. She was swaying slightly, as if she was drunk.

"Good evening," he said.

She said nothing. Strange that she didn't speak. He decided familiarity was a better tack.

"Hello," he said.

The woman went on staring at him. He walked across and put down his tools on the counter, jogging the metal base of the ink-well as he did and causing the lid to fall shut. The sharp noise made the woman start.

"What can I do for you?" he asked. He had never seen the woman before. Her clothes reeked of turf smoke. There was also an odour about her that reminded him of ammonia. She was drunk and had wet herself, he decided. Probably a tinker, he thought.

"Where are you from?" he said, softening his voice. He detected anxiety, or something even worse in her muteness.

The woman shook her head. She wore large gold hoops in her ears.

She was definitely a tinker, he decided. Only tinkers wore the sort of jewellery she had on. Now he thought about it, he remembered seeing a couple of them the day before. Colonel Hutcheson let them camp in the back lane of his demesne, just beyond the Monaghan crossroads. She was one of them, and doubtless she had come to report some brawl.

"Why have you come in here?" He spoke with extreme clarity as if she were deaf.

But no, she wasn't deaf. She had heard him. He could tell from the movement of her eyes. Only now, she didn't open her mouth, as he expected. Instead, she raised her arm and pointed in the direction of the fire burning in the grate.

What was she getting at? Perhaps she was telling him there was a fire somewhere. No, that couldn't be right. If there was a fire, he'd have heard her shouting, "Fire! Fire!" in the street outside. That's what people did. She hadn't shouted. She had come in like a ghost.

He stared at her closely. The woman wore a grey jacket with black piping, no gloves. She had small hands, rings on the fingers and thumbs. Then it occurred to him that of course she was not pointing at the hearth, but rather at what lay in a straight line four miles beyond the barracks' gable – the Monaghan crossroads. The Hutcheson demesne was just a few hundred yards beyond these. Oh, yes, it all made sense. She was a tinker and that was where she had come from.

"So, the crossroads?" he said. "What of them? What has happened?" He still spoke carefully, unable to shake off the idea that she was deaf.

The woman looked back at him, swallowed and nodded once. Her eyes were dead. Her skin was quite white. There was no pink or red anywhere about her face. She was like a lump of wax, with features roughly impressed on it. This was fear all right. It took something away and left the person less than human.

"Why don't you tell me what it is?" he said, very gently this time. "I have to know."

The woman let out a loud, sharp cry. It shocked him so much he took a step back, involuntarily. The tinker woman saw that he was confused. He saw she saw. The next instant she had turned and was bolting from the day room.

"Don't go off," he shouted after her.

He glimpsed the back of her black jacket, and then the door to the porch was slamming shut behind her.

Did he run after her? He heard the thwack of a rein. He would still catch her if he ran out.

Then he heard the rumble of iron-bound wheels. The tinker woman was going north and east – towards Crossmaglen and Newry. She was going in the opposite direction to the one in which she had pointed.

The noise of the wheels in the street outside grew fainter.

There was nothing else for it. He had to get himself to the Monaghan crossroads and see for himself what was there.

Constable Cleary found the barracks orderly asleep at the table in the kitchen. Cleary touched his shoulders and the fellow opened his eyes.

"Get the keys for the gun rack," he said.

The orderly stood and said, with a yawn, "An orderly's work is never done."

Always the same reply, thought Cleary, but he said nothing, just ran up the stairs to the unmarried quarters on the first floor and banged on a door. In the middle of the door was a brass square, a piece of paper tucked inside it with the names of the policemen who slept within. Even by candlelight, he saw the way the paper slip quivered with the force of his blows.

"Quinlan!" called Cleary. "And you, O'Neill. Get up."

"What is it?" one of the sub-constables shouted from his bed inside.

"We're going out to check something."

"Now?"

"When else if not now?" shouted Cleary. He was irritated. What did they imagine was the purpose of waking them? he wondered, and then, remembering that his life might soon depend on one of these fellows, he added, speaking in a softer voice this time, "Mr Quinlan, I don't want to go out now any more than you do. However, it can't wait until tomorrow morning. We do this now."

A few minutes later, the two sub-constables appeared in the day room yawning and rubbing their eyes.

"Look at that!" exclaimed Quinlan, pointing at the round mahogany clock ticking on the wall behind the counter. "Three o'clock."

"Your buttons aren't done right," said Cleary.

The constable clicked his fingers and Sub-Constable Quinlan glanced down the front of his slop jacket. In his haste he hadn't put the right buttons in the right holes and now the front of his tunic was out of alignment.

"There's no real need to re-do them, is there?" asked Quinlan, cheekily. "No one's going to see us at this unearthly hour." However, before Cleary was able to bark back a command, Quinlan already had his fingers to his neck and the first brass button was undone. This was a typical Quinlan routine. First he appeared to challenge a regulation and then he assented just before the order came. On another occasion Cleary might have warmed to the comedy, but not tonight.

"You do something right because it's right," Cleary said bluntly, "and that's all there is to be said."

"Course you do," the sub-constable agreed; his tone was pleasant and compliant. "The uniform must be perfect, whatever the circumstances."

31

This pleased Cleary. He couldn't have put it better himself. His standards were clearly rubbing off on the younger man.

"Right, Mr Quinlan," said Cleary jovially. "You'll be coming with me." Despite the quips, he preferred Quinlan to O'Neill. He trusted Quinlan. He did not trust O'Neill. "Mr O'Neill, you mind the shop."

"Right-oh, Mr Cleary," said O'Neill promptly, careful to keep his relief disguised that while his friend Quinlan marched around the country with Cleary on this freezing frosty night, he would drowse by the hearth.

While O'Neill contemplated his luck, the two other policemen buckled belts over their tunics and checked that they each had handcuffs, whistle, memorandum book, pencil and baton. Then each man checked his pouch; that there were three rounds in each of the pockets at either end of the pouch, and a further fourteen in the pouch itself, wrapped in glazed brown paper and tied crossways with narrow green tape.

The orderly unlocked the gun rack.

Constable Cleary and Sub-Constable Quinlan pulled capes over their heads, put on their forage caps, and pulled the chin straps into place.

The orderly extracted two carbines with socket bayonets fitted over the end of each barrel. He handed each man his weapon.

"Load," ordered Constable Cleary. Under normal circumstances, carbines were carried unloaded; however, Cleary had decided that tonight it would not be safe to leave the barracks without arming their weapons. As the senior man in the station, Cleary was free to give such an order so long as he noted it in his report.

Each man now took a shot from his pouch. It was a piece of rolled-up cartridge paper that contained a charge and a ball at the end held in place with a twist of paper. Each man bit the back off the cartridge to expose the powder, dropped it down the barrel and then rammed the thing home with a ramrod. Then each man fitted a percussion cap over the nipple below the hammer.

"Right," said Cleary, shouldering his rifle. "We're going to take a look at something." He handed the orderly a sealed envelope containing a note of his proposed route and destination.

"Will this be pleasant?" said Quinlan, stepping ahead of the older man through the door and into the porch. O'Neill (who was the gardener in the barracks) grew chrysanthemums out here in the summer. The petals of last year's crop lay scattered along the window-ledges and the chalky scent of the flowers hung in the air.

"Don't be daft," said Constable Cleary, following his subordinate and sniffing. He liked the porch smell: it conjured up a sense of the long evenings and warmer months that lay ahead. "It's never pleasant if the Constabulary are involved. Never."

They slipped out and Cleary closed the outer door of the barracks behind him.

"Arm," he said.

There was a click as each man pulled back the hammer on his gun.

"Armed," said Quinlan, from the darkness.

Cleary's lungs were stinging, a sure sign of low temperatures.

"Bitter!" Quinlan observed, and Cleary heard his colleague stamping his feet in the street behind.

He looked along the dirt street. A sheet of frost covering the surface that was perfect except for two dark parallel lines: these were the tracks left by the wheels of the tinker's cart. With the moonlight streaming on to it, the frost glowed like silver dust and Beatonboro', Cleary thought, looked lovely.

"We stay four yards apart, no more, no less," he ordered. "Also, let's try to stay out of step, shall we?"

According to the *Standing Rules and Regulations for the Government and Guidance of the Irish Constabulary* (Cleary read his copy once a year), four yards was the optimum distance between each man on a patrol; furthermore, they were to avoid moving in step. This, apparently, made it harder for anyone to hear them coming. Sub-Constable Quinlan knew the form but he didn't mind being reminded. Cleary was like that – a stickler, but always clear, always consistent.

"I know the drill," he agreed, with a smile. That was another reason Cleary liked the man. He could be quite charming when he wanted.

"Course you do," Cleary agreed with his subordinate.

The two policemen began to walk. Their footfalls echoed off the sides of the silent houses of Beatonboro'.

"Mr Cleary, can I smoke?" asked Quinlan.

Constable Cleary considered for a moment. A pipe glowing in the darkness gave a man something nice to aim at. On the other hand, the local Lodge had burned out three tinker camps in the previous year and in their written warnings the Lodge described all tinkers as dirty bloodsuckers. It probably wasn't Ribbon style, was it, to get a tinker woman to lure the peelers out? Probably not, his thoughts trickled on, in which case this was strictly a recovery operation.

Besides which, on a moonlit night like this, an assassin hardly needed the red glow from a pipe to guide his aim. Any half-competent gunman would see them coming at a hundred paces. If fired on, the pipe wouldn't make a ha'porth of difference.

"Course you can smoke. Go ahead," he said.

He stood and waited while Quinlan took a pipe from his pocket, then fished out a match and struck it on a wall. The noise this made seemed unusually loud because the village was so utterly still.

Quinlan now carefully lifted the burning match to the bowl and pulled. The tobacco caught. Cleary noticed the red glow from the bowl and how it lit up his colleague's face. Quinlan had a small mouth and curly hair. He was also smiling, Cleary saw.

They started moving again. Cleary noticed the other's walk. There was a fluency to it. It had bounce. Quinlan was happy to be out whereas his colleague, O'Neill, renowned for his feet-dragging, would have left his superior officer in no doubt that he resented being out in the cold and in the middle of the night.

They left the village and passed into the countryside. They did not talk. Sometimes their boots dislodged a stone and sent it clattering along the frozen road, but otherwise the only sound was the irregular tramp of their booted feet on the ground, their breath going in and out, and saliva bubbling in the pipe stem. Now and then Cleary smelt his colleague's tobacco and he thought it was like burning hay. Skirting Lough Drum, he heard something splash and then the wing tips of a duck beating against the water. Finally, after they had been walking for nearly an hour, the Monaghan crossroads came in sight.

"We've arrived," muttered the constable.

Cleary stopped and peered ahead. He saw the dark sky and the glittering stars spread across it, he saw the abandoned house with its gaping windows, he saw the milestone standing up like a big square boulder, and he saw there was something leaning against it.

It looked like a person although he couldn't be quite certain; but after he had moved round and forward, he saw that indeed it was as he had expected, it was a man.

In one single, fluid movement, Cleary slid the carbine from his shoulder and curled his finger around the trigger. He heard Quinlan repeating the process in the darkness beside him and then Quinlan was at his side and pointing at the body. The man sitting against the milestone was abnormally still.

Something moved furtively in the hedgerow at the side. It was a small animal, a rat most likely. Cleary pointed at the abandoned house. Quinlan nodded. He understood.

The sub-constable began to move forward. By putting his heel down first rather than the toe of his boot, Quinlan moved almost silently.

Quinlan reached the little gate. Cleary watched as the policeman swung it slowly open. Cleary was waiting for a squeak but nothing came. Now he watched as Quinlan moved up the path, overgrown with shrubs and bushes. A bare branch touched the man's shoulder, and when Quinlan moved on, Cleary saw that a line of frost had now transferred to his cape.

Quinlan slipped through the blank, black doorway and disappeared inside the ruin. It was just four stone walls, roofless. Cleary caught a glimpse of the sub-constable through one window, and a flash of a bayonet through another. Then Sub-Constable Quinlan reappeared in the doorway and waved. House clear. Cleary waved in return. Quinlan moved back inside and a second later the barrel of his carbine with the bayonet on the end appeared through a window that overlooked the crossroads.

Cleary began to move forward slowly. His breathing was slow. He didn't like the stillness or the silence of the man sitting on the ground.

He stopped and glanced along the Monaghan road to his right, the Cootehill road that stretched ahead, and then the smaller road to his left, the road that ran down to Shercock. Frost lay like dust on the roads and hedgerows that rose on either side of the roads. Apart from himself and Quinlan and the man by the milestone, there was not a soul around.

Cleary curled his finger around the trigger, and gripped the barrel of the rifle. Two steps further on and his foot knocked against something. As he stumbled, he heard Quinlan call to him, "Watch out!"

Cleary looked down. He saw that what he had walked into was a stone. It was flat underneath, round on top. It was a large stone, about the size of a loaf, and it was the sort that farmers used to cap a wall. Which made it somewhat strange, he thought, that he hadn't noticed it earlier. Yes, given its size and the moonlight, he really should have noticed it, lying there right in the middle of the crossroads.

Then he saw that there was a large square of white paper under the stone. He shoved the stone sideways with the side of his boot and bent forward. A skull and crossbones were drawn at the top and beneath this were written the words: INFORMERS BEWARE.

Cleary looked up again at the figure leaning against the

milestone, so still, so silent. He knew now to expect the worst. Well, he thought, better get it over with.

He clipped across the road. Drawing closer, he saw that the man's head was lolling at a curious angle and that his back was leaning against the milestone. There was something in the mouth of the man. It was white, like a pipe – so what else could it be? Frozen spit? He thought about the idea. It was ludicrous. No, it had to be a pipe.

Two steps more and he saw that the thing in the man's mouth had some pink in it. His heart began to race and the next moment he felt something sticky under his right foot. He sniffed the air and registered the iron smell that hung there, and then Cleary knew at once what it was: he had stepped into blood.

His eye darted back over to the milestone. He saw the trousers about the knees, and then he saw that the blood had come from the dark space between the man's legs. He lifted his eyes and he knew what he was going to find. He saw the slit across the throat, the penis clamped between the teeth. He recognised the face of the dead man as that of Joseph O'Duffy.

Constable Cleary stepped quickly up on to the verge. The grass was long here, and stiff with frost, and it crackled under his feet. He began to clean his boot on the grass.

Quinlan, standing in the abandoned house, saw his superior cleaning his boot. He decided to join his comrade.

As he swept his boot backwards and forwards, Cleary heard the other man running up behind. It occurred to him that he should turn and shout, "Stop!" or "Don't look!" yet by the time he had turned Quinlan was not only right behind him, Quinlan had seen. Next thing, Quinlan bent over and, with a great retching sound, his dinner flew out of his mouth and on to the road. Here it steamed for a moment or two in the cold night air.

"All right there, Quinlan?" he said, tenderly.

"Oh, God!" muttered Quinlan. "I thought the fellow was drunk or knocked cold. I didn't imagine this." He retched again. He was half bent forward, one hand on his knee, the other holding the stock of his rifle.

"They must have got the tinker woman, shown her, sent her on to fetch us," said Cleary. His boot looked clean but he went on rubbing it anyway.

After a few moments, Quinlan straightened up and spat.

"Should we go after her?" he said.

"The tinker woman?" said Constable Cleary. "I don't think so. She's had shocks enough for one night, and so have you for that matter."

Cleary and Quinlan returned to the barracks and the constable, following standard procedure, noted the details of their journey in their Patrol Book, got Quinlan to sign this, wrote a longer report in the Patrol Diary, and then wrote a letter to District Inspector Love in Monaghan, once again as the *Standing Rules and Regulations* stipulated:

12 January 1854

Sir,

Shortly before three o'clock on the morning of Tuesday, 12 January, a distressed tinker woman appeared in the day room of the Beatonboro' police barracks. Although her distress was so great that she could not speak, I understood from the gestures that she made that the police should go at once to the Monaghan crossroads.

I woke Sub-Constables Quinlan and O'Neill. I selected for the detail and instructed O'Neill to stay behind. I had two carbines broken out of the gun rack and ordered they be loaded before leaving the barracks. Then, with Sub-Constable Quinlan, I made my way to the crossroads. Here, we discovered the body of Joseph O'Duffy located on the west side of the location leaning against the milestone. The deceased was dead and had been for some hours. His body was badly mutilated about the groin.

Having covered the body, I proceeded with Sub-Constable Quinlan to the back entrance of Colonel

Hutcheson's demesne. It was from here that I believed the tinker woman had come when she came to the barracks. We found a fire and some pieces of clothing on a hedge but otherwise the lane was empty. We surmised that those responsible for this outrage woke the itinerant family who were camping there and instructed them to alert the police.

The deceased, Joseph O'Duffy, was well known to the police in the Beatonboro' area. He first came to our attention six years ago when he was the driver of the hired car in which the local publican, Mr McGuinness, was assassinated. It is believed O'Duffy provided details of Mr McGuinness's movements to the assailants.

He was an active Ribbonman and recently spent several days in custody on suspicion of involvement in outrages against cattle in Cullaville. He had also served a short sentence for threatening behaviour in Monaghan jail last year.

No arrests have been made but inquiries into the crime are continuing.

Constable John Cleary

Cleary sealed the letter, addressed the envelope and wrote 'C' in the top left corner, another part of the procedure in the case of an outrage. Then he summoned the orderly, and asked for the letter to be sent on to District Inspector Love at the county police station in Monaghan town.

Later that morning Cleary went through to the kitchen and asked for a cup of tea. The orderly hung the kettle on the crook and swung it over the fire.

"Did you hear the news about Upton?" the orderly asked.

"What is it?"

Mr Upton, once the agent on the Beaton estate, had left abruptly before Christmas. During his years in Beatonboro', Cleary had often come on the man sitting by the side of the road with his notebook and pencil, sketching away. Mr Upton had always answered Cleary's questions about art and the constable had liked him, although he assumed he was a poor agent.

"What about Upton?" said Cleary again. He was still waiting to hear.

The orderly was standing on the hearth. His face was lit from below by firelight.

"You didn't hear?"

"No."

The orderly drew a finger in a savage line across his neck.

"Did away with himself," said the orderly. "Drowned. Presumably it was the disgrace," he added.

Cleary shrugged. Of late, each New Year had made him sad because each New Year reminded him he was a year older, and yet once again he had failed to make progress in the Constabulary. He wondered now if perhaps it wasn't so much the disgrace of dismissal but a sense that he wasn't going anywhere that had driven Upton to do what he did.

Cleary shrugged again and the orderly, seeing that Cleary wasn't in the mood for talk, took the broom and shuffled out off to the wood-shed. There was a pile of sawdust to sweep up and mix with the kindling.

There was a newspaper lying on the table and Cleary opened it out. His eyes roamed across the columns of newsprint and at last settled on a story in a corner. Two years earlier, he read, the first St Patrick's Day march had taken place in New York. Now, according to the newspaper's correspondent, attendance at the soon to be forthcoming third event was expected to be well up on the first and second parades, and the organisers pronounced themselves happy with this state of affairs. "Increased numbers would draw attention to the Irish cause," one of them was quoted as saying.

"Cause!" Cleary muttered, and laid the paper down.

Then he spat. His spittle landed in the fire, sizzled for an instant and turned into steam.

chapter four

The brakes came on: the iron wheels of the engine locked and then skidded along the rails, and made a dreadful shrieking noise. The carriage began to shudder a little, and Thomas French, sitting in his seat, realised they were coming into a station. According to his calculations this was his stop, Cullaville.

Thomas stood up, pulled down the glass and put his head out of the window. There was a dense, thick fog outside that was cold on his skin. Although this should be Cullaville, there was an element of doubt in his mind because he didn't know the line. He hoped for a glimpse of a sign with the name; however, all he saw was the ghostly shape of a hand-cart, its rails sticking up in the air, and a couple of dripping milk churns that looked like oversized skittles. He decided to ask, and ducked back into the carriage.

"This is Cullaville, isn't it?" he said aloud.

Before any of the passengers in the compartment had time

to answer, the train jerked and Thomas fell back on to his seat again.

"The driver can't seem to make up his mind if he's stopping or going." The speaker was the man in the seat opposite Thomas.

The train had stopped and from outside came the sound of doors opening back, followed by the scuffle of feet.

"Is this Cullaville?" said Thomas again. The railways were always putting up temporary halts.

"Oh, it's Cullaville all right, don't you worry," said the man who had spoken before. As he spoke he wiped one of the compartment windows.

"Thank you," said Thomas. He got up and pulled his bag down from the rack.

The passenger took his sleeve away from the glass. He had made a porthole in the condensation on the back of the window but it was no aid to vision. The fog outside was so dense, it was impossible to see more than a couple of feet.

"It must have been a little like this when the locusts blocked out the sun in Egypt," said the passenger suddenly.

Thomas was sorry suddenly that he hadn't spoken earlier to this fellow, who sounded interesting.

"My name is Barrett," said the man. He was big with a red face and very thick wrists. He was dressed in the clothes of a minister.

"A pleasure to meet you," said Thomas.

"Now you'd better hurry or the train'll be off," continued Barrett. "They don't hang around at Cullaville. I should know. This is my home stop but today I have to go on to Castleblaney. Church business."

Thomas put his hand through the open window, and turned the slippery brass handle on the outside. He opened the door and stepped down. He swung the door shut behind.

Half-way down the platform, Thomas joined the stream of passengers going through a door and proffered his ticket, but the ticket collector paid no attention. Thomas moved on, found himself in a room with a couple of benches, a wall with a grille in the middle, and a timetable that was a jumble of figures and numbers. He passed through another door and out into the fog again. He could taste the wet of it at the back of his throat.

"Mr French."

Thomas turned and saw the speaker. He was jerking himself forward from the wall against which he had been leaning. His face was long and he wore a moustache which seen at a distance was shaped like a gull, two curves that met together at the middle. The speaker removed his hat.

"Mr French," he said again. "I was sent. Mr Laffin sent me."

Mr Laffin was the bailiff. In a letter he had written to Thomas the week before, he had promised to have the agent collected at the train station when he arrived.

The speaker was fumbling with something, a pipe. He was shoving it in his pocket.

"Has that got a cap?" said Thomas. He registered the man's slightly puzzled expression. "Your pipe, I wouldn't put it in your pocket like that." Then Thomas said, "Take it out. You can smoke."

The man took the pipe out and tapped it against the wall. Everything tumbled out of the bowl.

"There wasn't much left to smoke," the man said, and then he added, "You're very welcome, sir. The car's just down here."

Thomas let the fellow take his bag and then followed him along the wall. He made out the head of a horse in the fog, then a wheel and the side of an outside jaunting-car.

"Do you work for the estate?"

"Oh, no, sir, I'm an independent tradesman. This is my business. Mr Laffin always has me to fetch our visitors from the station."

The driver lifted Thomas's bag and set it in the well lying between the two seats, which faced outwards, then lifted back the footboard which covered the seat on the right. Thomas climbed up and he felt the car sinking under his weight; it was like stepping into a boat. Then, a moment later, the driver climbed into the seat behind and Thomas sensed the car righting itself. He pulled his coat over his knees. The driver slapped the reins against the rump of the horse. They began to move.

"How far?" asked Thomas, turning and calling to the driver across the well. He saw the outlines of a bare dripping hedge as they turned from the station yard.

"Six miles," said the other man, turning and calling back across the well to him.

"And I shan't be seeing much."

"No, sir." Then the driver said, "Will you be staying long?"

Thomas felt like saying, "Oh, about five years," but then he remembered what the driver had said outside the station. He had called Thomas a visitor. The driver did not appear to know he was the new agent. Now, why would that be? Thomas listened to the horse as it trotted along, felt the axle turning underneath him. In Beatonboro' he would be known soon enough, and then the demands would start. But as a visitor he was guaranteed peace for a short while. Well, for at least as long as the journey lasted.

"I don't know how long I shall be staying," he said, and with that he turned his back on the driver again and faced outwards once more. The grey wall of fog slid past. Yes, he decided, he already liked Mr Laffin very much.

As he stepped through the door of the estate office, the first thing that Thomas saw was the grey-haired man at the desk looking up from the ledger in which he was writing.

"Mr French," said the man, pen poised above the page of ruled, feint blue lines, "I am Michael Laffin." The bailiff laid his pen carefully in the groove in the plate to which the ink-well was attached and stood up. "Good morning," he said.

Thomas found himself looking at a man he judged to be in his fifties. Micky Laffin's hair was grey, thinning at the front, his nose prominent, his eyes grey. Lion, he thought, his mind throwing up the match without his thinking about it.

"How was your journey?"

Micky got up, arm stretched out.

"I didn't see much with the fog," said Thomas. He took the bailiff's plump, warm hand and shook it.

"You're very welcome," said the bailiff.

"You didn't mention to the driver who I was." Thomas smiled and pointed with his thumb in the direction of the street beyond the window.

"No, I didn't."

"I didn't get asked one question. It was marvellous." Thomas smiled again.

"That was the plan. A journey without talk. Your presence will soon be known, and then the talk won't stop."

Thomas looked around the room. It was square, with a door at the front and a window on either side overlooking Beatonboro' main street. There was a desk in the corner, a cupboard nearby, the doors hanging open, the shelves inside loaded with papers, deeds, manuscripts, folders. The whole of the wall opposite was given over to shelves and these too were packed with papers of all kinds. There was a clock on the wall above a door to another room, and a calendar below, which gave the day's date, 24 January 1854.

"This is the estate office," he said, which was not particularly original, he knew.

"Indeed, the estate office. I sit there."

Micky gestured at the desk he had sat behind.

"And through here lies your den."

Micky threw open the door at the back of the room under the clock, and Thomas found himself looking into a smaller, square room. There was a desk with a safe behind it, an enormous map of the Beaton estate pinned to the wall, a corner gun cabinet, and a long single window. A white bank of fog pressed against the glass and prevented him from seeing the view outside. A yard, he presumed.

Thomas nodded. "It looks congenial."

"The fireplace smokes a bit."

There was a black grate in the corner where turf embers smouldered gently.

"What are they?" Thomas asked, and went forward. Various

objects were laid out on the mantelpiece above the fire.

"Your predecessor's," said Micky, following Thomas across.

Lined along the black smooth surface of the mantel Thomas saw a huge pine cone, positively the biggest he had ever seen, the lower jaw-bone of a sheep, set with square yellow teeth, the red head of a dried poppy, an orange butterfly fixed with a pin to a small piece of cardboard, two green bottles, two square lumps of granite, a flattened piece of candle-wax in the shape of France, a coil of wick from a colza lamp, and a piece of railway track about three inches thick.

"He was an artist," Micky continued.

Thomas picked up the pine cone. Each segment was thick and fat and reminded him of a piece of meat.

"Well, perhaps not an artist," continued Micky behind him, "but he liked to draw, he liked to paint, and he was never without a sketchbook or a paintbrush. You'll notice on the estate map there are crosses everywhere."

Thomas looked across at the map to which Micky gestured. He could see crosses, like small black flies on the white paper surface.

"Each of those marks the spot where he made a sketch."

Thomas had heard a little about his precedessor from his previous employer, Mr Hazzard, who in turn had heard from Mrs Beaton. Reginald Upton had trained as an engraver and later worked as a bookseller in Belfast. The family lived above the shop. One night it had caught fire. Mrs Upton died, her husband and their two children survived. Without a business to support himself, Mr Upton went to work as estate manager on his sister's farm outside Larne. Apparently he made a good job of it; then he applied for the post in Beatonboro', and was accepted. He left his children with their aunt and came down. He had come full of good intentions but gradually these fell away – alcohol was involved – and he spent more and more time sketching and painting watercolours. Rents were not collected. Mrs Beaton grew disturbed. Upton's sister intervened and pleaded on behalf of her brother. He was newly widowed, he was still grieving. Mr Upton was given a second chance and a third and a fourth, and then Mrs Beaton told him to go. He returned to Larne, to the house of his sister. Two weeks later, he filled his pockets with stones and walked into the sea.

"He was here five years?" said Thomas.

Micky nodded.

"And he didn't do the job?"

"At the end he did nothing."

"Why didn't Mrs Beaton act?"

"I don't know."

"She knew?"

"She knew."

"You told her?"

This was a key question because it was about loyalty and where Micky's lay – with employer or agent.

"I told her," said Micky without, Thomas noted, a second's hesitation. "Well, eventually, I had to, didn't I?"

Thomas considered what he had just heard. This man Upton had come to do a job but hadn't. Yet for years nothing was done about it. When you thought about these things, they seemed incredible, impossible. But when you were inside a situation, what was extraordinary to others had a way of becoming normal.

"Let's sit," he said.

He saw Micky glance towards the straight chair in front of the desk. Micky – assuming this was the start of their official business and that Thomas would go behind the desk and that he would take the chair – was about to step forward when Thomas took his arm, stopped him. "No," he said, "here's more comfortable."

There were armchairs on either side of the hearth.

Thomas draped his coat over the back of one and sank down. Micky, he noticed, took a less comfortable position, more on the front and edge of his seat.

"Have you heard how I intend to handle matters?"

Micky looked straight back at him and nodded. "I have."

"And you don't think very much of it."

Micky looked at Thomas slowly.

"If a man can't pay his rent, I say buck him out."

Thomas took the pine cone down from the mantel, broke off a fat kernel and threw it in the fire.

"It makes a very agreeable smell, a pine kernel."

Thomas saw the other man was waiting for him to explain himself. In Thomas's experience, the best way was always the most direct, but Thomas didn't know a man alive who wasn't adverse to a little flattery first.

"I hear you're a very capable bailiff."

"I don't know about that."

"It's said you're invaluable."

"If Mrs Beaton says so."

"She says so."

Thomas saw the grey eyes of the older man, watchful and patient.

"You've been here a long time, haven't you?"

"Came here, well, not here, to the stables up at the house, as an under-groom, aged twelve. Forty years on and I'm still here."

"Since when you've risen," said Thomas, with a faintly deferential nod. The man had travelled far and it wouldn't do any harm to let him know he admired that.

"So they say. But I still have a common touch, I hope."

"Do you like your job?"

"Must do."

"Any enemies?"

"Must have."

The man was fencing, Thomas thought. He wasn't going to get any further by this route, so he decided to go straight to the difficult matter.

"What have you heard about how I plan to do things?" he asked.

"Just a bit," said Micky, a touch obtusely, Thomas thought.

"What do you think?" Thomas persisted.

"Well, they're not going to like it, you know, the tenants."

"Why? Surely everyone'll want rid of their debts."

"That's true. No one wants debt. But no one wants the agent to calculate the tenant right and for it then to always come out at what they owe. They'll say it isn't fair."

"But it is. Your arrears are scrubbed, you keep what goods you have to sell, and you get free passage to America for yourself and your family. I'd have thought that's incredibly fair."

Micky smiled. "Look, a tenant is always going to think his place is a gold mine. He's always going to think his farm's tenant right is ten or twenty or thirty times the rent. You know how these people are. They get preposterous ideas into their heads. Then you come along and say, 'Paddy, I'm giving you, let's say for the sake of argument, four or five times your rent and that's it, that's your tenant right.' It might be exactly what Paddy'd get on the open market, but that won't stop him thinking he could and should have more."

"But they're getting their arrears wiped out in return. The alternative is eviction, which would leave them with nothing."

"Well, it is and some may see it that way. But there will always be others who are going to say, 'Ah no, he should pay more tenant right. He's cheating us.' You know how tenants are? You give them the moon, you give them something for nothing, they're still never happy, they still love to complain."

"And is that how you see this? They're getting something for nothing?"

"If a man can't stand his ground and pay his rent, I say – buck him out," said Micky, firmly but politely.

"And so you think, I suppose, why let the tenant off the arrears and pay for him to go to America?"

"I didn't say that."

"But you think it?" Thomas said. As he stared at the other man, waiting for an answer, he heard the door of the other office opening, the bell above the door pinging, and then the door closing. Micky stood and looked through the doorway into the front office. From the expression on Micky's face, Thomas sensed that the caller was both expected and unwelcome.

"Someone's here to see you," said Micky, in a curt voice.

"Already?" said Thomas. "I've hardly arrived." He stood, reached under the sleeves of his jacket and pulled down the cuffs of his shirt.

"A tenant," explained Micky.

"Oh."

"He made this appointment last week when he heard you were coming. Wanted to be the first to see you."

"How does he know I was coming? I thought no one did."

"No one does except this one, who knows everything."

"And what does he want to see me about?" asked Thomas. "Do you know?"

"I don't like him," said Micky firmly. Apparently it was more important to state his opinion than answer the question.

They moved towards the doorway, the bailiff slightly ahead of him.

"Why don't you like him?" said Thomas. This time he wanted an answer and this was clear from his voice.

Micky stopped. "We'll be right with you," Micky called out through the doorway into the room where the visitor, as yet unseen by Thomas, stood waiting. Then Micky closed the door and looked at Thomas.

"He's always saying 'Good morning, Micky', 'Good day, your excellency.' "

"So?"

"It's always the friendly ones who stab you in the back. Ever noticed that?"

Micky didn't wait for Thomas to respond but opened the door and stepped out into the outer office. Thomas, alone now in his office, was puzzled as well as eager to meet this man whom his bailiff so disliked.

Thomas went out after Micky. On the other side of the room, on the mat in front of the door, he now saw the object of Micky's dislike. He was a man in his middle thirties, slim, wiry, with thinning hair, a cudgel neatly tucked under one arm, his hat carefully gripped in the hand that wasn't holding the cudgel. The man had an open, pleasant face, he was smiling.

"Good day," said Thomas, carefully. He moved forward to the middle of the room. He heard Micky going behind his own desk and sitting down.

"Good day," said the stranger. He carefully wiped one boot and then the other, and then took two paces forward. There was something ungainly about his walk, a just perceptible limp.

"I have only just arrived, I am not certain I can help."

"Will you try?"

Thomas was aware of a pair of eyes somewhere between blue and grey staring across the room at him.

"I will try, yes."

"Good," said the other man, with a confidence that faintly surprised Thomas.

"I am Thomas French. You are?"

"Isaac Marron."

"A subversive," muttered Micky from his desk, where he scratched with his pen along a piece of paper.

"Yes, thank you," said Isaac. Then, he added, with a smile, "Mr Laffin."

There it was again, thought Thomas, that confidence.

"So, Mr Marron," said Thomas, and as he spoke the name he remembered the girl with the seal's face – she was Marron as well, wasn't she? That explained both the visitor's fore-knowledge and the appointment that he had made before Thomas arrived.

"I need some gates," said Isaac.

"Oh, yes."

"And the last agent promised me gates. He wrote to Mrs Beaton."

"And what happened?"

"Mrs Beaton wrote back saying I was to have the gates," said Isaac, pedantically.

"You know rightly, Isaac, you'll get them," said Micky behind him, his tone tetchy.

"No, I don't," said Isaac charmingly. At the same time he

swapped his cudgel from under one arm to the other.

"They are a special size. They are being made," the bailiff explained. This was for his benefit, Thomas sensed.

"It's been six months since the letter. Are they smelting the ore?" said the visitor.

That was cheeky, thought Thomas.

"They're coming from Portarlington."

"Via Patagonia, is it?"

Cheeky again, but uttered in a cheerful voice which removed the insult.

"You're not going about this the right way, Isaac," said Micky. Now, he sounded weary and irritated.

"Surely, in time they will come?" said Thomas. This was a sensible comment, he thought.

"I need those gates now."

There was that confidence again.

"You shall have some gates soon," said Thomas firmly.

Isaac smiled, his face widening, his mouth opening a little to reveal a line of clean white front teeth. "Good," he said, happy – it seemed – that he had secured the word of the agent.

Thomas decided – in view of the man's good humour – to broach the difficult subject.

"How are you with your rent?" asked Thomas.

"Up to date. Me, I'm as good as gold."

"Good as gold," said Thomas, which he thought was a very strange thing to say.

"I'm staying put. No surrendering my land and off to America for me."

Yes – Mrs Beaton had told the maid and the maid had told her brother everything.

"You sound as if you disapprove," said Thomas.

"No, I don't disapprove. What's meat to one is something else to another."

"Poison," said Micky, from behind the desk.

"No, not poison. I can't think what," said Isaac vaguely. His voice was mild. He sounded utterly sincere.

There was silence. Isaac smiled. Micky stirred in his chair. Neither had anything more to say to the other, Thomas decided, and there was nothing more that he could say either.

"Goodbye, Mr Marron," said Thomas.

"Mr French, it's been a pleasure."

Isaac turned, stepped up to the door, went out, and closed it again. The coil and the bell shook above the door. Thomas listened to Isaac's footsteps receding outside. When he couldn't hear them any longer, he spoke.

"That was rum," said Thomas.

He looked at the older man, and the older man looked straight back at him. "I don't like him," said Micky.

"He pays his rent."

"Oh, yes. Isaac doesn't make mistakes. Isaac is perfect. Just don't cross him."

Thomas pointed at himself. "Me?"

"No, not you. He's mostly a danger to the other tenants."

"What's he do? Beat them with his cudgel?"

"Not personally. He has others do it for him. The peelers think he's a Ribbonman, but who knows? All I know for certain is that he's obnoxious, awkward, and I don't trust him."

Micky stared into space. His face had changed, the jaw had come forward.

"We're not going to quarrel, are we?" said Thomas. "When tenants surrender their leases and I buy their tickets to New York?"

Micky went on looking into space but at the same time he moved his head from side to side.

"The tenants might grumble like hell about their tenant right," said Micky, "but we won't quarrel. It's sensible, prudent, getting our farms back, reorganising. You're doing the right thing. I just resent paying even a farthing to these wastrels who've had places rent free, and done nothing. I'm old school, you see – no pay, see you in court. But we won't quarrel, I promise you that, absolutely."

chapter five

Helena had stayed behind in Hazzardtown clearing out the house where she and Thomas had lived. She arrived in Beatonboro' a fortnight after her husband; it was a further two weeks before she sat at the desk in front of the small parlour window, which overlooked the garden, picked up her pen and began to write to her oldest friend:

Dear, dear Virginia,

You must be wondering why you haven't heard from me. (I feel very bad about this because I remember, and only too well, that when you went to Weymouth, last year, I had a letter from you within a week.) Yes, I confess it, I am a poor correspondent – this is true – but also, and I am sure you can appreciate this, I have been overwhelmed by events. To leave one house and to settle into another – well, I'm sure you can imagine this involves a great deal of work and effort. However, enough apologies, enough excuses, and now on with the business of hard information.

My journey here was pleasant enough, until I got to Dundalk. My train from Dublin was late and I missed my connection on to Cullaville. I took rooms in a hotel on the edge of the town. It was rather late in the evening and I was in my room when I heard a good deal of shouting. It was coming not from the street but from the back of the hotel. I sent Maggie down to see what it was and she came back with a long white face and she wouldn't tell me, and so I had to go down and see for myself. In the yard I found a small crowd watching something in silence. As I appeared the crowd parted, and as I walked forward it occurred to me that they all wanted me to see what was happening.

When I got into the middle of the crowd I found three men in long shrouds, which were actually inside-out women's shifts, with ribbons of different colours sewn all over, and pointy hats which covered their faces. There was a couple as well, a man and woman both in their forties, a husband and wife, someone in the crowd told me, all their clothes on the ground, blankets over their shoulders. They were sitting on chairs and one of the men in the shrouds was barbering the woman's hair with sheep shears. The husband's hair had already been cut off and it stuck up in tufts.

I asked what was going on and someone in the crowd told me to mind my manners or the Ribbonmen would see to me, gentlewoman or no, but that if I watched quietly, no harm would come to me. I asked why the Constabulary hadn't been called and the man who was working the shears called back, in a most good-humoured way, that the peelers knew better than put their noses into business that didn't concern them. I asked him what had earned the unfortunate couple his enmity, and merited the treatment he was meting out – taking first their clothes and now their hair – and he replied that their crime was over-zealous collection of church funds on behalf of an obnoxious parish priest in a village three miles out of town, and furthermore, that the couple had always known that this would be their punishment. Then the man with the shears, he began to whistle. It was a jolly tune – it was a polka – and as he whistled, he went on butchering the unfortunate woman's hair. Her hair was thick and black and it took him a while to get it all off. Then he stood back and he looked at her, as if he was admiring his handiwork. It was nothing to be proud of, I thought. The woman, who had been quite beautiful before he had set to work now resembled a bird that had fallen out of its nest. He must have thought otherwise; for after looking at her for a moment, he went back to work again, snipping away at several tufts that were sticking up, before declaring himself satisfied.

The fellow with the shears, he was obviously in charge, now stood the woman up and pulled the blanket away from her and one of his fellows did the same with her husband. Then the man with the shears warned them that they were not to collect money on behalf of the priest. If the people wanted to give, they would give, but it was not for them to go about worrying the parishioners on account of obnoxious Father Hubert. Then the man with the shears told the couple to go home. They had received their punishment and the Lodge would not bother them again, providing they did not repeat their previous errors. Suddenly, the wife, who I think until this point had been too shocked to take in what had been happening, began to shake like someone waking up; she put her hand to her head and, feeling all her hair was now gone, she burst suddenly into tears. The crowd stirred as if they were moved by this and the husband put his arm tenderly around his wife. Then, together, they walked through the crowd and out of the yard, and disappeared up the road into the falling darkness. The crowd now began to disperse and I turned to find the assailants had gone, and that all that remained as testimony to their actions was the hair that was now blowing across the cobblestones. I asked later in the hotel and they told me the couple had been drinking in the bar when Ribbonmen, as they are called, and who are active in the area, and who often mete out this sort of treatment to miscreants, came into the bar and removed the couple to the yard, some twenty minutes before I arrived. When I asked the manager why he didn't summon the Constabulary, he told me that incurring the wrath of the Ribbonmen usually proved fatal.

I got to Beatonboro' the next day and found that Thomas had moved into the agent's house on the outskirts of the village. Thomas had been sleeping there for the previous two weeks, sleeping on a makeshift bed in a dressing room and eating alone at the kitchen table, mostly bread and cheese, cold meats and preserves. A girl had come in, ostensibly to clean, but the house was filthy, thick dust on the pine floors, stinking bottles piled to the ceiling in the scullery, the larder, the back kitchen (all left by the previous tenant I hasten to add), terrible scorch marks up the wall over the fire in the good front bedroom, and, most disgusting of all, a trap in the back hall, the shrivelled-up carcass of a long dead rat caught in the steel jaws, which, amazingly, my dear husband had failed to notice.

I now set to work with the help of a man called Tim Traynor; Micky Laffin, the bailiff, found him, and he came highly recommended by the bailiff as a man from a family who always paid their rent. We spent three days scouring, sweeping, washing, cleaning and dusting. I then had the wall with the singe marks repainted and I decided the blue of the hall was depressing and had the whole repainted white. Then we unpacked the boxes and trunks of clothes, cloths, towels, household items, plates, cutlery and pictures. Then I spent three days moving the furniture around with the help of Tim, who proved a most useful asset. Then, and only then, did I feel I had earned the right to sit down and put pen to paper.

I suppose you ought to know what Thomas has been up to, because Mr Hazzard will be on to you for intelligence as soon as he sees my envelope arrive. Well, tell your dear husband that my dear husband is running around introducing himself to every tenant on the estate (he claims that within a month he will know all the tenants and their families by name and sight) and attempting to get a sense of the financial position; that is to say, he is attempting to find out who is up to date and who is in arrears as a first step towards buying out the debtors. But you know all about the process, don't you? So much is set in stone, it seems, especially where my Thomas is concerned.

The letter has gone on long enough. Let me leave you with a last picture. I am at the window, the red Chinese curtains hanging down, you know the ones I mean, the garden stretching away towards the road, and the redoubtable Tim Traynor (whom I have to say I have grown to like immensely) hacking away at an overweening rhododendron.

Write soon with news, news, news. I miss our talks, I miss you, I miss Hazzardtown and Cork.

Your dearest friend,

Helena.

After blotting the last page, Helena folded the letter away and addressed the envelope. Then she opened the window – it ran from the floor almost to the ceiling like all the windows on the ground floor – and stepped straight out into the garden. She walked along the path, the gravel crunching under the leather soles of her shoes, and down the avenue to Tim. He was dressed in knee breeches and boots and a shirt. He was sawing at the branch of a rhododendron. A patina of green mould from the tree was smeared on the blade.

"Good morning," said Tim quietly to Helena, when she stopped a couple of feet from him.

"Tim, take this to the post."

Helena handed over her letter and a coin to pay for the stamp. Tim put both carefully in the pocket of the coat hanging over the wall.

Then Helena told him that his lunch would soon be ready

in the kitchen, and that he was to go there when Maggie rang the bell. Tim nodded and went on sawing away at the branch he was at work on. With a crack the branch fell.

Helena turned and walked slowly back towards the house.

chapter six

Tim Traynor had met Kitty McKenna the summer of the previous year when he was out walking the lanes one Sunday. They had begun to talk and the talk had lasted all day. They met again the following Sunday and the one after that again. Then Tim declared his love and Kitty accepted it.

Since that time the young couple would meet secretly most evenings. This was the procedure: Tim would wait for Kitty under the pine tree that grew near the cottage where she lived with her mother and father. As darkness fell, Kitty would leave the house with the water buckets. Kitty went to the well for water each evening before the cottage door was locked and the McKennas went to bed. She would also cold-wash clothes or pans or plates or cutlery in the spring water, so her parents never thought it unusual if she was away for a while.

In his place under the tree, Tim would see Kitty coming out of the house. He would check that Daniel and Bridie, Kitty's father and mother, were not around, and then he would slip from his hiding place and follow Kitty down to where she fetched the water.

This was a spring well about thirty yards along the lane and tucked into the side of a hill. Sitting on the low round wall, which held the spring water that bubbled from a rock, this was where Tim and Kitty did their courting.

The McKenna cottage was above them but between the well and house there was not only the side of a hill but trees and bushes as well. Kitty and Tim could talk away and her mother and father in the cottage above would never hear them.

Furthermore, which made the place yet more private, the McKennas' cottage was also the last on the lane, with the next family half a mile away in the Beatonboro' direction and they had their own water anyway. So no one except Kitty came to draw water in this place. However, if people did pass – and they did occasionally – or if Tim and Kitty wanted to be more private still, they would retreat into the small, dense copse of alders that grew immediately beside the spring.

The alders grew in a ring about thirty feet across, and in the middle of the ring there was a small space that was open to sky with a large, flat, moss-covered boulder. Tim and Kitty called the copse the Green Room and the rock the Throne. Hidden in there, they fumbled with each other's clothes, and touched the intimate parts of each other's bodies.

The physical aspect of their courtship was secret, of course, but the very fact that they knew and liked each other was also kept from Daniel and Bridie. This secrecy had nothing to do with Tim and everything to do with Kitty. She was an only child. Her father had struggled hard. He was something of a success among tenant farmers. He had forty-eight acres. He and his wife imagined Kitty was going to marry someone like himself. They had always made it clear that this was what they expected. For this reason Kitty believed her mother and father would not allow her to marry Tim, who had almost nothing.

However, Kitty, also believed the exact opposite of this. In the end, she was certain, she would have what she wanted because of family history. Her mother, Bridie, came from a family of eight who had lived in a cabin in the mountains and scratched a living from a half-acre. Her own father, Daniel, had married Bridie against the wishes of his father, her grandfather, old Henry McKenna. The marriage was a success and as her grandfather, Henry, lay dying, he grudgingly acknowledged this.

Her father, Daniel, she compared to an old fire: beneath the old ashes hot coals burned still. Inside her father's dour exterior there lurked the tender-hearted nineteen-year-old who had married Bridie. Yes, Kitty admitted to Tim, when they talked about their future, her father was a hard and sometimes boorish man, but when he saw she was repeating his pattern, he would understand and he would forgive because of his own experience, and, in the end, he would allow her to marry Tim, he would bless the marriage, and the farm would be theirs.

Alongside these irreconcilable beliefs there was a third, emphatic certainty: Kitty believed she must avoid confrontation, at all costs. Her thinking was simple in this respect; confrontation was coming, one day, so there was no need to seek it out. Again, her father was the example. Daniel hadn't asked her grandfather for permission to marry Bridie because he knew her grandfather was going to refuse. Her father married behind his father's back. At first this seemed like the height of disrespect, but in the end the act became the proof that Daniel really and truly loved Bridie.

Kitty's plan was neither to tell her father, nor to elope. Kitty's strategy was to wait until her father and mother found out about herself and Tim. When this happened, as was inevitable, Kitty believed the months of secret but dedicated courtship would touch her father's and mother's hearts. They would be angry at first, of course, but then they would see the couple were deeply in love. How could they fail to? And eventually they would consent to the marriage. This was how Kitty saw the future – hard times but with a happy ending. The fact was, she wanted her parents' blessing and she wanted the farm.

Tim did not disagree with Kitty and how she saw the way ahead. He was happy to go along with it. He was in love with

Kitty. He was besotted with Kitty. He was also overwhelmed by his physical attraction to Kitty. In Tim's mind everything was mixed up. Desire and longing, lust and hope. The truth was, Tim did not think. He trusted Kitty; he believed that what she said was going to happen. In the meantime, he found her irresistible and as long as Kitty let him have what they called "his way", he was happy to go along with her plans.

It was a dry March evening. Tim and Kitty were into the ninth month of their deception. Tim had spent the day in French's garden, weeding beds and cleaning ditches, and now he stood in his usual place beneath the pine.

There was a smell of wet earth and wet grass, and a moist and gentle wind. The days were growing longer, he had noticed, the climate warmer. Snowdrops were showing under the wall in front of him. The white petals glowed eerily in the fading light. It was not yet spring but the end of winter was not far away. He was filled with a sense of the force under the earth, coiled and ready to push.

From here, Tim's mind ran forward to the summer. He imagined himself and Kitty walking hand in hand along one of the brown tracks across the bog behind his cottage. Then he thought of the low hills behind the bog. They were lovely hills, rounded and wooded. Then a picture came into his head of himself and Kitty in the woods there. He saw her standing against a tree, her clothes on the ground, her long white thigh as she stepped towards him . . .

Kitty said there was only one thing that he ever thought about and perhaps she was right. When she said this it was always with a smile, so he did not take it as a rebuke. Very often she had exactly the same thoughts as he did, although she was always more cautious than he was about acting them out.

From across the lane Tim heard the grumbling of the cottage door. From his position under the pine, he could not see the front of the cottage only the gable end. He had to rely on his ears rather than his sight. The front door, he knew, was in two halves, upper and lower. The bottom edge made a peculiar squeak as it rubbed on the threshold. Over nine months of waiting and listening, he had come to know this sound very well. Now he strained his ears for "The Bonny Labouring Boy" (with its lyrics so close to their experience – "Cruel were my parents who did me sore annoy, They would not let me tarry with my bonny Irish boy"). If Kitty sang this, it was agreed between them, Tim was not to come forward because her parents were around. Tonight, happily, he heard no song.

Tim stepped forward from the pine tree and vaulted over the wall. In the beginning of the courtship he never ran out like this. He waited until he saw Kitty on the lane and that she was alone. But over nine months, he had grown confident. If she sang, the parents were about; if she didn't, he was safe. She just closed the door and sauntered with her buckets down the path that connected the cottage to the lane. The system worked. Throughout their courtship so far, Kitty's parents had never once caught sight of him. And tonight there was no song. He was safe. Tim was certain of that.

Then, to his immense surprise, it was not Kitty but her dreaded father Daniel whom he saw coming down the path towards the lane, jauntily swinging the buckets just as if he was her. Tim wondered if there was time to turn and run but the old man had his head up and Tim knew he was seen.

"I am not my daughter, Tim Traynor," the older man shouted at him, his tone both angry and triumphant.

Tim was bewildered. They had been seen, he realised, he and Kitty. They had to have been. But by whom and when he had no idea.

"You're to stay away from Kitty," the older man shouted. "I won't have you around her, do you understand? Do I make myself clear?"

Tim felt an unexpected sense of calm. Here it was, at last. The truth was out. Kitty had always said this moment was going to be terrible. However, after anger, understanding and forgiveness were to follow, once Daniel saw, as inevitably he would, the similarity between his own and his only daughter's life. Daniel had married for love, so how could he stop his daughter marrying for love? Kitty always said so and Tim believed her. This was not the end but a station along the way. At this stage Daniel was bound to be furious.

And now, by rights, Tim should have shouted back but he rejected the idea. What was the point? He knew the future. Kitty had told him. Instead, he opted for silence. Words would fan the flames. No words could be interpreted as a sort of respect, provided he didn't smirk. However, Tim didn't want to seem like a coward either, a man who was too cowed to speak. Therefore, in order to suggest he had courage, Tim stood, legs apart, feet firmly on the ground, and stared up at the older man, while the older man, in turn, stared back at him, each meeting the other's gaze.

Tim's face was pale and smooth, his hair was thick and black. He had grey eyes and thin wrists. He was twenty and it was his sense that he was handsome.

Daniel was broad across the shoulders. A worn brown leather belt was buckled over the front of his paunch. His legs bowed slightly. He had thick, solid wrists and brown eyes. His face was criss-crossed with deep lines and his nose was red and crooked. It was Daniel's father, Henry, who had broken it; this was in a fight thirty-five years earlier, when Henry McKenna discovered that his son had married Bridie in secret.

After the fight, Daniel fled home and went to live with his new wife in a shack that he built in the woods. Four weeks later, Henry fell from the roof of the cottage – he had been clearing the chimney – and broke both his wrists. A day or two later, word came: Daniel was needed at home to work the farm and he was to bring his new wife with him. Henry didn't like this but he needed his son's help: he couldn't have earned any money to pay the rent otherwise. As for Daniel's nose, a month or so had passed since it was broken and it was now too late to do anything about it. It had to be left as it was, the crushed bone of the bridge sticking out sideways in both directions, and the cartilage, which ran down the middle, curving to the left side like a sickle. Because of the damage

Daniel could never breathe again properly through his nose and every night of their married life, without fail, Bridie warmed two balls of wax between her knees, and when they were soft and pliable, plugged these into her ears to keep out the roar of her husband's terrible snoring.

"You are not and never will be a fit suitor," Daniel McKenna suddenly shouted down at Tim.

The younger man tried to think of something to say but his mind was blank. He felt suddenly intimidated by both the age and the anger of the older man.

Now he felt angry himself. How dare the old man roar at him like that? Then Tim reminded himself that of course Daniel McKenna was going to be angry at this stage. Only later was that going to change. The best policy, undoubtedly, was to continue as he had started and say nothing.

So, without saying a word, Tim turned and began to walk away up the lane towards his home. The older man was relieved that the younger man had gone off without a row. He strode off down the lane in the opposite direction to Tim, whistling a jig.

The next evening, Tim waited again near the pine tree. He heard the door of the cottage opening but he did not move forward. Instead, he crawled on his knees over to the wall that separated the field where the pine tree grew from the lane. He heard the sound of boots scuffing on the path. He peered through the hole that he had made in the wall earlier, and he saw it was Kitty's father again.

Daniel McKenna had reached the point where the path from his front door met the lane.

"Tim Traynor," the old man boomed along the darkening lane, "I knew your father. I even had your father working about my place. I have nothing against the Traynors except when it comes to Kitty."

The old man turned and walked off down the lane. Again he swung his buckets and again he whistled.

They were still in the angry stage, thought Tim, but they were on their way to the happy future, as Kitty predicted.

The third evening, the old man came down the path from

the cottage and stopped again at the point where it met the lane. Tim was behind the wall already and he peered at the thick, slightly stooped form of Daniel.

"Tim Traynor," the old man shouted up the road, "I know you're there."

Tim held his breath. Daniel McKenna was bluffing. Daniel McKenna was not able to see him.

"Tim Traynor," the old man called mockingly, "Tim Traynor. Come out and show yourself, you little rascal. For nine months you carried on with our Kitty behind my back. But no secret will keep in this world. You were seen and now you're stopped."

The old man started to giggle. It was an unpleasant, high-pitched noise from the back of the throat.

"You rascal, Traynor," he bellowed. "You've got no staying power. Kitty doesn't show up for three evenings and you're gone. You're not a suitor, you're a fly-by-night." He stopped and shook. "Don't waste your breath, McKenna, he's gone," he said.

Daniel McKenna turned and began to walk down the lane. It struck Tim that the old fool really did think he was alone.

Suddenly, Daniel stopped in the middle of the lane, turned and retraced his steps. Tim wondered what he was doing.

"Hey!" Daniel called up towards his house. From his place behind the wall, Tim saw the gable end of the cottage, the lane running away into the darkness and Daniel in profile shouting up the path.

"Hey!" Daniel called again. Tim heard the door opening, then saw Bridie McKenna bustling into view.

"Bring my daughter out," he shouted at his wife.

Bridie McKenna went back inside the cottage. From his place behind the wall, Tim heard Bridie McKenna and Kitty shouting at one another inside.

Mrs McKenna reappeared, dragging Kitty along by her arm. Through the hole in the wall, Tim saw Kitty at the top of the path, looking down on her father, and Daniel in the lane looking back up at his daughter.

"He's not here, daughter," shouted the old man. "He'll show two nights but by the third your lover's gone. That's how much he cared for you, Kitty. We told you he was worthless. Now we have the evidence."

Kitty appeared to shake her head, but with the darkness coming on it was hard for Tim to be certain. He thought he heard her sobbing, and he very much hoped she was. At least if Kitty cried that was proof she loved him; at least if she cried, her failure to defend him against her father didn't matter. The fact was, Tim was hurt. Why had Kitty said nothing to defend him? Why hadn't she said that he did love her and she did love him? The plan was to prove that they loved one another. But if she said nothing, and Daniel's lies went unchallenged, then their separation was guaranteed.

However, Kitty said nothing, just turned and walked back in the direction of the cottage door.

"I hope you've learned your lesson," Daniel McKenna shouted after her. "I hope you see now that he was worthless. I hope you will never deceive us again as you have these last months."

She must say something, thought Tim, his face reddening. Then he saw Kitty stop, turn and run back to the top of the path where her mother stood.

"I will never learn my lesson," Kitty shouted down at her father.

Tim felt a warm glow of pleasure. Yes, she loved him. She must.

Bridie McKenna's arm came up, and half a second later her hand connected with her daughter's cheek. Tim heard the smack and Kitty's surprised cry of hurt. Mrs McKenna turned her daughter round to face the house, kicked her twice from behind, then shoved Kitty viciously towards the front door.

"I'll be with you presently," Mr McKenna shouted up ominously.

Tim heard another cry, the door closing and the noise of the bolts as they were drawn inside.

Now there was silence except for the sound of Daniel McKenna as he walked to the well and filled the buckets. Then he walked back up the lane, climbed the path to the cottage, and knocked on the door. Mrs McKenna let him in and bolted the door after him.

Not long after this, Tim heard a whack followed by a scream which he judged to be Kitty. There were several more screams. McKenna was beating his daughter with his belt. He heard Kitty shouting, "I'm twenty, I'm twenty," and crying with rage and pain.

Tim slid from his hiding place behind the pine tree, clambered over the wall and on to the lane.

He could run up there and batter on the door, but they would not let him in, and he was not strong enough to force the bolts.

He could smash a window, of course. There was always that route of entry.

Then he remembered that Kitty's father kept guns over the door and had done ever since the business with his sister and her husband . . .

Daniel's sister, Mary, married David, a small tenant farmer in Roscommon. Despite being warned not to do so, David took on three extra acres from which a family had been evicted. He made hay on the land. The local Ribbonmen warned David they were going to burn the hay unless he gave up the land. The land belonged to the evicted family, not him. David refused. The family were gone, he said, to America. Why shouldn't he have the land? He needed it. He only had seventeen acres. He called the Constabulary. As a detachment of policemen arrived, the Ribbonmen ran out, set fire to the hay and ran off. David was warned again to give up the land and again he refused. On Christmas Eve, four men with flour sacks pulled over their heads broke into the cottage where David lived with his family, woke the couple and their children. The men tied the children up. They beat the couple with cudgels. Then the ring-leader said, "Your music-making days are over." David was well known as a fiddle player and his wife a singer. They often played together at local weddings and parties. The Ribbonmen spread David's hands on the table and with the pestle pulped in turn each finger-end. Then they laid Mary on the table, like a patient. Her mouth was levered open with a wooden spoon; then a red hot coal was picked out of the fire with tongs, carried across and dropped into Mary's mouth. Her saliva steamed and rose around her into the air. The Ribbonmen ran off then.

The coal burned away the skin inside Mary's mouth. The skin became infected, the infection turned to gangrene and Mary couldn't eat. She died a month later. David quit his farm, sold his stock and possessions, and went with his children to America. He found employment in a mine in West Virginia where the other miners called him Fingers on account of his splayed finger-ends and broken nails.

After the attack, Daniel swore that if anyone ever came he would be ready for them. He bought two pistols from a soldier. He hammered wooden pegs into the wall over the front door and hung the pistols on these. Every morning, after he came in from milking the cow in the byre, he reprimed and repacked the guns, so there would be no possibility of misfiring.

Tim remembered Kitty telling him about this. She had smiled as she did but there was also a serious purpose to her words. Her father was a nervous man. He kept his guns where he could easily reach them. If someone came to the house and he didn't know who they were, or he didn't feel happy about them, his pistols were always ready. And if he tried to break in now, Tim decided, Kitty's father would try to shoot him.

All he could do was wait for Kitty to persuade them, wait for Daniel to see how like himself his daughter was. In the meantime, Tim was going to return the next night, and the next, and the next. Eventually Kitty would go back on bucket-filling duty and he would be waiting.

Tim turned and started walking up the lane towards his own miserable cottage that lay in the hills two miles away.

chapter seven

The first Beaton, Colonel John Alexander, received his grant of two and a half thousand acres in 1612. He moved to Ireland bringing his wife. They produced three children. The eldest son, Alexander John, fell in love with a local woman. Leonara was the daughter of a small Catholic landowner, who had managed to hang on to some poor mountainous land in the hills to the south of Beatonboro'. Leonara converted and married Alexander and in time became the mistress of the ugly towered and gabled house built by the Colonel.

Fifteen years into the marriage, Leonara, passing through the yard one evening, overheard two men whispering in Irish in one of the barns. She gathered that the house was about to be attacked, and that this was part of a larger scheme, a rebellion. Some of her clansmen, augmented by mercenaries, were to be let in through the back door. They were going to take her husband and hang him from his own front door. That was the plan.

Leonara hurried inside and found her husband. There was no time to flee and none of the servants could be trusted, she thought, to fight for her husband. Instead, she suggested that Alexander hide in the well in the kitchen. He agreed. She lowered him down in a basket, secured the basket to a hook, then slid the huge coping stone into place. Minutes later the back door was opened and her clansmen with their forces streamed in. They surged through the house searching for Alexander. They found Leonara in her bedroom at the top of the house. She had gone there in order to be as far away from the well as possible. Under questioning, Leonara said her husband was in Dublin, called there unexpectedly on business. A Scottish mercenary, who was dubious about this, slashed Leonara with a dirk; he thought this would encourage her to tell the truth. Unfortunately, he misjudged and cut the artery in her neck. With blood spurting and pumping round the room, the mercenary threw Leonara out of the window, set fire to the bed and departed.

Closeted in the well, Alexander heard the shouting above, the pounding of feet, and then the terrible roaring sound as the fire spread from the bedroom through the entire house. He hung on in the darkness, reciting the psalms and hymns he knew by heart. When he got to the end of what he knew, he would start the cycle again.

At last, when there was no longer any noise coming from above, Alexander knocked on the coping stone and waited for Leonara to come and lift it away. When no Leonara appeared, he managed to worm the small knife, which Leonara had given him, through the crack and then lever up the stone from underneath. Once there was a space into which he was able to get his fingers, it was just a matter of slowly inching the coping stone away and then climbing out.

It was early morning. The kitchen floor was covered with a carpet of ash. As he trod around his footsteps appeared in the ash. It might have been new powdery snow that he was walking in, except that the colour was grey and black. It was also very hot. The walls were still warm from the terrible heat of the fire. He took off his coat and set out to explore the rest of the house. He discovered the upstairs floor and the roof had burned away, but his four walls, the windows and doors were still intact. Then he went outside and found Leonara.

Alexander slipped away to Scotland and returned six months later with twenty mercenaries. He slaughtered Leonara's father, her three brothers, their wives and all their children.

The remainder of the father-in-law's land passed over to Alexander and was marked on the estate map, Leonara's Bounty. However, by the time Thomas arrived, more than two hundred years later, most of Leonara's Bounty was gone. Over the centuries it had been sold off or exchanged for other pieces of land closer to the main estate. Now, only one mountain farm remained, leased to a man called James McNally, known as Jimmy; the McNally family had been tenants on this farm for over a hundred years.

The incumbent tenant was a small man with a big voice. Jimmy was in arrears and Thomas believed there was a good chance he would surrender the lease. Thomas had calculated the tenant right he was prepared to offer as five times the annual rent, which exactly covered the back rent Jimmy owed to the estate. Jimmy also had some stock and other goods, and by selling these, Thomas estimated, Jimmy could raise sufficient funds to pay back the shopkeepers in Beatonboro' who had given him credit over the previous years. The cost of passage to America for Jimmy and his family the estate would pay. So far Jimmy hadn't decided but he had come to the estate office today to give his answer; irritatingly, however, Jimmy's answer was that he had not quite made up his mind.

"Just give us a week," he shouted. "I'll come in here in exactly seven days and you'll know for certain then and I'm certain it'll be the answer you want."

"All right," said Thomas. "You have a week. But I tell you what. We'll come out to you and hear it from you in your house."

Jimmy shook his head from side to side. "I always come

into the estate office," he explained, "if there's any business to be conducted. The track through the hills to my place would ruin horse or car. And Micky will back me up there."

"It's not great," Micky agreed. He had not been out to Jimmy's farm more than half a dozen times during all his years with the estate. "But I have managed to get out on a few occasions," he added.

"When were you out there last?" Jimmy asked enthusiastically, in his booming voice.

"It must have been before . . ." Micky pondered. "Before . . . when your father was still alive."

"He died thirteen years ago," said Jimmy. "You can't have been out since 'forty-one so."

"Yes," Micky said. The road really was terrible, he remembered.

"I have to look at the place," said Thomas. "We'll come out to you, this time, seven days hence."

Jimmy's face lengthened and darkened. He didn't want to agree but he had no choice. Then, despite his initial resistance, Jimmy left the estate office in good spirits, promising his guests extensive hospitality.

It was a dry afternoon the following week, when Micky and Thomas arrived by horse and car at the start of the track which was to take them across the country to Jimmy McNally's place. The track, at least the part they saw from the road, was filled with holes and strewn with stones. Micky suggested they leave the horse and car and make the rest of the journey on foot.

Thomas agreed. Within a couple of hundred yards the stones became boulders and the holes became pits.

"We'd never have done this in the car," said Micky, breathing heavily, for the road was steep as well as rotten. After a couple of paces he added, "He'd better be in when we get there."

There was a small pit in front of them. As they skirted around it, Thomas noticed a squirrel floating belly up in the black water in the bottom.

"Course he'll be in," said Thomas. "He stood in the office last week and said, loud enough for everyone in Beatonboro' to hear, 'Thursday next, four o'clock, if you come to my place, you can have my answer.' "

"Here's hoping."

Thomas ignored this remark. In his mind he rehearsed the arguments he was going to use if the decision was not the one he wanted.

"Tell me," said Micky, interrupting his thoughts, "why does it take so long for the man to make up his mind? When he came in last week, Jimmy was supposed to have decided. It was the same story the week before. Does he or doesn't he want to go? If he doesn't, then he must pay his rent or face ejectment."

"We're asking him to give up everything," said Thomas slowly. Over the preceding weeks he had come to see that, although his proposal to take back the leases made economic sense, attachment and a sense of belonging counted for more with the tenants. Micky, on the other hand, was now an enthusiastic convert to his plans.

"Jimmy gets free passage," he heard his bailiff saying, "plus whatever he gets for his moveables. He should do it and no more mucking about."

"I think I'd hesitate," said Thomas. "Once he goes to America, he'll never see this again."

"Oh, yes," Micky agreed sarcastically. "Leaving all this will be a wrench." He pointed at the hill that rose on one side. It was brown with old bracken and covered with small black pathways that wound by different routes towards the summit. There was a man near the top leading a donkey with a pannier on its back. "You'd really miss this place," Micky continued.

The track they were tramping curved violently. When they came out on the other side, Micky and Thomas saw a small lane on their right. It was dead straight, which was a surprise in the middle of this bumpy landscape. It led from the track to a hollow that looked as if it had been scooped out of the earth by the hands of a giant. In the middle of the hollow, half hidden from view, stood a dwelling, and this was the home of James McNally.

Thomas ran his eye over the fields in front of the dwelling. The land was ridged and lumpy, sure sign that cattle had tramped the ground when it was too wet to support them. There were ragwort and rushes and thistles growing every-where, and in the damp corners he thought he saw the broad green leaves of wild irises. A scrawny calf suckled a solitary cow.

"The place is a mess," said Thomas.

"A mess is right," agreed Micky. "I don't know what Jimmy thinks he's doing." He lifted his arm and pointed at the blue smoke wriggling from the bent chimney and escaping into the spring sky above.

"Well, praise be the Lord, someone's at home," he said.

"There's a wife, isn't there?" asked Thomas.

"Oh, yes, there's a wife."

"And?"

"I've actually never seen her." Micky thought about this for a moment. "No, I haven't. Come to think of it, no one's actually seen her. Now there's a strange thing. The man's married twelve or thirteen years, and I've never seen his wife, and I don't know anyone who has. I have a vague idea her people were called Clerkin and they were from the Blayney direction but . . ." Micky shrugged his shoulders to emphasise his ignorance and the two men turned on to the lane and began to walk towards the hollow with the house in the middle.

There was a stone wall on either side of the lane and stacked against it were fantastic pieces of gnarled bog oak, bits of broken machinery and chipped slates. There were even half a dozen headstones, corners flaking, their inscriptions long worn away.

"I might buy a couple of those if he sells up. I could have them made up – 'Michael Patrick Laffin. Born 1805, died . . .' and I leave that blank and the wife fills it in."

"Brilliant," said Thomas, "but why stop there? Get one for

each of the family. Solve all headstone problems at a stroke."

" 'Laffin was always laughing.' Is that a good epitaph?"

They had reached the dwelling. It was a small, crooked cabin, with a warped, thatched roof, a battered front door, the paint peeling away and two tiny windows, both planked up inside. Micky knocked with his stick on the door and called, "Hello."

From inside the house there came neither a reply nor the sound of footsteps.

"Strange. The fire's going. You'd think the wife or the children or someone would be here at the time we said we were coming."

Micky rapped on the wood this time. Thomas pulled the fob watch out of his waistcoat pocket and opened it.

"It's ten past," said Thomas. "Do you think when we didn't show on the dot of four o'clock, Jimmy ran off?"

Micky nodded. "That would be typical, and he could put off the decision for another week."

"I suppose we'll just have to wait." Thomas turned and stared along the dead straight lane with the pieces of wood and stone and other debris stacked along the edges.

"It's a tragedy," said Micky. "I remember in Owen's day, he was Jimmy's father, on those few times I was up here, there were flowers all along this lane, daffodils and hollyhocks, irises and snowdrops. If Owen came into town, he'd always leave a bunch at the estate office for old Mrs Beaton, that's the mother-in-law of our Mrs Beaton. Now, look, all Jimmy grows are weeds."

A few minutes later, the two men saw a flat cart bowling along the track above. It was going in the opposite direction to the one they had come from. The driver was standing up and alternately shouting at his donkey and singing to himself at the top of his voice. Two passengers sat in the back, their legs dangling.

At the top of the lane, the driver hauled on the reins. He turned in and drove the cart down to where Thomas and Micky stood waiting. The figure stopped and jumped off the cart. It was Jimmy McNally, with his twin sons sitting on the back. His boys were twelve years old.

"I haven't kept you waiting," he shouted. In the estate office, when Jimmy shouted in the same way, Thomas had assumed it was nerves or deference towards himself, but apparently it was habitual.

"Not at all," replied Thomas. "You haven't kept us waiting."

"You're very good," Jimmy boomed again. His face was so delicate; pale blue eyes, a small nose, and a forehead scored with thin lines. A worrier's face, thought Thomas, if ever he'd seen one; also a dormouse face. What didn't fit was the voice.

"Right, lads," Jimmy shouted at his sons. He told one son to water the cow and the calf in the front field, and the other son to take a headstone to a woman who had bought it for her husband's grave.

"I dabble in everything," Jimmy said, as the son drove the cart away, a headstone on the back laid on a bed of dirty straw.

"Time to make hay," he said enigmatically, and he clumped towards the window-ledge. "The sun is shining but not for long."

Micky and Thomas met one another's gaze. The voice level was extraordinary.

There was a box of earth on the window-ledge with a couple of green shoots sticking out of it. Jimmy lifted the box and removed a key from underneath. It was very large and black. At some point, twine had been bound around the handle and the body.

"You know my secret now," he said. "You'll be breaking in for my gold next, I know it."

"I don't think so," said Micky. "I promise, we don't want your gold."

"Hah!"

Jimmy inserted the huge key into a hole at the side of the door. It wasn't keyhole-shaped, but oval and uneven; the hole looked as if it had been hacked out of the wood with a knife . . . .

"I can probably trust you, probably."

Jimmy laughed uproariously at this and turned the key. The mechanism clicked inside.

"Welcome to my humble abode."

Jimmy swung the door open. Thomas and Micky found themselves staring at a wooden screen, with a chipped Holy Water font hung dead centre.

"Go in to the right," instructed Jimmy.

The two men stamped their boots on the ground and then followed the corridor down to the end and into the room beyond. It was very dark because of planks nailed over the window. The holes in the planks were small, they were no more than nail holes, and they let in very little light. It was a moment or two before their eyes adjusted to the gloom, and then, to their great surprise, they saw a woman sitting on the floor in front of the fire. She wore a dark red dress and her feet were bare. The woman jumped, as if their entrance had startled her, then recovered and stared back at them in an odd way. She did not speak.

"Hello," Jimmy shouted at the woman, this time in a voice so loud it made Thomas and Micky jump with fright.

The woman stood up in a single elegant movement. Micky and Thomas saw her face, her forehead broad and wide, her moist grey eyes, her small neat mouth. Her hair was long and turning grey and it hung down over her shoulders and stretched down her back. She was the same age as Jimmy, mid-thirties but she looked older, or was it sadder? Both Thomas and Micky assumed this was the wife.

Jimmy strode to the fire and pointed at the soot-covered kettle and then at the dresser, which stood against the back wall. The woman swung the kettle over the embers.

"Sit, you must sit." Jimmy dragged two chairs from the table and put them one on either side of the fire. As there were no other chairs, he put himself standing between the two visitors. 'We'll have some refreshments knocked up in a second," he said.

While Micky and Jimmy talked about mutual acquaintances and events that predated his arrival, Thomas watched Jimmy's wife. She was standing at the dresser with her back to him. He watched as she mixed up some dough, rolled it flat, cut scones out of it with a cup, put the scones on a griddle and finally carried the iron plate by its hoop handle to the fire and set it on the embers. She did all this with extraordinary rapidity and without speaking a single word.

Within minutes the room was filled with the smell of dough baking. Again working wordlessly and at great speed, Jimmy's wife laid the table with her best crockery and made the tea in a brown teapot. The scones were taken out of the fire and carried to the table.

"Right," said Jimmy. "Tea-time."

Thomas and Micky carried their chairs to the table. Jimmy went out and came back with a box which he up-ended and sat down on. His place was between the two visitors.

"Tea?" Thomas realised it was the wife who had just addressed him. The voice was flat and guttural, with no music or melody. What was the matter with her? She didn't seem right in the head.

Jimmy's wife poured the tea into his thin china cup.

After the scones were devoured and the tea was drunk, Thomas cleared his throat and said, "We have to talk about what we have to talk about. We can't put it off."

"No," Jimmy agreed.

The wife, Thomas noticed, was at the dresser once again, back to them all, furiously kneading more dough.

"Have you made up your mind?"

"I have," shouted Jimmy. "I have. It's probably the best thing to do."

"What?"

"We'll go," said Jimmy, "we'll go."

"You'll go?"

Thomas looked over at the wife. This was a momentous decision: Jimmy had just agreed to give up the farm which the McNallys had worked for generations. Wives always had something to say about these things but there she was with her back to them, busily making dough as if nothing was happening.

"Have you spoken to your sons about this?"

"I have, course!"

"What do they say?"

Jimmy swiped the air with his hand. The decision was made; the children were going to fall in with it and that was that.

"And your wife?" said Thomas politely, and he pointed to the woman on other side of the room. "Is she happy with your decision?"

Jimmy shook his head.

"Ellen! Ellen!" he shouted over at her.

Ellen went on working, quite oblivious to his calls.

"Ellen!"

Again, no response.

Jimmy got up and went over to Ellen. He turned her round and pulled her over to the table.

Ellen, assuming she was to pour more tea, said, "Tea?" in her flat voice. Her hands were covered with flour and she brushed them frantically against the side of her dress.

"No tea," Jimmy shouted. He turned his wife's head so that her eyes and his eyes were locked on one another and then he said, "A-mer-i-ka."

As Ellen stared back at her husband Thomas understood at last. She wasn't stupid: her problem was that she couldn't hear.

Jimmy pointed at the boarded-up window.

"A-mer-i-ka! We go."

"Tea?" said Ellen again.

Jimmy shrugged at Thomas. He had made his point. His wife was deaf. He pointed at the dresser. Ellen made a clumsy attempt at a curtsy and went back to kneading dough.

"The night of the wedding," said Jimmy, sitting back on the box, the volume of his voice lower, for now he was speaking like a man who did not want to be heard, "we were in her people's house, and the bean-beggars were coming to entertain. They came, when it was dark, crept up the lane in their straw outfits, their faces black with soot. They were expected but not one heard them coming. They hid in the bushes outside.

"You see, there was some sort of dispute between Ellen's

folks and those ones which went back years and years – it was
all to do with a cow and a well and a dispute about water, this
was years and years ago, mind – but you know how they bean-
beggars never forget and like to pay off old scores? – well,
didn't the bean-beggars think it hilarious this night to fill a
little wooden cask – it was a tiny thing – with gunpowder and
stones and lower it down the chimney by a rope into the fire,
and the wedding party dancing in the house. What good sport,
they thought, make a big bang and scare the living daylights
out of the guests.

"So didn't they lower it down, and no one in the wedding
party was paying any attention to the fire, and wasn't Ellen
sitting by the hearth, watching the dancers, and didn't it then
explode, bang, right beside Ellen's head, right here."

Jimmy clicked his fingers loudly beside his ear.

"In the beginning it was just the hearing. She went as deaf
as a post, like that," he clicked his fingers again, "overnight.
But she wasn't always like this, like she is now. When the
twins were born, she seemed happy. She wanted more
children but God never blessed us with more. Then the boys
got grown, and I think a sadness crept into her. She started to
drift off in her head. She started leaving the house in the
middle of the night and tramping the roads. If she took a
fancy, she'd strip off and run up the mountain. She went
down to the river and jumped in. She can't swim. A
neighbour man fished her out. Another time she tried to
jump into the well at the back.

"I had to lock the door after that. I had to board the
windows. I had to watch her all the time. In the night, if she
moved beside me, I'd waken up. I was terrified she was going
to get out and harm herself. It's been like that, I don't know,
for years now, and she has me run ragged, that's the truth, and
I don't know what the matter is. She can't tell me. I have my
ideas. I think she'd like to be away from this world, and if she
got down to the river or over to the well, she'd jump in and
make an end of it."

Jimmy moved the crumbs on his plate and pondered.

"Are you worried about the journey?" Thomas asked quietly.

"Oh, aye. That's why I couldn't say yes. I'd have taken your offer long ago only I know the crossing will be a hard station. We'll be on that ship for days with nothing but damned water everywhere we look. But I think I've got a solution. This was the boy's idea, just the other day in fact, which is how come I'm saying yes now. Tell me what you think."

Jimmy sprang up and ran over to the wall where some sort of leather contraption with reins hung from a nail. He took it down and the contraption began to jingle because there were bells attached to it.

"Ellen," he boomed. "She can't hear but sometimes she'll feel the voice," he explained, but not this time it seemed.

Jimmy rushed over to his wife and turned her round, then held up the contraption for her to see. Ellen nodded and stepped forward. Thomas was reminded of a horse opening its mouth to take the bridle. Jimmy dropped the contraption over Ellen's head. It landed on her shoulders. Thomas and Micky saw that it was harness, with bells stitched all over it.

Jimmy went behind his wife and fiddled with a buckle out of sight. He picked up the reins, which hung down at the back, and Ellen began to walk around the room in a circle like a horse in the ring.

"What do you think?" asked Jimmy. "With this laddie tied on, there's no chance she'll be jumping ship."

Thomas and Micky mumbled about it seeming to be a very good idea. The harness came off and Ellen – she had finished the dough – started to peel potatoes in the corner. Thomas and Jimmy agreed on a date for the surrender of the lease, and a date for Jimmy and his family to sail to New York. Now that arrangements were finalised, there was nothing more to say. The men stood and shook hands. The visitors waved to Ellen. She did not see because she was engrossed in her peeling. Thomas went over and touched the woman on the shoulder.

She lifted her face towards him. He looked into her eyes and she stared back blankly. Perhaps she had passed beyond despair and was now in a place where she understood nothing. She smelt of earth and potato skin. He held out his hands. "Good luck," he said.

Ellen cleaned her hand and held it out for Thomas to squeeze. It was still damp to the touch and there were grains of earth along the fingers.

Thomas wished her good luck again, then Micky came over and shook her hand.

Then the two men fled from the dark room. Outside they found it was a warm spring evening, the sun slanting across the landscape and lighting up the underside of the bare branches of trees, the grass in the fields, the stones in the walls.

"Now I know why I was never out," said Micky. "Jimmy wanted to keep her hidden."

"Are we doing the right thing?" asked Thomas, when they were half-way down the lane.

"Oh, no," Micky exclaimed wearily. "You're not after going and getting a fit of conscience on me, are you?"

They walked on in silence. At the end of the lane, at the point where it met the track that led down to the road, Micky and Thomas stopped, turned and looked back. They saw the cabin in its hollow, with its sagging roof and bent chimney, smoke curling out and rising into the sky.

"The place is a mess," said Micky. "The land's a disaster, the roof's about to go any day, and he's up to his eyeballs in debt. But with any luck Jimmy'll have a few pounds left after he's sold everything off and paid his debts, it's not costing him anything to get to America because you're paying the family's passage, and once he's over there he's going to get what he'll never know in this place, and that's a fresh start."

"I suppose you're right," agreed Thomas. In his heart he wasn't certain but with his head he knew his bailiff was right. He wondered about the deaf woman living in the city of New York. That had to be better than living on the hills, he told himself.

The two men walked in silence to the Shercock road where their car was waiting, the horse tied to the gate.

chapter eight

Home from work in Mr French's garden, Tim stood in the bigger of the two rooms that made up his cabin.

It was an oblong, eight foot wide and twelve foot long, a fireplace at one end, a single tiny window with no glass beside the crooked stable door at the other.

The hearth was a square rough space, a fire arm on the right-hand side with a sooty crook. A kettle hung from the end of the crook by a chain, and a small nest of turf coals burned underneath it. The black cooking pot stood on the dirt floor in front of the hearth. He did all his cooking in this pot.

There was a salt hole above the fire, containing a lump of salt in a twist of paper, a loaf of bread baked by a neighbour woman, his shaving kit, his writing things, his rosary, and a broken crucifix that his mother had brought with her when she married his father and came to live in this tiny house. The enamel washing bowl hung on a hook beside the salt hole.

The only furniture in the room was a table and a chair, and the box in which he kept the turf that he burned. The box had once held salted cod and it still smelt of fish.

His tools stood in the corner, a pick-axe and a spade, a scythe and a small hook. He had stood them there when he had come in from work. He had spent the day cleaning a ditch, a job he detested. Inevitably, water had got into his boots and he had worked with cold, wet feet all day.

A straw St Brigid's cross hung above the door. An old flour sack, which he used as a towel, hung on the hook behind the door, and a heart-shaped stone lay on the window sill. He had found the stone when he was clearing the acre he rented up in the hills.

The door to the bedroom was behind the fireplace. It was warped and crooked. The door was ajar and through the doorway he saw the wooden frame of his bed, his lumpy mattress stuffed with scratchy straw, the bolster lying across the top of the bed, the blanket folded over the end.

On the other side of the bedroom, underneath the tiny window, was the box where he kept his other shirt, his good trousers and his jacket.

These clothes and the other things lying about the two rooms were all that he owned in the world.

He squinted now at the kettle. It was late afternoon outside and although it was not dark, there was not enough light for him to see if there were wreaths of steam curling from the spout.

He listened to hear if the lid was flapping, as it did when the water boiled inside, but the only sounds he could hear were the murmur of the fire and the wind blowing through the ash tree that grew in front of the cabin.

He glanced at the window to check the light and gauge the time. It was grey outside. He should get a move on, he thought, if he wanted to be sure of getting down to Kitty's before darkness. The water, whatever its temperature, would just have to do.

He filled the washing bowl and took off his shirt. He

noticed then that he was filled with an odd sense of hope. Kitty might have spoken to Daniel and Bridie, he thought. For all he knew, it was settled and he was accepted.

He stropped the blade a couple of strokes then lathered his face. The soap was like egg white, dense yet light. He began to shave. His fragment of mirror was about three inches square and he could only ever see part of his face at any one time. Also, with the light failing, the image in the glass was murky and indistinct. He had to work the blade up and down his face with extreme care. He wanted to rush the job yet he knew he must go slow. He wanted to do this extremely well. He wanted to look his best.

Then he told himself that his optimism was misplaced. Daniel was going to need longer than four days to accept that his daughter was following in his footsteps. Of course. Yet because there was a possibility that he might have come round, Tim felt it was vital to clean himself up as well as he could. If an opportunity arose to make an impression, he planned on making the most of it.

He tilted his head back and began to move the cutting edge towards his Adam's apple. That was when he registered the tiny jab of pain. A moment later he saw a thin line of blood in the foam.

He wiped his neck with a flour sack and saw the nick. It was tiny, yet blood was streaming out of it. It was extraordinary that so much blood was able to squeeze itself out through so small a hole. He realised then that he would have to wait until the blood had dried before he put on his good shirt.

The pine tree came in view, a black, jagged shape against the darkening sky behind. Tim went to the wall, sat on it and went as if to swing his leg over. Then he heard voices.

He got down from the wall and moved noiselessly down the lane. The cottage stood on the high bank to his left. He stopped and looked up at it. It was a long, low building, with a door and four windows all with glass. Two of the windows looked into the main room in the middle of the house, while the single ones at either end gave on to the bedrooms.

Daniel and Bridie McKenna slept in the room on the right-hand side, close to the byre. This was so that Daniel was able to hear his animals in the night. Kitty slept in the bedroom at the opposite end of the house.

The previous Christmas Day, when the McKenna family were all at Mass, Tim had crept up to Kitty's window and looked in. He saw Kitty's iron bed, the crucifix on the wall over it, the statue of the Blessed Virgin on the window-ledge, the grey work-dress hanging on the back of the bedroom door, the iron chamberstick on the floor beside the bed with half a tallow candle stuck in the holder in the middle, and a black stocking lying nearby.

Tonight, however, the McKennas were at home. He saw the light of a tallow candle spilling from one of the windows that gave on to the main room. He guessed the candle lamp was on the table in its customary position.

The front door had two halves and the top half was ajar, allowing him to hear the voices inside. Tim went over to the bank, and angled his head.

"I will, I've told you that I will," he heard.

This was Kitty and the sound of her voice made him tingle in his legs, his back and his chest.

"Only I don't want you spying on me," continued Kitty.

He felt the tingle again. This time it was in his stomach behind his belt.

"It's a pity we didn't keep you under observation these past nine months," shouted Daniel, and then he added, "You will do what you're told."

Tim wondered, was this a question or a statement? Then he heard Kitty saying, "Do I have to repeat myself? Yes, I will! But don't spy, that's all I say, don't spy. I'll do what you say," and Tim decided this was a statement and this made him feel anxious.

"You will do what we have told you," said Kitty's father a little threateningly. "All right, go out and fill the buckets."

"Yes," said Kitty.

Tim felt the tingling sliding down from his stomach and towards his groin. Kitty was coming out to the spring.

"No spying," said Kitty again.

"You needn't worry, there'll be no need of spying," sighed Bridie. He saw the mother's plump shape moving behind a window. "If that young hero is anywhere near you, I'll smell him off you."

The tingle had moved into the bone at the bottom of his pelvis. He was getting hard. He imagined taking Kitty's hand, sliding it under his belt and down into his trousers, and him begging her to do it quickly.

My little spear, Kitty called it, when she took it with her hand and pulled and pushed at it until the milky seed came out with much shuddering and gasping and ran over her hand and her arm and her skirt.

Once they were married, she would do more than hold him in her hand, or in her mouth, as he had recently persuaded her to do. Once they were married, he would have her in his bed every night, and she would be naked and he would do what he wanted, and so would she.

Tim pinched his ear lobe and then slapped his cheeks a couple of times. He had to. This was not the way to think. Not now, not at this moment. He reminded himself that tonight he had to find out what was happening and he had to exclude everything else from his thoughts. He had come to find out. What had she told Bridie and Daniel? What had Daniel and Bridie said? He had shaved and put on his good shirt because of the remote possibility that everything was settled and he was invited in. However, judging by the conversation he had just overheard, that wasn't going to happen, which was disappointing. On the other hand, he was going to see Kitty, whom he hadn't seen for three days.

In the McKenna house the talk had stopped. There was a bang and then a squeak. Tim recognised the sound of the handle on one of the buckets as it was picked up.

There was time to spring back up the lane, climb the wall

and get into position by the pine. However, as he went to turn, it occurred to him this was unnecessary. Kitty was coming and Daniel and Bridie were not going to spy. They'd said that, hadn't they? And there was somewhere else to hide besides the pine, somewhere much, much better, a spot that would allow him to effect a marvellous sudden appearance.

Tim turned and ran on down the lane, the bank rising on his left, the cottage disappearing from view, and he kept running until he came to the well.

The spring well was some thirty yards down the lane. It was set into the side of the bank, and there was a circle of stones that Kitty's father had built to hold the water after it bubbled out and before it flowed away.

There was a bank at the back and on top of this there grew an apple tree in what was the end of the McKennas' garden. It was an apple tree that had yet to produce a crop. Bridie hung her washing on the branches. The cottage lay behind, and although it was not in view, everything said up at the cottage was audible down at the well, yet from the cottage, any talk down by the well was inaudible. It was a mystery that no one understood.

"Out you go now, Kitty," Bridie ordered her daughter. Hallelujah, thought Tim.

"You close the door," Kitty called. "You can trust me to go down to the well by myself. I've agreed what you wanted me to agree. I'll say my piece. Now will you please close the door."

There had been much of this sort of talk from Kitty. Tim registered a faint sense of dread as he wondered what she'd agreed to say.

One of the McKenna parents shouted something back at their daughter, which Tim didn't catch. Then there came the sound of the lower half of the door scraping shut.

He heard the sound of Kitty's bare feet as she padded down the stony path. She appeared on the top of the bank. She held a bucket in each hand. She did not see him. She was staring towards the pine tree that stood further up the lane.

"Tim?" she called quietly.

He saw Kitty screwing up her face and looking around in a puzzled way. Why did she think he would be in the usual place? Perhaps, he thought, she was so desperate to see him, she had called out towards the pine tree before stopping to consider that he probably would not be there. Or perhaps she thought he was a creature of habit. He thought that was more likely.

She moved down the path. Any moment now she would be on the lane, heading towards him. He stepped up to the well. The side of the bank would hide him here. He could hear Kitty coming. He slipped sideways into the copse of alder trees, which grew at the side of the well. He took two strides and then squatted down.

From this position, he saw the wall built into the slope of the bank. He saw the boulder in front of the wall and the small jet of spring water that shot miraculously out of the middle of it. He saw the spouting jammed into the rock underneath. He saw water running along the spouting, dribbling off the end and tumbling into the pool below. He saw the circle of stones around the edge of the pool. The level of the pool never varied because as quickly as it filled, the pool emptied along a fissure into a ditch a hundred yards down the lane, and flowed away as a small stream known as the Waters of Mary.

He heard noises in the McKenna house. He heard Kitty. She sang as she walked.

"Feather beds are soft," she sang. Her thin voice wavered and trembled. He felt his penis hardening.

"Painted rooms are bonny,
I know who I love,
But the Lord knows who I'll marry."

Kitty arrived at the well. She stepped up to the pool. She put one bucket down on the edge of the circle of stones. She hung the other bucket by its handle from the spouting. There were two prongs on the end of the spouting to prevent a bucket falling off as it filled up.

Kitty straightened up. She threw back her shoulders and

stared up at the sky. He saw her pale face with its small, straight nose. Her eyes were grey with thin, rather beautifully arching eyebrows above them. Her cheeks were ever so faintly ruddy and there was a small indentation in Kitty's chin. Her mouth was even; her upper lip was thinner than her lower lip. Her hair was in a bun, held in place on the back of her head with an ornamental comb. When she was at rest, as she was now, her habitual expression was dreamy. On the other hand, when she wanted to say something important, or when she was either happy or troubled, her dreaminess would vanish and she would look directly at Tim with her dark grey eyes.

Kitty began to yawn. She patted her mouth with her hand. He might as well do it now, he thought.

He got up and came forward. "Boo!" he said.

Kitty turned towards him, a look of alarm on her face. A second later, layered over her appalled expression, was the look of relief as she recognised him. He was grateful for this, but Tim also knew that it would do him no good. Recognition would in no way lessen her anger.

"Jesus! You gave me the scare of my life," Kitty hissed. "What do you think you're doing?"

He took a step towards her then half a step back.

"Just here to say hello. Like I am every evening, 'cept you keep avoiding your faithful servant."

As Kitty said nothing, Tim decided to press on.

"Where've you been for the last three days, and why's your father been out here in your place?"

"You gave me a terrible fright," she said.

"Sorry," he said.

Tim moved towards Kitty. She didn't move back from him so he reached up and touched her cheek where her mother had struck her. There was a shiny purple bruise between the lower eyelid and the top of the cheekbone. Tim touched the bruise, waited for Kitty to wince, and then, when she didn't, he began to stroke his finger backwards and forwards across the plum-coloured mark.

"It must have hurt when your mother whacked you," he

said. "I saw that," he added quickly.

Turning her face away from his finger Kitty said, "Father and Mother's up at the house."

Of course they were. Daniel and Bridie were always up at the house – that was why he and Kitty did their courting down here, and in the middle of the alder trees below.

"So what?" said Tim.

"He has a pretty good idea you might be here."

"Yes," he said, sarcastically. "And what's that mean? I should be shivering in my boots?"

"We were seen you know, here, last week."

"Oh." With his tone he hoped to suggest insouciance, indifference.

"Emily Johnston," she said.

So that was who. Emily, known as Creeping Spot because of her habit of moving around noiselessly, was an old and unhappy spinster who lived a solitary life, avoided by pretty much everybody unless they were suffering from cystitis, or the "bride's complaint" as it was called, and for which Emily had the cure.

In her youth Emily had loved a man who had abandoned her on the morning of their marriage. She was literally left standing at the altar while he was shipping on a boat out of Dundalk. He drowned a year later in the Bristol Channel, and since then, Emily believed his ghost followed her around. They had long conversations, Emily and her ghost. Like the rest of Beatonboro', Tim thought she was harmless but definitely mad.

"Who'd believe a word she says?" he said.

"Old Mrs Gallagher did, and she told them above and now they know everything."

Kitty sounded very angry. There was no doubting that. What was impossible to tell was with whom she was angry. Was it him? or her parents? or old Mrs Gallagher?

"Your bucket's full," he said, and it was. The excess water was spilling over the top and running down the sides.

He lifted the full bucket off the spout and set it down on

the ground. He picked up the second bucket, the empty one. Suddenly, as he lifted it towards the spout, Kitty snatched it away. "I can manage on my own," she said.

He tried to get the bucket back from her but she wouldn't let go of it.

"All right," he said. However, he did not let go of the handle. He held it very tight, with his left hand. At the same time he slid his right hand up the handle of the bucket and onto Kitty's hands, and then from her hands he went across her knuckles, and wriggled his fingers under her cuffs and began to touch her wrists.

"Do you enjoy saying no?" he asked. He stoked where blue veins traced across the thin skin. He could feel her pulse bumping underneath. "You are driving me absolutely out of my mind."

This was not what he had come to say but to hell with it. The words were coming. "I cannot, cannot, cannot wait any longer," he said.

"No," she said.

"I don't have to wait any longer. It's a yes!"

He put his hands straight between her legs and lifted. He felt the springy hair on the other side of her skirt, and behind the hair he felt the bone, and it was his sense that as he lifted she was pushing back against his hand.

Once he had got her drunk on poítin, he remembered, one evening late the previous summer. They were in the old quarry half a mile up the road. No one went there. She had let him undress her completely, and when she was naked, she had let him lay her back, and then she had let him open her legs. He had stared at the small pink slit for a while and then he had reached forward and touched it with his finger and she had smiled. Then he had bent forward and kissed the top of this slit and she had smiled again, and then he had pushed his tongue against her and she had unexpectedly sat up, covered her breasts and told him that she had to get dressed and go home. He tried to get her to lie back down again but she wouldn't. She undid his trousers and pulled him off on to her breasts.

Then she said she wanted to go home, stood up and began to get dressed.

It occurred to him at this moment that the memory was a warning. If he pushed too hard now the spell would be broken, as surely as it was when he touched her with his tongue. She would remember who she was and where she was. She would shake herself free.

Yet at the same time as he had this thought, he was also lifting Kitty's skirt. He held his breath. He had her skirt as high as her thigh. He felt her bare skin. She cried out, tugged herself free and stepped away from him.

"No," she said.

He pointed up at the house. "They'd put anyone off. Let's go in here," he whispered.

He took hold of her arm and tugged her towards the stand of alder trees.

"No." She spoke with much more force than before.

"Come to my house," he said.

"No, never."

"Is this because your parents hammered you the other night?"

Kitty said nothing.

"I could hear. He took the strap to you."

Kitty sighed. Perhaps it was wrong, he thought, to suggest the beating had achieved the desired result and that she had now given in to them.

"What did they say?"

"What do you mean?"

"Mrs Gallagher told them about us?"

Kitty moved her head up and down slowly, once.

"And what about your plan? You always said, at first your father would be furious but then he would see that your path and his were the same."

Kitty was looking down into the pool of water where her watery silhouette floated on the surface. Why wasn't she looking up? Tim did not like this at all.

"What happened? We had a plan. What happened?"

"I can't see you any more," she said slowly.

"It's not just no now, it's no for ever?" He affected a light, jesting tone. He didn't believe what he was hearing.

"I think so," she said, and then, straightening up and staring at him with her grey eyes, she continued, "Yes."

"Yes?"

"Yes," she confirmed.

She was still looking him in the eye as she did when she had something important to say. She meant it.

"All right."

Meanwhile, he thought, Why not? If the plan was to prove that she trod the same path as Daniel went down twenty years before, then why not go all the way? Why not do what Daniel had done against his parents' wishes?

"Marry me," he said.

"No." She delivered her reply, plain and straight.

"But I love you," he said.

Silence.

"And you love me."

Silence again but he was going to finish now he'd started. Tim lifted his shoulders and held out his hands, as if to say — What are we waiting for?

"There is nothing to wait for," he heard Kitty reply, and then she swallowed. "I have told my father, I have promised him, in fact, I won't."

"What?"

"See you. It is now over. Finished. I have promised him."

"Promised him what?"

"I won't see you any more, or talk to you, or say hello if we pass in the street in Beatonboro', or anything."

"Not even tumble with Tim any more?"

He put his hand between her legs. For a moment she stood still — and he wondered if she was about to give in — and then she stepped back and he realised why she had delayed. She wanted him to know that though she liked him or loved him, she was still not going to see him again.

"I've promised."

"Why don't you just drop the buckets and we'll go?"

"I can't."

"You can."

"How much have you in your pocket?"

Tim put his hand into his trousers pocket and pulled out all his change.

Kitty looked at the coins in the middle of his palm. "Three farthings," she said staring at the round, brown shapes, "plus an acre of mountainy land, and you think we can live on that?"

"Yes," he said defiantly.

The truth was, no, he did not. The future as they imagined it was that he married Kitty and then he took over the farm from Daniel. When he had said to Kitty, "Marry me," and when he had defiantly answered her question about living off his acre, he hadn't envisaged the two of them living in his cabin for ever. If they married and went there – and he believed there was now no alternative – their stay was going to be temporary, rather like Daniel's stay in the woods with Bridie until his father's accident and the call to come home. He and Kitty had talked about this for nine months, although now, alarmingly, it seemed as if they had never had these conversations.

"What about the plan?" he said again. "Your father was always going to be angry, but then he was going to come round, he was going to see that we were the same mettle as him."

Kitty exhaled, a signal, he sensed, of short temper and a weary self-disgust.

"If we marry my father and mother will never speak to me again – ever," she said. "If we have children they will never speak to those children – ever. They have made this plain to me."

She had never said anything like this before. It was an alarming development and Tim didn't know what to say. So he shrugged and said, "When they beat you the other night, they told you all this?"

"Yes."

"So, everything you said when we talked in the past, none of it has happened?"

"No."

"Why not? I thought Daniel was going to be angry and then he was going to come round."

"I was an idiot, I was wrong, I was a fool," said Kitty. "I never realised they would be as angry as they were."

Tim was incredulous. "I believed you."

"They were so angry. I never thought . . . they were so furious. They said, and I knew they meant this absolutely, if, if, you and me, that was it, for ever, I would never have sight of them, and any children we had, they would never have sight of their grandparents."

"Well, forget Daniel and Bridie."

"Your parents are dead," said Kitty crossly, "but I can't cut myself off from mine."

He was starting to feel angry. A few taps of the strap the other evening and Kitty had caved in. It was as if everything she had said over the previous nine months had never happened.

"So, the wedding's off?" he said.

Kitty said nothing but stared down at the water again. Mixed with his anger were huge feelings of desire.

"They're inside," he said. "We're free. Pull me off by hand," he said.

Tim kissed her neck and rubbed her breasts through her jacket. Kitty stood quite still. She was going to let herself go, he hoped. Then she moved back. It was the same as in the quarry when she had come out of her drunken reverie and sat up.

"No, stop it," she said. "Yes. It's off. That's it. Goodbye."

"But we can have such a good time together," Tim pressed. "Come home with me, we'll light a fire, undress, sleep, see the priest tomorrow, have the banns read, marry in six weeks."

"*No*. We will not marry. I cannot. And I cannot see you again. It is over, finished, that's it."

"They beat this into you, didn't they?"

Kitty was still staring downwards.

"They whack you a couple of times and you never want to see me again."

Still nothing from Kitty.

"You can't ever have been that keen if they could put you off me that easily."

"You have no idea what you're talking about. I was a fool ever to think they'd let us carry on, and now I see that. Yes, they thumped me, but it's what I heard that counted. Try and understand, from now on, it's as if you and I don't exist. That's an order." Kitty glared.

"Bastards," he muttered. "Bastards."

"Don't," said Kitty, more irritated than angry.

"We make each other happy, have our whole lives ahead of us."

"You haven't listened, have you, Tim?"

She still sounded irritated and in turn that now irritated him.

"I have listened."

"You haven't."

"I have."

"If you had listened, Tim, you'd have understood."

"I've understood," he interrupted her. "I've no land, that's why your father doesn't like me. And that makes him lower than cow-shit in the fields."

"Always one for the choice language."

"Don't tell me how to talk."

"Then don't insult them."

"I've only one acre to his forty-whatever-the-number-is," he began, uncertain where this was going, "and that's why he and your mother won't countenance me."

"You're wrong, all wrong!" she scolded.

"Oh, yes." His face was flushed. To be judged like this because he was poor. He wanted to shout, I'll work, I'll prove them wrong, I'll take a farm, I'll make money. Daniel didn't know him, other than by name. Daniel had never spoken to him. How dare he! How dare the old fool with his broken, ugly nose and his fat ugly stomach, lay down the law and tell him, Tim Traynor, he was not to marry Kitty, or talk to Kitty, or even look at Kitty.

As well as fury, there was a cool realisation on Tim's part that now he had to find something to say. Something which would shock Kitty and prove that her father could not treat him like this. He needed to show her that he could teach the old fool a lesson. The question was, how? His mind raced. What could he say that would put the fear of God into the old bastard?

In his mind there was a vague image of men in pointy hats and inside-out dresses trailing ribbons. He was just a boy of eight. He was in the classroom in the school. Four of these men in pointy hats came in with sticks and cudgels and bill-hooks. Ribbonmen. They overpowered the master and three of them dragged him out of the room. Tim watched, terrified but not surprised. His father had warned him there was going to be trouble with the master, and that when it came he was neither to say nor do anything. He was to sit tight.

It was a dispute over shooting rights. This was the back story. The master had recently begun to rent a piece of land from old John Hutcheson, the present Colonel's father. It was a piece of land on which the landlord had always permitted free shooting. Unfortunately, and carelessly, old Hutcheson had not retained the shooting rights when he leased the land. The shooting rights were the master's now. The master's lawyer had advised him that the rights were his to do with as he wished. The master wanted to keep them to himself. The master put signs up on the trees along the edge of the land, No shooting. The locals ignored these and went on shooting. The master pleaded with Hutcheson to tell the locals that their old rights were now suspended, but the landlord ignored his letters. The locals pleaded with Hutcheson to tell the master to allow the old tradition to continue, but the landlord ignored their pleas as well. Hutcheson was angry. If only his agent had retained the rights in the letting agreement, none of this mess would have happened; the locals would have gone on shooting the land and the master couldn't have got on his high horse. However, now, he, the landlord, was stuck between two angry parties, each of whom believed right was on their side. It was going to end with blood spilt. Old Hutcheson knew it.

One day the master came on a group of men on his land. They were there to shoot. The master told the men to leave. The shooting party refused. The master wrenched a gun off one of the men and threw it into a ditch. The ditch was waterlogged. The gun sank down into the muddy slime. The owner retrieved his gun. There was filth all over the weapon. The owner held the gun upside down in front of the master and a black mess trickled out of the barrel. The shooting party left threatening revenge, and the Ribbonmen who appeared in Tim's classroom were that revenge. The master had said the land was his land to do with what he wanted. Well, they were going to prove him wrong. The master threw the gun in the ditch. Well, now they were going to teach the master a lesson.

Three of the Ribbonmen took the master out of the classroom and closed the door behind them. A fourth stayed behind. Outside, Tim could hear the terrible shouts of the master and the Ribbonmen laughing. Then Tim heard the small school gate opening and the unmistakable sound of the master being dragged out on to the road and towards the lake on the other side.

Meanwhile, inside, Tim could hear the fourth Ribbonman, the one who had stayed behind, pacing up and down in front of the class. Tim, who had his head bowed, lifted his eyes towards the front. There were two eye-holes cut in the pointy hat that hung down over this Ribbonman's face. The hem of the dress that he wore stopped a little above his knees. His muddy boots and spattered trouser bottoms showed beneath this. He had very big, very clean hands. The ribbons tied on the dress were red and green and blue.

Suddenly, the fourth man stopped, then turned and opened the doors of the cupboard. The lower shelves were empty. This was where the slates and chalks were kept, and these had been distributed among the children and were now on the desks in front of them. On the upper shelves were the master's books – Shakespeare's plays, the poems of William Wordsworth, Homer, Caesar's Gallic Wars, a Bible, as well as the master's pens and paper, and a jar of ink.

While the shouting continued outside, Tim watched the Ribbonman take the master's books and lay each of them open on the master's desk. Then the Ribbonman took the large jar of ink and pulled out the stopper with his teeth. He spat the stopper into the fireplace where a small fire burned. He tipped the bottle over the master's desk. When there was not a drop of ink left in the jar, the Ribbonman hurled the bottle at the fire. It hit the back of the hearth and exploded. Tim's heart started to beat faster. All the children were silent. The screams and roars of the master were continuing but now they sounded further away. A drop of ink plopped into the puddle on the floor. Suddenly, the shouting stopped.

The Ribbonman clicked his fingers. The class stood. No child said a word. The Ribbonman pointed at the window. Forty-five children moved over the pine floor to the glass.

When he got to the window, Tim saw that the three other Ribbonmen were on the jetty on the other side of the road. It was the master's jetty. He used it to fish for pike and brown trout. He kept a boat tied here and sometimes, if the weather was fine, he took the children out for rides in the boat after school. The master took his fiancée out in the boat as well, and Tim was certain he had seen the master and Irene kissing while they drifted across the black, still surface of the lake on Sunday afternoons.

Tim saw the three Ribbonmen were now holding a big brown sack. The sack was struggling and moving because there was something in it. Two Ribbonmen took the sack, one at each end.

"One, two, three," the third Ribbonman shouted. He seemed to be in charge.

The sack flew through the air and landed on the surface of the water with a splash. For a second or two the sack was afloat and struggling on the surface. Then it sank.

The Ribbonmen walked back towards the school. The fourth Ribbonman slipped out of the class without any of the children noticing and joined his colleagues outside. In the classroom, Tim and the rest of the children remained, gathered at the window. He was as uncertain what to do now as everyone else: were they to stay as they were? or were they to leave and run home? or were they to risk running out and trying to get the sack out of the lake?

The Ribbonmen outside saw Tim and the children at the window. Tim saw that they saw and waited, holding his breath. One of the Ribbonman raised an arm. The Ribbonman was pointing at him. The Ribbonman pointed back at the lake and then he pointed his finger back at him again, or that's how it seemed. The message was unmistakable. He was not to go down to the lake. He was not to move. No one was. Everyone was to stay in the classroom.

The Ribbonmen walked away. Every now and again they looked back at the school, at the children standing at the window. Then the Ribbonmen went around the bend in the road and were gone. The class remained silent. The lake, Tim saw, was still and calm. A wind blew and moved the rushes at the side. The master's boat moved slowly sideways and bumped the jetty. There was no sign of the sack. Tim returned to his desk and sat down. The other children in the class returned to their desks and sat down. No one said a word.

In the late afternoon, when Tim did not appear at home, his mother decided to go down to the school. As she walked along the road, she met other mothers who were also going to the school because their children had not come home.

When Mrs Traynor and the other mothers arrived, they found their children sitting silently in their classroom without their master. The fire in the grate was dead and the master's books were on his desk and there was ink all over them. Mrs Traynor guessed what had happened although nothing had been said. She took her Tim's hand and led him out of the room.

There was no school the next day because there was no master to take the class. Four members of the Constabulary dragged the lake and found the sack. They got it in the boat, rowed to the jetty and carried the sack up to the school garden. Here they cut the sack open and lifted it up. Out tumbled several heavy stones, the master and a long, thick fat eel. The eel had eaten the master's lips and cheeks and ear-lobes. The constable who was in charge of the search got his boot on the eel and cut off its head. The body went on writhing for some while. In Beatonboro', when the story went around, it was said the eel writhed for minutes rather than seconds, as was actually the case, because eating human flesh gave it special powers.

The master was buried three days later. Tim Traynor's mother and father did not go to the funeral. Nor did any of the parents from the school. This was not because the Ribbonmen had warned the population against going. It was simply that all the parents, including the Traynors, knew that to be seen at the funeral would suggest they sympathised or agreed with the dead master and disapproved of the Ribbonmen, and although they might privately, it would be fatal for that to be known publicly. Only Hutcheson attended (as an Anglican he usually shunned Roman Catholic funerals, but in this case he felt he had to go), as well as a couple of Beatonboro' shop-keepers who felt they were above the fray, and of course, Irene, the master's fiancée. She threw herself down on the coffin after it had been lowered into the grave in order to stop the earth being spaded in. The two gravediggers had to lift her off and carry her away. After the funeral, the will was read; the master had left everything, including the land, to a cousin in Pomeroy. However, the beneficiary wanted nothing to do with it. He thought the land was cursed because it was connected to the schoolmaster's murder. So he gave it up and the land went back to Hutcheson, and in due course free shooting resumed on it.

In Tim's boyhood, the master was feared by children, and revered by the parents. The only ones who did not fear or revere him were the Ribbonmen. The master took something away, they wrested it back. So there was the answer to the question — what would put fear into the old bastard McKenna?

"You can tell him and your mother," said Tim, "I shall be joining the Ribbonmen."

"You can't be serious," said Kitty, ferociously.

Because of the way she said this, Tim couldn't help smirking like a schoolboy who had been caught out. He remembered seeing three cows the previous summer. They belonged to a farmer who earned the displeasure of the local Lodge. The Ribbonmen had come in the night with billhooks and slashed the hamstrings of the animals. When Tim came on them, very early one morning, they were lying where they had fallen, moaning and roaring, their splayed legs flopping about uselessly on the ground, the grass around them smeared with their blood.

From this an imaginary picture jumped into his mind. It was Daniel's cow — he called her Josie — lying in her stall. In his mind's eye Tim saw Josie and her legs were slashed, or houged as it was called, and Daniel was standing over the animal with his precious pistols pointed at her head. He was about to kill her. When a creature was hobbled like that, there was nothing else to do but kill it.

"They're a pack of villains," started Kitty, "who go around —"

"But they want me," interrupted Tim, "which is more than you do."

This was a lie but he felt so angry he knew there was going to be no difficulty convincing himself that it was true.

"Slashing, killing, maiming, to make themselves important, and mostly it's ones like us they do this too, and then every now and again they bump off a policeman or a landlord and we're expected to shout, 'Well done! Hurrah for Ireland!' "

"They're trying to do something," he heard himself shouting, which was feeble, he knew, even as he got the words out.

"Was that just 'something' they did to my aunt Mary and uncle David?" snorted Kitty.

He'd forgotten about that. However, he'd started now, he'd have to brazen it out.

"They took land that they shouldn't have taken," he said insolently. "They broke the rules."

"Those three acres going beside their farm, the family was gone."

"You told me evicted," he said. He wasn't going to let her get away with substituting "gone" for "evicted".

"Yes, all right," she said tersely. "They couldn't pay their rent. So they went. The landlord offered the land to David. Why shouldn't my uncle have had them?"

Tim shook his head. It was a point of principle. The land belonged to the evicted family. If nobody took it, the landlord would have no choice in the end but to give it back to them. That was the logic, although he knew there were also plenty of instances, when families were evicted, that their farms were re-let, and no one minded. As the inconsistency struck him, he wondered first how this was explained, and then he found himself hoping that Kitty wouldn't get on to this.

To his relief, her next words were, "O'Duffy. Look what they did to that boy, O'Duffy."

"What about it?" said Tim weakly.

"They cut him off and left him a girl. That was disgusting. You wouldn't treat an animal like that, let alone a man."

Perhaps, after all, it would have been better if they had been arguing about inconsistency, how sometimes a man could take a farm and no one minded, while sometimes a man took a place and everyone minded.

"He was an informer," said Tim, and swallowed. He managed to sound fierce when he spoke although he felt anything but fierce.

"Would you, could you, do that?" Kitty said forcefully. He met her gaze. Whatever happened, he must not blink. If he blinked she'd know he was lying but if he returned her gaze she would believe he spoke the truth.

They stayed locked as they were, staring at each other for several seconds. Tim did not blink.

Something changed in Kitty's face. The anger drained away and tender curiosity appeared in its place.

"Tim, is this my Tim that I'm hearing? I don't think so. This is someone else."

"No, we're the same." He didn't like this talk.

"You're just trying to frighten me."

"No, I'm not."

"This is a ploy. This is you, getting at me."

Not for the first time, he was struck by how sharp Kitty was, and how quickly she was on to him.

The thought must have shown because Kitty's face changed again. Her perplexed, puzzled look vanished and back rushed her furious look.

"Don't get at me," she shouted. "This is not my doing. None of it is. If I don't do what my parents say, I will never see them again. Do you understand that? Do you understand what that means? I can't cut myself off from them, not for ever!"

"They've been on at me to join for months," he began coolly. "They always regretted not signing the father, and they don't want to repeat that mistake with the son."

"Your father despised them."

Tim decided to ignore the remark, although it was true.

"You've chosen your road – go back home," he said.

"This is just to get at me. I know it."

"No, it isn't," he said. He had not forgotten that he had only arrived at the idea of threatening to join a few minutes earlier, but now that he had, he genuinely felt it was the right course of action. When this had occurred, he didn't know; obviously, just moments before. What he did notice, however, was that he felt much better now he knew what he was going to do.

"Kitty, Kitty . . ." The voice of Daniel drifted from the cottage overhead.

Suddenly Kitty began to cry. "I don't believe it. I can't stand this. You and my father . . ."

Tim saw a last chance.

"Come to America," he said.

"We couldn't afford the ticket for one of us, let alone two."
Tears showed in her eyes and one trickled down her cheek.

"You have to choose," he said. He tried to say this as gently as he was able.

"Don't," she shouted back at him. "That's not fair."

It occurred to him that of course it wasn't fair. Then he reminded himself that it was her parents who had beaten her and then told her she had to choose. Not him.

"Now," he said. "Me or them."

"Kitty," Daniel shouted again from the cottage above.

"This is not fair," she said. "This is not fair."

"Who's it to be? Choose."

"I won't."

"Fine," he said.

Kitty picked up the empty bucket and hooked it angrily over the end of the spout. "You must not join," she said, suddenly calm. Noise came from the bottom of the bucket like rain on a roof. "You know how it'll end."

Tim frowned, as if to say, Don't be silly.

"Your choice," he said, and at that moment he believed it. She had left him no alternative. If she turned him down, he would join. He had told her this. It was her choice.

He looked at Kitty. He was trying to see if she had understood this. Most unhelpfully, she was looking down at her bucket and the water flowing into it. Inwardly, Tim decided to count to three and if by that time she hadn't said anything, then he would assume her answer was no. No to America, no to him. Which left him only one choice.

One, two, three, he counted. Not a word from Kitty.

"Goodbye," he said.

"Kitty," Daniel shouted, "you're to come in right now, Kitty."

"He's calling," said Tim. "You'd better go in to him."

"You know why I came out here?" Kitty turned and looked at him. "I could have just never seen you again," she said. "That would have been the easy way. But I decided that way was also cruel. I decided I *must* tell you myself, and I persuaded them that was the right thing to do. That's why they let me out tonight. It is wrong to be cruel and you are being cruel now."

He decided there was nothing to say in reply to this. He also decided that Kitty was stupid. She had to be stupid if she failed to see how cruel she was to come and say she would never see him again. She was also stupid for having imagined Daniel would say yes. The miserable old bastard was never going to say yes, never, ever.

But at least he knew what to do now. It was going to terrify the old man when he threw in his lot with these ones that Daniel so feared that he loaded his pistols every day in case they came. Oh, yes, once he, Tim, the rejected suitor, was in the Lodge, the old fool would have a few unhappy hours. It was wonderful, a certainty in fact, and at the thought Tim began to laugh.

"Goodbye," he said, and still laughing he turned and began to walk away. Daniel, he noticed, was on the bank looking down on the lane. The two men looked at one another for a moment.

"McKenna," Tim called up, mock-respectfully, "one day, you're going to learn a lesson you're never going to forget."

Daniel raised his right arm. He was holding his pistol. He pointed the gun at Tim's chest.

"I'm leaving," said Tim, "but I can't promise you won't ever see me again. Goodbye, Kitty," he called down the lane. Then he walked on, waving a hand like a lord while at the same time keeping his back towards Daniel and Kitty as they stood and watched him go.

When she came into the cottage a few moments later with the buckets, Kitty found her father sitting at the table.

Daniel glanced at his daughter.

"What did you say?" It was Bridie who spoke.

Daniel began to spread butter evenly across the piece of bread on the plate in front of him.

Kitty put down the buckets of water in the place where

they always went by the door.

Bridie was standing in front of the fire. She had lifted her skirt at the back. Bridie felt the heat of the fire on her thighs. Her rump and the tops of her legs were often cold but never her hands or her feet. This puzzled her. Properly speaking, she thought, it should have been the extremities where she felt the cold, rather than her middle.

"Has he agreed, do you think?" Bridie asked her daughter. "Do we think this is the end and that whippersnapper shan't be bothering you again?"

Kitty went and sat on the chair by the dresser. It was in the corner of the room furthest from the table and the hearth.

"I hope I shan't just be hearing the sound of my own voice," said Bridie. She was irritated by her daughter's silence.

Daniel spooned blackberry jam from the dish to his bread and started to spread the dark jelly with the jam spoon.

"Don't use the spoon, dear," Bridie called over.

"Oh, sorry," said her husband.

Kitty watched her father lick the spoon and put it on the plate.

"Tut, tut," went Bridie. Her husband was meant to put the spoon back in the dish without licking it.

"I think you'd both like me to go to bed," said Kitty.

The bread went to her father's mouth. He bit off a piece. He began to chew.

Kitty felt disgusted. She had told Tim she would never see him again. Yet her parents were unimpressed.

"Why go to bed?" her father said, with a full mouth. Then he swallowed. "It's early."

Because that's what dutiful daughters do, Kitty thought. She felt a great rush of heat in the middle of her chest and on her face.

"Do you know what I have done?" she said. She only just managed to stop sounding angry.

Her father, bread in hand, looked across the room at her, open-mouthed.

"I've told the man I love that I will never see him again and you say nothing. It was hard, it was awful for me."

"Don't talk to your father like that," said her mother, crossly.

Kitty stared at her father's face. At the end of the broken lump of his nose, the nostrils were moving in and out, sure signal of anger.

"Now just you wait a minute little lady," he roared.

He threw his bread down with all his might on the table. The slice disintegrated and crumbs and pieces of bread covered with butter and jam flew in every direction.

"I've nothing against him as a man. He's just the wrong husband. He's been chasing you for nine months behind our backs and I won't have it any more."

Great hot tears leaked from Kitty's eyes and ran down her cheeks.

"Do you know what your father is saying?" called Bridie. "I don't know if you're old enough to understand, but this is for your own good. A crooked house and an acre of spuds – that boy's a nothing, a nobody."

Kitty wanted to tell the truth. Kitty wanted to shout, I love him. Instead she said, "You don't know what you're talking about."

"You might be due another tap with the strap, young lady."

Her father began to pull the tongue of his belt out of the buckle. His hands shook.

"I think you should go to bed," said her mother quickly.

"I won't see him again," said Kitty, just as quickly. She didn't want to be beaten again.

Daniel looked across the room at his daughter.

"That a promise?" he asked, coldly.

"I promise."

Kitty went to bed. As she lay huddled under her covers in the darkness, Kitty started to cry. After she had cried for several minutes, the bolster became wet under her cheek. She developed a pain in her throat and a pain in her stomach. These felt as real as if she had been punched in these places – which she had not. She understood that this hurt was what older people meant when they spoke of heartache.

As she wept, almost all of Kitty's attention was absorbed by her pain. However, she was also dimly aware that there were intimate memories hovering on the edge of her thoughts. His arms enfolding her, and her enfolding him in her arms as they embraced. Moving her hand up and down his penis, his moan, his seed running over her fingers. It was warm but soon it went cold and she wiped her hand on the grass. Lying in her bare skin the time in the quarry and the stars swirling in the velvet sky. Then another time, pushing back the funny skin with her tongue and the end of him tasting salty when the skin was right back . . .

These thoughts were faraway, like sounds in a distant room. Yet it was impossible to escape their effect. As she wept, her breasts started to tingle, her nipples went hard. Her thighs trembled. She felt first tender and then moist between her legs.

She was crying from hurt and, at the same time, she was wanting Tim. She wanted him to hug her and she wanted to hug him back.

There was a place between her legs where she had touched before. Tonight she touched it again and, instead of stopping as she'd always done before because she felt it was wrong to do this, she went on doing it while thinking about her moments of intimacy with Tim. After several minutes, she felt a great wave of pleasure washing towards her. She had always known that the wave was there, waiting to break, and sometimes when she had been with Tim, she had felt it approaching; but always, at the last moment, the same as when she was alone, she had shied away from it. Tonight, however, her feelings of desire and hurt and longing were so overwhelming, she reasoned with herself that she should just let the wave come, and then she would sleep. So she let herself go and it washed across her, and the last thing she imagined was Tim's smiling face and then she went to sleep.

From around the edges of the closed shutters Tim saw there was light leaking out into the darkness – firelight, candlelight, even the light from a colza lamp, perhaps. Isaac was still up, thank goodness.

Tim knocked on the door at the front of the house and waited. From inside came the sound of footsteps and then a man clearing his throat.

"Who is it?" the voice came through the wood.

"Tim Traynor."

"What do you want?"

"Can I talk to you?"

"What about?"

"I can only talk to you inside."

"You can come back tomorrow if it's that important. I'm going to bed."

"It's only early," Tim called back. Then he added, in his most persuasive voice, "Please let me in."

"No. Go away."

He only had the one chance and he had best make his case now, Tim thought.

"You know I'm getting to know the new agent very well," he said. "You know I'm working for him."

There was a long pause at the end of which Isaac said, on the other side of the door, "Yes, you are."

"I think you should let me in," Tim said.

"All right."

Two bolts were pulled inside; a key was turned in a lock; finally the door was pulled back.

Isaac stood on the threshold holding a brass tinderbox with a candle in the socket on the lid. It was a spermaceti, its light hard and white. Isaac wore a clean white shirt with a cravat tied around his neck. His hair was cut short and the scalp underneath had a white sheen to it. His eyes, which were normally blue shading to grey, were almost black in the candlelight. His demeanour was, as always, quiet, calming, almost priestly.

"Come in."

Tim stepped in and the door closed behind him. The bolts were rammed home again and the key was turned in the lock.

113

They were in a vestibule, the walls panelled with wood. Isaac pointed to the door at the end. Tim went through it. He found himself in a room with two cupboards built into the wall, the doors thrown open, gleaming plates displayed along the shelves inside. Wood crackled as it burned in the fire grate. On the mantelpiece there were two Staffordshire china dogs. Isaac lived alone and kept his house immaculate.

"You were saying?" said Isaac, who had appeared noiselessly behind him.

Isaac crossed the room. He was lolloping as he moved, almost limping, the result of a kick from a stallion he had received as a child. Isaac sat down on a chair by the fire. Tim stood and waited to be invited to sit in the chair opposite; however, to his surprise, Isaac put his feet up on the chair that Tim had imagined he would be invited to take.

"You were saying?" said Isaac again. He fiddled with a clay pipe, tamping down the tobacco in the bowl.

"Swear me in," said Tim suddenly.

"Why?"

"I'm up for it."

"Are you now, up for it?"

"Yes."

"And are you up for jail or your own death?"

Isaac lit a twig in the fire, then lifted the burning end to his pipe and sucked the flame down.

"I don't understand," said Tim.

"The world is full of brave men," said Isaac, "and their hearts are full of passion when they talk at moments like these in front of the fire."

Isaac threw the twig back into the embers. Tim watched as it caught and then flared.

"The fact is, the choice is jail or death."

"I'm not brave," said Tim.

"That's novel." Isaac exhaled a cloud of smoke.

"I'm not brave at all," said Tim, emboldened by Isaac's reaction.

"Oh, don't overdo it," said the older man.

"I don't want to go to prison but I'd rather jail than the gallows."

"None would disagree," said Isaac.

"I want you to take me. I will be extremely careful. I will . . ." Tim couldn't think what to say next.

"Go on," said Isaac.

"I will do everything in my power not to get caught."

"How?"

"Neat appearance, attention to my work –"

"Polite to the peelers?" interrupted Isaac.

"Oh, yes, always polite to the peelers," agreed Tim. "You don't want to get on the wrong side of the peelers."

"No, you don't. Very bad idea, that. But we don't want to be too friendly with them, either," said Isaac. "That's a very, very bad idea."

"Yes."

Isaac stared into the fire and pondered. A young man with whom he had never had much contact had turned up late at night with the familiar request with which young men came to him. Isaac nearly always turned these young men away. The only reason he admitted Tim this evening was because the fellow had reminded him that he worked for the new man, French.

In Isaac's experience, when men came at this time to see him, they were very often drunk, and they were always extremely angry. Invariably something had gone wrong in their lives and they wanted to join because they believed this would be a first step towards making their lives better again. More often than not, what was wrong in their lives was personal and domestic and would in no way have been made better by following the course of action Isaac was interested in. However, with this fellow Tim, Isaac wasn't certain: he might be one of those; on the other hand, he did work for the agent and his thoughts now turned to the new man.

After French had had his interview in Dublin with Mrs Beaton, Isaac's sister had written and told him what she had heard. Then the agent had arrived in January, since when Isaac had kept his ears and eyes open. The new man had been talking to those tenants who were badly in arrears and, just as his sister had written, the agent had a novel but appalling proposal.

Traditionally, when a man gave up a farm, the incoming tenant gave the outgoing man a multiplication of the yearly rent, tenant right. This repaid the outgoing man for all the improvements he had made, and gave him money to pay off any debts he had, and there wasn't a tenant in the county who didn't owe money to some shop-keeper or other.

But what French proposed would scotch all that. What he was saying was that he would take farms back from those with big arrears and he would pay the tenant right. Then he was calculating the tenant right as, say, four or five times the annual rent and arriving at a figure more or less the same as the tenant owed in arrears. This was what Isaac had heard, anyway.

The trouble with what French was offering was that it wasn't the full tenant right: he was undervaluing tenant right – so any tenant who accepted would end up being swindled. But those tenants who accepted would not be the only losers: in the end, everyone would lose out if this scheme went ahead.

The real iniquity with the plan, as far as Isaac was concerned, was the bad precedent it would set. If tenant right went down from, say, a multiplication of fifteen times to five times the annual rent, then all the good tenants who stayed behind on the estate and didn't ship to America would find their farms were worth less than they had been. A lot less.

Now, of course, as Isaac would have been first to admit, it was still possible that nothing might happen. There had been many hare-brained schemes proposed during his life that had never come to pass; on the other hand, as he would also have acknowledged, it was often the case that when a new man came in, sweeping changes often followed.

So now as he sat staring into the fire, turning these thoughts over in his mind, it seemed very clear to Isaac that it might be very useful indeed to have Tim in place, just in case they had to move.

He lifted his gaze from the hearth and looked across the room at the youth. Tim was standing quite still, his cap in his hand. Seeing how the older man was staring at him, Tim smiled back. Then he averted his gaze and politely looked at the china dogs on the mantelpiece.

Isaac liked the way the boy deferred. He also liked the caution he sensed in him. Brave men were not useful. Careful men were useful. He liked Tim's calm. Tim wasn't sweating or shaking; he wasn't bursting with talk. He liked Tim's silence. That was rare and welcome. When Isaac was pensive, as he was now, most men in this situation − mistaking silence as an invitation to talk − would jabber and chatter and try to persuade him to take them on. What these eager fellows failed to understand was that while sometimes a man must put his case, at other times he must shut up and let events take their course. The sign of a mature man was that he knew the difference. And this boy Tim, Isaac mused, might be just such a man.

"All right," he said. Isaac lifted his feet off the chair on which they rested and put them on the floor. "You can sit down."

Isaac leant forward and brushed away the specks of dirt and earth that had fallen off his boots on to the seat of the chair.

chapter nine

An advertisement appeared in the local paper. On Saturday afternoon there was to be an auction at the house of James McNally. All stock, household contents, stonework and fuel were for sale.

Isaac walked out to the place in the evening a couple of days later. He found Jimmy in the shed, splitting great lumps of wood with an axe.

"I hear there's to be a sale, Mr McNally?" said Isaac. He only knew Jimmy by sight.

"That's right."

"I'm looking for gates," said Isaac. "The agent promised gates but I've been waiting for months. Upton was awful, and I think this new man French, he promises the world but at the end of it all he can't come up with the goods."

Jimmy's axe made a neat arc in the air and hit the round of timber on the block. The split ran neatly down the middle and two halves fell to the floor.

"I don't have any gates," said Jimmy cautiously, "and I like him. I think he's a good man."

"Has he been decent to you?"

"Oh, yes."

"You're leaving, I take it," said Isaac.

"Oh, yes."

Jimmy lifted up another piece of wood and set it on the block.

"And who's coming in here, or what's happening?"

"We're off, passage paid to America, arrears waived, and any money from the auction staying in my pocket. I don't know what Mr French is going to do with this place. Fix it up, I'd say."

"What about your tenant right?"

"Oh, tenant right, tenant right," said Jimmy. "I'm up to here in debt." Jimmy held his hand over his head. "It'll take more than tenant right to get me out of this."

This was wrong to Isaac's way of thinking. Instead of taking whatever the agent was giving him, Jimmy would surely get more from a proper farmer. However, he knew there was no point arguing this with Jimmy.

Instead, he wished Jimmy luck and said he had to be off.

Isaac smiled as he left but as soon as he was out of sight the smile vanished.

Tenant right was the most valuable asset a tenant had; he could sell it, he could use it as security for a loan (although not from the bank); he could even will it.

McNally was wrong to do what he was doing but, then, obviously the agent had said, "Accept my terms or see you in court." Judges didn't accept tenant right. It didn't exist in law. So Jimmy took the lesser of two evils.

It was short-sighted of McNally, not to mention selfish, but could Isaac blame the man? Not really. He was frightened, Isaac guessed, and panic-stricken and he had no idea what else he could do. French had him over a barrel. French was the wrong-doer in all this.

The agent had no right to trade arrears and passage to

America in return for the lease. If a tenant fell into arrears, then it was up to the agent to come to some arrangement to clear the debt that didn't involve putting the man out. It was also a point of principle with Isaac that the man who rented a farm should remain in possession, if possible. And if he did leave, this had to be on a voluntary basis and, furthermore, he made his own arrangements with the incoming man regarding tenant right. It was preposterous for the agent to pay it.

Isaac had reached the end of the lane. He turned and looked back at Jimmy's farm. He saw two bad fields and the cabin, smoke curling out of the crooked chimney, and more bad land beyond. What did Jimmy pay for his place? he wondered. It was thirty acres, wasn't it? Nine pounds a year, perhaps? Well, the tenant right, bad as the place was, it had to amount to sixty or seventy pounds, didn't it? And what was Jimmy getting? He'd heard a figure of forty-five pounds mentioned.

Isaac walked on, his mind racing. Yes, there was a plan here, and the more he considered the matter, the more obvious it became. French's intentions were not just to sort the estate out, and get rid of the bad tenants. Over the years to come his plan, obviously, was to separate all the tenants from their ancient right. He wanted to take away the only thing they had. He was after power, complete power, and if he reduced the size of their tenant right, or got rid or it, then power was his. Every farmer borrowed against his tenant right. Even Isaac had. But if tenant right was drastically reduced, or even abolished, then how could farmers borrow to see them through the lean times? They wouldn't be able to, of course, which left them with two alternatives – they would have to give up their farms on the agent's terms, or face eviction.

Isaac stopped beside a hole in the road and gazed at the black water in the bottom. If this thing got going, it would end with every tenant being cleared off the estate, wouldn't it?

It surprised Isaac that he hadn't already seen the point to which the agent's scheme was leading. He should have seen this when he got the letter that his stupid sister wrote; the one where she told him what she had heard and then whined about having to eavesdrop. The moment French got Mrs Beaton to agree to his scheme, his plan to get every tenant off the estate was set in motion.

Isaac asked himself the question again. Why hadn't he seen this before? Was he going soft? Was he getting slow? No. Soft was closer to the mark. His problem – and Isaac saw this now with extraordinary clarity – was the goodness of his heart. As usual, it held him back. French was malevolent from the start but Isaac had wanted to give the man the benefit of the doubt. He had wanted to see what he was like. He hadn't wanted to jump to conclusions. He had waited to see what was going to happen. And he had chosen not to see the obvious, although it was staring him in the face. Well, those times were over. There was to be no more tolerance. Now, it was war.

Walking on, these thoughts rattling in his head, Isaac worried at the skin at the side of his thumb. All the way back along the terrible track he worried away. By the time he reached the Shercock road the skin had started to bleed. Isaac put the thumb in his mouth. His blood tasted like iron.

After Tim finished his work at Mr French's, he put his tools away and set off along the road for Isaac's. He had been instructed to appear before dark. Isaac's farm was a couple of miles from the agent's house.

After walking for a few minutes, Tim came to a straight stretch of road with high hedgerows on either side. In the distance he saw Emily, of all people, walking towards him. It was Emily who had seen Kitty and himself at the well, and who had told old Mrs Gallagher, who in turn had told Daniel and Bridie.

He often met Emily on the roads. Everyone did. She was a fixture. As Emily drew closer, he saw her shout back over her shoulder at the imaginary groom who marched behind.

"Don't you know, it's water!" Emily shouted mysteriously.

She paddled the air in front of her face as if batting away flies. Or perhaps she was swimming. It was hard to tell.

Tim glanced along the road beyond Emily. He rarely said anything when they met, and he saw no reason to change his policy today. She lived in a private world and there was no point telling her she had ruined his life with her gossip.

They drew level. Although he was looking into the distance, at the corner of his eye he became aware that Emily had her finger pointed at him, and her dark eyes fixed on him.

"Listen to me," she shouted, and stepped up to him.

Rather than the everyday voice she used for the groom, she spoke in her prophetic voice. It was slow, like an incantation. Emily clearly modelled herself on the priests she had heard over the years.

"The Mills of Louth," she boomed, "will be turned three times by blood rather than water before the land will become ours again."

Tim was familiar with the prophecy. He had heard his mother and father speak of it when he was a child. He didn't need reminding. He went to step around Emily but she stepped sideways and blocked his path.

"It could be our own blood that turns the millstones," she said.

Now he saw that he would have to speak to her, he said, "Oh, really."

At the same time he wondered why she had stopped him of all the ones she might have stopped? Did she know that he had joined? Was that possible?

"It's not a matter of Ireland rising against England," she continued.

"Isn't it?"

"The Catholics who haven't the land will have to go against the Protestants who have."

In her cracked way Emily made a sort of sense. "But we will win," said Tim.

"The Protestants will be fierce when their backs are against the wall."

"Go on."

"There will also be Catholics who will join them."

He felt himself being drawn into the conversation although it wasn't what he wanted. Emily had that power.

"Maybe," he said.

"Then the Queen's army with their cannon will come. The people won't have a chance then," she said.

"Wait until the big war comes," he replied. This seemed a reasonable answer. He wished Isaac could hear him now, sounding bright and confident. He also found it puzzling; at this moment he was certain of the future, yet at other times he felt despondent. "Then we'll see what happens," he concluded, cheerfully.

A peal of sarcastic laughter filled the space between the hedges. Emily stepped away from Tim and hurried up the road.

"You'll see, you'll see," she shouted, but it was unclear if she was talking to him or the groom.

Tim walked on. There were butterflies in his stomach. Instead of the usual mad muddle of words, Emily had addressed him just now as a Ribbonman. She knew he was sworn in. Had to. Hence all her talk about the Mills of Louth. In which case, he thought, was it possible that she might inform, and worse, that she might be believed? After all, when she blabbed about himself and Kitty, someone had believed her then.

The butterflies vanished and Tim felt as if everything in his stomach had curdled. Any moment now he felt he would retch.

This was no good, he thought. He had to stop this. He had to get himself under control. He asked himself a question: did he seriously believe that Isaac, who had sworn him in, might have told Emily? Or told someone who had told Emily? No, both ideas were inconceivable. The logic was faultless and Tim soon felt better. It was just a coincidence, the talk about the Mills of Louth, that's all.

Half an hour later, Tim knocked on Isaac's back door.

The door swung back and he saw Isaac standing inside.

"Well, lucky me, you're on time. Come in," said Isaac.

Tim said nothing. He didn't know this man well enough to banter with him.

123

Tim climbed the steps and entered the back kitchen. It was a dark room with shelves. There was a wooden table and a wooden washing-up bowl. The door closed behind him. There was a tallow smell. Usually Isaac burned spermaceti candles but tonight he was preparing to burn the cheaper tallow ones. Half a dozen of these coarse, dull-coloured candles lay on the table, the ends carefully pared, ready to slot into the holders of the tinplate chambersticks that were lined along one of the shelves.

"Sweep the parlour floor and lay the fire," said Isaac in his calm, almost monotonous voice. Tim had come to get the place fixed up for a meeting, so the order was not unexpected.

Tim sprinkled water on the parlour floor to keep the dust down and began to sweep. The floor was covered with pipe ash, dung, dried earth and straw.

When the dirt was in a heap he used a goose wing to transfer it to the ash bucket.

Then he cleaned out the grate, transferring the grey ash and the black clinker to the ash bucket with a small iron shovel.

Isaac was singing in the back kitchen when Tim came in with the bucket, on his way to empty it outside. Isaac sang:

"I am a bold undaunted youth, my name is John McCann,
I'm a native of old Donegal, convenient to Strabane,
For the stealing of an heiress, I lie in Lifford jail,
Her father swears he'll hang me for his daughter Mary Neill."

Tim said nothing, went out of the door and stamped over to the disused pig pen where the ash bucket was always emptied. Isaac put the clinkers on the paths around his land, where they acted like gravel, while the ash proper went on his vegetable garden. Isaac was a fastidious man and he wasted nothing.

Tim returned to the back kitchen. The candles were in their holders and he found Isaac with a long spoon. He was getting pickled onions out of a jar and putting them in a bowl. He would eat these later at the meeting.

"I hope you're ready," said Isaac.

This sounded ominous to Tim.

"What for?"

"I've two fellows lined up for French," said Isaac jovially. "You're going to be their eyes and ears. Hurry up with the fire, there's plenty more to do."

Tim left the kitchen with his thighs fluttering. What exactly was Isaac talking about? Eyes and ears? Tim wanted to go back and ask but that would be pointless. Isaac would simply stare without blinking and say something like, "We don't have time to dither, we've got visitors."

Tim opened the door of the cupboard under the stairs where Isaac stored and dried his kindling. He gathered a handful of small sticks and threw them in the pail. His hands shook slightly.

The next moment he was aware of an unpleasant memory. All day it had lurked in a distant corner of his mind, and now it scuttled forward into his thoughts.

On Monday, when he went into the kitchen in French's for his meal at midday, he had found Mrs French and Maggie at the big table. They paid no attention to him as he came in. There was a ball of brown dough on the bread board between them.

"They cut it off and left him a girl," said Maggie.

Tim knew at once what they were talking about. It was O'Duffy, the boy who was dumped on the Monaghan crossroads.

"What?" said Mrs French. As she stared at the housekeeper her face shrank. It was as if a stopper had been pulled and some air let out of her head.

Tim went over to the side table and sat down. Cold potatoes, ham and brown pickle were laid out for him on a white plate. He heard Mrs French say, "Oh, God! That couple in Dundalk got off lightly."

After lunch, when Mrs French went out on an errand, Tim

went and asked Maggie what she had meant. Maggie blushed. She was peeling a large green cooking apple. There was flour in her hair.

"I can't say," she said.

He knew he didn't want to know and yet he went on asking her. In the end Maggie gulped and told him about the couple who were stripped and shorn and put out on the road. Their crime, she told him, was that apparently they were too officious when they collected money for the parish priest.

Tim went back outside into French's garden. He took a saw from the shed and went up to the copse at the back. An old elm had blown down the previous winter and he began the slow business of cutting it into lengths for the fire. He liked to saw and usually he was able to lose himself in the action of the blade sliding backwards and forwards. This afternoon, however, all he was able to think about were the couple without their hair, O'Duffy without his manhood, and the master at school, bundled into a sack and thrown like a litter of unwanted kittens into the lake.

Before he joined, Tim had kept his nose clean and avoided trouble; punishments and murders were always something that went on somewhere else; they were at a distance from him. Since he joined, however, and although nothing had happened yet, he knew he was no longer unconnected.

In Isaac's musty cupboard under the stairs, Tim felt his head spinning. It was all Emily's fault, he decided, with her talk on the road about the Mills of Louth. What did she know about anything? Damned lunatic.

He heaped more sticks into the bucket. He must not give in to these thoughts. He must busy himself. That was the only way to keep bad thoughts at bay.

He rushed to the parlour with the pail and knelt in front of the fire. He broke a handful of kindling and tossed it in the grate. Yet his hands shook, and despite these efforts, another thought now rushed forward. Since that night in March, he had had no contact with Kitty whatsoever. She had no idea that he had actually done what he had threatened to do and joined up. For all she knew, he was studying to be a priest.

He threw a brown, gnarled sod on top of the bed of kindling. Because of a moment of anger towards Kitty, he had talked his way in here, but it wasn't going to get her back, was it? If anything, it was going to keep them apart. She loathed everything to do with the Lodge. He must have been mad, he thought, to get himself into this. Quite mad.

But he had a policy, he reminded himself sternly, and he must stick to it. He had told Kitty what was going to happen and then he had done it, as she had known he would.

In time he would take part in an action. Fairly soon, if he wasn't mistaken. Afterwards, he would let her know he had been part of the operation. He looked forward to seeing her face then. He imagined it going white – then he reminded himself that that was why he had joined; so that he could see this. One day, he might even help to put down a farmer with the same acreage as her father. And wouldn't it be wonderful to tell Kitty he had been part of that operation? That would really put the wind up the McKennas.

Yes, Tim had to agree with himself; yes, this was what he wanted, wasn't it?

He reached down the brass tinder-box from the mantelpiece, opened it and took out a piece of very dry cloth which he laid on the fire; then he took out a flint and a steel. He began to strike the flint and the steel together furiously. Sparks fell like shooting stars on to the dry cloth. A spark set a thread smouldering. He blew on it and the cloth caught fire. He put a twig into the flame and when it had caught he inserted it carefully into the middle of the fire, where he had put the driest, thinnest kindling. After a few moments the kindling began to crackle and he stared at the flames as they spread through the network of twig and branch. They were going to ask him to do something. He knew it.

"You look like a lovesick girl staring at the fire," barked Isaac, behind him. "Come on, hurry up, there's work to be done."

Tim jumped. He hadn't heard Isaac coming into the room behind. He pinched out the flames on the cloth and put it back in the tinder-box. Panic gripped him. Was it possible Isaac had seen his face and read his thoughts? Then, as Isaac gave him a list of other tasks to perform, it became clear to Tim that there was no cause for worry, the fears were all in his mind.

When Tim had finished his tasks he went and found Isaac in the kitchen where he was washing eggs. The older man told him to go home.

"What about the meeting?" said Tim. As he had cleaned the parlour, he thought the very least he could expect in return was that he got to stay on and listen to what was said. And didn't he need to know what was planned, especially as it involved himself? Isaac, however, saw things differently.

"You're on probation," he said.

"I thought I was on for something," said Tim.

"That's right," Isaac replied nonchalantly. "But you don't need to know anything yet."

Tim was burning to know. It was cruel of Isaac, he thought, first hinting, as he had at the start of the evening, and now packing him off like an apprentice. Tim put on a grumpy expression. That would show Isaac what he felt. However, if Isaac noticed he did not show by his expression that he had, but kept his face blank.

"Go home," said Isaac. "I'll be up to see you with a couple of fellows some time soon. I'll send word when to expect me."

Tim stamped off into Beatonboro'. He called in to Dolly Walsh's public house and ordered a glass of whiskey. He swallowed the liquor in a single gulp and asked for a second. Dolly, behind the bar, saw that Tim wore a furious expression. So did the other customers in the room. Nobody spoke to him. Everyone was puzzled. Tim was normally such a mild-mannered fellow.

When his money was spent, Tim left Dolly Walsh's. His humour was worse than when he arrived. His intention was to go home but then he changed his mind. He went to Kitty's cottage instead and stood in his old spot under the pine tree, behind the wall.

The candle lamp was burning in the main room of the McKennas' cottage. He saw the yellowy light of the candle streaming into the darkness. Later he saw the paler light of a naked candle burning inside Kitty's room and he was filled with a sense of sadness and longing.

A few minutes later all the candles inside went out and the cottage went dark. He walked home, his mood black, yet to his great surprise he was able to go to sleep easily that night.

When he woke up the next morning Tim realised how much he missed Kitty. He missed her desperately.

While Tim drank in Dolly Walsh's, and later while he stood sullenly outside the McKenna cottage, Isaac sat in his parlour with Alex Ward, Thady Burns and Turk McEneaney. They were all tenant farmers on the Beaton estate. They had all seen the advertisement. They had all guessed what it meant. Isaac described his conversation with Jimmy McNally to the others. Alex, Thady and Turk made noises of disapproval. They did not like this. Isaac proposed doing away with French.

"No, not yet," said Alex. He was a powerful man with a sour face and big hands. "The biggest problem we have is Philips, he's the one we must sort out." He fiddled with his left ear as he spoke. Alex had been born with a curious crease that ran from the top of his left ear down to the lobe and he liked to put his finger in the groove when he talked and run it up and down like a bolt.

"The exciseman?" Isaac let out a snort. "He's small fry. It's got to be French." He selected a pickled onion from the bowl on his lap and popped it into his mouth. The vegetable was cold and smooth. He pinched the onion between his teeth and split it in half. The lovely sharp taste of vinegar filled his mouth.

"Philips is a devil," said Alex plainly. He explained how the exciseman worked with a telescope, how from vantage points he would carefully survey the countryside, how smoke in unexpected places always drew the unwelcome attention of Philips.

"He smashed a still last month," continued Alex, who was sore about the destruction of his property. He heard the sound of crunching inside Isaac's mouth.

Now Isaac swallowed. The others were waiting for him to speak. Turk and Thady sympathised with Alex but they believed Isaac talked more sense. This was Isaac's impression anyway.

"Instead of always thinking of yourself," said Isaac, "think of what French is doing."

"All right," said Alex grudgingly, like a man who knew he had lost the argument already.

"You can't pay your rent, you go to him."

"As one does," said Thady cheerfully. He was a man with a compact and powerful body, and a pleasant face. He wore his blond hair cut short, and his eyelashes and eyebrows were almost white. But he was not an albino. His eyes were a deep greeny-blue. Thady was the peacemaker in the group.

"You say to Mr French," continued Isaac, "I can't pay. 'Never mind,' says nice Mr French. 'How much do you owe? Three years' back-rent. Let's see. What's your tenant right? On a place like yours, I'd say three times the annual rent. I tell you what I'll do for you, Alex. I pay three years' tenant right because the place is coming back to me. We'll put that against your arrears and that'll clear them, so now you don't owe me anything. All right? All you have to do is sign here. The farm comes back to me. Here's your passage to America.'

" 'Oh, but Mr French,' you protest, 'my tenant right is ten times the annual rent, not three. It's unfair. You're under-paying.'

" 'Well,' says bold Mr French, 'whether I am or I'm not, either you agree to my terms, or I'll see you in court.'

"So, poor old Alex, he has you over a barrel. He evicts, you end up with nothing. At least this way you have something. 'All right,' you say finally, and you sign. Mr French gets your land back and you and your family trot off to America where we never hear tell of you again."

"But I'm not in debt," said Alex. "I won't need to go to him, cap in hand, like you say."

Isaac raised a hand. "Stop thinking of yourself. You aren't the only one who's affected. He's trying to take tenant right away and impoverish us all – don't you see that? And once that's done, we'll all end up going to him cap in hand, because we'll none of us be able to borrow any more. We'll all get into debt at some point if we can't borrow."

Alex was silent.

"I'll end up there, you know, same as everyone else. 'I can't pay, Mr French.'" Isaac spoke in a whispering voice like a girl. "'Oh, never mind, Isaac, here's three years' tenant right.' 'But I should have much more, Mr French.' 'Shut up, Isaac, I'm being very generous. Why, I'm letting you sell your stock, your implements, everything you have, and I'm paying your passage to Boston. What are you complaining about? You want to go to court, do you? You want me to throw you out?'

"'Oh, no, Mr French, please don't do that.'

"'Right, just sign here. Thank you very much, Isaac, glad to have the acres back. Now get ye to America and don't bother me again.'

"McNally's taken the bribe. More families will take the bribe. Five, I hear tell – but there'll be many more, you can be sure of that. New tenants will come in. They won't be local. They could be Protestants. Rents will rise – you can bank on that. Meanwhile, our tenant right goes down. Our position gets worse and worse, credit gets harder and harder, until eventually there'll be nothing else *we* can do, *we'll* have to go to the office and accept the offer. What French is doing is dangerous. It's our land and he's trying to claw it back. We can't let him do that. We must stop him."

"Why don't we put Micky Laffin out of the picture?" Although he didn't think Isaac would agree to this, Thady wanted the semblance of a discussion with all possibilities aired. He rubbed his white eyebrows.

"Laffin, Laffin, who's Laffin?" said Isaac. He held out the

bowl of pickled onions. Each of his guests waved their hands. Nobody wanted any. "A jumped-up Paddy who's turned Prod," continued Isaac. "Small fry."

Thady murmured approval. He agreed with this yet he decided to say something more. The more discussion, the less likely Alex would get grumpy.

"Laffin's a spy," said Thady. "He reports to French. Get rid of him and the fellow French can't operate."

"Later, later," said Isaac. He put the bowl of onions on the mantelpiece. "First, the keystone of the arch and that's French. With him gone, everything tumbles."

"All right, agreed," said Turk, the fourth member of group. Turk was so named because of his dark skin and his incredibly thick and incredibly black curly hair and his black eyes. His real name was Paul. Turk had only spoken now because he was tetchy. This conversation had gone on for so long, it was beginning to bore him. Turk became bored very easily.

"Gentlemen?" said Isaac, looking at Alex and Thady. It was time to demand a decision now that Turk appeared to support him.

"Agreed," said Thady, after a pause. Although he believed this was the right decision, he was careful not to sound too enthusiastic. It was important Alex did not think he was alone against everyone else.

"What about you, Alex?" said Isaac.

Alex put his finger in the groove in his ear again. "All right," he said finally, "if you say so."

"So now we draw lots for who shall do it," said Thady quickly. He wanted to move the conversation on to specifics.

"There's no need," said Isaac.

Thady was surprised and so was Alex.

"But we always do," said Alex. "That is the rule and the law."

"I say we use the same pair we used with Sheridan."

"Oh, yes," said Turk. "They were discreet, efficient, thorough —"

"They were expensive," said Alex, interrupting.

"Yes, they were, but so what?" said Isaac. Why was Alex so

132

obstructive? Why couldn't he just agree?

"How much?" Thady wanted to know. He always asked these precise questions.

"Fifty should start them off," Isaac said quietly.

"That's expensive," said Alex predictably. "Why don't we do it ourselves?"

"Alex Ward, where are your brains tonight?" Isaac said, and he touched his forehead. "Sheridan was so brilliant because they did not know him, and Sheridan, he did not know them. Now, can we say that French does not know you?"

"No," said Alex slowly.

"Does he know you, Turk?"

"Of course," said Turk enthusiastically. He saw where the questions were leading.

"What about you, Thady?"

"I was in his office just yesterday."

"Exactly. He knows us. I too was in the estate office just the other day, looking for some gates I've been promised. But French doesn't know these men. They are strangers in these parts. They can saunter in and out of the estate office. They can drop in on the Petty Sessions. They can even call up to French's house and ask for a cup of water. French won't know these ones from Adam. Plus we have Tim. He's working in French's garden. He'll be their eyes and ears. I say, these three are the ones to do it and we keep out of it. Murder is a machine," he ended. "Assemble the parts, wind them up and off it goes – and this one is going to run like clockwork."

Isaac had prepared this sentence before the meeting and he was delighted to have the chance to say it.

"Fair enough," said Turk quickly.

Alex and Thady nodded assent.

"We have to give French a warning, haven't we?" said Turk.

"Why? What for?" said Alex. Just because he had agreed to Isaac's first suggestion, he wasn't going to just assent to everything else that was proposed.

"We always give notice," said Isaac mildly. He wanted no more bad temper.

"Absolutely," Turk agreed fiercely. He thought Alex was being obtuse. There was always a warning, and Turk saw no reason to abandon the tradition. "You won't have my consent to put him away unless he's fairly warned," Turk continued.

"I don't know," said Thady pleasantly. Thady knew that warnings reflected well on Ribbonmen and made them seem like men who believed in fair play. On the other hand, he sensed Alex smouldering. At least let them have the semblance of a discussion. "Why does he need to know he is condemned to die," said Thady, with a smile, his blond eyebrows moving, "when he's going to find out anyway?"

"Because those are the rules," said Turk, his dark eyes glowering. Turk was growing more and more irritated with the drift of the conversation.

"Give it yourselves, then," replied Alex bluntly, finger in his ear again. Alex stared across at Turk on the other side of the hearth with an expression that was more sour than usual.

"And while you're about it," Alex continued, "tell him everything else – our names, and where we live, the works. Then collect your informing money and run off to America with it jingling in your pockets."

There was a pause.

"I say we warn him," said Turk furiously, "and I'm as true a patriot as you." Turk was furious. How dare Alex imply that he might inform?

Isaac took another pickled onion from the bowl.

The reason they were so quick to accuse one another of informing was not only because it was their deepest fear; it was also O'Duffy. His fate was what made the word so potent, and that was Isaac's work. He had not only taken the decision; he had supervised the job himself.

With Puck and Rody, the two men he was proposing to use this time against French, he had picked up O'Duffy from his home on a winter's night. He told Mrs O'Duffy they would bring him back later, safe and sound. Then they walked him to the crossroads where they planned to put the body.

It was freezing cold but with a bright moon. "What have

you brought me here for?" O'Duffy demanded. He was blithe and unaware of his fate.

Isaac produced the piece of paper from his pocket that he had prepared. There was a skull and crossbones drawn on the top and underneath the two words, INFORMERS BEWARE. "You can't be serious, I'm no informer," said O'Duffy, when he had read the paper.

O'Duffy had been held by the police before Christmas for drunken behaviour and assault. He had served ten days in the jail. After O'Duffy was released, the policeman, Cleary, had told Isaac mockingly, when they had passed one another in the street, that O'Duffy was a brilliant talker. This left Isaac no alternative. He had to act.

"I told the police nothing when they had me in the barracks," shouted O'Duffy, as Isaac laid the paper down in the middle of the road and put a stone on top to keep it in place.

Rody snorted and told O'Duffy to undo his belt. O'Duffy began to cry and whimper and the astringent smell of his pee floated on the cold night air. Rody agreed to slit his throat first and then do the rest of the business.

Rody told O'Duffy to lie down on the frosty road, and because he had only obedience to offer as proof of his good character, O'Duffy threw himself down on the cold, hard ground.

Rody pulled something from his pocket, wrapped in a brown rag. It was a large knife with coarse brown twine wrapped around the handle. The blade was eight inches long.

As O'Duffy saw the steel flashing in the moonlight, he realised that his obedience counted for nothing. He began to beg for his life. He promised he had said nothing to the police, either before, during or after his period in custody. He had said nothing in the jail.

"That policeman Cleary says you're a great talker," said Isaac, "the best ever." He didn't want to hear O'Duffy's pleas. He just wanted to finish this.

O'Duffy shouted that from the day he delivered

McGuinness into their hands he had done nothing of which he was ashamed.

Puck stood on O'Duffy's arms and told him that talk only made it harder. Isaac stood on his chest, and Rody, holding O'Duffy by his hair to stop his head moving, dug the knife in at the side of the neck and began to pull it round.

It was a slow job, more a case of hacking than cutting the throat, blood shooting everywhere – some even went inside Isaac's boots – while O'Duffy writhed and struggled. At last, with a horrible gasp that Isaac imagined was the sound of O'Duffy's soul jumping through the gash and flying towards the stars, he finally went limp and they knew he was dead. Then they got the breeches down. Isaac took the foreskin and pulled hard, stretching the penis out. Rody cut through the flesh close to the bone at top. He said it was like the neck of a chicken. Isaac opened the man's mouth and clamped the penis between the teeth.

They walked over to the lane at the back of Hutcheson's demesne and woke up the tinker woman. She thought they wanted to lie with her and mentioned a price. They pulled her back to the milestone where the body was propped up. She became hysterical and, like O'Duffy, she wet herself. She would not carry a message to the police, Isaac thought. He feared they were going to have to wake someone else.

Puck slapped the tinker woman across the face, twice, and she came to her senses. Isaac told her she must fetch the peelers. They walked back to the camp. The tinker woke her children. Isaac and the other two helped her to load her cart. They lifted her sleepy children on to the back and the tinker woman set off for town.

He paid off Puck and Rody and walked home. When he took off his boots he found that O'Duffy's blood had not only got inside them, it had even managed to get between his toes. The blood was brown, sticky, like jam between the fingers, he thought.

It was a dirty, tiring business but now, several months on, here in his own front parlour and before his very eyes was all the proof he needed that his action had been worth it. Isaac had elevated informing into the worst crime these men could imagine, and he had made it impossible for them to contemplate it because the penalty was so terrifying.

"Look at it this way," said Turk. "When he learns he's going to be put down, French might just decide to take off. Then, without a struggle, everything would be back the way it was before French came."

"That's not right," said Alex. He did not sound quite as certain as a moment earlier. "French won't go. All your notice will do is warn him and then he won't be so easy to get at. I hear tell he can shoot well, and telling him is just going to make it harder for us."

"Listen to me, Alex," said Turk. Isaac was curious to know what Turk was going to say. "We're having these two men we had before?"

"Yes," said Alex.

"They're handy with the gun, aren't they?"

"I think so," agreed Alex, uncertain where this was leading.

"How about the knife?"

"I suppose."

"The cudgel?"

Alex only moved his head this time.

"They're expert, agreed? This is their field."

"I suppose."

"We're going to pay the two of them fifty pounds?"

"Right."

"To put French away?"

"Right."

"They're going to be on the job day and night?"

"I suppose."

"But given their expertise and all the hours that they'll dedicate to the job, you're telling us you don't actually think they can do it. French is too good a shot, or something. In which case, what are we paying them for?"

"You've taken me up wrong."

"He's got to be warned," said Turk, "and I'll draw it up

myself. It'll be on the chapel doors, Sunday."

"Good, gentlemen," said Isaac, smiling and rubbing his hands. Everything was agreed. "But no one will shoot French until after Thursday next. I'm finally getting those two fine iron gates I've been promised these last months, no, years – supposedly – and I might as well have them before he dies."

After this it was decided to put Tim at the disposal of the gunmen and to set in motion the purchase of a blunderbuss. Turk said he had wind of one for sale in Crossmaglen. Isaac agreed to look into the matter.

The meeting closed. Each man drank a glass of beer. Alex, Thady and Turk went home. Isaac bolted his doors and went to bed.

On the Sunday morning of the following weekend, Micky woke early. He needed to shave before he went to Mass but when he went to the water pail, he found it was empty.

Micky took the pail and slipped quietly out of the house. His wife was still sleeping. Outside, he found it was a still spring morning. Grey and white fluffy clouds lay across the sky, and the horizon was brightening with the rising sun.

Micky went through his gate and on to the lane. Oak and elm trees grew on either side, tall old trees with great branches that reached across to one another. As he walked underneath them, it seemed to Micky that he was moving down a long tunnel. It was a grey tunnel now but in the summer, when the leaves were on the trees, it was a green one. He heard the cawing of the crows who roosted on the branches overhead. He felt strangely subdued this morning, although there was no reason why he should be.

At the bottom of the lane, about fifty yards from Micky's home, there was a spring in the ditch. The spring water flowed from a rock and fed into the ditch. The ditch carried the water down to another stream.

Across the road from the spring was a small cabin where the church caretaker lived, and beyond the cabin stood St Patrick's chapel. It was a grey stone building with a Celtic cross on the apex of the roof. The chapel grounds were surrounded by a grey stone wall and near the gate there was a gantry with a large blue bell that the priest used to summon parishioners to Mass. The land on which the chapel stood had been given by the Hutcheson family; the cost of building the chapel had been met by the Beaton family.

Micky set his pail in the ditch directly underneath the water flowing from the rock, and as the pail started to fill he heard someone calling his name.

Micky turned and saw the huge figure of Croker Flanagan standing on the chapel steps. Known as Haystacks, because of his truly enormous height and weight, Croker had the mind of a ten-year-old child, an awful temper, a small talent for professional pugilism and a reputation for piety. He never missed a Mass and he was always outside the chapel at least an hour before the caretaker unlocked the doors. If it was raining Croker would wait in Micky's kitchen. Micky liked Croker but he always treated him with great care because of his capacity for violence.

"Hello," Micky called back to Croker. He saw the huge fellow was gesturing at him to come over.

Micky went across the lane and through the chapel gate. Looking ahead, he saw there was a piece of paper, about a foot wide and two foot long, nailed up on the chapel door. He saw a skull and crossbones at the top of the paper and writing underneath. It was bad, whatever it was about, and perhaps this explained his mood.

"Look at this!" Croker called. The giant spoke slowly and without inflection, and he pointed with one of his enormous fingers at the paper.

Micky climbed the steps.

"Good morning, Croker," he said.

A smile creased Croker's enormous, stupid face. "Hello," he said.

Micky's eyes darted to the poster. The skull and crossbones were drawn in a strong and firm line. The message underneath was written in a square, neat hand. Micky swallowed. This was to do with McNally and the agent's intentions. He was certain.

"What does this say, this?" Haystacks asked, in his childish way. He was excited. "Is it from the priest?"

" 'Thomas French, take note.' " Micky began. " 'Your insatiable desire for depopulation must stop. On pain of death you are forbidden from evicting tenants, executing decrees, serving process, distraining for rent, rescinding leases and putting on new tenants in farms you have taken back to the estate. This is not an idle threat. Recollect the fate of Patrick Vokes Sheridan, on this his anniversary, 23 May 1854. General Starlight, Beatonboro' Ribbon Lodge.' "

"Oh," said Croker. He stroked the paper. "It's nice writing."

It was a typical Croker remark: no harm intended but absolutely inappropriate.

"Was anyone about earlier?" Micky asked innocently. "Did you see who put this up?"

"No," said Croker, in his careful, slow way. "I saw no one. I haven't been here long."

The notice was nailed up with tacks. They were only banged in half-way and the heads stood proud above the wood.

"Can you get those out?" asked Micky.

With an enormous finger and thumb, Croker effortlessly pulled out the tacks.

Micky rolled up the warning and put it in the pocket on the inside at the back of his coat.

"What about these?"

Croker held out a palm with the four tacks lying in the middle.

"Keep them," said Micky.

Croker beamed. He dropped the tacks into his hat and put the hat back on his head.

Micky walked back to the bucket. It was full, the excess water running down the sides. He stared at it for a moment and decided he was not going to Mass.

★

Micky shaved, combed his hair and ate a piece of bread and cheese. He said goodbye to his wife and set off for Beatonboro'. He walked smartly down his lane, then followed the road across a landscape of rounded hills and small trees. He walked fast and he was breathing heavily when he arrived at the gates to the agent's house. To his surprise, he found the gates closed and Tim inside with a pot of black paint touching up the metalwork.

"I see they like to keep you busy."

"Yes," Tim agreed, keeping his eye on the brush.

Micky went to the stile. This was set in the wall at the side. He put his foot on the first step.

Tim was an industrious young man, thought Micky, and industry was a quality the bailiff admired. He had an idea that Tim had an acre of the appalling land Hutcheson had up in the hills. Perhaps the estate should offer Tim something? he thought. One of those farms that were coming back? Since McNally agreed, a further five families had said they wanted to take up French's offer. He should have a word with Thomas about it.

He climbed to the top of the stile, swung his leg over and, as he did, a new thought struck Micky. It was fear of a mass clear-out that had prompted the warning in his back pocket. Furthermore, he could be certain that there was a copy of the same notice on the door of every other chapel in the district. By midday, there wouldn't be a soul in Beatonboro' who didn't know that Thomas was under sentence of death. Indeed, word had already got about for all Micky knew.

He jumped from the stile to the ground below. The sun never shone in this spot and the grass was still wet with the morning dew. Drops of water spotted Micky's boots. The leather, where the drops landed, went dark brown.

"You didn't go to Mass, did you?" Micky asked.

Tim glanced at the bailiff who was coming up at his side. "Why?" Tim asked.

"I didn't either," said Micky, "but I'm sure He knows we're both doing something important."

The remark was a strange one and it made Tim wonder, Why was the bailiff here on a Sunday morning?

"I'm going up to the house," said Micky.

"I might as well come up. I have to clean the brush."

The drive forked beyond the gate. The left fork led to the front door. Micky and Tim took the other fork. They followed the drive around the side of the house, passed the room with the bureau and the chair where Helena wrote her letters, and arrived at the rear. Here they filed through a gate, went down stone steps, which were so old and worn they dipped in the middle, then walked across the flagged yard to the back door. The yard was bounded by the house on two sides and by outhouses and walls on the other two sides. The air here was very still because it was enclosed and warm from the sun. There was a smell of mould and stone. In the kennel at the side, two red setters sat with their raspberry-coloured tongues hanging out of their mouths.

Tim turned the handle of the back door. It opened into a vestibule with shelves for boots, and huge trunks for storing turf and potatoes. A door ahead led to the office, and another door on the right opened on to the scullery. This room connected to the kitchen. In this room there was a large open fire and a range for cooking.

Thomas was in front of the fire, reading a novel. He often came here to read on Sunday mornings, when the room was quiet except for the whisper of the fire and Maggie was at Mass. As he heard Micky coming in from outside, Thomas read the line, "I could with pleasure have destroyed the cottage and its inhabitants and have glutted myself with their shrieks and misery." Next thing Micky hurried into the kitchen proper and Thomas looked up. "What's the matter?" Thomas asked, and seeing Micky's expression he closed *The Modern Prometheus* or *Frankenstein* by Mary Shelley, and stood up.

There was no point, Micky realised, in breaking the news gently. His face already said that he had come to say something awful. The best thing to do was to get it over and done with.

"I've got something here you're not going to be very pleased about," said the bailiff.

Micky took the warning out of his pocket and opened it on the table. To stop the paper curling, he put a wooden piggin from the dairy at the top and a heavy iron salamander at the bottom.

Thomas read what was written. "Oh, God!" he said.

He felt giddy. He had faced antagonism and hostility in his time. He had had arguments and rows. He had had stones thrown at him. He had had two men attack him in a back lane in Cork with cudgels. He had been punched, he had been kicked, he had been jostled. He had been sworn at. He had been spat at. He had been threatened verbally with death and mutilation and damnation. As had his sons, as had Helena. Every agent had. It was what happened to agents. They did things to tenants and tenants hated them for it.

But never before had he received a notice in writing like this, in black and white, an unequivocal sentence of death. And unless he packed his bags and went away, or unless he persuaded Jimmy McNally and the other families to remain on their farms and issued a public statement that he would be taking back no more leases and that tenants who were in arrears could stay on their farms, there was no way to have the sentence lifted. But what was he thinking? he wondered. These were not alternatives. Even if he wanted to go, why should he? His policy was fair, he was convinced of it. It gave tenants the opportunity to start afresh in America and, goodness, how many people got a second chance like that in life?

That initial feeling of giddiness gave way to something heavier and darker, more like anger. How dare they respond with this threat, he thought, to his perfectly benign and reasonable policy? Damn all bloody tenants.

He was about to say something, when he heard the scuff of a boot. He noticed Tim in the scullery. Tim was cleaning his paintbrush with a rag. The sharp smell of turpentine hung in the air. It occurred to Thomas that it was critical he remain calm, from now onwards. In the weeks ahead, everyone in

Beatonboro' would be watching him and trying to gauge whether he had succumbed to panic or not, had lost his wits or not, and he must give no one the satisfaction of knowing he was overwhelmed.

"Shall we sit down and have a quiet chat about this?" said Thomas slowly.

"I think that would be a good idea," said Micky. "I'll make some tea."

In the scullery, Tim heard these words. He had finished cleaning his brush. He put it back in the box on the window-ledge with the other brushes. There was a fine film of oil all over his palms and fingers.

He slipped out of the back door. A white butterfly careered past and sailed into the house. He found the low stool on which Maggie sat in the sun. Maggie was Scottish and called it a creepie. He moved it over to the door and sat down.

"Who was Sheridan?" he heard Thomas asking from the table in the kitchen. Tim closed his eyes. The sun passed through his skin and warmed his eyes.

"He was a farmer," said the bailiff.

"What happened?"

"Someone broke into his house looking for ·guns," explained Micky. "Patrick reported the fellow and he was arrested. Patrick was warned not to testify but he wouldn't hear of it and the fellow was sent to prison on his evidence."

"Time passes. One evening, knock at the door. It's a pie-seller and his wife. 'Do we want a pie?' Sheridan shouts to his wife in the kitchen. 'Yes,' she shouts back. 'Yes,' says Sheridan. The pie-seller reaches into his basket, pulls out two pistols, shoots Sheridan. The pie-man and his wife run in. They find the gun box, smash the lock, take the weapons. They make Patrick's wife look at their faces. She has no children but she has a sister with three and they say to Mrs Sheridan they *know* where that sister lives. Later, there are arrests but she won't pick anyone out of the line, assuming the culprits were even picked up. Then Mrs Sheridan sells up and last I heard she was in Manchester."

"Her husband shouldn't have kept his guns locked up in a box," said Thomas grimly. "He was defenceless."

"I suppose he must have known that once he gave evidence they would come for him. He should have had them handy, all right."

"That's right."

"So you have to keep your weapons about you at all times," said Micky quietly, "day and night."

"And I don't suppose he thought the pie-man was a threat," mused Thomas.

"There's another lesson," said Micky.

Thomas agreed. "From now on, anyone and everyone I meet, he might be the one who wants to get me."

"Or she. The accomplice was dressed as the pedlar's woman but it was a man."

"Or she," Thomas agreed.

In the yard outside, Tim took his pipe out of his pocket and put it in his mouth. He sucked and air came into his mouth that tasted of tobacco and ash.

"Imagine living like that," said Micky, "always on your guard. It must be intolerable."

"What's the alternative?" demanded Thomas. "I hole up in a cell in the barracks, and you send food in to me every day?"

Micky snorted. "They'd get it poisoned in the end anyway," he said glumly.

Now Thomas snorted. "Have you ever been in anything like this before?" he asked.

"Oh, yes," said Micky, "with McGuinness," and he told Thomas how his friend had been murdered at the bend in the road as they came out of the alder wood.

"Go back to the moment when your car turned. Your friend Hugh took it in the face."

"Yes."

"What happened then?"

"He fell on me."

"Where?"

"Across my lap."

"And?"

"He was screaming. O'Duffy, the driver, he got down. He opened the door at the back. We got Hugh on to the road. I got out. I wiped his face. He couldn't see with the blood."

"How long since the trigger was pulled?" Thomas interrupted.

"I don't know."

"A minute?"

"Could have been."

"Could it have been more than a minute?"

"Might have been."

"What then?"

"I saw the men running towards the wood. I knew that if they got into the wood then I'd've lost them. I got up and ran after them."

"But you didn't get them?"

"No."

"But you might have," said Thomas excitedly.

"Yes, I might have got the slow one."

"No. You might have got the fastest one."

"No, I couldn't."

"Yes, if you'd gone straight after them as soon as they jumped the wall, you'd have got the leader."

"But I was in the car. How could I jump down? I had Hugh lying across me, screaming his head off. He was drowning in his blood."

"If you'd jumped out of the car, the second they fired, you'd have got one. And that's what we're going to do."

"How so?" said Micky. He didn't follow Thomas, but Tim had a very good idea what was coming. He felt like running straight to Isaac and telling him what Thomas was going to do, but he knew he must wait and listen and then go on with his day as if he knew nothing. In the evening, Isaac was coming with the others to see him. He would tell Isaac then what he had learned.

"Micky, think what happened." This was Thomas again. "Your friend Hugh gets shot. What happened then? You didn't abandon him — of course not — and they knew that for a minute or two after they fired, you'd be with him and that gave them the time they needed to get away. And that's what always happens, I'm sure of it. A man goes down. His friends rush to his aid. They run off. Then the friends give chase. But then it's always too late! So this is not what we're going to do.

"From now on, wherever I go, you go with me, and if I'm shot, under no circumstances do you come to my aid. If I'm shot, you just get your pistol out and go after them, straight away. What is more, you will make it your business to tell everyone in Beatonboro' what our plan is. Regardless of any pain or suffering I am in, you are going to get them, and shoot them, or bring them back and hang them."

There was a pause and then Micky said, "I couldn't have left Hugh crying. It would have been heartless."

"The murderers got away. That was just as heartless. Do you think Hugh didn't want them caught?"

"I couldn't desert him straight after he was shot."

"When it's me, you will," said Thomas grimly.

"Your eyes are shot out, you're crying out for the priest . . ."

"Forget me," said Thomas, "I'll make my own arrangements with God. Shoot them or hang them. That's what I want."

"I can promise now," said Micky, "that at the sound of the first shot, I go straight after the man who pulled the trigger. But at the actual moment, I'm likely to forget."

"If we can't agree," said Thomas, "the alternative is that I pack up and go back to Hazzardtown."

"All right," said Micky, slowly. "I can't have you give them the satisfaction of leaving. And I'm going to make a couple of home visits tonight, take in a pub or two. Put the word around."

"Good, rattle them," said Thomas. The white butterfly that had come in earlier was battering its wings against the glass of the window.

"I just hope I can do this," said Micky plaintively.

"Just remember, they can't afford to lose good men. We put

the wind up them, they may never get a chance to fire."

Tim stood and stretched himself; then, whistling loudly, he walked in through the back door. From the front of the house came the sound of a piano.

"Mr French, sir," he called. Micky was lifting the sash window and Thomas was shooing something out.

"Go on," said Thomas, and the white butterfly dropped away from the glass and darted out into the open air.

"At least we've done one good thing today," said Micky, closing the window.

"I'm going to do those flower-beds," said Tim.

As he walked back out of the room, Tim heard Micky saying, "We'd better check the windows and the doors up here and then I'll get this notice down to the police station. And you'd better load your hunting pieces. They'll do until we get you properly armed."

When he got home at the end of the afternoon, Tim built a fire and boiled a kettle. He made a cup of tea. He sat in the chair with the cup in his hands and stared into the flames. He felt cold. Apprehensive as well.

His door swung open. He looked across and saw Isaac standing in the doorway in a clean coat and clean trousers and polished boots. There were two strange men standing behind him.

"Can we come in?" asked Isaac.

As Tim gestured to his visitors that they should come in, he wondered why he hadn't heard the sound of approaching footsteps, or at the very least why old Mrs McCarney's dog hadn't barked. The only way to his cabin was past Mrs McCarney's and the dog faithfully warned him of the approach of every caller. It was the first time he had known the dog not to do this.

Isaac kicked his boot against the lintel although there was no mud to shake off his sole. It was a dry evening. He stepped forward. The strange men also kicked their boots and stepped into the room. The taller of the strange men closed the door.

The other, who was a little smaller, said, "Hello."

"This is Puck Garrett," said Isaac, and he pointed at the one who had just spoken. "And this is Rody Donohoe."

The tall man nodded in Tim's direction. His nose was very long, with a kink at the top. His eyes were dark, the colour of wet slate, and his cheeks were covered with the shiny bumps and pockmarks that were the scars left by smallpox. The other man, the smaller one, Puck, had a very pleasant, even face and close-set eyes. As Tim stared at this man, Puck stared straight back at him without blinking. Tim felt uncertain. Was he simple? Or hostile? Then it occurred to Tim, after he realised there was no force of feeling behind the look, that the man was neither of these things. He was simply passing the time by looking at him and waiting for something to happen.

"Right, Thomas French," said Isaac quietly.

Tim stood and offered his chair to Isaac which the older man declined. Tim put a plank on top of the turfbox and this time Isaac sat down. He pulled out another box from under the table and gave it to Rody. Finally, Tim offered the chair – which was the only one he had – to Puck but the one with the intense stare said, "No, I prefer to stand." Puck scrutinised the salt hole and then went back to the door where Tim's tools stood in the corner.

"Can't you sit down?" Rody called.

"No, I'm restless."

Puck picked up Tim's spade and weighted it with both hands.

"I can't stand it when you pace around."

"I'm not pacing around," said Puck fiercely. "I'm just looking at some tools. That's not a crime, is it?"

Tim caught Isaac winking at him. Isaac raised his hands. His palms were white with deep dark creases running across them.

"Let's talk about Thomas French."

"You work for him?" Tim heard, and he realised Rody had addressed him.

Tim nodded. He explained his work in the garden. Then he reported what he had overheard in the yard that morning. He spoke quickly. He felt proud. Here was news, real intelligence, and he was the bearer.

He finished expecting a compliment; a warm word or two. But instead Puck exclaimed, "We should never have put up those notices. I don't know why we always have to do that."

"Oh, don't start," said the other man, Rody, gruffly.

"Everyone gets a warning," said Isaac, "everyone gets their one chance. That's the way it's done."

"Telling him is just going to make it harder for us," said Puck, crossly.

"When you agreed to take the money," said Isaac, "you knew the terms. I don't want to hear any complaints."

There was a chill in Isaac's voice that Tim had not heard before. It seemed to have an effect. The smaller man, Puck, put his hands in the air and said, "All right. From now on, you won't hear another word from me on the subject."

Next, the weapon was described. It was a blunderbuss, English made. "I'm waiting for word to collect it," said Isaac. Then Rody asked Tim some questions. What time did Thomas leave for the estate office in the morning? Did he walk to the estate office or did he go by horse and car? What time did he arrive at the office? If Tim gave a reply that was imprecise, Rody made him clarify the point.

Meanwhile, Puck continued to walk around the room. He opened the door and peered into the bedroom. Rody paused for a second and Puck called across to Tim, "That's a small bed."

"There's just myself," said Tim. "I sold the bigger bed," he added, "when my mother died."

"I see," said Rody archly, "you sold the other bed, the big bed, when your mother died."

The three men laughed and Tim went red in the face. He wanted to say something smart but his mind was blank. Embarrassment always emptied his mind and left him defenceless.

"Is there a sweetheart?" asked Puck suddenly.

"A sweetheart?" Tim wondered if further humiliation lay behind the question.

"Yes, a woman."

"There was," said Tim.

"Oh," Isaac said. "Who is she?"

Tim shook his head. He was keeping Kitty's name to himself for now. Then he had an inspired idea. He would extricate himself from this awkward situation with the Kitty story – or at least a version of the story.

"We had to stop," he said smugly. "We couldn't go on."

Three faces looked at him from different parts of the room.

"What happened?" Isaac pressed. "What did you do with her?"

"I just realised . . ." Tim sighed. "I couldn't do this *and* have her. She was only going to be hurt. So, when I started this I ended it, like that." He clicked his fingers to emphasise the sense of sudden and permanent separation.

"So you gave up your hole for Ireland," explained Puck. "You made the supreme sacrifice."

"Puck!" This was Isaac.

"He's only messing," said Rody. The man with the pockmarks glowered at Isaac.

There was a short silence. Tim offered tea and apologised he had no sugar.

In the evening, sitting in the drawing room in front of the fire, Thomas told his wife about the notices posted on the chapel doors. Cleary, the constable, had told Micky that a total of five had been recovered by the authorities. When he finished Helena sniffled and her eyes filled with tears. She pulled her handkerchief from her sleeve and blew her nose.

"Oh, God!" she said.

There was a cushion on the sofa beside Helena. She picked it up and put it over her face. He heard a wrenching cry. He went over and tried to pull the cushion away but Helena wouldn't let go of it.

"Why did we have to leave Hazzardtown?" he heard her saying from behind the cushion.

"Oh, come on," said Thomas, "we're in a mess." Put down

the bloody cushion, he thought, and listen.

"What are we going to do?"

If she listened, he thought grimly, he'd tell her. He had a plan and Micky, at that very moment, was setting that plan in motion. But Helena was moaning.

He tugged at the cushion and this time Helena let go of it. He saw a red, wet face with strands of hair stuck to the forehead.

"It's going to be all right."

She looked at him dubiously.

Thomas explained his plan and that Micky, at that moment, was spreading the message.

Helena stopped crying and wiped her eyes. She said nothing.

"Well, what do you think?" asked Thomas.

The wind in the flue moaned.

"I don't know."

"You don't know. You must think something."

"You could give up this policy with the leases and paying the tenant right and sending the tenants to America."

"That's not very helpful."

Her brown eyes filled with tears. He knew that this time she was not going to wail from behind a cushion. This time she was going to sit and stare. All their scenes followed the same pattern. First, the explosion, then this, when she carried her hurt in pained silence.

He threw two blocks of wood into the grate. The wood was wet and it hissed as the flames heated it from below.

"Do you want to play cards?" he said eventually.

Helena put the toe of her shoe on the fender and slid it up and down.

"Cards?" he repeated.

Helena said nothing. She got up and moved to the card table.

They played a round of whist. Helena won. Thomas poured her a glass of port and took it over to her. After the first sip a pale pink wash appeared on her upper lip. He pulled out his handkerchief and wiped it away. Helena smiled weakly. He fetched the cribbage board. One of the ivory pegs was missing. The replacement was a small wooden peg which he had carved himself.

"You take the ivory," said Helena. "It's luckier."

He smiled and dealt. The sound of the cards as they landed on the baize reminded him of leaves falling on snow.

In the cribbage game he started well but soon Helena's brown wooden peg had overtaken his smooth, white ivory peg. She won, handsomely.

They went to bed. He put out the candle. The wick was red for a fraction of a second and then there was darkness. The case on the bolster was fresh and smelt of lavender. He felt Helena take his hand under the covers. She stroked the soft flesh between his forefinger and thumb, then touched him seductively in the places between each finger. He kissed her cheek, and then her mouth. Her breath carried a faint aftertaste of port wine. She allowed him to lift her nightdress and helped him to climb on to her. He wanted to undress her completely as he had done when they were first married, but she did not seem to like that any more. He pulled his foreskin back and wet the end and pushed himself into her. Helena folded her arms tightly across his back and hugged him to her chest.

He remembered the drunk girl with the gloves that were coming apart, the one he had met as a student what – oh, years before, and the hotel room and the breath of the girl. He hardened. The memory was exciting. It was also wrong. He nosed Helena's hair spread out beneath her. There was a smell to it that was all Helena, sharp and female. He must bend his thoughts to his wife, he thought. No one else. Not here, not now.

After twenty-five years of marriage, he and Helena knew each other well. Their love-making was not exciting but it was eloquent. She was squeezing him again and this was Helena speaking. She was apologising for her reticence earlier, because she knew how much it infuriated him, and as he moved inside her, he too was apologising, in his case for his sharpness and his anger and his impatience. Suddenly, he was filled with supremely tender feelings for his wife. She had wanted to make love; she had made this possible. He began to pant. She put her tongue into his mouth and touched the end of his tongue, and he came.

They lay still for some moments then rolled apart. Helena turned on her side and pushed her back against him. Her flanks were cold and he rubbed them. She murmured, "Good night," and within a few moments she began to breathe evenly as she drifted towards sleep. The lace collar of her nightdress prickled his cheek. He slid his head back. He felt sleepy. With his mind's eye he saw himself walking in a street. There were wide pavements, red-brick houses, windows, fanlights, cobbled roads, a cart going along, a girl selling flowers – it was a street in Dublin or Cork, unnamed, unrecognised, at a quiet time in the afternoon when little was going on. He came to a kerb. He put out his foot to meet the cobbled road below but suddenly there was no road. It had gone. His leg jerked and now Thomas was suddenly wide awake.

Damn! he thought. The very second that sleep was about to arrive, it had been driven away. Why did that happen?

He fumed for a second or two, and then, to his great surprise, he found himself recalling a series of disconnected memories from his schooldays.

He saw the grey gate lodge and old Francis Hughes, the gateman, with his shining red face, and a shining red growth the size of an apple bulging from his cheek. He saw the entrance of Champion Hall, white pillars, hideous oil portraits of old headmasters, and the names of all the scholars who had gone down to Trinity in Dublin written in gold leaf on a plaque on the wall. There were boyish cries and from the stairs came the sound of trunks being bumped up and down. This was the work of the porters, the McMullen brothers, three squat, terrifying troglodytes.

Thomas felt exasperated. He was wide awake in his bed, Helena asleep beside him, and back at school, his mind filled with memories of the biggest event of his teens.

He was in his second year at the school. He was fifteen years old. The old headmaster Mr McGinty retired and in his place came the dreadful Mr Magee. What a name.

Mr Magee was a thin, wiry man in his early forties, with yellow, leathery skin. His eyes were grey, his stare was intense, and his manner was nervous. He wore his grey hair long, swept back from his forehead. There was a rumour in the school that Mr Magee was once a poet; hence the coiffure.

Mr Magee's first action was to place a thermometer in the dining hall, a second in a classroom, and a third in a dormitory. Mr Magee recorded the results and posted them each week on the notice-board by the front door underneath the list of Trinity scholars. The boys assumed this was simply eccentric behaviour. It was the sort of thing to be expected of a man who was once a poet. Then, one October morning during assembly, Mr Magee made his announcement. There were to be no more fires in the classrooms or the dormitories. He argued that the mind was improved and sharpened by cold, whereas it was addled and confused by heat. He had made the decision, he said fiercely, for the benefit of the boys. It was to make them better scholars. Within six months, he said, they would see an improvement in their minds.

That day, the fires went out in every hearth in the school with the exception of those in the kitchens. The whisper went around that Mr Magee had sold the school's winter supply of turf and the school's turbary rights in order to augment his income. It was believed he had old gambling debts to pay (poetry and gambling were synonymous activities in the minds of the boys), and the appearance one morning, shortly after the announcement, of a mysterious man in black confirmed these suspicions.

Autumn advanced, temperatures fell. In the early mornings, the first task for the youngest boy in each dormitory was to smash any ice that had formed overnight inside the pitchers of washing water. On Mr Magee's instructions, small hammers were bought by the school for this purpose. Boys and masters went to class wrapped up in coats and scarves and mufflers.

Writing with a pen while wearing gloves became a necessary skill.

Meanwhile, it had not passed unnoticed by the school that in the headmaster's quarters off the front hall, where Mr Magee lived with his wife and four children, there was a fire in the parlour every evening. It became a school fashion for boys to jeer at the porters, the McMullen brothers, when they carried turf into the apartment in the mornings, and for boys to gather behind Mr Magee's parlour wall in the evenings and warm themselves against the bricks that became lukewarm from the fire on the far side.

Each morning, milk from the school farm was heated in the school kitchens. At eleven, all boys were given a mug of hot milk in the quad. This was a school tradition. A month after abolishing all fires, Mr Magee decided, as an economy, to serve the milk cold. Then, three weeks later, he cancelled the milk altogether. Water instead was handed out, a pint to each boy. Mr Magee decreed that each boy must drink his entire pint. Water was good for the kidneys and the bowels, said Mr Magee. Boys who tipped their water into the drain or spilt it on the floor of the quad received three strokes of his rod on the hand. At the end of each morning, it became common practice when boys peed away their water ration to hold their freezing hands in the warm stream of urine.

After the Christmas and January holiday, Thomas and the boys returned to find all the kitchen staff were gone. Mr Magee reported that they had been caught stealing and consequently he had dismissed them all during the holidays. The new cook was Mrs Magee, his wife. At first her meals were hot, but as winter wore on, there were fewer and fewer soups and stews, and more and more plain bread and jam or cheese. As spring came round, the diet became fixed; bread and jam for breakfast and lunch; bread and cheese for supper. Butter was served only on Sundays and it was usually rancid anyway. Tea vanished from the menu and the only drink was water. Mr Magee was especially proud of the spring water, which came from a well under the kitchen floor. On the

Sunday closest to St Patrick's Day, his first as headmaster, Mr Magee delivered a Sunday evening talk in which he argued that Ireland's first saint had certainly visited the site of Champion Hall to drink from their spring. None of the boys on the benches in front of him paid any attention.

Champion Hall had a large armoury of carbines, pistols and hunting pieces. As Easter approached, Thomas received the supply of powder and shot that he had written to his father and asked for. He was now sixteen, the age when Champion Hall boys were allowed to hunt on the grounds and on the school farm. Mr Magee had not yet abolished this privilege and Thomas's intention was to shoot food to eat.

One warm Saturday afternoon in April, Thomas and a dozen other boys enjoyed a successful afternoon's hunting. They shot twenty-eight rabbits. They built a fire and cooked the creatures immediately.

Afterwards, as they sat around talking and sucking on the animal bones, someone suggested that instead of going back to the school they just stay where they were. Another voice pointed out that there was a small ring fort in a corner of the wood. It consisted of a perfect circle of trees, which grew out of a high earthen bank. There was a single gateway with two huge stone piers. If they were going to stay in the woods, the speaker suggested, why not live there? Seal the gate with gorse and thorn and the place was impregnable. Everyone thought this was a brilliant idea. Several boys were sent back to the school to steal utensils, blankets, candles and every hand lantern in the place. Late that afternoon, the boys established themselves in the ring fort. Someone even made a flag and flew it off a tree.

In the evening, when Thomas and the other boys did not appear at supper, the three McMullen brothers were sent out to find them. It wasn't long before the porters found the boys camping in the ring fort. As the McMullens drew close, Thomas fired a warning shot over their heads. The porters ran back to the school. Mr Magee was called from the dining room and told that some of his boys had rebelled.

In the ring fort the boys prepared for battle. They hid themselves in the trees and behind the bank. Their plan was to make the place appear deserted and so lure Mr Magee's forces forward. Then, when the enemies' forces were so close there was no possibility of missing them, Thomas and his school-friends were going to pop up and shoot the porters dead. Unfortunately, Mr Magee did not attack. He got one of his small children to watch the fort from inside a hollow oak tree behind the ring fort. As darkness fell, the child crept out of the tree and carried the news of the boys' plan back to Mr Magee.

At dawn the following morning, Mr Magee appeared. Besides the McMullen brothers, and Francis Hughes, the gateman, who carried a large drum, he had a dozen more men, each of them armed.

Mr Magee ordered his men to circle the fort. They did so with a great deal of noise while Francis Hughes beat loudly on his drum. When his men were in position, Mr Magee shouted at the apparently deserted ring fort that he knew Thomas and his friends were holed up inside. "You may be hidden now," shouted Mr Magee, "but once you fire, I will know where you are, and then my men will shoot. I want you to know, once you show yourself, you're dead!"

Mr Magee ordered his party to arm their weapons. Delicate but ominous sounds filled the air as powder, wad and ball were rammed home, then hammers were cocked.

"Fix bayonets," called Mr Magee.

The noise of metal grinding on metal now filled the wood as ring bayonets were fitted over muzzles. Crouching behind the grassy bank of the ring fort, or concealed in trees, the boys heard everything and were terrified. What were they going to do? Nobody knew. Every boy was waiting for someone else to take the lead. Thomas realised they were stuck with their plan because there was nothing better on offer.

The drum started again. This went on for ten minutes and then Mr Magee repeated what he said before. The boys might be hidden now, but once they fired, his men would know where they were and his men would shoot them dead.

This was the pattern for the morning – drum, message, drum, message. Gradually, each boy came to believe he was about to die. Finally, a young lad called Andrews threw his weapon over the bank and came out with his hands up. Other boys streamed after him. Thomas was last. He carried his rifle over his shoulder like a soldier.

Mr Magee marched the boys back to school with their hands over their heads. Mrs Magee fed them bread and cheese in the dining room. Mr Magee appeared in cap and gown at the door when the meal was over.

"Let it never be said that I beat a boy on an empty stomach," he said.

Helena murmured in the bed beside him, and the picture before his mind's eye vanished. Thomas sat up in bed and lit a candle. Then he shifted round and holding the candle he looked down at his wife. Her face always changed in sleep. The lines at the side of her eyes lost their depth, and her skin became shiny and healthy. In sleep she looked ten years younger than in life.

A new thought struck him. What exactly had Mr Magee done? Why, yes, he had filled the boys with terror. He had convinced them that once they struck they would die. Which was exactly what Micky and he were hoping to do. Unwittingly, his plan was a variation on Mr Magee's scheme. He may have had Thomas beaten until his backside bled, but the man had given him something, after all, and it might save his life.

Thomas got out of bed and padded across the floor to the window. He lifted the metal bar and opened the shutter. He looked out. He saw the moon in the sky, the copper beech tree that grew outside, and the faint shadow of the tree on the ground. He saw the avenue, he saw the gates, he saw the stone wall that separated his property from the road. He saw that nothing moved, yet perhaps, at that moment, he thought, someone was out there, watching and waiting.

"Come back to bed," Helena called.

He closed the shutter and went and lay down beside her.

★

Rody entered the grounds of the agent's house around one o'clock that same night. There were no lights showing. He investigated the chicken roost, the turf shed, the laundry house, the ale house where ale was no longer made but extra turf was stored, the kennel where the dogs slept, the covered well, the back yard, and the stable where a pony drowsed.

Then he tramped the grounds and examined the flower-beds, the two garden sheds, the paddock where the milking cow lay in the moonlight, a rickety-legged calf sucking on her udder, and finally the copse with its neat stacks of cut-up wood. Rody knew this work was Tim's.

Having finished with the garden, Rody walked around the entire circumference of the demesne wall. He found the door at the back that opened into a wood. It was locked. Tim had warned Rody about this. There was only one key, which Helena kept on her belt. That left only one way in and out, and that was through the front gate. Rody didn't like that. Restricted access always made things harder.

Now Rody made his way to the rhododendron bush he had noticed earlier. He entered at the back. He pushed aside the branches and made his way forward. Underfoot, the ground was soft with rotting twigs and mouldering leaves.

When he reached the other side of the rhododendron, he had a side-on view of the agent's house. He stood and watched it. He saw the shutter moving and he saw the figure appear behind the window when the shutter was pulled aside. He hoped it was their man and that French was unable to sleep and that he had come to the window to check on his grounds. He hoped their man was worried; he hoped their man was fearful. The more unsettled he was, the more tired he became, and then the more likely he was to make a mistake.

Rody slipped away from the rhododendron, climbed over the wall at the back of it and jumped into the field on the far side.

He set off. One or two sheep looked up at him as he crossed the field. They did not move. They did not appear to be frightened. He heard an owl hooting, far away.

He reached the wooden gate at the bottom. He opened it, slipped out and closed it carefully.

Two hours later he arrived at Mellontown. This was the name of two rows of terraced houses in the middle of the countryside, miles from anywhere. They had been put up by the landlord five years earlier to give local people employment and an income. It was nearly dawn. Light was beginning to bleed from under the horizon and spread up across the night sky.

Rody went to his house. It was a stone building with a door and a small window on the ground floor and two small windows above. The door opened directly from the street. He opened the front door and stepped into the hall. There was a staircase ahead and a door to his right.

He closed the front door behind. He smelt burning turf and wood. Perhaps Geraldine had waited up. Perhaps she had only just gone to bed.

"Geraldine?" he called softly. "Geraldine."

A child murmured upstairs but not Geraldine.

He felt his way along the passage and then opened the door and went through to the downstairs room. Embers glowed red in the fireplace.

He lit a bit of tallow candle and found an apple. It was old, with wrinkled skin, one of the last he had gathered the previous autumn and which he stored in the cold shed at the end of the garden.

He peeled the apple and threw the skin into the fire. As he ate the fruit he watched the skin shrivel and hiss. He expected the room to fill with the smell of apple, and when it did not he felt cheated.

He went out of the back door and peed at the end of the garden in the nettle patch. He came back in. He took his bit of candle, now jammed in a cheap tinplate holder, and went upstairs.

On the landing, Rody stopped at the first door and listened. He heard Geraldine's three children snoring behind the wood. They were called John, James and Patrick and they were not his children. The father, Geraldine's husband, was a soldier from Exeter called John Lumford. His Devonshire regiment were stationed in Monaghan when he met Geraldine. They married, the children were born. Then Lumford and his regiment were sent to Gibraltar where Lumford was bitten by a monkey. The wound turned septic and then gangrenous in the heat, and Lumford died.

Lumford was buried in Gibraltar. The Colonel of the regiment wrote to Geraldine with the news and five guineas subscribed by the officers and men. Geraldine raged and wept and began to drink. It was two years after this that Rody first met her.

It was August and he was working with a gang of mowers who were moving around the country renting themselves out to bigger farmers. They called in to a pub at the end of the day. Geraldine lay outside, unconscious with drink, sick down her front, her youngest child, Patrick, sitting on the ground beside her, snuffling and weeping and trying to rouse his mother.

Rody fetched a pail of cold water and poured it over Geraldine. This woke her and cleaned her up at the same time. He brought her home, to the house that the local landlord had built. The older boys were with neighbours and Patrick fell asleep on the bench near the fire. Geraldine went upstairs to take off her wet clothes. Rody took his boots off, waited a minute and climbed after her.

When he opened the door, her first instinct was to scream and her second was to pull the blanket off the bed and cover her nakedness. However, because Rody just stopped at the doorway and did not move forward, and because she was still drunk, she then noticed how still everything was. They stood like this for some time. After a while, she noticed Rody's smell. It was a mixture of sweat and grass, and the oil the mowers used to wet their whetstones. She felt vague stirrings of desire, which she had not felt since before her husband's death.

Rody slept downstairs that night, on the bench, but the next morning, instead of returning to the gang of mowers, he accepted Geraldine's invitation to stay. She had a cow and a bit of a garden, and in return for his accommodation and his food, he worked for her; he milked the cow, he dug the garden, he fetched her turf from the bog. She liked the company, she liked his effect on her children, and she liked him. She stopped going out to shebeens and public houses. She began to comb her hair at night. She clipped her nails and washed her hands. She bought a white apron and a lovely new shawl shot through with red threads. A month after he had started living in the house, Geraldine and Rody became lovers.

Soon after Rody and Geraldine started to live together, the curate visited. He urged the couple to regularise their relationship. Geraldine said nothing but Rody agreed. The curate left. Then Rody denounced him as an interfering, meddling fool. Geraldine felt uncertain. In childhood and early adulthood she had believed. However, bereavement and alcohol had burned away her faith. She had not set foot in a chapel since she started drinking. She was sober again but she didn't know what she believed any more.

The curate's first visit was two years ago. He came regularly in the months that followed. He continued to urge marriage. Rody always agreed, and afterwards did nothing. Geraldine's early acquiescence began to change.

Why did Rody resist the ceremony? she wondered. She began to think he had a sweetheart somewhere else. Or, worse, that he was already married to someone else. Rody denied both possibilities. He had no sweetheart. He had no wife. He loved her and only her, he said.

Then May came – this was the year before, they had been together eight or nine months now – and Rody disappeared. Geraldine did not know where he was, or what he was doing.

Rody returned after a week. He was dirty and dishevelled but he did not smell of drink. Under the dirt he was remarkably well. She asked him where he had been. He gave her a cock-and-bull story about sleeping up in the hills and hunting for game birds without any success. Now Geraldine was certain. He had been with his wife or his sweetheart. She was absolutely certain. That was why he would not marry her. He had someone else. She threw clods of turf at him. She threw the milk jug. She threw the iron. She wept and screamed.

Rody denied everything, said he was working, although he couldn't say at what. That was a secret. She didn't believe he was working. He showed her the twenty guineas he had earned. Geraldine tested each one by biting gently into it. The coins were real enough. They were gold, solid.

So what had he done? she asked again, now she believed the money was real. He wouldn't tell her. He refused point blank.

He put the money in a bank at an abysmally low rate of interest. Life went on, but not as before. The curate stopped coming. He had decided the case was hopeless. They were a lost couple.

Meanwhile, Geraldine decided she must marry. She wanted Rody to be hers for ever. She calculated there was only one way to make this happen. She had to get pregnant. They had to have a child.

It was nearly a year since she made this decision. So far, no luck, no conception but Geraldine was determined to keep trying.

Another murmur behind the door. The children were sleeping soundly, he thought. Rody moved on down the landing, one foot against the wall, the other tight against the banister rods. He wanted to avoid the boards in the middle of the floor. They creaked and he did not want to wake Geraldine up.

He pushed open the door of the front bedroom, their bedroom. He saw the shape of Geraldine's body under the blanket. He set the candle in its holder down on the mantel. He lifted Geraldine's apron from the chair. He brought it to his nose. It smelt of flour.

"Hello," she murmured. She always woke, whatever time he came to bed. "Where have you been?" she asked.

He said nothing as he sat down on the side of the bed and began to unlace the boot on his right foot.

"It's late."

"It's late," he agreed. In fact, it was nearly dawn but he decided to say nothing about this.

Half awake and soft with sleep, Geraldine felt the straw of the mattress move as Rody slid under the covers beside her. She turned over to face him. The straw crinkled and rustled underneath. She pressed her waist against his waist. His breath smelt of apple as she kissed him on the mouth. She put her hand under the waistband at the back of his long johns and tugged his pelvis towards her pelvis.

"I thought you were sleeping," said Rody, trying to sound sleepy. She pressed against him again. "Oh, all right," he said.

Rody's preference was for sleep but at least if he made love, he thought, she would not ask him where he was all night.

Kitty woke up. It was Monday morning. She did not open her eyes, however. She kept them closed. This was what she did nowadays when she woke up.

Ever since that March evening, when she and Tim had said goodbye, she always woke up in the mornings with a sense of hurt, and her first task in the morning was to judge how bad it was.

In her own private language there were three categories. The worst day she compared to a bad tooth; this was because the worst physical pain Kitty had ever known was when one of her back teeth went bad. Her father had pulled it himself with pliers. The tooth had shattered as he tugged. Little bits of enamel filled her mouth. By the time her father had everything out, her gums were raw, her jaw ached, her mouth was split at the corner. Her tongue tasted of blood and it stayed like this for days. Thus a bad-tooth day was the worst for her. Next was what she called a splinter day. Third was a bruise day. So, how did she feel?

As she had discovered over the previous months, hurt not only hurt, it was also a weight that had to be carried around. Pain made it harder to get up and get dressed. Pain made it harder to sweep the floor and peel the spuds; pain made it harder to churn the butter and to stamp the blocks with the little wooden stamp that left the imprint of a swan, which was how they marked their produce. Far less energy, however, was demanded on a bruise day than on a bad-tooth day.

In fact, sometimes, on the bruise days, she even forgot about Tim as she kneaded the dough, or carried the chamber-pot outside and emptied it behind the hedge.

And on one or two very rare occasions, she had even felt the way she used to feel before all of this happened. She became the old Kitty again, the Kitty who smiled, the Kitty who sang as she worked, the Kitty who always joked with the man who came to buy their eggs.

These episodes did not last very long, and they always ended in the same way. As she was doing something, she would suddenly notice that she was cheerful and that the pain wasn't there. And there was nothing like this self-consciousness to bring the pain whizzing back. But even to be on holiday from herself for a short period was something.

So now, this morning, how did she feel? She waited and wondered, Was this going to be a bad as it could get, or as good? Oh, yes, she was getting a sense now. Today she fell between the two extremes. This was a splinter day.

Also to be considered was the fact that this was now the fourth morning in a row that she had woken up feeling like this. Until recently her feelings had swung between extremes. If that was no longer the case, was it safe to assume there was a pattern emerging? Wouldn't that be wonderful? Pain at this level for some weeks, and then a drop to the next notch. She would live with that for a while and then the pain would go altogether, for ever. How wonderful.

In the room next door, the room with the fire, the room where they lived and cooked and ate, someone was moving. She recognised her father's tread, the clatter of the ash pail, as he put it down on the floor. Then she heard the sound of the spade. It scraped on the hearth as he scooped up the ash. Then there was a pause. That was the moment when he held the spade over the bucket and the fine, grey turf ash slid from the spade and dropped into the bucket, landed almost silently in the bottom, and a cloud of ash rose upwards that stuck to the skin. At least when she cleaned the fire, as she did throughout the day, this was her experience.

Now she opened her eyes. She was lying on her side. She felt her feet lie one on top of the other, and where her skin touched there was a lovely warmth.

Suddenly, her father was beating with his knuckles on the other side of the bedroom door.

"Are you awake?" he called.

"Yes."

"Well, then, get up."

"I'm getting up."

"Don't go back to sleep."

"I'm getting up," she said.

She put a leg out from under the blankets and reached down to the earth floor and touched it with a toe. It was hard and though it was not cold, it was not warm like the bed either.

One, two, three, she thought. If she went at it at a run, it was never as bad as if she dawdled.

She threw back the covers, and swung her legs sideways. She put her feet on the floor and stood up.

"I'm up," she shouted, "I'm up."

"Good," her father called back.

First thing, that Monday morning, Thomas and Micky went through to the back office where Thomas worked. Thomas went to the table with the green leather top and the two drawers. Micky went to the gun cabinet in the corner, an oblong box, a foot deep, that ran from floor to ceiling.

Thomas opened the drawer on the left, reached into the back and felt around.

"Ah," he said, when he found the key under a piece of blotting paper. He pulled it out and held it up. The key to the gun cabinet was large, brass, the colour of fudge.

"Is the drawer really the place to keep that?" asked Micky

gently. If anyone broke in looking for weapons, the first place they'd search would be the desk. It wouldn't take them long to find the key. Yet Micky's words carried no hint of rebuke. This was quite deliberate. If he and Thomas were to be a unit, if they were to act as one, he knew he must neither irritate nor annoy the other. They would have to be like a perfect marriage, always harmonious, always polite.

"Yes, you're right," said Thomas, grateful for Micky's tact. He should never have left the key in his desk and it was better to admit wrong than brazen the matter out.

Thomas, too, had given attention to their partnership. His life depended on the older man, so it was imperative the older man not only like but respect him. Arrogance alienated; modesty had the opposite effect. "You're absolutely right," he repeated.

He was in their sights now. The proclamations on chapel doors the day before told him that. The battle was about to start. In a moment he would unlock the gun cabinet with the key. He would check the weapons with Micky. Later he would lock the cabinet, but instead of going back under the blotting paper, the key would go on the ring with other keys in his pocket. From here on, his was to be a life of care and vigilance.

He inserted the key into the lock of the gun cabinet and a rather dismal thought now crossed his mind. There was no logic. This was nothing more than very bad – extremely bad – luck.

The mechanism turned inside and he swung the door back. There were hunting pieces and rifles along the floor. These were held in place with leather ties. The upper portion was filled with pistols. These were hung up on hooks by their trigger guards. Along the shelf at the top lay piles of cartridges and tins of powder and a mass of shot in boxes with the different sizes of the shot written on the outside. There was a smell of oil.

A double holster hung down from the hook on the back of the door. It was made of a leather that was a very dark, chestnut brown colour.

"I remember this," said Micky, lifting the holster down.

"Mr Beaton got it in Sicily. It was made by a cobbler for a man whose life was threatened. He needed to go about armed. The man was actually killed when he was on his way to the cobbler's to collect it, and Mr Beaton picked it up a few months later."

"I hope I have better luck," said Thomas. He unbuttoned his coat and hung it over the chair. He held out his arms and Micky slipped the straps over his shoulder.

"You know, when I was at school, at Champion Hall," Thomas started, "something happened not unlike this."

A strap creaked and the distinctive smell of leather drifted up.

Since the night before when he had lain awake, the memory of these events had never been far from his mind.

"The old headmaster went and the new man was an animal. No heat, no food, it was intolerable."

He began to buckle the straps at the front.

"So we holed up in a wood in the school grounds in an old ring fort – you know the sort of thing? – and we refused to go back to school."

"Yes," Micky said as he selected a pair of pistols. Their curved, snug stocks were the colour of brandy. The barrels were iron and black.

"The new headmaster came with the porters and some other men to winkle us out. He could only see trees."

Thomas took a pistol.

"We were well hidden."

He fiddled with the holster near his heart and slipped the pistol inside.

"He told us that once we fired, he would know where we were, fire back and kill us."

Thomas reached with his right hand and pulled the pistol out abruptly, testing the holster for smoothness of draw.

"That's how he broke our resolve – by insisting that some of us would die."

Thomas pointed the gun at the fireplace. He pulled back the firing arm.

"I was beaten over a wine barrel in the cellars. Bled for a week."

Thomas pulled the trigger. The arm came forward with a dull click.

"You will have to be with me, always, from now on." He turned to face Micky.

Micky slipped the second pistol into the other holster. "I think we'll be all right."

From the street came a burst of song; the voice was a tenor, young and fresh:

"My heart is nearly broken from the clear daylight till dawn,
And I never will be able for to plough the rocks of Bawn."

"I hope so," said the agent.

"I think we're going to be all right," repeated Micky.

It was afternoon, two weeks later. Tim passed a man walking two greyhounds along the road. The animals were brown, with white stomachs. Each animal quivered as if stretched like a string between the tip of the nose and the end of the tail. They were energetic animals and they pulled on their leads as they strode ahead of their master.

"Good afternoon," the man called out, and Tim glowered back grumpily. He went on. A bee buzzed lazily across his path. A thrush fluttered at his side in the hedgerow.

Tim was going to Isaac's house. He had a good idea why. Puck and Rody had spent the last fortnight following Thomas around the estate. Only the gun to do the job was missing, and Tim suspected they were to receive the weapon this afternoon.

He was filled with apprehension. While Puck and Rody simply stalked their quarry, the attack was theoretical. But once they had the weapon, the deed became a certainty. They would kill French, and then what? It was this next part that really troubled Tim.

Once Thomas was dead, Puck and Rody disappeared, but Tim, who would have supplied all the details of the dead man's movements, Tim could not disappear. That would only arouse suspicions. Tim would have to continue to go to work, and this, inevitably, would bring him face to face with the grieving widow.

A cat with a white belly and a grey back ran across his path. It jumped up on to the bank and began to run along beside him. Tim pounded on, and now an image of Helena appeared to him. He saw her as she was now, in the garden among her roses, cutting blooms, laying them in a basket, her face broad and a little plump, her expression trusting and open, wearing a red day dress.

From this his thoughts moved to the future and he imagined the scene after Thomas's death. He saw himself in the kitchen of the agent's house. He saw Maggie with her apron over her face. He heard her muffled sobs. He saw Helena, eyes red-rimmed, face long and drawn, wearing a black day dress. He saw himself standing in the middle of the kitchen floor. He was clean-shaven, hair combed flat, and he wore a black armband. His cap was in his hands and he turned it nervously, round and round and round.

Next he imagined himself saying, "I'm sorry for your trouble."

He thought he said the words in his head but to his surprise he heard he had actually recited them out loud as he strode along the road.

"Oh, I'm sorry for your trouble, Mrs French," he continued. "It was terrible that thing that happened to your husband."

Had anyone heard him? He looked back. The man with the greyhounds was a good way down the road, thank goodness.

Tim tried another sentence, addressed this time to the cat. As he spoke, he monitored himself. Did he sound convincing? Did he really sound as if he meant what he was saying? Or did he sound insincere and, if so, would Helena see through him?

He saw himself in the agent's kitchen again. He delivered

his condolences. Helena looked back at him and shrieked furiously, "Liar, liar." Maggie dropped her apron and stared furiously at him. He heard Helena demanding to know why he had done it. Why had he helped the two men who had killed her husband? Why had he told them where Thomas was going so they could ambush him? Why? Why?

In his imagination, Helena's voice grew louder and louder. Suddenly the back door flew open and the policeman, Cleary, rushed into the kitchen with his baton drawn. Now everyone in the kitchen was shouting at him. He was a betrayer and a collaborator, a murderer and, worst of all, a Judas. Tim denied receiving money. He said it was only Rody and Puck who were paid. He was simply the look-out, the scout. "Liar," the others in the kitchen shouted back at him. They didn't believe he wasn't paid. The others were paid so why wasn't he? Nor did they like his tone. Trying to make out he was just a small cog in a big machine. He told the murderers where Thomas went. He told them what Thomas did and at what time. He made it possible for Puck and Rody to kill Thomas. It was meaningless to say he was just the look-out. The blood of Thomas was on his hands, shouted Helena, Maggie and the policeman, Cleary, as surely as it was on the hands of the men who pulled the trigger.

Then, in his mind's eye the scene slid from the kitchen to the square in front of Monaghan jail. He saw a crowd of silent men and women. He saw the iron balcony on the jail wall where men were hanged. He saw a rope, thick and brown with a noose on the end, hanging from the metal bar over the balcony. He saw a figure standing on the balcony whom he recognised as himself despite the bowed head. He saw the noose on the end of the rope, and the way the noose was fixed to the rope with careful turns. He saw the hangman slip first the bag and then the noose over his head. Tim saw the bag pulsing and throbbing as his condemned self sucked in air through the fabric. He saw the hangman tighten the noose around his neck. He saw the trap in the balcony open and himself tumble through. He saw the crowd shuddering. Then he saw his very own boots on the body that hung in the air. He was wearing the same boots this afternoon. They were black with brown laces. They were clean this afternoon, but the boots before his mind's eye had dry mud on the edges of the soles. The petal of a dandelion was stuck in the mud. The boots hung several feet above the stone flags of the square. The legs which stretched up out of the boots swung limply backwards and forwards. He tried to imagine the body below the neck, and the head on the other side of the noose lolling sideways. But he could not.

Tim stopped. He felt his heart beating, beating very hard and pushing against his ribs. He put his hand up to his head. He felt hot. He began to breathe in and out very slowly. He went on.

And what about after the murder? After French, would they promote him from look-out to assassin? On the next job would *he* have to use the gun? Tim imagined himself with a weapon, crouching behind a wall, a horse and car coming towards him, an indistinct figure holding the reins. At least he could aim to miss. But in the situation he was in at the moment he had no such get-out. He could neither lie nor withhold the information Rody and Puck demanded and, once he had given it, he knew they would act on it, ruthlessly.

He lengthened his stride and increased his pace. Physical activity was one way to keep these thoughts at bay. But he must do more. He opened his mouth and began to sing. First he mouthed nonsense, singing "La, la, la, la . . ." then the song, "The Lambs on the Green Hills" came to him.

Two children, a brother and a sister, sat on a wall by the side of the road. Each chewed a piece of grass. They heard Tim's voice in the distance. They heard:

" 'Stop, stop,' said the groomsman, ' 'till I speak a word . . .' "

Tim came into view. The children heard:

" 'Will you venture your life on the point of my sword? For courting so slowly you've lost this fair maid . . .' "

Tim passed by and disappeared around a bend, but he sang so loudly the children heard him still:

" 'So begone, for you'll never enjoy her.' "

Isaac closed the shutters over the window and dropped the metal arm that held them shut.

"It's all gone dark," said Puck, in his comedy voice. He sat with his chair tipped on to its back legs. Rody sat opposite, Tim between them.

Isaac said, "We don't want any prying eyes, do we?"

Puck screamed suddenly, lurched forward and grabbed the table. The front legs of the chair banged on the stone flags of the floor.

"Will you just quit that?" Puck shouted across at Rody.

"What? What did I do?" the other shouted back, all mock innocence.

"Tried to tip me back with the toe of your boot, is what." Puck kicked out with his own foot under the table and Rody slid back.

"Settle, gentlemen, settle," Isaac shouted from the hall. Tim heard the key turn in the front-door lock, then the bolts sliding over.

"Your quiet is much appreciated," continued Isaac, as he passed through on his way to the back kitchen. Again, Tim heard bolts drawing and a key turning.

Rody snorted.

"Be quiet," Puck urged, with mock officiousness, "or the master will be cross."

"I shall be going upstairs for a moment," said Isaac, gliding back into the room. "Can you sit here without squabbling?"

"Course we can," said Puck. He winked at Tim conspiratorially. "We're not children."

Isaac clumped up the stairs. A muffled sound drifted down of a door opening and closing. Puck began to giggle. Rody followed suit. The mood was infectious. Tim felt his own face creasing.

Laughter filled him, the feeling huge and generous, the knot in Tim's middle vanished, and the thoughts that had assailed him on the road half an hour before suddenly seemed stupid and trite. He had nothing to worry about. He was just going to pass on a little information. There was no way the authorities would trace anything back to him. Weren't there lots of people who knew of French's schedule, not least his wife and Micky Laffin? Absurd to let himself get into the state he had got into on the road. As for imagining his own hanging! That was just plain ridiculous. He was not going to hang, and besides, he had to remember why he was doing this.

Isaac's feet sounded on the stairs.

"Quiet, quiet," urged Rody. This had the reverse of the desired effect, of course. Inside each man, laughter swelled again and broke free.

Isaac appeared in the doorway. He saw Puck, Rody and Tim around the table. Each man was bent double. Isaac smiled.

"Come on," he called gently, delighted by this merriment. Laughing together like this, they would make a good team.

Isaac carried a sack in his two arms like a baby. He laid it on the table and sat down. The laughter lasted for a few moments more and then stopped.

"Oh, God! I don't know what's got into me." Puck wiped away the tears that showed at the corner of each eye.

"You're three daft fellows." Isaac untied the twine with which the mouth of the sack was bound. He reached with his arm inside the sack and sang, "De, de, de, le, de, de – ee," exactly as the band had played in the Belfast theatre he visited once, each time the curtain was about to rise.

All eyes stared at the mouth of the sack. Isaac let the silence last. Finally, when everyone was quite still, he began to pull. From out of the brown mouth of the sack emerged first the brown wooden stock with a patch-box on the right side, then the trigger and the trigger guard, then the firing mechanism – an S-shaped hammer and a nipple below over which the percussion cap fitted snugly (this was a flintlock that had been modernised), and finally, the brass barrel that ended in a broad, trumpet-like mouth. It was a blunderbuss, with a spring-operated bayonet on top of the barrel, which snapped forward on release of a catch.

Rody whistled and Puck clapped his hands. Tim said nothing. He felt awed. It seemed to Isaac just like the moment in the theatre when a pretty girl comes out to sing.

"It's got a very interesting history, this weapon," said Isaac.

He laid the gun on the table carefully. He opened the patch-box. Normally this was where the wadding, the waxed patches and the shot were stored but it was empty.

"It was bought in England by a man named Hope."

Tim stared at the barrel. In the shiny brass he saw his own smudged reflection staring back. There was a faint smell of gun oil in the air, and the bitter smell of powder. He had worked for Colonel Hutcheson as a beater sometimes and he knew this smell. After day in the smoke of guns, one reeked of it.

"This man Hope brought her over to Ireland," continued Isaac.

He reached into the sack again and pulled out a pewter box with pictures of birds and flowers scored into the metal. Isaac flipped the lid back. The box was filled with percussion caps.

"Hope sold it to a man named Phoenix in Antrim."

Isaac reached into the sack again.

"And, the story goes, this Phoenix fellow, he didn't want anyone to know he had her. Frightened of being caught with it, you see."

Isaac pulled out a tin with something rattling inside.

"So Phoenix kept this beauty under his shirt next to his bare skin."

The top came off the tin. It was filled with lead balls of shot of various sizes.

"The tarnish from the alloy made a sore on Phoenix's belly."

Isaac's hand went back into the sack.

"The little sore got bigger and bigger . . ."

Isaac felt with a finger in first one and then the other corner of the sack.

"... and bigger, until his whole stomach was like a rotten black potato. And we know all about those, don't we?"

With his arm still in the sack, buried as far as his armpit, Isaac looked from one face to the next around the table.

"Finally, the rotten skin split, Phoenix's guts spilled out. Thinking on his feet, he caught them in a chamber-pot, but there was no way he was going to get them all back in again, and so he died."

"Ha, ha, ha," said Puck. "You expect us to swallow that, do you?"

"Course." Isaac pulled his arm from the sack, bringing with him a powder flask and a device for making shot. He brushed away the wisps of hessian entangled in the hairs on the back of his hand. "I couldn't make up something as good as that," he said, and then he continued briskly, "What are we going to do for wadding until I can get some? I thought there was some in the sack but there isn't."

Here, thought Tim, was an opportunity to shine.

"What about some of these old rent receipts of my father's?" he said.

He pulled a crumpled fistful of papers from his trouser pocket.

Isaac took one and read, " 'Receipt for rent paid for the year by Philip Traynor – signed, on behalf of Robert Rudd, the agent, by Cormac Hanratty, clerk to the Beatonboro' Estate – the first of November, eighteen thirty-five.' It really is the real thing."

"I found a sheaf of them," Tim explained, "tucked up in the roof."

"Only they won't do as wadding, I'm afraid." Isaac handed the paper back to Tim. "Imagine the gun is seized and these are stuffed in it."

Tim felt stupid. The receipts would be a giveaway, of course. He wished he'd kept his mouth shut.

"I've got a copy of *The Times* of London," said Puck, in the

West Country accent that he always adopted when he spoke of England. When the Devonshire regiment were garrisoned in Monaghan, he drank with one or two of the soldiers and learned how to mimic them. "I found it in the gutter in Beatonboro'. Someone had just tossed it aside. Thought it would make good kindling."

Puck pulled a folded newspaper from the pocket in the coat-tail of his frock coat. He opened it out and spread it on the table. The front page was covered with tiny black letters.

"Oh, yes," said Isaac, with a smile. "This'll do for now. We can use it to bundle up some shot as well. Course, when you're on the job, lads, you must get some stocking or something and tie the shot up properly. It's got to be a snug fit in the barrel."

Rody nodded.

"But this'll do as wadding for the time being as well. *The Times* of London. That'll confuse them." Isaac chuckled again.

Now Tim felt grumpy. First his idea was rejected; next Puck was praised because he happened to have an old newspaper in his pocket. Tim chewed at the corner of his lip.

"I like your wit, though, Tim." It was Isaac again. "Old receipts from the estate, it would be beautiful to use those as wadding. Poetic justice. Trouble is, what if the peelers ever got their hands on the loaded gun? They'd have you into the barracks so fast, Tim, your feet wouldn't touch the ground." Isaac clicked his fingers. "Like that. And you're far too important to lose, Tim Traynor."

The older man squeezed his arm. Tim's grumpiness of a moment earlier dissolved like mist before sunshine.

"Sorry to intrude, but what's the point of the story about this man Phoenix that you just bored us with?" The speaker was Rody. It was the first time he had spoken since Isaac appeared with the sack.

Isaac said, "That's obvious, I'd have thought." He lifted his hand away from Tim's arm.

"Don't sleep with her, Rody, or you'll get a nasty rash."

"I'll try," said Rody. "Can't promise. Of course, if She were in your care, Isaac, there'd be no problem, would there, seeing as She's a she?"

"Just keep her as shiny as if she were in the police barracks," said the older man. "For God's sake." Although Isaac smiled at Rody as he issued his instruction, the tone of irritation in his voice was unmistakable.

chapter ten

Beatonboro' main street was filled with cattle and horses which had been brought there for sale. It was fair day. Isaac and Tim, along with Rody and Puck, had placed themselves behind a large horse immediately opposite the estate office. It was a chestnut mare. Rody held the bridle and studied the animal's face. Puck, pipe in mouth, gazed along the street. He gave a good impression of a man who was fascinated by what he saw, the people, the traders, the animals. Isaac held the back leg of the chestnut and carefully looked at the hoof. Tim stood a few feet away. He listened to a fiddler, who was sitting on the doorstep of a shop and playing away.

"Here comes French and his poodle, Laffin," said Isaac nonchalantly.

The door of the estate office opened. Thomas and Micky emerged.

Isaac dropped the hoof. The vendor hurried forward. A sale was in the offing, perhaps?

Isaac dropped the hind leg and stepped away from the horse. Thomas and Micky moved off along the street. Isaac let them get a ten-yard start and then ambled slowly in the same direction. Tim followed. Puck and Rody drifted after them. All four men had their eyes focused on the brown felt broad-brimmed hats worn by both the agent and the bailiff, which bobbed in the crowd ahead of them.

"Did you see the bulges under the man's coat?" said Puck quietly.

"Quit complaining. Your gun is better." This was Isaac.

"He should never have been warned."

"I thought you promised never to mention the subject again."

"Did I?" murmured Puck.

The men spoke gently; they were countrymen on a fair day exchanging pleasantries.

"Have you heard what Micky Laffin's been blabbing?" Puck continued.

"I forget, why not remind me," said Isaac, who knew perfectly well but had decided to play dumb.

The felt hats of the agent and the bailiff came to a halt by a pen full of goats. The four men following stopped and carefully began to scrutinise the display in a haberdasher's window. Tim, who hated goats, could smell their sharp, distinctive odour.

"Apparently, after we put French down," explained Tim, "Micky won't go to his aid, he'll come straight after us." This was puzzling. Why was he having to explain this again?

"From the horse's mouth, is it?" said Isaac.

Isaac's feigned ignorance was a ploy, Tim decided, intended to defuse the threat. What couldn't be remembered wasn't worth taking seriously. Tim could sort of see the sense of it.

The man selling the goats and the agent, mouths open, were laughing. The bailiff took off his hat and wiped his head with a handkerchief.

"It's what Laffin's been saying around the pubs," said Puck, grimly.

"We'll just have to be more careful then," said Rody.

The bailiff's hat went back and the two hats moved off through the crowd again, and the four men who were following moved after them.

"What's French like?" said Rody.

"How should I know?" said Isaac. "You should be the expert by now."

"I thought you knew him."

"I've had dealings. I don't know him. He's an agent. What else do you want to know?"

"Just what's he actually like," said Rody calmly. "In your opinion."

"Decent enough."

"What else?"

"Married, four grown sons."

"In Dublin, thank goodness," interrupted Puck. "But they've got the same instructions as Micky Laffin. Once we fire, they're coming after us."

"What's Mrs French like?" asked Rody.

"Well, Tim, you know her better than we do," said Isaac, and smiled.

"A couple of years younger than her husband. Plays the piano a lot. Green eyes."

"Oh, quite the poet, aren't we?" said Isaac.

"I'm just relating what I know."

"Just a bit of sport, Tim."

"French is a magistrate, isn't he?" interrupted Rody.

"Yes, you'll find him at the petty sessions," said Isaac.

"We must drop in some time," said Puck.

"Does he hunt?" asked Rody.

"A little, doesn't he, Tim?"

"Snipe, a bit of woodcock, that's it. Strictly for the pot."

"A devil with the gun, though, I hear," said Puck.

"As you have said, several times," said Isaac.

"Dogs?" This was Rody.

"A couple of setters."

"I know that."

Rody had seen the setters asleep in their kennels on the night he visited the agent's house.

"He's just got himself a bloodhound."

"Oh, Jesus," moaned Puck. "That'll be the size of a small pony."

"Noisy. Has this strange booming cry. You'll hear it coming for miles. Doesn't bite."

"You mean it hasn't bitten you," said Puck quickly and almost gleefully.

The felt hats stopped again and the four men following stopped as well.

"Is French going round the estate much nowadays?" asked Isaac, quietly.

"All the time," said Tim. "But he always has Micky with him now."

"Who's got his instructions, of course, but I won't repeat myself," said Puck, and Rody snorted with amusement.

"You will just have to be *very* careful," said Isaac.

"And patient," Rody added. He didn't want Isaac to think he was on Puck's side.

"That's right," Isaac agreed, "and don't forget, in the end he'll make a mistake. They always do."

The hats floated away again and the four men went after them, to see what was going to happen.

It was an August morning, mild and moist. Rody and Puck sat on a boulder in a field, silently smoking their pipes. A cow in the corner of the field dropped her head. The two men heard the noise of grass ripping and teeth grinding. The cow was pregnant and Rody idly wondered when she would calve.

"Here he comes," murmured Puck. He touched his colleague with his elbow.

Rody looked over the stone wall and along the lane. A pony and car was coming towards them. It was a quarter of a mile away. The pony moved at a slow trot.

Rody and Puck got up and ambled over to the wall. They'd chosen an open stretch of country with no trees or hedgerows.

"Is he alone?" Puck asked this from the ground where he knelt in front of a sack. The end of the sack was tied with twine.

"I believe he is."

"Are you sure?"

Rody looked at the car. French sat sideways holding the reins. The bloodhound stood up on the seat beside him, head into the wind. The seat opposite was empty. French was alone. They'd got lucky at last.

"No sign of Laffin," confirmed Rody.

"Happy days. We're ready to go. You wave."

"I wave," said Rody. "I jump over the wall. I put my hand up. French stops the car. I ask the time. He undoes his coat. He gets out his fob."

"I pop up," continued Puck. "I fire. I drop the gun. We run down the field behind us, cross the river, disappear into the woods on the other side."

"Right," agreed Rody.

"Sure there's no sign of Laffin?"

"None," confirmed Rody. "No Laffin. We can proceed."

Puck undid the twine and put his hand into the sack. He pulled out the blunderbuss. Puck pressed down the percussion cap on the nipple. He cocked the trigger.

"Oh, Jesus!" Puck heard Rody whisper suddenly above him.

"What?"

"Put the gun away, now!" ordered Rody.

Puck removed the percussion cap and released the hammer. He slipped the blunderbuss into the sack, and tied the end with twine.

"Stand up," said Rody, "and wave."

The rumble of wheels sounded just beyond the wall.

Puck stood up. The car was just a few feet away. French held the reins, and Laffin, who hadn't been there the last time he looked, sat on the seat opposite the agent. Micky shouted something at Thomas.

Puck waved expansively, a countryman greeting the quality.

Rody smiled. He found it hard to act when he was frustrated, like he was now.

The car passed by. French and Laffin waved. From the back of the car, Puck and Rody looked to Thomas and Micky like two labourers who greeted them from behind the wall. They paid no attention to the men's faces. Puck and Rody were like hundreds of people that they passed every day on the roads.

"You know what?" said Rody, as the car rumbled away.

"What?"

"The bastard Laffin was kneeling in the car and tying his laces or something. That's why we didn't see him before."

"Jesus!" Puck spat on the ground. "We're never going to get at our man. He's always got Micky with him, and if it isn't Micky it's someone else."

Puck stared grumpily after the back of the disappearing car.

"We just have to wait for him to make a mistake," said Rody. "One day, he'll be alone. One day. And then we'll have him."

Puck picked up the sack with the blunderbuss and swung it over his shoulder.

"Let's get this out of here and put it somewhere safe."

The two men followed the line of the wall towards the gate.

From the Patrol Diary of Constable Cleary

28 September 1854

At ten o'clock in the morning, Thomas French and Micky Laffin were fired on as they passed a small orchard four miles north of Beatonboro'. The assassins, they numbered two, placed themselves inside an empty barrel which stood inside the orchard wall. As Messrs Laffin and French passed in their car, a man stood up from inside the barrel and fired. A second man then helped the first out of the barrel and the two made their escape through the orchard. Messrs French and Laffin pursued the pair but found their path obstructed by apple pickers who allowed their ladders to fall in their way.

News of the assault was received at Beatonboro' police station an hour later. I proceeded at once to the orchard with two sub-constables. Mr Laffin and Mr French were certain the orchard workers had personal knowledge of the attack before it happened and deliberately contrived to foil their attempt to capture the assassins.

With Mr French I went and spoke to the foreman, Mr Paul Handley, a Belfast man. His team numbered about twenty, men, women and children. They had previously worked in Armagh, he explained, and just five days before had come down to Monaghan to work for Jeremiah Barnett, who has a large orchard in the area. They had never worked for Jeremiah Barnett before and anticipated being in the area for two more weeks.

I pressed Mr Handley that his employees, perhaps with his connivance, had agreed to facilitate the two assassins and to assist in their escape in the event of the attack failing.

Mr Handley denied this charge vehemently. It was hardly possible, he said, that in a mere five days, his workers, all newcomers to the area, could have got involved in a murder attempt. Besides which, two of his people were Protestants who wouldn't have anything to do with a plot like this in the first place.

I asked to speak to Mr Handley's employees. He agreed that I could do that but only in his presence. I interviewed all of them. They seemed decent enough and at first I found it hard to imagine that they might have been involved. However, I then discovered that the two Protestant members, who are both women, had been sent away for the morning to purchase provisions in a shop some miles away. I wondered if there had not been a deliberate plan concocted to get them out of the way. Didn't Mr Barnett, their employer, I mooted, provision the gangs who worked for him? And furthermore, was it not a fact that there was a shop a quarter of a mile away? When Mr Handley explained, in his reply to my questions, that there were goods needed which Jeremiah Barnett did not provide (new boots, for instance) and it was to buy these that the Protestant girls had been sent off, I began to suspect someone, somewhere, was not telling me the truth.

I pressed the employees again, one after the other, that they had foreknowledge of the attack and had willingly obstructed the path of Mr French and Mr Laffin. Every man, woman and child denied the charge. The vehemence of the denial only confirmed my suspicions.

Towards two o'clock I stopped to talk over matters with Mr French and Mr Laffin. The latter, a slightly circumspect but highly intelligent man, had been examining the barrel. He brought me over to look at it. It was old and the wood was green. It had been in the orchard for some years, neglected and quietly rotting, but the spot where it had lived during these years was not near the wall overlooking the road, but in a ditch behind the orchard. The barrel had been moved, and according to some of the work party, its sudden appearance beside the wall that morning had surprised them a little. However, they assumed this was the doing of the owner so they thought nothing more of it.

I went and examined the barrel myself. This was my second examination. I rolled it away from the spot where it had been stood and I found the grass underneath was green and fresh, rather than white and decayed as would have been the case had the barrel stood there for months. So it had just been moved. The workers were telling the truth about that at any rate.

At about this time one of Mr Barnett's servant girls arrived with cans of tea, and bread and butter wrapped in muslin. The workers stopped their labours and gathered under a tree to eat their lunch. Two of them, meanwhile, sloped away from the party and came over to me at the barrel. These were the two Protestant women. One of them, Amy McCardle, requested a private word with me. I walked them down the lane to where the car of Mr French and Mr Laffin was parked. Miss McCardle explained that she had heard the gang talking; they wanted to tell me the truth but they were worried I would not believe them.

What was that truth? I wondered.

First, she and the other girl had been sent to the shop together, not to get them out of the way but because the foreman, Mr Handley, had thought that with the two girls coming from a similar background they might enjoy an excursion in each other's company. Furthermore, she added, two had to go, in order to carry back several heavy items.

As for the events of that morning, she said, the gang had been hard at work when they heard a single shot, followed by shouts and imprecations. Next thing, they saw two men running after two other men; the pursuers had guns, as far as they could see, whereas the men who were being chased did not; from their ladders they failed to see the assassins carried a blunderbuss; apparently, all they saw in the hands of one of these men was a sack. Assuming the front runners were in danger, they acted without thinking; they blocked the path of Mr French and Mr Laffin and it was only later that they realised the seriousness of their actions. Had they known, Miss McCardle stressed, there was a Ribbon conspiracy against Mr French, they may have tried to apprehend the assassins but would more likely have stayed where they were in the trees and done nothing. Ribbonmen command a healthy respect amongst the working population.

Very shortly after this conversation, Mr Laffin and Mr French returned on foot. They had been to the local shop, the one a quarter of a mile away, and they had discovered that indeed it was closed, and had been since first light, as the owner's sister was being buried this day in Keady. Why had no one mentioned this at the start? I wondered, and Miss McCardle ventured that close questioning by members of the Constabulary after an attempted murder, provoked such anxiety in the minds of everybody, this detail was overlooked. This seems amazing but I subsequently confirmed with Mr Handley that he had known about the funeral and so had sent the girls to the more distant shop to buy boots, gloves, twine and shears.

I conclude there was no conspiracy to help the assassins but conclude the gang of workers in the orchard, misreading the situation, intervened to help those they assumed were the victims. However, I greatly regret the action in Mr Barnett's orchard; Mr French remains under sentence of death and the conspirators remain at large.

Cleary put down his pen and blotted the last page of his copy. He watched the ink in the shape of some of the letters on the page bleed through the blotting paper.

For a moment, when he arrived at the orchard, he had thought he had a conspiracy, but his suspicions came unstuck when he began to look at the detail, as was so often the case in Ireland. This was a worthwhile observation but it was not, he decided, the sort of thought that would have made an appropriate conclusion to an entry in his patrol diary.

He closed the book and – as the *Standing Rules and Regulations* specified – he locked his diary away in the drawer of the day-room desk. A visit was imminent from District Inspector Love of the Monaghan station. They were already in correspondence about the Ribbon conspiracy, and he had no doubt that this superior officer would want to see his patrol diary.

"There's good news," said Rody, "There's a chink in his defences."

Rody sat on a box, his back flat against Tim's hearth. Puck, who had walked out of the rain and into Tim's cabin just a moment or two before, now stood in the middle of the floor, legs apart, his feet planted on the hard earth. It was a Sunday afternoon and winter had come.

"Well, about time," exclaimed Puck. He took off his coat and shook it. Drops of rainwater landed on the embers in the fireplace and hissed. Outside, rain was falling.

"I thought I was going to be lighting a candle in the chapel on this one," he said. Puck hung his coat on a wooden peg near the door.

"They've made him a Guardian," said Rody. "Two evenings a week, he walks across to the meetings at the Union, alone, no Micky." Then he added, "Right, Tim?" The younger man, on the other side of the fireplace, was staring upwards and apparently paying no attention.

"It is," said Tim.

"Tell us the route, Tim." The current mood of the younger man was abstracted and dreamy. Rody believed this was on account of the woman Tim had once loved, this Kitty about whom, just recently, he had spoken quite often.

"The route, Tim," repeated Rody, "the route."

Tim took a breath and spoke his piece quickly. "French comes out of the estate office on Tuesday and Friday at seven, goes down the street to the church, goes up the entry at the side to the wasteland at the back, and crosses over to the poor-house gates."

"Every week for the last three weeks," said Rody, with genuine delight, "without the Laffin trotting behind. Yes, Tim?"

"Yes," agreed Tim.

"Very good." Puck pulled out his pipe and fiddled with the bowl. "So, he doesn't think we'd dare do him in Beatonboro' town."

"So that's where we shoot him."

There was a pause. Outside, the rain fell with a whisper from the sky, trickled down the thatch and dribbled from the eaves.

"I have an idea," said Puck slowly. "Tim, get an envelope – don't use one of your own, get it from the agent's house, or get it from somewhere else, and write on it 'Thomas French Esquire, Beatonboro' Estate Office, and so on.' Can you do that?" Tim was literate, he could write, while Puck and Rody could only read their names and make out odd words.

Tim was looking at the warped boards of his ceiling again. He thought he could hear a mouse scratching above, but then again it might be wind or rain. The weather was ferocious.

"Tim, did you hear?" asked Puck.

"An envelope," he said, "with a name on the front."

"Whose?"

"Thomas French."

"What's the matter with you?" asked Rody.

"Nothing."

"Your mind's not on what we have to do."

"Yes, it is," said Tim.

"Is it this old love, Kitty?"

"It's nothing," said Tim. "It's nothing."

That night the temperature dropped and the land froze. Throughout the following day there were flurries of snow that covered the ground in patches. When he arrived at work, Tim's first job was to hack out the ice that had formed in the water trough in the yard. Later, Helena gave him a pair of fingerless mittens and sent him to the shed to saw and chop wood. That day she wanted a fire in every room in the house.

That night, when he finished work, Tim went and sat in Dolly Walsh's public house for an hour while snow fell outside. When he came out he saw the snow had settled and everywhere he looked he could see it gleaming eerily in the darkness.

He put his hands in his pockets and made his way to the old forge. This abandoned building – windowless, doorless, gaping holes in the roof – stood on the outskirts of Beatonboro', and overlooked a piece of wasteland divided up by a few broken walls. Originally farmland, it was the intention, fifty years before, of the Beatons and the Hutchesons and the worthies of the town, to build a market house on the site. The plan fell through, however, due to lack of subscriptions, and the land became a dump where Beatonboro' householders threw stones and unwanted building materials, and the town orderly put the dung and rest of the rubbish he cleaned from the streets, rather than carting it away to the old quarry a mile from town as he was meant to. The poor-house, where the Union held their meetings, was a stone building set on a hill above the wasteland. The Guardians believed this was a healthy, airy location. The view from the poor-house was of the back of Beatonboro' main street.

When he arrived at the forge, Tim found Puck and Rody waiting in the building. The snow had even got in here through the open roof.

"Did you bring the letter?" asked Puck.

Without saying a word, Tim took the letter from the back pocket of his coat and laid it on the palm of the pale hand he made out in the darkness.

"That feels good, substantial," exclaimed Puck, weighing the envelope with his hand. The weight came from the three sheets of blank paper with which Tim had packed it.

"Feels right," continued Puck. He turned the envelope over in his hand and touched the back with his fingers. "Oh! A seal," he continued. "Good touch."

Until this moment, Tim had successfully managed to avoid thinking about what they were about to do. Now Puck's remark changed all that. Tim was overwhelmed by a sense that in a few minutes, after months of waiting and many failed attempts, they were finally going to kill Mr French.

As soon as he realised this, Tim became fearful. He was not frightened of being caught – that was not what crossed his mind at that moment – but rather than his employer would recognise him in the moments before his death and know that Tim had taken his wages and, at the same time, betrayed the man who paid them. Tim wanted his part in this action to remain unknown; he wanted this more than he wanted success, he realised. Even if they had to run away, he thought, it wouldn't matter, so long as Mr French didn't know the part he had played.

Tim watched as Puck wound his scarf around his face and he decided to do the same.

"Right," said Rody. "We all know what to do? You go in first, Puck. I get behind him. You watch my back, Tim. You present the letter, Puck. The agent takes it, he starts to open it, that's when his guard will be down, and that's when I run up and pull the trigger."

Rody removed the blunderbuss from the sack in which he had carried it there. He folded the sack and put it in the pocket in the tail of his coat. He cocked the blunderbuss.

"If he's the least suspicious," continued Rody, "if we get a smell of a policeman, or Micky, we run. But, happily, I think that tonight we're going to get him, at last." He laughed gently, and added, in his sincere voice, "God rest his soul."

"That's right," said Puck. "Let's go." To Tim's ears Puck sounded not so much like a man who was anxious to get on with the job as a man who was excited and even eager.

The three men went and stood behind the oak tree that grew in front of the forge. The bark was rough. The air was cold and there was a meaty smell; a fox had passed that way not long before, Tim guessed.

After a few minutes the light of a lantern appeared on the far side of the wasteland. It swayed from side to side as the carrier moved away from Beatonboro' and towards the poor-house and the three of them as they waited. Rody touched Puck with his elbow.

Puck moved away into the darkness. He found the path that snaked across the wasteland and along which he knew the agent was coming towards him. Snow gleamed ahead of him on the ground. He placed himself by a bush where the agent couldn't see him. He heard the snow compacting beneath the agent's boots as he drew closer.

When the agent was half a dozen paces away, Puck stepped out from behind the bush and called ahead, in his polite voice, "Sir, excuse me, sir, is that you? Mr French, sir, I've been looking for you . . ."

He saw the agent hesitate and stop, lift the lantern up and peer across the darkness at him. Puck had wrapped his scarf around the bottom of his face; he had pulled his hat well down over his forehead. Only the eyes and the temples and the bridge of his nose were showing, but it was Puck's assumption that this should seem normal. On a freezing cold night, with snow on the ground, what man wouldn't cover his face?

"Who's that?" called the agent.

Puck heard something else as well as the agent speaking: his two accomplices creeping through the darkness somewhere behind the agent. A fox cried somewhere. It was an eerie sound, like a moan of pain.

"You don't know me," said Puck quietly.

"Get back."

"I have something for you. Something very important."

"I'm not interested."

"A letter."

"Get away from me."

Puck thought he saw the shape of his two accomplices moving along a wall to his left in a wide sweep, which would eventually bring them behind the agent.

"I was told to put this in your hand. It's urgent. You must read it," said Puck. His tone was conciliatory. He must keep the agent talking until the others were in place.

"Go back to Beatonboro'. Put it under the office door. I'll read it tomorrow," said the agent unhelpfully.

"I'm a poor man," said Puck. This was not an inspiration but the line he had decided on in advance. "This is worth sixpence to me."

The agent had been fiddling with his buttons. Now his coat was open. The hand reached under his clothes and came out with a pistol.

"Is it worth your life?" said the agent.

"No." Puck swallowed. "No." The crucial thing was not to panic. He had lost sight of the other two. He presumed they were watching; he presumed they had seen the pistol come out. If Rody was to succeed, he must make the agent take the letter and open it.

"I mean no harm," said Puck, and he took a step forward.

"Back off," said the agent. He cocked the hammer. Now Puck took a step back.

"I'm just an honest man making an honest sixpence," said Puck. He drew his slight, slender body to its full height, maximising his size. He was an innocent with nothing to fear from the man with the pistol. He would offer his whole body as a target for the agent to shoot at.

He saw the agent hang the lantern on the little finger of the hand that held the pistol. The agent rummaged with his free hand in one of the waistcoat pockets and came out with something between his fingers.

"Take that, then," said the agent. He flung something, which landed with a faint plop in the snow on the ground between them.

"What was that?" Puck asked.

"I've doubled your pay. That's a shilling. Take the letter to the office."

Puck looked at the small dark hole, bored by the coin through the snow.

"You must read it now," he said.

"No."

"I was told you must have it now."

"I'll get it later," said the agent grimly. "Bring it to the office."

"No, I was told you must have it, this instant."

The free hand dived back through the slit in the coat and came back holding a second pistol.

"If you won't take it from my hand," said Puck, "then you must have it by your own."

He threw the envelope carefully. It floated through the air and landed, address upwards, a couple of feet from the other man's boots. The agent lowered his lantern and peered down at it.

"No, you pick it up," said the agent finally.

The agent carefully kicked the edge of the envelope and sent it skittering back across the snow in Puck's direction. "I said, you pick it up," he repeated.

The mechanism of the second pistol clicked as he cocked the hammer.

"There's one ball for you," he said, "and one for whoever's behind me."

Snow, Puck noticed, had begun to fall again. A soft flake

landed on his eyelash and he blinked it away. He wondered when the snow had started, and why he hadn't noticed that it had started. The part of the scarf which was closest to his mouth had been warmed and dampened by his breath. The edges of this warm patch were beginning to chill in the cold night air. "You don't understand," said Puck, finally.

"I do."

"You don't."

"Pick it up,"

"I can't. You must. It's addressed to you."

"You won't, but you can."

"I won't," said Puck.

"A shilling to carry that back to the office – that's not bad."

"The snow's wet the envelope," said Puck. Several flakes had landed on the paper and melted.

"But not so's I can't read the name," said the agent.

Puck peered at the writing on the front of the envelope. He saw, by the light of the lantern which the agent obligingly held forward, that in some places the copperplate script was clear and strong, but in others, where the water from the melted flakes had mixed with the ink, the letters were disappearing.

"And it's your name," said Puck, in his most persuasive voice. "It's for you."

He was surprised when he heard the agent bark across the darkness, "Tench is not my name!"

"It must have smudged," said Puck, which he thought was an inspiration although he could not actually read what was written.

"Whoever addressed that letter wrote the name Tench quite clearly on the front," said the agent, delightedly. "They wrote Tench, not French. Now, who would write a letter that was so important and then write my name wrong?"

Until this moment, Puck had believed they were evenly matched. Until this moment he had believed he might get the agent to pick up the envelope and open it, and so allow Rody to get in. Now he realised the balance had tipped in the agent's favour. Puck felt his mouth going dry.

"Who gave you the letter?" said the agent, pressing his advantage.

"I don't know," said Puck, trying to think what to say. "It was dark. I didn't see him clearly."

The agent moved back from him, the snow crunching as it compressed under his weight.

"You know exactly who wrote it."

"I don't," said Puck. He gave his answer in a strong, clear, ringing voice; he was innocent, blameless.

"Course you know who gave it to you. It was a Ribbonman. Well, you can keep the money and the letter. I don't want them. It's French, not Tench, Thomas French . . ."

There was nothing more to be said. This episode was over. Puck knew that. The agent moved slowly backwards from Puck in the direction of Beatonboro'.

The snow was still falling. Puck saw flakes trembling in the light of the lantern. He dropped the scarf from his face and felt a flake on his cheek and another on his lip, each a smooth, cold prickle on his skin. He wondered about Rody. Was he going to leap out suddenly and fire? He entertained the idea for a second and then he decided, no, that wasn't going to happen. That wasn't the plan they had agreed upon and it wasn't Rody's style to improvise like that. No, Rody was there in the darkness and, just as he was, Rody was watching the agent slip through their fingers again.

Puck bent down. He found the shilling and then he picked up the letter. He pocketed the coin and then wiped away the snowflakes that had fallen on the envelope, and this further smudged the address. In the distance he saw the agent turn and begin to run back towards the safety of the town, with its police barracks and townspeople. The snow was falling even more heavily now and he felt flakes touching his face.

"You imbecile," Puck shouted. "You worked for this man and yet you can't spell his name. Now he knows my face."

In a corner of the forge, Tim shuffled on the spot, the snow that had come through the holes in the roof crumpling under his feet. "Surely it was too dark to see you?" he offered, lamely.

"He had a lantern. He read the envelope. Of course he could see my face. And, what's more, he now knows my voice as well."

Rody sat on a stone in the middle of the floor. He held the barrel of the blunderbuss over his lap and shook the gun. Out tumbled the wadding, then the shot bundled up in a piece of old stocking, and finally the powder. The shot and the wadding he put away in the patch-box in the side of the stock; the powder he scattered on the floor. It formed a grey stain on the snow.

"Let's not forget, we've got a job to do," said Rody mysteriously.

"Yes, yes," said Puck, pacing up and down, glowering angrily. Tim wanted to run but Puck stood between him and the door. Kitty now came into his mind. He imagined her sitting at her kitchen table at home, staring into the embers of the fire. If they hadn't argued he wouldn't have joined, he thought, and if he hadn't joined, then he wouldn't be standing in the corner of this derelict building with two furious men.

Tim's thoughts were interrupted by the word, "Sorry," spoken with terrible vehemence.

The speaker was Puck, just a couple of feet away and staring at him. He was glad he couldn't see Puck's eyes. When Puck was furious, his brown eyes went black. At the same time his small, slight frame was filled with energy. He became a man who could hurt.

"Sorry," continued Puck furiously. "Can I hear the word sorry?" Puck held the envelope in front of his face.

"I don't know how it happened," said Tim. "I know he's French. I just don't know how I wrote that other name."

"I'll tell you how," Puck shouted. "Thinking about Kitty! Kitty this, Kitty that, Kitty I miss her."

"That's not true," Tim shouted, his face reddening. He was grateful for the darkness that hid him. "I never think about her. My mind's totally on this. I haven't thought about her since I started."

"Tim," said the other man, "every now and again you go all still and soft and you drift off and I know what you're thinking about then. Her. Has to be."

"I never think about her."

Puck let out a derisory snort. "You gave her up, for this caper, you said. You told me yourself. So of course you still think about her. Don't be ridiculous."

"I've put her completely out of my mind," Tim repeated.

"I wish I could put you completely out of my mind," said Puck grimly.

"We'd better have a talk," said Rody, from the floor.

"Yes," Puck agreed, "we had. Turn and face the wall, Tim."

Tim blinked, uncertain whether this was an order or a joke.

"I said, turn and face the wall."

Tim turned.

"Nose against the stone."

Puck pushed Tim's face against the cold, wet wall. Smell of mould and mortar.

"Put your fingers in your ears."

Tim plugged a forefinger into each waxy hole. Wind and bark of distant dog were blotted out and in their place he heard only his anxious breathing and a rumbling, like an iron-bound wheel on cobbles. He wanted to pee. Hoped he wouldn't wet himself. Puck and Rody somewhere behind. Impossible to tell where exactly.

Were they talking, perhaps, about him? What was he thinking? No perhaps about it. Course they were. Deciding what to do. Whether or not to tell Isaac, weren't they?

Legs trembling and a drop of pee leaking into his trousers. He felt the wet fabric against his skin. He imagined Isaac's parlour, a fire burning, the gleaming Staffordshire dogs on the mantelpiece, Isaac in his chair, bringing his fingertips together and then separating them over and over again as he ruminated, and the awful, unbearable, suspenseful atmosphere. Oh, Kitty! What had he done? What had he got himself into?

Something tapped his shoulder. He turned, pulling his fingers from his ears. Saw Puck and Rody standing side by side.

Rody touched the release on the blunderbuss and the bayonet which lay flat along the barrel flipped forward and quivered. Two-foot length of iron with an evil point on the end.

"Hands up, Tim," said Rody. He motioned upwards with the bayonet. "Put 'em up," he said again.

"Hey!" said Tim, bewildered. "Put that thing down." He remembered Rody unloading it, but perhaps, while his face was to the wall, Rody had reloaded it. The hammer was cocked all right. But was there a percussion cap underneath it? Too dark to see.

"Put your hands up in the air," said Puck coldly.

Surely this was a joke, Tim thought. They couldn't be pointing a loaded gun at him. Course it was a joke. Had to be.

"You know you must never point one of those things unless you mean to kill," he said, sounding rather like Isaac.

"Which we do," Rody said, quickly and lightly.

"But I'm one of yours. We're on the same side."

"No, you're not." This was Rody. "The Ribbon Court have weighed you in the balance and found you guilty of incompetence, malingering, back-sliding."

His knees trembled and his groin, he noticed, had become a small hard nut and shrunk back into the bony point on the end of his pelvis.

"Guilty," said Puck, with a smile. "And you know how we treat incompetents? Like we treat land-grabbers and informers."

This was preposterous. What were they talking about?

"I'm not an informer," said Tim swiftly. He never was nor would he ever be that terrible figure, a man who told, a man who betrayed his people to the peelers.

"Guilty," Rody muttered.

"Guilty," Puck pronounced.

"Come on, boys," Tim said. "A joke's a joke."

"We're not joking," said Rody bluntly.

Surely he was. Surely this was all put on.

"Rody Donohoe, we're friends," said Tim.

"No, we're not."

What did he say next? A pause. Rody looking at him. Blunderbuss levelled at him. Bayonet point levelled at his heart. Snow pouring through the roof, swirling around the dark interior. A duck flew across the sky, its quacks rolling across the frozen land. Puck twisting and reaching into his coat pocket. What was he getting? Now pulling something out. What? Couldn't see. What was that? A metal blade grinding across another. Oh, yes, he knew now what it was.

"Captain Blue!" said Puck, in the manner of a Ribbon proclamation. "I have the shears."

"Have you the sharpening stone to hone the blade?"

"Oh, aye," said Puck, although Tim saw no stone, just the terrifying implement, sheep shears − two blades, about nine inches long, with black wooden handles, joined at the top by a half round of springy metal.

"Cut off his balls?" Puck murmured, speculatively. "No. Tongue and ears, I think, don't you?"

"Boys," said Tim, and swallowed, appalled. He shrugged sideways. If he could just get outside, he could dash across the wasteland faster than Puck or Rody, and once he made Beatonboro' main street, he was safe from harm.

Puck reaching forward to grab his shoulder. He swerved away and Puck failed to grasp him. Angled himself and struck out for the dark oblong in the middle of the wall that was the door. Two steps and then a stinging slash. The bayonet lay flat across his chest. A hand tight on each shoulder. Rody and Puck pushing him back, and now he was standing against the wall, exactly as he had been a couple of seconds earlier.

"We have a job, remember?" he stammered quickly. "French − I mean, the agent." That was the term they preferred, wasn't it? "You've been paid. I'm your scout, your aid, your eyes. You can't harm me."

"You are useless," said Puck. "You are sluggish. But most of all you are stupid."

So it wasn't informing this was for. No. It was incompetence. Well, that was something. He could defend himself on that count, at least.

"I'm trying my hardest," Tim said. A fair enough proposal, surely.

" 'Tench.' That was trying your hardest, was it?" shouted Puck. " 'Tench!' "

Yes, he had written Tench. Why? No explanation, unless of course – no! Appalling idea. The mistake was intentional. He hadn't seen because he hadn't wanted to see. And the reason for that? Obvious. He wanted the ruse to fail. He wrote a name that was almost but not quite right. Oh, God! Then he folded his sheets away and sealed the flap at the back with a nub of sealing wax.

The thought set his heart racing. Palms hot, sweating, wet. Must not, under any circumstances, let the other two get wind of that. Must think of something to say. But what? Had to come up with something that showed they were all on the same side. Had to. But what?

Yes. Rody's gnomic comment, when he was on the stone unloading the gun. "We've got to remember the job," said Tim. "Didn't Rody say that just now?"

"Plans change," said Puck. "New job now."

They'd guessed. Knew he'd tried to sabotage the operation by writing the wrong name. Somehow, some way, worked it out. Certain of it. Time was up. Oh, God! They were going to do something terrible.

"Oh, my God," said Tim.

"You can forget Him where you're going." This was Puck, gruff.

Thighs trembling, heart booming, racing, fit to burst. So why not? Nothing to lose. It was the end. Speak the truth.

"I want to see Kitty," he said. Very quiet this, and at the sound of her name, he suddenly felt much better. "I haven't seen Kitty these last months," he said. The truth, but he didn't care whether he was believed or not. "I must see Kitty. I have to say goodbye." They couldn't fail to be moved by that.

"Had you used your brains, none of this would be happening." Puck again.

"I want to say goodbye to her. She is all I have in this world."

"On your knees." Rody pointed the bayonet at the ground.

"Will you carry a message to her?"

Only one thing mattered now, that she knew he loved her.

"That you've gone to the devil, certainly I'll tell her." Puck, in humorous mode, laughing. "Kneel!"

Tim knelt, crossed himself, muttered, "Dear God, please forgive me, please."

"Save your prayers," said Puck. "Sing!" He pondered. "Sing, 'Rule, Britannia'." Rody chuckled.

What was this? Test of loyalty? What?

"I don't have the words," Tim said, which was true.

"All right, 'God save the Queen'," said Puck. "Everyone knows 'The Queen'."

So it was true. This wasn't devilment. They suspected he was disloyal. This was to find out.

"I made a mistake with the envelope. I can't know how. I didn't mean it."

" 'The Queen'."

"I can't," said Tim. He moved his head at the same time.

" 'The Queen', come on." Puck's tone impatient. "You've got a lovely voice."

Tim again shook his head. Heard the song, yes, drifting out of Orange Halls. Never sung it, though. Why would he? They must know that.

"I'm waiting." This was Rody. Blunderbuss tight in his arms.

"I can't."

"Sing," said Rody.

Opening mouth, taking a breath. What else was there to do? If he managed the first note, the next might follow, and then the third after that? Puck clicked the shears, metal sliding over metal. No alternative.

He sang, "God . . ." Voiced wavering, tuneless. Didn't care. Had the next word. ". . . save . . ." Now the third. ". . . our . . ." It worked. He had the fourth. ". . . gracious . . ." Miracle of miracles, now he had the fifth. ". . . Queen . . ." Done it. First line. He could do this. He just had to keep going. He took another breath and sang on:

"Long live our no-ble Queen,
God save our Queen.
Send her vic-tor-i-ous,
Happy and glor-i-ous,
Long to reign o-ver us,
God save the Queen."

There was silence when he finished. The wind moaned outside the stone forge walls. A flurry of snow chased through the roof and down towards the ground. He waited. He had finished. He'd sung badly. Very. Without any enthusiasm. But that spoke volumes about his loyalty. Wasn't that right? He'd done what they'd asked. This was over. He was free to stand. Surely?

Rody pushed the bayonet on the gun into the ground. Got the blade down far enough so the gun stood up. Tim tried to interpret the act. One weapon less. Surely a good sign. Any second now the shears would disappear. Rody'd offer him a hand. Help him up.

Rody turning from the gun and coming back towards him. Oh, yes, the hand was coming. There it was, reaching for him. But what was this? Rody taking his ear, pulling it away from his head. Something touching the lobe. Oh, God! The cold point of the shears.

Stomach fluttering and a trembling running from heel to groin.

"Tim, I'm sorry," said Puck, his voice quiet and reasonable. "Let's do the hard bit first, shall we?"

He felt this man's thin fingers at his mouth, parting the lips, lifting the teeth.

"Stick out your tongue. Come on, Tim," Puck continued, reasonable, quiet and reassuring. "It's got to come out. Don't be a bold boy now . . ."

He was to be punished. That was what happened if you made a mistake. But at least when they finished he would have his life and his manhood. At least he wasn't getting the O'Duffy treatment. Best thing now was not to struggle. Might make them angry. Just get it over and done with. That was it.

Felt his tongue tentatively offer itself. Puck's fingers pinching his tongue. Funny taste. Brass? Oil? Vague idea Puck polished the gun up earlier. That must be it. Tongue sliding forward over lower teeth. Puck was pulling but he was complying.

The trembling in his legs had moved to his trunk and then up to his neck. Must control it. Whatever happened he mustn't let them see this. Bad enough to be a fool, but to be seen as a coward as well – oh, God! Ordered his limbs to stop shaking. But nothing happening. Spasms worse, if anything. Beyond his control. Like his tongue, trembling also. And his whole body. But he was out, above his body, looking down from above on what was happening.

"Come on." This was Rody now. "Get it out. Open wide."

Rody now pinching his tongue, Puck letting go. Taste of powder, bitter and sulphurous on the new man's finger-ends.

"Right, then," said Puck. "This won't take a second."

Shears clicking. He closed his eyes. Didn't want to see the dirty blades come towards him or the blade close around his tongue.

"Bloody shears," Puck saying suddenly. "Bloody stuck."

Puck struggling. Blades scraping suddenly for a second or two then stopping again.

"Bloody shears. Bloody stuck."

"No," said Rody, disbelieving.

"Stuck!"

"Bloody shears." Rody, appalled.

"Bloody shears, bloody stuck."

"Bloody hell."

"Bloody, bloody shears." Puck struggling again, breathing angrily.

"Bloody shears, bloody worn out."

"No bloody good trusting any bloody tool."

"Too bloody right."

"No bloody, bloody good."

"Bloody hell." Now Rody sounding amazed.

"What's the bloody world coming to?"

"It's a bloody mess."

"If your bloody shears won't do the bloody job," said Puck, finishing the other man's sentence.

"Bloody awful."

Sounds of exertion again and then metal grating over metal.

"Bloody marvellous, look!"

"Bloody hell. One moment they bloody don't work . . ."

A sharp intake of breath from Puck, and then he said, "And next moment they bloody don't work."

Strangest thought. His own mouth with just a stump in it, and Kitty's lovely long pointed tongue reaching in and stroking the cut, ragged end of the wet muscle.

"This is too bloody much." Rody this time. The image of Kitty's kiss vanished. He was back on the floor of the forge, his trousers damp at the knees, body trembling, tongue pinched between Rody's powerful fingers.

"Too bloody right," said Puck.

The shears worked again.

"Bloody hell."

"That's a look-up for the books."

"Better do the bloody job before the thing bloody packs up again."

"Hey, Tim. Better do the bloody job, right?"

A moment or two before he realised. Puck speaking to him. Don't, he wanted to say. Spare me. Give this up. But couldn't speak if he wanted to. Tongue held too tightly, stretched out from his mouth. Saliva all dried in the cold night air. He was parched. Suddenly, a prick. A snowflake, landed, melting. Tasteless. Silence. Then another snowflake. And a third.

"Lost your bloody tongue, mate?"

Rody laughing, whole body moving with huge guffaws, hand shaking, wrenching the tongue between the fingers.

"That's a bloody good one." This was Rody. "Lost your bloody tongue."

"He's not laughing," said Puck.

This was a joke, wasn't it? Long, very complicated, and unpleasant but a joke none the less. He just had to keep kneeling and waiting. They would have their fun. Then it would be over.

"He don't get the bloody joke," said Rody.

A joke, yes, but something deeper as well. A dreadful test of his mettle. Only one requirement. Keep himself under control. Do this for long enough, in the end he'd pass some invisible point. They'd tell him then to open his eyes. They'd be impressed. They'd know then that he had courage, and finally, then, he'd be one of them.

"Why aren't you laughing, Timmy?" This was Puck.

Mustn't move, mustn't respond. Stony silence – best proof of his character.

"He's got no bloody sense of humour, has he?" said Rody.

"He should be laughing," said Puck. "Why isn't he laughing?"

Give them nothing. Keep eyes shut. Don't speak. Above all, mustn't make a show of himself. Be a blank.

"Yes, why isn't he?" said Rody gruffly.

End of this getting closer. Surely, had to be?

"Because you're holding his tongue."

"Right enough."

The fingers pinching the end of his tongue suddenly seemed not to be there. Tentatively, he curved the tip towards his upper lip. Yes, no fingers holding and stopping him. He was released.

"All work and no play," murmured Puck, "Timmy's humour flies away."

Tap now on his cheek, not hard, affectionate. That was it. He'd passed. Crossed the line. This was over. But he kept his eyes closed. Didn't try to stand although his knees ached and he longed to get his weight off them. Let them make the moves. He'd stay still.

"I don't think he sees our funny side," said Rody.

"No, he doesn't."

"And we've been to such trouble," said Rody. "We try so hard."

"That's right," said Puck. "We try so hard." Silence, and then Puck said, "Open your eyes."

It was really finally, finally over. He opened his eyes. Immediately in front of him, knees of Rody's breeches with snow behind falling and swirling. He had survived. He was unhurt. Great, sweet feeling of relief. One day, with his tongue, his whole tongue, he would touch Kitty again, as he had that time in the quarry.

Now that it was over, suddenly he felt the full import of what had almost been. They had been going to cut his tongue back, clip off his ears. Staggering, the awfulness of it. Terrifying too. A great sob formed in his belly, rose to his throat, and before he could stop it, had pitched out into the darkness.

"Oh, no," said Rody.

"He's crying."

Hot and salty tears of relief running down his cheeks.

"Look what you've done." This was Rody.

"Not my doing," said Puck, mock-seriously.

"Yes, it was."

"No."

"Only joking, Tim." Rody again. Felt the man's hand squeezing his shoulder.

"Just a bit of harmless fun," said Puck, and Tim felt Puck squeezing his other shoulder.

chapter eleven

That winter afternoon Tim clumped along the Boho road. It ran across the land in a straight line, rising and falling exactly as the land which it crossed. He approached the lime kiln, a dark, square stone building with pigeon-grey smoke pouring from the chimney. There was a smell of woodsmoke and lime. He looked for Eyes, as Davy, the old man who tended the kiln, was known, because one eye was blue and the other was brown. Eyes, however, was nowhere to be seen.

Tim walked on. Largy Lake appeared, also known as the School Lake because of Tim's old school that stood at the far end. The water was still and black this winter afternoon, and he saw the surrounding hills reflected in the water. How was so dark a surface a mirror? It was a mystery.

The road bent to the right, following the lake shore, and there was the school on his left. It was a stone building with two rooms and high windows. Inside the porch he glimpsed row upon row of muddy boots, lined along shelves. A stone tablet above the door gave the name as Woodvale School. Inside, childish voices were chanting and he joined them: "Five times five is twenty-five, six times five is thirty, seven times five is thirty-five, and eight times five is forty."

He shifted the spade to the other shoulder. The jetty off which the master was thrown into the lake was below him. He had not looked at the rickety wooden structure, nor would he. He never looked at it when he made this journey.

However, his memory was less amenable to control, and the next moment he couldn't help but imagine the man inside the sack, pinpricks of light showing through the material, the coarse smell of the thing, the fibres itching his nose, and then the awful sense of falling, the water closing in, and the desperate hopeless struggle to breathe, before sinking under. As these pictures floated before his mind's eye, Tim felt a sense of panic.

And, on top of everything, the distant past was mixed this afternoon with recent events, with memories of himself kneeling on the floor of the forge with eyes closed, the evil clacking of the shears at his ear, his tongue pinched between dirty fingers, and the taste of gun oil, brass and powder in his mouth.

As the memories jostled he went hot and cold and then hot again. He realised he must banish these thoughts, and he gulped and blinked.

The voices of the chanting schoolchildren faded behind him as he marched on. Yet his case was different from the master's, he thought, quite different. The master disobeyed and was punished, whereas he had made a mistake and was given a chance to recover his reputation. He had proved himself. It was a triumph. Out of disaster, out of writing the wrong name on an envelope – and he was still at a loss to understand how he had failed to notice the mistake – had come a game, a prank, from which he had emerged with his standing higher than before.

The master had it coming, he told himself, whereas in his case it was just a bit of sport, and a test of his mettle. He thought of the young coopers, rolled through Monaghan inside barrels filled with mud and nettles when their apprenticeship ended, and of the young mill girls before they married, coated in flour and eggs and left tied to railings in the square for hours. Surely what happened in the forge was the equivalent, the end of his apprenticeship?

For hadn't Rody and Puck taken him afterwards to Dolly Walsh's? Hadn't they stood him several glasses of whiskey, toasted his health and praised his courage? He was one of them, they said. He hadn't flinched or broken. They clapped his back. They squeezed his shoulders. It was the first time in the nine months they had worked together that he really felt they liked him.

Oh, yes, he had reasons to be cheerful, didn't he? It was awful in the forge for a few minutes but he had survived the experience and everything was much better now, wasn't it? He agreed with the proposition. He felt warm; yes, he felt almost happy as the road wound upwards and he began to climb with it.

Two hundred yards further on, the road levelled out. The land here was poor, the soil thin; it supported coarse grass, whin bushes and stunted ash trees. It was a favoured hunting place, however, with the landowner, Colonel Hutcheson, and Tim had often seen him around here when Tim was on the way to his garden, stalking through the undergrowth, or heard the Colonel calling to his dogs, or the retort of his gun.

This afternoon, however, there was no sign of Hutcheson on the rough land beyond the wall. All there was to see was a cow, which stared back at him. Her ribs showed under her black pelt, and on her small, tight pink udder, there was mottling like lichen on a stone. After a second or two, the cow lost interest in him and dropped her head back to the ground.

Animals were like children in that way, he thought, unable to concentrate; always moving on to whatever caught their attention next. The cow belonged to Croker Flanagan, Haystacks as he was known, which guaranteed the beast was even more stupid than the average animal. Now the head jerked up. Tim heard grass ripping from the ground and teeth closing as the cow began to chew. The cow was looking at him again.

The air was still, and a lid of low grey cloud stretched above. There were old brown ferns by the roadside and two rowan trees, their branches standing out against the sky behind.

He wondered vaguely where Haystacks was. The man was a liability as a neighbour: he didn't control his animals properly; he let his animals and particularly his goats go everywhere. When farmers went to complain about an animal trespass, Croker's size – he was six foot eight and he weighed over seventeen stone – tended to settle disagreements in his favour. Croker was not a man worth fighting with. He had a terrible temper when he was angry, and he had two brothers who were the same size as he was. If Croker's herd got into your barley or your bog, it was unwise to order him to remove them or, worse, to take the law into your hands.

The Brady family – they had five acres further along the road – had made the mistake of driving Croker's goats off their cabbage patch and putting them on to a piece of scrubland, which backed on to the top of an old quarry. As it happened, no goats fell over the cliff; none the less, Haystacks decided the Bradys were mischievous and wanted his flock to tumble to their death.

A vendetta started. When he passed Mr Brady on the road, Haystacks whispered threats. When the whole Brady family were away visiting relatives, Croker borrowed a bull and locked him in the Bradys' turf shed. The animal kicked down a wall as well as the bank of neatly piled fuel. One winter's night, he plugged the Bradys' chimney with a wet blanket, and when the Brady family fled from their smoke-filled house, Croker and his brothers pelted them with eggs. His worst deed was to canter a pony at the Brady girls when he saw them on the road. They had to jump into a ditch filled with enormous nettles, got badly stung, and one, Marie, the eight-year-old, had to go to bed for three days.

The parish priest attempted mediation but Croker denied there was a feud. He said the Bradys were his neighbours; he said he would never harm a hair of their heads, let alone pelt them with eggs or try to run them down with a pony. Croker sincerely believed it himself when he told Father Smyth that he loved the Brady family, and he only remembered that he hated them the next time he saw them.

Fortunately – the thought now crossed Tim's mind – he had never fallen out with Haystacks. He touched the wooden shaft of his spade and asked inwardly to be spared this fate.

The rough, boggy ground had given way now on either side to a network of small fields, separated by grey stone walls; the land, which was better here than lower down, was divided into small parcels and let to landless people like himself. It was Hutcheson's conscience land.

There was a whiff of goat in the air. Tim squinted along the road. It bent sharply to the left at the point where his plot lay, and so he was looking straight on to the side of his property. When he first took the land, two years earlier, the wall was low and tumbled down in places. The previous man had neglected it. Not so Tim. He picked the land clean and used the stones he took from the dark earth to build a formidable wall, over five feet high. A horse would have been hard pressed to jump it. There was no gate. The only way in was over a stile at the corner. This was to keep out freelance graziers.

This afternoon, however, he noticed that instead of the even horizontal line that was the top of his wall, and the normal vista that greeted him, the wall was bowed; it was tumbled.

His heart raced and he felt tears behind his eyes. He took the spade from his shoulder and holding it like a spear, he began to run. He ran on as far as the edge of his plot, to where grey, flattish stones lay heaped on the ground. He noticed the small, shiny, tell-tale droppings, and registered the rank smell of goat in the air.

He looked over the wall. First, he saw that the beautiful ridges of dark earth that he had lovingly made over the previous weeks, and sown with early beans and peas and kidney-shaped potatoes, had been scuffed and trampled underfoot, and peppered with holes that could only have been made by hoofs.

Next, he saw that the pots and leaves with which he had crowned and covered his rhubarb and his asparagus shoots, to protect them both from the cold, had all been kicked aside and scattered, and that the tender shoots of the plants, which were exposed, had been chewed to the ground.

Finally, he saw four goats in the corner, eating the long green grass that flourished there. They were plump, bow-backed creatures, each with a skirt of hair hanging down from its belly. There was something about this hair that he found mildly obscene.

Croker's goats, he thought. Had to be. He moved forward over the scattered stones. A goat looked up and stared without blinking. The eyes of the animal were yellow with a black line down the middle, and as always with goats, he had the feeling that each eye saw him separately, rather than the two eyes working together. And as the goat stared it went on eating, and the beard under its chin trembled in motion with the eating. This struck Tim as the height of impudence and insolence.

He felt a surge of rage. There was only one way to get through to Croker, he thought. That was to hit him where it hurt.

He ran towards the animals, wielding his spade like an axe. He wanted to slash the leg of the first goat, to hough him.

Within the time it took Tim to make two strides, the goats, as one, leaped up on to the wall.

Tim threw his spade towards the furry back ends of the animals. By the time the spade had covered the distance between him and them, the goats were off the wall, stones tumbling after them. Next thing, the spade clattered to the ground on the far side of the wall.

Tim let out a shout, doubled back to where the wall was tumbled and ran on to the lane.

The end of his spade was stuck in the ground like a spear, while further on, between the stone walls that rose on either side, their legs kicking back towards him in a way that was both lewd and triumphant, the goats fled away along the lane.

A second later, Tim found himself running after them with the spade in his hand. Their infuriating rumps and their maddening back-kicking legs were receding further and further away from him, yet he could not help himself. He would keep going; he might just catch them if they stopped somewhere.

Ahead he saw a corner. The goats went round it and were gone. A few seconds later Tim went round it himself, and when he emerged on the other side, he saw the lane stretching ahead again. He saw the goats, and he saw there was a figure beyond the goats. It was a huge man. His heart leaped. Haystacks was coming his way.

It was time to hit Croker hard, he decided, and hurt him bad, but the very thought made him tremble with both fear and excitement. Tim might knock him to the ground, but what if Croker got up and came after him? The fellow was a giant and there were those awful brothers as well. Except, said Tim's inner voice, he was not alone, was he? He remembered what happened in the forge and afterwards in Dolly Walsh's. Puck and Rody had welcomed him as an equal. He had others to help him now. He was more than just plain Tim Traynor; he was a Lodge man now.

He saw Haystacks raise his arms. This was to stop his animals swerving sideways. Next he saw Haystacks glance at him. Then he saw the enormous head shift as the giant refocused on his beloved goats. Beautiful, thought Tim, this gave him the advantage.

"Whoa there!" he heard Haystacks shout.

The goats, caught between the two men, now put on a spurt of speed. Haystacks dived for the mane of a grey and white female, missed and fell heavily.

"Damn you," shouted the big man.

He lay sprawled on the ground. Tim was almost upon him

now, and an instant later, he swung the flat of the spade towards the big man's face. The big man brought up his arm. The spade struck. Tim felt the impact as the metal of the spade connected with the bone. He heard a tremendous cry from Croker.

"Jesus!" the big one shouted.

"You bastard," Tim shouted back. He lifted his spade again.

Croker put his hands and his arms over the top of his head. "Get away, will you!" he shouted.

Tim brought the bottom of the spade down on Croker's knuckles and heard another terrible wail of pain. "That's for your goats ruining my place," shouted Tim.

"Get away!" Croker shouted back.

"And that's for my wall." Tim delivered another blow, this time to the back of Croker's head, and then yet another, this time to the ear.

"Nothing to do with me," shouted Croker desperately. "I don't know anything about your wall," he shouted, which was not true. He knew everything.

There was a lull. Tim turned the shaft half a turn and held the edge of the spade over Croker's head.

"I'll break you in two," said Croker, his voice full of menace but his eye on the spade, which hung over him like an axe blade. Tim watched the big man slowly begin to move his head. Tim realised he had hurt him very badly indeed.

Croker lowered his eyes towards him.

"Get away from me," he heard Croker say gruffly. This wasn't a warning so much as an appeal.

"You're a damned nuisance," Tim shouted in return. His voice was shrill and he hoped his excitement did not show. If Croker tried to get up, and Tim thought he might, then he would have to strike with the edge of the spade. That would cause real damage: there would be cracked skin, blood and splintered bone. So what he hoped now was to make his point, and when that was done, to walk away.

"You graze your filthy animals," Tim continued, "wherever you want, and you thump whoever complains. Your damned goats have ruined my garden. You're worse than a land-grabber."

He thought that was a nice touch, setting Croker even lower than those who took land from which others had been evicted.

Croker moved his vast face from side to side to emphasise the negative, this wasn't his doing, he wasn't to blame. He had a sparse beard on his chin. His upper lip was clean-shaven. His skin was reddish, with an oily sheen to it, and there were freckles scattered over the upper half of his face. There were even pale brown discs on the giant's eyelids.

"I said, I had nothing to do with your blooming wall. If the goats were in, I'm sorry, but they did it themselves. They have a mind of their own, those ones."

"You put the bull in the Bradys' turf shed," Tim shouted back. "You may say you didn't but everyone knows you did. You lied about that and you're lying about this."

"The Bradys are my friends," said Croker.

"You drove the Brady girls into the ditch. Marie, the youngest, was in bed for three days with nettle stings."

Croker stared at Tim's boots.

"Try and get this through your thick skull," began Tim. "The days you threw your weight around are over. We won't have it."

"Oh, fighting talk," said Croker.

"We won't have it," said Tim. "Do you understand?"

"Really?" said Croker, in what for him was a sarcastic tone of voice, and then he added quietly, "I'm going to have you."

He looked up at Tim again, looked him straight in the eye. "I'm going to have you," he said again. "You're going to be minced meat, Traynor."

Croker stood up slowly, and dusted his behind. Then he began to walk away in the same direction as his goats had fled.

"I'm going to have you," Croker shouted back, when he'd gone half a dozen yards.

Tim said nothing as he watched the big man slope off. He felt good. He had just enjoyed the first fruits of being a Lodge man. He had trounced the infuriating Haystacks.

Tim returned to his field. He began to clean out the rhubarb and asparagus roots and to turn to ridges where the potatoes were. Later, he would go on to his wall.

Cleary was on duty in the day room when Croker came in. The constable was surprised to see Haystacks with swollen hands and a battered head. Croker might have received one or two blows in his lifetime, but never anything like this. He was always the one who inflicted the punishment.

Constable Cleary was even more surprised when Croker told him the assailant was Tim Traynor.

The Tim that Cleary knew was the mild-mannered only child of old Philip Traynor and his wife Louise. They were tenants on the Beatonboro' estate, fairly decent, fairly poor, and fairly honest people.

In 1848, the couple had died of typhus within hours of each other. It was the second year of the blight. Tim was fifteen at the time. He was away from home, working for a boat builder in Enniskillen. His parents were anxious he acquire a trade.

Tim returned for the funeral and expected to take over the farm. Unfortunately, his father Philip had made no arrangements. Although many were dying of hunger and illness at the time, Philip Traynor had never expected that he or Louise would be among them. The first year of the Famine they had lived off corn and milk very comfortably. Old Philip Traynor saw no reason why he and his wife should not continue as they had, and furthermore, he had a countryman's resistance to wills and last testaments. They tempted fate, and so, he argued, matters were better left to a later date. He was not alone in thinking this; almost every neighbour thought likewise. Therefore, there was no codicil of understanding between Philip Traynor and the old agent who preceded Upton, Robert Rudd; in consequence the farm reverted to the estate on his death and was let to another family. All Tim was allowed to hold on to was the cabin where he lived.

If Tim had been older, he might have fought this. However,

he was young, he was confused, and he was in mourning. He accepted his fate; he began his new life as a labourer and later Hucheson rented him an acre. He worked for several of the big farmers in the district. These men were happy to give work to him rather than hundreds of others who were clamouring for employment, firstly because Tim had lost everything and they felt sorry for him, and secondly because he bore his troubles with exceptional good humour. He also proved to be a fastidious workman and a good time-keeper. After several years of this, Micky had nominated Tim as the new agent's gardener and general help. He knew Tim was hard-working and would do the job well; he also regretted the way in which Tim had lost the land that his father farmed. Tim had worked for the French family for nearly a year now, and Constable Cleary understood that Mrs French thought highly of him. This was what he knew about Tim, and now he was being told the young man was an assailant. Anything was possible, but as Tim had never been in trouble before, Cleary thought it was unlikely.

Constable Cleary took up his pen, dipped it in the ink-well and asked Croker to tell him what had happened. Croker told the story in his usual halting and half-witted way. Cleary took down the details in the Station Note Book. The story, as Constable Cleary understood it, had strong and familiar outlines. This sort of dispute was routine in the country.

After Croker left, Cleary noted the details of the assault in the Register of Crime, or Outrage Book as it was also known, and after he closed the book, he pondered. If Tim had used just his fists and boots, well, a warning would have been enough. Next time he saw the boy he would have ticked him off and that would have been sufficient. However, to use a spade and to use it repeatedly, Cleary didn't like that. He wondered if Tim, pleasant and good-tempered Tim, was like one of those perfect dogs who serve their master unfailingly and then, for no reason at all, suddenly turn savage one day and start to bite. And then there was the rumour regarding the company Tim was keeping. Until this moment Cleary had dismissed this talk. So what, he had thought, if Tim Traynor was seen occasionally in the company of the detestable Isaac? It didn't amount to anything. However, having heard Croker's story, both his instinct and his experience as a policeman told him that he was going to have to pay Tim a visit.

Small spurts of flame danced up from the three sods piled in his hearth.

There was a threatening knock at the door and Tim heard a voice outside shout, "Open the door. Police."

Tim pulled open the door and saw a policeman standing outside, a livid winter sky behind him, clouds heaped and twisted, red and purple streaks of colour over the hills. The policeman wore a forage cap, the strap tight under his chin, and there was another policeman behind him with a carbine hanging on his shoulder by a leather strap.

"Good evening. Tim Traynor?"

"Yes," he said. He aimed to sound confused and vague. He had a pretty good idea what was coming. Croker had blabbed. That's why the peelers were here to see him.

"There's been a complaint, Tim Traynor."

He was right. His heart thumped yet he managed a slight smile. Charm was always important with the police, as were good manners. He remembered Isaac's words to this effect during the talk they had had before he joined.

"I'm sorry," said Tim. "A complaint?"

"Oh, come on!" exclaimed the constable. "You know exactly what I'm talking about."

"No, I don't."

"So you don't know why I'm here. You've no idea?"

"No."

Tim looked straight back at the policeman. The man had a wide face, a small mouth and mutton-chop whiskers on his cheeks. His eyes were blue and penetrating. They were boring into him. But he had nothing to be ashamed of. At least, he must act as if he hadn't. So he went right on staring back, although taking care to ensure his expression did not seem insolent.

"I said, I don't know why you're here, no," Tim repeated.

The policeman's face, he now realised, was familiar. He knew the man. He had seen him around Beatonboro'. They had spoken, although Tim was unable to remember precisely when. This policeman was called Cleary.

"Where were you yesterday afternoon?" asked the policeman.

"Up in the hills. I have an acre up there," said Tim.

"Did you meet Croker Flanagan?"

The policeman, the one behind the one who was speaking, had stopped listening to the conversation. He was looking up at the sky. Tim looked at this policeman's profile, guessed he was bored with the halting, strained answers that he was coming out with. Now Tim looked at the sky himself. There was one cloud, he saw, like a clipper, rigged out with full sails that were fringed with red light. To complete the image, there was purple sky below the ship, and this was the purple sea on which she floated.

"Did you meet Croker Flanagan?"

"Yes, I did," said Tim, shifting his stare from the sky back to the face of Cleary. "Yes, I did."

"He alleges assault."

"He knocked down my wall. His animals ruined everything." The words were out before Tim was able to stop himself.

"So you knocked him down, is that right?"

Instead of thinking things through, and considering the consequences, Tim had let himself get carried away by his anger – he was still angry with Croker – and now he was trapped. He didn't think. Kitty always said so.

"We had an argument," he said sullenly.

The policeman pulled out his notebook and wrote something at the top of a clean page with a pencil.

"What was the argument about?"

Inspiration came to him now; how to retell the story to his advantage.

"When I asked him to repair the damage, he refused, he

laughed in my face. I asked him again. He started to swear. I thought he was going to hit me. He has a reputation for scrapping and he's a big man. I was all alone up there in the hills and I was certain one of those huge fists of his was going to come piling into my face. I saw him step back. I knew the position. He was getting ready to swing. The spade was in my hand. It was up and I'd struck him on the side of the head before I thought what I was doing. He fell to the ground. I tapped him once or twice on the shoulder and he begged me to stop. He went off then, promising to come back and repair the damage. I waited but he must have changed his mind and gone down to yous instead."

Cleary's pencil floated across the paper as he continued to write, the noise quite distinct to Tim. A thrush warbled from the ash tree in front of his cabin. Tim was pleased both with his invention and that his words were being so fastidiously copied out.

"Croker Flanagan alleges he was on the ground when you came up and struck him repeatedly about the head without any warning."

"That's a lie," Tim said, and he looked the policeman straight in the eye as he knew he must. "I tapped him to save myself. The ground only came into it when Croker crouched and fell."

"But you don't deny hitting him?"

There was a very long silence and then Tim said finally, because he saw there was no way out of this, "No, I suppose I don't, but I was provoked."

"Have you got any writing materials in your house?"

"What do you mean?" Tim managed to sound innocent but he knew exactly what the constable was talking about. Because of the huge incidence of threatening letters and proclamations, the police had special powers to search for pen and ink, paper and envelopes. Knowing this, Tim had taken the precaution of removing from Helena's bureau the stationery he needed for the entrapment of French, and leaving his own paper, pen and ink with a neighbour.

"No writing materials of any kind in here," he said. He

stared back at the policeman confidently. "But come in and look if you don't believe me."

The policeman said nothing. He closed his notebook and returned it along with his pencil to the pocket he had taken it from.

Tim felt a strange sense of anti-climax. Why wasn't the peeler saying anything? There must be something the policeman wanted to say about his story, or his invitation to search the cabin.

"You will be hearing from us presently," said the policeman. "You may need to come to the station to make a further statement. Or," he added ominously, "you may receive a summons."

"But what have I done?" said Tim.

"That remains to be seen. Good evening."

The policeman turned and walked away, followed by his colleague. The two men went along the path to the gap in the hedge and slipped through to the lane beyond. Tim listened to the sound of the men's boots as they disappeared.

"I hear you've been a bit of a naughty boy," said Isaac, as Tim passed behind the older man.

Tim was not surprised by this. He had been expecting the worst. As Maggie, the Frenches' cook, had told him only that afternoon, after leaving the police station, Croker had gone straight to Dolly Walsh's public house, cadged drinks and told everyone what had happened. Within twenty-four hours, everyone in Beatonboro' knew the story, Isaac included. So, of course, he was going to get a ticking-off. It was inevitable.

"Get on with what you need to do now," said Isaac. "I'll talk to you later."

Tim moved from the scullery, through the kitchen and out to the back hall, his face suddenly quite red. Temporarily, the inevitable was postponed. Isaac was happy with that state of affairs, of course. For the next few minutes, Tim realised, he would worry, and that was as much part of the process as whatever Isaac said when he finally got round to the subject.

In the front room, Tim lit a taper from a candle and then knelt down in front of the hearth. He held the waving flame to the kindling. A twig caught and then a second and a third. The wood crackled as it burned. It was good and dry. Then, suddenly, as if by magic, the flames leaped from the corner and raced across the kindling piled in the grate; there was a sudden whoosh as the chimney roared.

Tim felt the heat on his face and on his eyes.

"Good fire," said Isaac, from behind.

Tim had failed to notice the older man coming into the room. Isaac carried a candle lamp. He set it down noiselessly on the mantelpiece above Tim's head. "A little bird tells me there's a summons with your name on it, and it's winging its way to you," said Isaac, quietly but menacingly. It was true; Tim had heard this as well.

Tim blew out the taper and stood quickly. Isaac smelt of soap. When Tim arrived earlier, he had found the older man with his arms in the wooden basin, carefully scrubbing his fingernails. The awful moment, Tim realised, had arrived at last.

"I haven't had it yet."

"It's coming."

Silence.

"You hit somebody."

Tim couldn't help himself picturing the awful moment that was looming – himself at his cabin door and opening it to find Cleary outside. The policeman put a piece of paper in his hands. He opened the paper. It was the summons. His name was written at the top. The time and date on which he was to appear at the courthouse were below.

There was no point in denying the truth.

"Yes," he said.

Why didn't Isaac just say his piece and get it over with? Why spin this out so long? To maximise Tim's discomfort, of course.

"It's nothing," Tim added, awkwardly.

"Have you forgotten what we discussed before you joined us?" said Isaac carefully.

"No," said Tim, still awkward.

224

Isaac's face was gentle, almost saintly in the firelight from below. "I think you must have forgotten."

"No," said Tim again. He had not forgotten, and that was why he now felt anxious. He knew it was a mistake.

"Well, if you haven't forgotten, why is there a summons?"

"It was only a small thing," said Tim. He wanted to run out of the room. This interrogation reminded him of school.

"That's not what I heard," said Isaac, and then he added, "Taper, please."

Tim handed him the taper. Isaac crouched and held the wick in the fire.

"It's just a dispute," said Tim. His mouth was dry. He swallowed.

"You attacked a neighbour." Isaac's taper caught.

"He put down my wall," said Tim. "He put his goats on to my plot and they trampled everything in my garden."

Isaac stood, one hand cupped around the wavering flame of the taper. His knees creaked a little. Once he was up, Isaac put the burning end of the taper to the wick of the candle in the lamp.

"Whatever he did, that's no excuse," said Isaac.

The wick caught and the flame burned white and bright.

"I lost my temper and I hit him." Tim hoped this admission would bring the conversation to a close.

"You didn't think." Isaac blew out the taper. "And that's not acceptable. We always think. Your behaviour is just not good enough."

There was a silence.

"Do you remember what I said when you came here? Once you are with us, your behaviour must be beyond reproach."

"I do."

"I don't think you do remember. If you remembered, there wouldn't be a summons."

They'd already been over this. Now he was starting to feel angry. How dare this grown man treat him, another grown man, like a schoolboy? He knew he was wrong. He had admitted he was wrong. He had listened to Isaac's criticisms without flinching. What else did he have to say or do to prove he was sorry? Apparently Isaac was unimpressed with everything he had said so far. Was the man ever satisfied? Perhaps it was not the summons that was really on Isaac's mind. It was something else.

"How are you going to plead?"

"Guilty," whispered Tim.

"Sorry?"

"Guilty."

"Can you pay the fine?"

"I suppose."

"You're not proposing to come whining to me for it?"

"I hadn't actually thought about it," Tim confessed. This was the truth. When he imagined his future, what he saw in his mind's eye was the summons, Constable Cleary, the courthouse. His thoughts had not gone further.

"You have a wage. You can afford it," said Isaac. The fire settled at his feet. "What about jail? Are you ready for that? You might get a few days."

Tim's face went red. "Prison." He had not thought about this either – although in this case, that was by choice. Of course, he had often passed the local jail when he visited Monaghan. It had high grey stone walls and no birds settled on these walls or flew anywhere near them. What he also noticed when he hurried by (and he always hurried by) were the noises that came from the other side of the walls, the wails and sobs, the screams and cries of the convicts. Even at night, when the town was asleep, there was always someone in the prison who was awake and crying in pain. Tim imagined the place as a form of hell, and now from Isaac came the reminder that he might be locked inside with the rest of the damned.

"I'm sorry," he said. He was now filled with the sense that he must accept his responsibility absolutely and apologise totally both to Isaac and the court. He must make both like him and, more importantly, trust him. They would both have to know that he would never do this again. Never, ever.

"I'm sorry," Tim said again.

"You have a job to do. You don't have time to sit around the barracks while the police interrogate you about some petty argument with a neighbour, or lie about the jail for a week when you're sentenced."

"I know."

"A Ribbonman concentrates on the job. He doesn't get into that kind of trouble with the peelers. It's stupid."

"I know."

"I'm disappointed."

"I've said I'm sorry."

"You're not concentrating."

"I will, I promise."

"Certain?"

"Yes, sir," Tim heard himself saying.

"We can do without the sir."

Isaac lifted the chimney and dropped it on to the ring that held it in place.

"You have a job to do. You are the eyes and ears on the French job."

"Yes."

"But there's something else I want you to do."

"What?" he said. He was right. There was something else on Isaac's mind.

His left leg trembled slightly. So far, he had simply provided information on Mr French's movements. Rody and Puck were the ones to do the business. Now he feared Isaac was about to ask him to do more than just report. Isaac was about to put him to work, properly.

"Listen, I know I can trust you."

Isaac settled his elbow on the mantelpiece and stared at his face. "There's maybe a leak in here. An informer."

The tremble grew stronger. The mention of informers filled him with dread. It was the fear of being mistaken for one, and the fear was inescapable.

"I thought we'd stopped it with O'Duffy," continued Isaac. "Now, I'm not so certain. Otherwise, how else do I explain that we haven't got the agent yet?"

Isaac stared deep into his eyes. Taking him into his confidence? Or trying to see inside his head? No, surely the first, Tim thought, the second was a preposterous idea. If he was under suspicion, Isaac wouldn't talk to him like this in the first place, would he? Would he?

"I want you to watch Puck and Rody," said the older man.

Yes, Tim told himself, this was a genuine request, had to be. He felt comforted and gratified and, most of all, he felt protected by the request.

He agreed to watch the other two.

There was a knock on the back door.

"Speak of the devil," said Isaac.

He floated out of the room.

The noise of bolts drawing and a key turning drifted through to Tim from the scullery.

He knelt down in front of the fire. Now the sound of voices came from the back of the house. Tim lifted a piece of turf from the basket and dropped it into the middle of the grate. He reached into the basket again and found it was empty. How had he failed to notice this before?

He lifted the basket by the two handles. Murmuring voices still drifted from the scullery. It was Puck and Rody. What was Isaac talking to them about? Suddenly, it struck him as a little odd. Isaac had just asked *him* to keep an eye on them. Now he was locked in conversation with them at the back door. Strange, thought Tim.

He moved silently out of the parlour, into the hall, and down towards the kitchen. He could hear one voice distinctly now, coming from the scullery beyond: Isaac's.

"This Tim here alarms me."

At the mention of his own name, he froze and held his breath. "There's a summons coming," said Isaac. "When the police get him in the barracks, or the jail, God knows what he'll say."

"Cut his thing off and pop it in his mouth," exclaimed Puck, humorously. "Same as O'Duffy. He won't blather after that!"

As the laughter of the three wafted from the scullery, Tim retreated to the parlour. He put the basket down and then, with a loud groan, he picked it up and walked into the passage singing. As he headed towards the kitchen door, he sang even more loudly, and when he opened the door, he was not surprised to see Isaac, Puck and Rody moving towards him from the scullery. Furthermore, judging by the expressions on their faces, they had heard him singing and they were clearly expecting him to appear.

"Who's a happy boy tonight?" said Puck.

Tim smiled and nodded. "Got to get the turf in before the dark falls," he said, as he bustled past. He bolted through the back door and closed it carefully after himself. Then he hurried across the yard and disappeared inside the dark turf shed.

He put the basket on the ground. He forced himself to breathe slowly. He could feel his heart racing inside his chest. He felt his knees sagging and his head was swirling. He gripped the lintel and steadied himself.

Why had he failed to see what was really on Isaac's mind when it was so obvious?

"There's a summons coming. When the police get him in the barracks, or the jail, God knows what he'll say."

O'Duffy, Tim remembered, had been in prison before he was done. He was sent to prison for something trivial. However, while he had been inside, it had been easy to make him give information. At least, that's what Puck had said when the subject had come up in conversation once or twice over the previous nine months.

Puck had said something else, as well. "Thank God, for the peelers, and especially the constable." After O'Duffy came out, Cleary had hinted that the prisoner had named names and arrests were imminent. O'Duffy's betrayal to the police of his fellow conspirators was inexcusable. Hence, two days after his release, O'Duffy was put away one frosty night. "He had to be done," said Puck, when he described the events to Tim, "because he was an informer." In the course of this conversation, Tim asked who had done it, but Puck had said he didn't know. It was certainly not himself, he added, and certainly not Rody. "It was probably that evil bastard Isaac," Puck had concluded. It was a rare moment of candour.

Tim lifted a couple of sods from the pile and threw them into the basket. He still felt queasy in his stomach and light in his head. Fearing he might fall, he gripped the lintel. He heard Isaac's words in his head. "There's a summons coming. When the police get him in the barracks, or the jail, God knows what he'll say."

But, of course, it now occurred to him, what if O'Duffy had said nothing? What if he was quite innocent, but because he was in jail, everyone believed what Cleary said? Then when O'Duffy came out, everyone assumed he was an informer and he was immediately done away with. Later, it turned out he had not named names because no one was arrested, but by then it was too late. They couldn't bring him back from the dead.

Oh, God! That was a dreadful thought. No, it couldn't be right, he told himself, but then Tim remembered something else Puck had said: "Thank God, for the peelers, and especially the constable." O'Duffy hadn't blabbed, but by praising O'Duffy for his candour, the policeman made it seem as if he had named names.

The next moment, Tim had a premonition of his future. The police were going to come for him. He could face them and receive the summons, or he could duck out the back of his cabin and hide in the bog.

Then his own story, Tim suddenly saw with awful clarity, would have the same pattern as O'Duffy's. He would go to jail. Cleary would put his evil rumours about, and then, when he got out, the others would kill him because that's what they did to informers.

He must leave now, at once, and hide. He knew that for certain. Otherwise he was dead. He kicked the turf basket aside.

And there was only one place he could go and one person to whom he could turn. He should have listened to her in the first place, he thought, flitting from the shed and melting into the darkness.

chapter twelve

Kitty approached the well. She saw that something was
tied around the spout, a cloth of some sort. She was late
this evening and it was dusk, nearly dark. What was this? she
wondered.

She set the buckets down on one of the big, bowed flagstones that were set in the ground. She bent forward. Now that
she was close to the spout, she saw that it was a handkerchief,
the sort a man might wear tied around his neck. Was it her
father's? But her father didn't like to wear anything around his
neck and he also did not come down to the well very often.
Kitty was the water-carrier in the McKenna family.

She untied the handkerchief and took it off the spout. The
material was clean. She could tell from the feel of the stuff
between her fingers. Her intention was to store it in her apron
pocket and bring it up to the cottage. But she lifted it up to
her nose instead and sniffed. It smelt of turnip and turf.

She felt a great rush of desire and nostalgia. There was only one person who smelt like this. But how could it possibly be that his handkerchief was here? Was it a sign? And, if so, of what? The continued warmth of his feelings? A token of his friendship? Did it mean that he missed her? Was that his message? He could have written a letter. But, then, so could she.

She missed him. Terribly. Did he ache for her, she wondered, as much as she did for him? She hoped he did. If he pined and longed, she thought, as she did, then it was still possible that they could start up again from where they had left off. But what if he had met someone else?

She shivered. She hated this thought. As far as she knew, he went to work for Mr French every day, he went to chapel on Sunday, and he slept alone in his bed at night.

So who was to say what the future held? One day she and Tim might meet again. One day her parents might soften. With every day that passed they were certainly getting older. It was still a possibility – Kitty and Tim – remote, but still a possibility.

This sequence of thoughts had sustained her for months and they did the same trick again this evening.

She put the handkerchief over her mouth and nose, this time completely covering the bottom of her face. The hand-kerchief was linen, and the material was cold on her skin.

She breathed through the material and smelt again. She thought about Tim's neck, and in particular the part under his ear. When Tim dropped his head sideways, the sinews here went tight, like pieces of string pulled taut. His smell was particularly strong in this spot.

She thought she heard something. She tilted her head and strained her ears. The noise came from inside the clump of alders. She heard water trickling from the spouting and plopping into the pool below. She heard the wind. She heard the pained, rasping bray of a donkey in the distance. She was certain she had heard the sound of someone clearing their throat. Surely she had? No, she was imagining it, she told herself. There was no one around but herself. Or was there?

"Tim?" she called.

From inside the copse his voice called back, "Yes, Kitty."

"Is that you?" she said, her voice louder now.

"Yes. Shall I come out?"

"Yes, yes," she shouted, and then, this time in a whisper, "Yes."

She heard a twig break, the rustle of leaves on the ground. A branch lifted. A figure stepped forward. The face was dark but the silhouette was unmistakable.

He was in front of her. His arms were up. Her feet flew forward. She threw herself against him. She folded her arms around his back. She put her face against his neck. This was a miracle. Her deepest and greatest wish, but one that she would never have dared to hope for five minutes earlier, had come about. Here he was. Tim. He was in her arms. She was in his arms. She was intoxicated and excited. She felt moist. She pressed with her middle against his middle. She felt his arms squeezing behind her back and pulling her tighter against him. She squeezed with her own arms and pulled him tighter against herself. She took her face out of his neck. Her lips brushed against his bristles as she moved her face against his. She felt his teeth under his lips, and a second later she felt his warm, wet tongue, touching her own.

After a few moments, he disentangled himself from her grip and slid backwards. He sat down wearily on the edge of the pool and sighed.

Kitty pondered. One moment, an ecstatic embrace, the next moment he was sitting half a dozen paces away as if they had just had a quarrel.

She stepped across and lifted Tim's hand from his lap. She wanted to kiss him on the knuckles. But before she could get his hand to her mouth, he tugged it away and put it between his knees.

"Tim?" she said.

He had appeared from the copse, they had embraced, and now this.

"What's the matter?"

Water trickled from the spout and splashed into the pool below. A bird settled on a branch in the copse. Finally Tim said, "Nothing," and dropped his chin on to his chest. "Nothing," he said again.

"Nothing," she said gently. "Don't put your face down there, look up at me."

He sighed again and said, "Leave me."

"We don't speak for nine months and then that's all you can say."

He sighed again.

"What is this?"

"Nothing."

"You're in trouble."

"No, it's nothing."

His denial told her she was right.

"Leave me alone."

"Can't. Won't. Shan't,' she said. "I made a mistake. I should have said yes, last March. Are you listening? I'm saying it now."

Another long silence. "Well, that's progress," she said. "At least you haven't said, 'Leave me alone!' Why don't we make plans, you and me?" she continued.

"Go away," he said finally.

"Oh, he speaks. Tim," she continued, and she stepped towards him, rolling up her sleeve. "I'm not wearing any clothes. I've taken all of 'em off and thrown 'em all on the ground. Really, truly, not a stitch. I'm bare. Here, give me your hand."

She took Tim's hand and put it on her wrist. He lifted his head and she smiled. "Only joking."

He put his face down again.

"Come on. Lift that head. Look at me. No. All right. This is how it's going to be. I'm going to tell the parents we're marrying. Whatever they say, I'll tell them, our minds are made up. That's it! We'll take our chances. They'll have to lump it. And they'll come to like you. 'Love is the only engine of survival', and it's true," she ended, quoting a poem she had read in the Monaghan paper recently.

Her words came out at a tumble. She hadn't intended to

speak so candidly or so quickly.

"I don't think we can," said Tim, and he looked up.

"We can."

"We can't."

"So, you swore in, is that it?" What other trouble, she thought, could there be?

"Yes," he said bluntly.

Until this moment she had only theoretically known; now it was a fact. It was the same as with the news of a death. First, one knew of the fact because one heard it, or one was told it, but there was always a little bit of oneself that thought it mightn't have happened. Then came the sighting of the corpse at the wake or the funeral, after which there was no alternative but to accept the appalling fact; this was the point at which true grief kicked in.

"If the Ribbonmen knew I'd told you I'm sworn in," Tim continued sadly, "they'd cut me up."

Her thoughts focused on the word cut. Bad enough that he had joined, worse was what this might entail. "Like the boy O'Duffy," she said, feeling suddenly sick to her stomach. "Have you done anything yet?" she asked.

She didn't want to know but she also had to know, she told herself, so that a plan could be worked out. "You haven't done anything bad yet, have you?" she added, in a hopeful tone of voice. She must know for certain that he hadn't done anyone any harm.

"No, nothing," he said.

"Well, thank goodness."

"I'm on probation now," Tim replied. His was the tone of a man who was irked at having to explain the obvious. "I'm on for the next job after French." Then he added, "I wouldn't do him. Not with me working there, I couldn't."

As it happened, this wasn't true. He had never actually been asked. The understanding had always been that on this job he would be just the eyes and ears. However, there was no need to tell Kitty that. This was a better version and, besides, he told himself, it could have been true.

"Sweetheart," she said. Now that she knew he hadn't done anything, she would tell him again, with vigour. "I'll go with you wherever you want, now," she said.

"Why didn't you say that before? We could have gone then."

"I'm saying so now."

"But I'm sworn in, I can't leave and I'm bound to obey." He used the same sad tone that he had used earlier when he had told Kitty what would happen if it was discovered what he had told her. It occurred to her that he felt impotent. He was caught in something and he did not think it was possible to escape from it. He was doomed, or at least he felt he was.

But surely it was possible to escape, she thought. Surely it had to be possible. She had to act.

"You'll do no such thing," she said. There was no point in remaining and obeying. She saw this with great clarity. If he remained, he would have to kill someone, or get killed.

"What use is love if you won't stick by the one that you love?" she asked.

Tim said nothing, uncertain where this was leading.

"I'll stick by you. Stick by me." Then she had her inspiration. "We'll go to America," she said. "They'll never find us there."

"You know I couldn't inform, even to win you."

His voice had changed, from sad to grim, with a faint edge of rebuke, which surprised her.

"Did I say anything about that?" she asked. Then she immediately answered her own question; "No, I didn't."

Tim replied by nodding his head.

She decided to appeal to his better instincts, to his wish not to do wrong. "Listen," she began gently, "what I meant was, leave, now, us, before the next job turns up."

He turned his face towards her. It was almost night. His eyes, his nose, the shape of his mouth were lost in the darkness. He was just an outline against a darkening sky. His silhouette, as she remembered it from other evenings out here by the well or inside in the copse, was always upright and firm and full, but tonight it was shrunken, crumpled. He was a sack with its contents emptied out.

"But how?" he said dismally. "How can we go? I hit a man a while back. There's a summons and there'll be a warrant."

She remembered her mother narrating with great glee the story when she had first heard it. Young bold Tim, as her mother called him, had assaulted the simpleton, Croker Flanagan, up in the hills. It was a dispute about a wall, a few goats and some trampled potato drills.

"You didn't hit Croker that hard, did you?" said Kitty. It was a minor altercation, she assumed, just a bit of pushing and shoving. She imagined it warranted a fine, but not a custodial sentence, surely.

"I hit him, and I hit him very hard, several times." Tim's voice was flat, with not a trace of bravado, which made his words more truthful in Kitty's mind.

"He'd wrecked my garden," continued Tim. "The wall was down, everything trampled, all my winter vegetables destroyed."

"Won't the court take that into account? Surely they have to," she said crossly. "The man Croker's been at this for ages. His comeuppance was due sooner or later, and he deserved what you gave him. Won't they see that?"

Tim shrugged and she saw despair in the gesture.

"And I'm bound for jail," he said, "and once I go to jail, I'm finished."

"Why?"

"Because I'm signed in, and once you're signed in and you go to jail, you're done for."

"Does anyone know you're signed in?"

Tim sighed.

"I wrote this letter," he began. He didn't want to speak, but he had no alternative; he just had to get the words out. "I wrote it for Mr French," he continued. "The plan was to give him the letter and when he opened the envelope and his guard was down, then the man with the gun would come up and shoot him."

Kitty burst out, "That's terrible." She felt sick again. She clenched and unclenched her fists.

"Will you listen to me?" he said.

However, what he meant was, don't judge me. She knew that. All right, she thought, so be it. Her face would be a blank. She would not speak. She would simply listen.

"Go on," she said, quietly.

He told her the story about the letter and how the plan went wrong and how he was blamed. When he finished, Kitty said nothing.

"The noose is around my neck, don't you see?" he continued. "I get the summons, I go to court, I go to jail, I'm dead when I leave. Or, I get the summons, I don't go to court, so they issue the warrant, the police come looking for me, they find me, then I go to jail, and I'm still dead when I leave, because once you've been in prison everyone thinks you've informed.

"Or, let's say we get money somehow, we decide to catch the boat to America. We start walking to Belfast. Somewhere between here and the boat, we'll meet the peelers, and they will have the warrant. They'll arrest me, they'll return me here, I'll go to jail, and when I leave, I'll be done for."

"We travel at night, back roads," said Kitty.

"There'll be peelers on the docks, even on the boat," he said. "Some way we'd be stopped, I know it, and then I'd be shipped back here, tried, and sent into Monaghan jail. It's hopeless, I'm done for."

Tim drew a finger across his neck.

"I won't – I can't let that happen."

There was a long silence and at last Tim said, "I am a fool. One tiff and I get myself into this mess."

She felt the huge weight of his distress. It troubled her to see Tim in such pain. She wanted to make him feel better. She also remained optimistic. Some way, somehow, they could find a way to go together, surely. She could even go to see Mr French. He was a magistrate. Her father had good relations with him. What about that as a solution?

"I'll get the warrant stopped," she said.

She said this more in hope than in reasonable expectation. It was also true that she said this just to pacify Tim, for on top of everything else, she now felt amorous.

Yet she was also terribly clear-sighted, and she saw that it was essential to bind them together so they would never part, she to him and him to her, and there was only one way to do that. It was risky but if she just let go, her feelings would carry her along.

"You won't stop the law," said Tim.

She wondered if he felt as she did. His shoulders were still bent. He was sad. Oh, well, she thought, this would make him happy.

"Who says?" she said, mechanically.

"I said I won't inform," said Tim.

"Did I say inform?" she said.

"No."

She was standing very close to him now. Her leg touched his arm.

"I'll do it," she said. "Don't worry." She put her hand on his shoulder and said, very quietly, "Itch me, itch my leg."

She lifted her skirt to show her bare calf rising out of her boot.

"Where?"

"Around the knee."

His hand followed the rising hem. He had not yet grasped what she was suggesting. He was never usually so backward. She assumed he had failed to notice because he was pre-occupied with his difficulties. This pleased her. She was coming to him, for once.

"At the back of the knee," she said.

Suddenly, he looked up at her. She couldn't see his face but she knew his expression was both puzzled and excited.

"Higher," she said, and she hiked her skirt again. Tim's hand went up the back of her thigh and under the edge of her drawers.

She bent her knees slightly and opened her legs so there should be no misunderstanding her intention. At the same time she pulled his head against her waist and squeezed him tight, squashing his ears.

"We might as well start as we intend to continue. Come on," she said, "I can't wait any longer."

They went into the copse. He took off his coat and spread it on the rock in the middle of the trees.

"If I leave, it means breaking a solemn oath," he said.

Kitty heard him as she took off her skirt and her underwear but she paid no attention and said nothing.

She lay down on the rock. She felt the hard, cold stone through Tim's coat. Goose bumps appeared on the back of her legs. He came up to her. She took his penis. It was hot and surprisingly thick. At the end it was sticky and damp. She pulled it into her. She expected it to hurt and it did. He pushed and she felt the tear deep inside. At the same time she was also warm and open. The manoeuvre was surprisingly easy to negotiate, she thought.

She felt Tim's face against her neck and his breath on her skin. She saw a few bare branches overhead and the black sky behind with a few pale stars shining here and there. She closed her eyes. The chill from the stone had passed through the coat and into her bottom, yet the rest of her body was hot. The cold hadn't touched it. She could have been in bed, she felt so warm.

Tim's breaths came faster and faster and his movements harder and harder. She felt his weight bearing down on her and a great swell of feeling inside. Her breasts tingled. She imagined his hand under her shawl and her blouse, touching them. She imagined his mouth around a nipple. Her nipples went hard at the thought.

She also tingled between her legs, and as he bore down she now moved up to meet him. They moved together like this for several moments, their bellies slapping against each other. She found the sound and the motion exciting. Then he let out a cry. She clasped his body in her arms. He held himself very tight for a few moments and then relaxed.

She felt his body slowly sinking down on to her. She wondered if there could be more to this. She still felt amorous and even if her bottom was cold, she was hot under her arms and all down her front. Wet as well. She could have gone on like this all night. She pushed and pulled with her waist but Tim remained quiet. He wasn't going to start again. She saw that.

She felt him pull his hand out from under her buttocks. He reached up and began to stroke her cheek. His fingers smelt of moss and stone. She opened her eyes. There were the bare branch ends waving above her, and there was the night sky with pale stars scattered here and there. She was no longer the person she was, she thought, when she had looked up before. She was different now, although it was hard to connect this enormous change from girl to woman with the rather modest event that had just occurred.

"Better to be damned for breaking an oath than for murder," she heard Tim mumble. This was exactly what she wanted to hear. Her feelings soared. It did not matter that she had not lost herself in the moment, there would be time enough for that.

That evening, Kitty smuggled two blankets out of the house in the turf creel. She brought them to the turf shed where Tim was waiting. There was a small platform at the back of the shed, just under the roof, and Tim slept there that night.

The next morning she woke up early, took half a loaf of bread and a can of milk, and slipped from the house. In the turf shed Tim and Kitty made love again. Tim's mouth tasted of milk and the bristles on his face scratched her chin.

It was still dark when they left the shed. Tim said he was going home but he would not go to work and he would come back that night. Kitty went and let the hens out of their coop; then she filled their trough with feed. When she went back inside the house, she found her father kneeling by the fire. "I did the hens," she said.

After he had got the fire going, Daniel went to sit at the table while Kitty made his breakfast. As she stirred the porridge, he could not help but notice that she sang as she worked and she kept smiling to herself. When the porridge was made and she sat down to eat with him, she continued smiling to herself. He thought this was odd as well as mysterious, because ever since the business with Tim she had only ever been moody and grumpy. Furthermore, she had blamed him for what had happened. She hadn't smiled in his presence for months – not that he could remember, anyway.

Now he was a harsh man, Daniel would be the first to concede that; on the other hand, there was nothing he could do about what had happened. It was done, over, no point moping about it. This Tim business was in the past, and in life you had to look forward, not backwards, he believed. Kitty would meet someone else, he didn't doubt that. And he assumed the smiles and the good temper this morning were a sign, long overdue, that Kitty had finally turned the corner. She no longer hankered after Tim. She had forgotten him. She was ready to face life. She was her old self again.

As Kitty cleared the plates he gave thanks that at last this phase had arrived. He would not have to put up with her sullen silences or her resentful sighs any more. She loved him again.

Daniel stood. He stretched. On his way to the door, he stopped behind Kitty. She was scraping the butter dish at the dresser. He touched her shoulder for a second. She did not turn and smile as she once might but she did not flinch and move away either, which had been the pattern for the last nine months.

He whistled as he walked out of the house and strode towards the byre.

The next morning, once again, Kitty got up before her parents were awake and went out to Tim. When she came back into the house she found her father lighting the fire. Daniel noticed the milk can as she put it away on the dresser.

"Did you feed the chickens?"

"Yes," she said, lightly.

She made the porridge, and as she ate it she kept smiling again.

One day of humour Daniel could understand, but two days in a row made him suspicious. Suddenly, in his bones, he knew something was afoot.

He had to check the cow, he said. He got up slowly, pulled on his coat and went outside. The chickens were in the yard at the back. They were gathered round the stone trough that was filled with corn meal. He looked at the feed. It was dry. There was no milk mixed with it.

He opened the shed where they kept the seed potatoes and the meal. The meal sack was closed up, and the meal shovel hung from its nail on the wall. He touched the shovel. Kitty had let out the chickens and then put their food out. But there was no milk mixed with it and yet she had come in from the yard with the can.

The third morning, Daniel woke in darkness. He had left his shirt and trousers and jacket on the end of the bed in readiness. He dressed quietly while his wife snored under the covers.

Then he went and stood behind his bedroom door. Time passed. The clock on the mantelpiece in the room next door chimed five times. He heard the noise of Kitty's bedroom door opening. It was a shy, cautious noise, secretive, and full of criminal intent.

Next he heard her take the handle of the milk can. Then he heard her feet on the floor, the key turning in the back door and then the latch whirring as she lifted it carefully. A moment later the door closed. She was outside.

He left the bedroom and went into the next room. It was dark except for the embers that glowed in the hearth but he knew the room well. He slipped past the table and the chairs and the dresser and got to the front door. He reached his guns down from the hooks overhead. The wooden stocks were smooth and cold. The guns smelt of sulphur and oil and brass. He touched the hammers and considered whether to cock the weapons or not. In the end he decided against this. He must wait and see what he was shooting at before he armed them.

He opened the front door and went out, closing the door after himself. It was a damp morning, misty and silent.

He crept around the gable end. The flagstones under his feet were wet and treacherous. His left boot creaked. The noise annoyed him. He stopped and listened. He thought he heard the sound of voices. He went round to the yard. He stopped and listened again. There was no doubt about it. There were voices and they came from the turf shed. He heard a woman's voice. That was Kitty, he assumed. He heard a man's voice as well. He cocked the guns.

Daniel moved carefully across the yard to the turf shed in the far corner. It was a stone building with a slate roof. It had a strong wooden door. The door fastened with a wooden bolt. When he got close to the door he saw the bolt was drawn back. He heard two voices. Daniel raised the pistols to shoulder level.

"All right," he said.

Total silence fell behind the door.

"Kitty," he shouted, "who have you got in there?"

The silence continued on the other side of the door.

"Yes, Father, it's me," said Kitty, finally. "What do you want?"

"Who have you got with you in there?"

"A friend, and he's hungry."

"What's his name?"

"Who?"

"Your friend's name."

"You know who it is, Father."

"You'd better open the door and come out. Both of you."

More silence.

"I have my guns. If you don't come out, I'll come in."

The door creaked back. Kitty came out first and smiled at him. Behind his daughter the fellow Tim slunk out. He held the milk can in one hand and a half-eaten lump of bread in the other.

"What's he doing here?" asked Daniel.

245

"He's hungry," said Kitty. "I was giving him something to eat."

"But what's he doing here?"

"He can't go home, you see."

"Why? He's in trouble?"

"He slept here last night," she replied, "and the night before, and the night before that."

"I'll go now," said Tim, but he did not move. "You won't say to anyone you saw me," he said plaintively.

In the darkness, with the weapons in his hands, Daniel continued to interrogate the two younger people. As they talked, the pistol stocks grew warm in his hands, and the first light of dawn began to show beyond the horizon.

When he finished explaining himself, and particularly his predicament with the warrant, and having repeatedly apologised for the wrong he had done in joining up, Tim took a bite of bread and began to chew while he stared into the distance. Daniel, seeing he was no threat, uncocked the guns, and pondered what he had heard.

"Why not get the warrant stopped?" he said finally.

"I can do that," said Kitty. "I can do that."

"Are you sure you're sorry?"

"What about, sir?" asked Tim, confused.

Daniel liked that word, "sir". "That you ever joined?" he said. "Are you sorry?"

"I am truly sorry, sir. It was a terrible mistake."

A little later the back door opened and Bridie came out to see what was happening. Leaving Tim and Kitty where they were in front of the turf shed, Daniel took his wife to the gable end of the house. The two old people had a long, whispered conversation. Daniel thought they could help Tim. They could hide him and help him to get away. Any action that thinned out the ranks of the Ribbonmen, he said, could only be a good thing.

Bridie was worried. What if Tim was discovered? The police were looking for him already and soon his associates were going to be looking for him. Discovery was inevitable.

Tim would be found in her house, surely. There would be a row and Bridie did not want to fall out with anybody over a man she hardly knew.

Daniel was adamant. They would not get into trouble because they would never be caught. How would anyone know about Tim? he asked. No one knew he was in their turf shed. If they brought him into the house, they could put him upstairs on the platform under the roof. They could have twenty visitors around the hearth and no one would know Tim was up there.

What was more, he argued, it was their duty to save him from the clutches of those who had caused their family so much hurt and pain.

It was light by the time negotiations were over. Daniel returned to Tim and Kitty. Tim could come in, he said. Tim could sleep on the platform. He was to stop up there during the day, or if there were visitors at night. Tim was to do exactly what he and Bridie told him. They would help him to get away.

Of course, Daniel had another reason for making this offer that he kept to himself. For the last nine months he had pined for his daughter's love, but until this moment he had not seen how he could get it back without abandoning his principles. Then, this morning had come, he had found Tim and Kitty together, and at last he had seen an opportunity to achieve a reconciliation without losing face and backing down.

On the face of it, his offer to help Tim did not constitute an apology or a climb-down from his previous position. He was offering to hide the young man, simply because there was no way he could refuse to help a reformed Lodge man, given what had happened to his brother and his sister-in-law. However, as Daniel also knew perfectly well, his proposal was going to transform Kitty's attitude at a stroke.

When he finished delivering the invitation, Kitty smiled at him and kissed his forehead. It was worth helping Tim, he thought, just for that. He kissed Kitty back. She squeezed his arm. It was like stepping back into a warm room after shivering in the cold for nine long months.

The McKenna family led Tim to the back door and invited him to step inside. Tim ducked through the door and stopped a couple of feet beyond the threshold, one hand clasped in front of the other. He reminded Daniel of a hired hand waiting in the square for a farmer to take him home. It was the mixture of silence and gracelessness, feigned indifference and hopefulness. Although it was light outside it was dark inside. Daniel lit the candle lamp and invited Tim to sit down at the table.

The younger man pulled out a chair and sat down brusquely, as if this was an order, and not an invitation. Daniel sat down opposite. Outside, he had not seen Tim properly because the young man had kept himself tucked in the turf-shed doorway, but in here Daniel could see everything by the clear white light of the candle.

The boy was pale and drawn and, most alarmingly of all, he looked like a toothless old man with nothing in his mouth. Did he have his teeth? A moment later, as if in answer to his question, Daniel saw Tim nervously dragging his upper teeth over his lower lip. So he did have them. Yet the sense remained with Daniel that here was a face falling in on itself. He realised this was the effect of terror and anxiety and fearfulness. Daniel had never seen anything like this before.

"Is the kettle on?" Daniel called out to his daughter. Kitty was bent over the hearth.

"Yes," she said. Her voice was bright and ringing.

"Boiled eggs for breakfast for both of us," Daniel called.

"Certainly," said Kitty happily. "Two each?"

"Yes," said Daniel, answering for both of them. He stared across at Tim. "You look absolutely terrible," said Daniel. "What can we do?"

"I know what to do," said Kitty. She held a large brown egg in one hand and a wet cloth in the other. She wiped away the feathers and muck that were stuck to the shell. "I'll go and see Mr French."

"Maybe your father should go," called Bridie. "He might be better than you."

"I might be," said Daniel, "but then again, I might not."

A couple of days later, Daniel walked into the police barracks in Beatonboro'. Ostensibly he went there to supply details of the acreage he had had under tillage that year: the police were collecting agricultural statistics on behalf of the government and all farmers were required to submit this information by 5 January, at the start of the new year, just a few weeks off.

Daniel found Constable Cleary in the day room. The policeman was alone. Daniel gave him the figures. Cleary wrote them down. Then Daniel coughed and began to chat. Cleary was bored. He was in the mood to talk. After a while Daniel asked about Tim Traynor. Now why ever would he ask about him? Cleary wondered aloud.

Daniel explained that at one time the boy was a suitor of Kitty, his daughter. This was months before.

Cleary nodded.

And now, continued Daniel, he had heard something about Tim and a fight and, well, naturally, he was interested because of the connection to Kitty.

"Didn't Traynor attack the simpleton Croker Flanagan with a spade," he asked slyly, "and give the fellow a dose of his own medicine?"

"Yes," Cleary agreed, "allegedly."

"So he hit Flanagan with a spade, did he?" Daniel continued, smiling. "That must have earned him a fierce fine!"

"There wasn't a fine," said Cleary.

"He was let off, then? Well, that'll make a lot of people round here happy. Croker made himself some wild enemies with his antics. I don't think many'd shed tears if Croker got a hiding."

"There was no fine, or anything."

"Oh."

"Traynor never showed up in court, which was stupid. Now there's a warrant for his arrest. It came down from Mr French."

"Oh, really," said Daniel.

"But I hardly see the point," the policeman continued. "I haven't seen Traynor this while. He's gone to ground, or run off."

"I wouldn't know," said Daniel. His heart thumped.

"I went up to his place yesterday," said the policeman. "There was no sign of him, and all the neighbours said they hadn't seen him for days."

"I wouldn't know," said Daniel again.

"He's probably more frightened of Croker than he is of us," said the policeman. "I think I'd hide if I was in trouble with that madman."

Cleary blinked and smoothed down his moustache. Now that he had said it, it occurred to him that perhaps this was what had happened. Tim had disappeared because he was petrified of Croker.

"If I see Tim Traynor, I'll send him down to you so," said Daniel.

"Thank you," said the policeman, and with a smile, he watched the older man turn and walk towards the door.

The next day Kitty called in to the estate office. Mr French was not there. Micky told her he was in Dublin. She asked to make an appointment. Micky asked the nature of her business. Perhaps he could help her? Kitty said that only Mr French would do. Micky looked at the calendar. Mr French returned at the end of the week. Would the following week, say Tuesday, four o'clock, be convenient? Kitty agreed and left the office.

The following Tuesday Kitty presented herself. Micky was behind his desk. He stood up and apologised. Mr French had been called away suddenly. Kitty offered to wait. Micky said he doubted if the agent would return before the end of the afternoon. He apologised and asked Kitty to come back at the

CARLO GÉBLER

start of the next week. Kitty left the office and went home.

The next week was a repeat. Kitty turned up. Micky said sorry effusively. Once more, the agent had been called away suddenly. Kitty wondered if Mr French didn't want to see her. Micky read her thoughts. "You must know that he will see you," said Micky. "It's just very unfortunate that the last two times you've come, he was called away."

"It'll be third time lucky, then?" asked Kitty.

Micky agreed that it would.

It was nearly Christmas and the new appointment was made for the next week just before the New Year. Kitty went home to find her parents waiting. She told them she had again failed to see the agent. Daniel was puzzled and upset. He was a diligent tenant farmer, he paid his rent punctually. So why was the agent unable to see his daughter? Why, after two weeks, had he failed to see her? Didn't his past record count for anything?

Tim said nothing. He sat by the fire, cleaning his nails with a twig he had found in the wood basket. He wanted to be on the road, to be reading off the falling mileages on the milestones as he marched towards Belfast. He wanted to feel the gangplank groaning and sighing beneath his feet as he climbed towards the deck of a ship. He wanted to watch the coast of Ireland grow smaller and smaller as his ship sailed away, until at last Ireland slipped below the horizon and was gone. He wanted all this desperately, and had done since the moment he had stepped into the McKennas' cottage. But nothing he could do or say would hurry this up. He would just have to wait until Kitty saw French and got the warrant set aside.

As he went on cleaning his nails, he remembered the weeks just past and what a torture they had been. First he and Kitty had had to prove to her parents that their feelings for one another were genuine; then he had had to sit through hours of agonised discussion about the future. Throughout the ordeal all he had wanted to do was to shout at everybody; if he did not move immediately, he had wanted to tell them, he would

251

be caught and he would be killed. Why were they so slow? Why did they not see that?

However, a still voice had always urged him to remain silent. He must not let them see his anxiety, said the voice. It would panic Kitty's parents. It would get in the way of the anti-Ribbon feelings that obviously played such a powerful role in their thinking about him. So Tim heeded this voice. He kept his impatience and his terror to himself and he imagined that Isaac was probably happy he was gone because Isaac had never thought much of him in the first place. And in the end he was rewarded for his self-control. The McKennas consented to his marrying their only daughter and to her emigrating to America with him.

He ran the point of the twig under his thumbnail. A wet sausage of dirt came away and hung from the point of the twig. It was shaped like a sickle. Or a maggot. He shook the stick and the dirt dropped into the fire.

He thought again about Isaac. The older man had never liked him, had he? No. So he was delighted to be shot of Tim, wasn't he? Tim liked this thought, a lot. He clung to it, in fact, and he had it many times each day. It was like a talisman, and it calmed him. But in the middle of the night, when he woke up on the platform under the eaves, with his heart thumping and his mouth dry, as was the case most nights, he knew the truth was altogether different.

Isaac, he guessed, was furious. Likewise Rody and Puck. He had run out on them. It was the action of a coward. It was only a step up from informing.

A noise disturbed him. It was the crook grating in its socket in the floor as Kitty swung the sooty kettle towards the fire. She gave Tim a wink. Despite this latest setback, her spirits were high. They were always high in fact. Throughout the weeks during which he had been hidden in the house, she had remained confident that she would see Mr French and he would stop the warrant. They would marry, as her parents had agreed. They would take the boat and go to America. They would begin a new life together in the New World.

★

When she woke up that morning, some days later, and she saw there were no tell-tale threads of light leaking in around the edges of her shutters, Kitty realised it was still dark outside. She lay quite still in the bed. The blankets were folded around her body. She felt warm and safe inside them.

Then she remembered the night before. She remembered she had put in a plug. Her periods were always absolutely regular and she believed her period had either started in the middle of the night or was about to start.

But had it? She wriggled in the bed, sliding her hips backwards and forwards. She expected to register the dull ache at the bottom of her spine but there was none to be felt. She lifted her torso off the straw mattress. She expected to feel the ache at the front of her body, but again she felt nothing.

Was it possible there was no period this month? There must be some mistake, she thought. She had miscalculated, surely. She got out of bed quickly, lifted her night-dress and pulled out the plug. It was moist. She saw that. But there was not one drop of blood on it, no russet speckle.

She threw the plug in the laundry bag where she kept her dirty clothes. She would wash it and use it again. She made another plug and kept it in all day and in the evening there was still no sign of her period. Nor the next morning. Nor the morning after that again.

Until this moment she successfully resisted the only possible explanation for this event. But this was now the third morning without blood, and it was impossible to deny it any longer.

So when had it happened? she wondered next. Was it in the copse? Or perhaps on one of the following mornings when they had made love in the turf shed.

After thinking for a few moments, she decided it should be, it must be, the copse. She liked the idea that she had conceived the very first time they were intimate. It was a sign of good luck, a sign that their relationship was blessed, a sign which promised a long and happy marriage, she thought.

That night, Kitty included a special request in her prayers. She asked for a healthy child.

It was three days after Christmas. Thomas stood in his office holding the cone of a Scotch pine between finger and thumb.

There was a quick knock at the door and a moment later Micky put his head around the lintel. "It's Kitty McKenna," he said.

"Oh. Hasn't she been here a few times already to see me?"

"Yes," said Micky.

"What does she want?"

"I don't know," said Micky, "she wouldn't tell me. It has to be you, she says, only you." He raised his eyebrows a couple of times.

"Do you think it's to do with her father?"

Micky doubted this. "I wouldn't have thought so," he said. The man was a prompt payer, up to date with his rent, a faultless tenant.

"Well, then, I'd better find out what she wants. Perhaps she's in love and wants my advice."

Micky snorted. "I'll search her first."

"No, just show her in."

Thomas pulled his pistols out of his holster and set them down on his desk.

"I thought we had a rule," said Micky, smiling.

"I don't think she's come to get me, do you?" Thomas sat down in his chair.

"You're probably right. But you know, I'd probably enjoy searching her," Micky added a touch lasciviously.

"I don't doubt it," said the agent.

Micky went out, and a moment later the door was pulled back and Thomas saw Kitty. She was a pale-faced girl with red cheeks and clear grey eyes. She wore a straight black skirt, and a grey jacket with a white blouse underneath. Her hair was piled under her hat and pinned up. Her neck was white. She walked towards him. Her movements were strong and her boots sounded on the floor. He sensed energy and anxiety, both only barely controlled.

"Who are you?" Although he knew perfectly well who she was, he asked this in a dreamy way that he imagined was disarming.

"Kitty McKenna. Daniel McKenna's daughter."

"Good afternoon."

She was lovely, he thought. She smiled. He saw her teeth. They were neat and white. A memory of the girl with the torn gloves, and the wine breath, drifted in and then out of his thoughts.

"And what do you want?"

"To see you. I made an appointment."

"She did," said Micky, from the doorway behind.

"Is it a farm matter? Does Micky need to get records or anything?"

Kitty glanced back at Micky.

"It's a private matter. A female matter," she added.

Every day visitors came to his office to talk of drains and ditches, walls and barley yields, turbary and trespass. Private matters, when they arose, invariably involved family feuds and farm transfers, wills and probate, valuations and inconvenient relatives. Now, here was a visitor who promised a story. Thomas felt an anticipatory flush of pleasure. He was going to enjoy the next half an hour.

"Won't you sit down?" he said.

She sat, tried not to but couldn't stop herself glancing at the pistols, then put her hands on her lap. She wore no gloves. Her fingers were clean and neat.

"Micky, would you mind stepping into the outer office?" Thomas called over to the bailiff.

"You don't want me to stay?"

"No."

"Are you sure?" said Micky.

Their visitor had stirred up his bailiff's interest and Thomas was not surprised. He also wanted to be near her and to listen to what she had to say. He too liked to be in the company of younger girls, drawn to them by their looks and energy. He thought of this appetite as the emotional equivalent of the desire, when he was cold, to put himself near a fire, but it was a yearning, not a lusting feeling, and he accepted it as part of the sorry process of growing older.

"I'm sure," said Thomas. He looked at Kitty. "You're not armed or dangerous, are you?"

Kitty said no. Micky strolled out, smiling. The bailiff's normal practice, when he left Thomas with a visitor, was to leave the office door slightly ajar, but this afternoon he closed it shut. Obviously, he had taken to heart Kitty's remark that she had come about a female matter. On the far side of the door, Kitty and Thomas heard Micky cough and the creak of his chair as he sat down. Thomas pulled open the top right drawer of his desk and put the pistols away.

"Could anyone hear us," Kitty asked quietly, "if they were outside?" She looked round and stared at the door.

Whatever she had come to talk about, it must be extremely interesting.

"Mr Laffin," Thomas shouted, "anyone in the front office?"

"Just myself," Micky shouted back.

"Admit nobody."

"Nobody passes me. Don't worry."

He saw Kitty look uncertain. Perhaps something about Micky's manner had suggested to her that the bailiff might eavesdrop.

"Don't worry, we're quite alone," said Thomas, "and Micky's got better things to do than listen at the door. Our conversation is in the strictest confidence. Now, would you like to tell me what you want."

"I've come about Tim Traynor," he heard Kitty say quickly.

"Oh, yes." So she had come about his vanished gardener. "What about him?"

"There's a warrant out for him. You signed it."

"Did I?" He remembered signing it perfectly clearly, of course. At the time he had even considered for a moment not signing it. Tim was a reliable employee and he liked the young fellow. "Do I have to?" he had asked Cleary. "It's assault," said the policeman, and Thomas had seen then that he had to do it.

"A few weeks ago," said Kitty.

"I sign so many," said Thomas. He felt a twinge of disappointment. He had hoped for a story from her. Now it seemed the actual purpose of her visit was petty and legal.

"I've come here to ask you to cancel the warrant."

"You're joking, of course," said Thomas grumpily. Her anxiety before about privacy seemed suddenly overstated. It was just a ploy, he thought, and her intention had been to mislead him by raising his expectations.

"No, sir, I'm not joking," she said.

"You can't seriously think that a magistrate would arbitrarily cancel a warrant?"

Her face reddened. The young, he thought, they were so vibrant, but they were also so easily hurt at the same time. He had spoken too strongly to her and he regretted that now. He decided on a change of tack. "Even if the request comes from a very pretty young woman," he continued, "a warrant can't be cancelled. And you are a very pretty young woman."

"With your help," she said very quickly, "Tim Traynor and I will marry." How very female, he thought, this prompt insistence on her marital intentions, as if she thought this was the way both to deflect any intentions he might have of flirting with her and persuade him to do what she wanted. Of course, what she couldn't possibly know was that he had no intention of doing either.

He asked, "What's marriage got to do with the warrant?"

"We want to leave the country, sir."

"Leave?"

"Only we believe he'll be arrested when we try to leave, sir."

"What's the charge?" He knew the answer but he wanted to hear it from her.

"Common assault."

"He'll get two months for that, minimum, with hard labour. He can serve his time. Then he can do whatever he wants." This was blunt and to the point; however, Thomas calculated that a certain amount of disinterest, such as he had just shown, was probably the best way to get her to tell him more.

Kitty moved on her seat. "Can I be absolutely candid with you?"

It had worked. "Of course," he said.

"My fiancé, the one I love and who I will marry, with your help, he is, or was, as they say . . ." and with this she swallowed.

"You can be assured that nothing of what you are going to say will go beyond these four walls," he said.

"He was active," she continued.

"Was he?"

"Yes, sir."

"In what sense?"

"Sworn in."

"Really."

"He's on probation."

"I see."

"He's on your case."

"My case?"

"Yes, sir."

"What exactly does that entail, being on my case?"

"He's just the scout. He couldn't put you away, you see."

"Why?"

"He knows you, sir."

He didn't believe this but he let it pass. "Is this Tim Traynor a tall young man?" Thomas asked this with feigned vagueness, although he knew the answer perfectly well.

"The same."

"He worked for us?" By pretending not to remember he hoped she would say more.

"That's him. I'm sure you remember he was a good worker."

"I don't remember anything at all," Thomas lied. "My wife dealt with him."

He remembered Tim cleaning the paintbrushes the time Micky arrived with the notice taken from the chapel door. That morning, Tim had sat outside the back door while he and Micky talked in the kitchen. Thomas had thought nothing of this at the time. Tim was enjoying the sun, he assumed. In fact, it now appeared he was eavesdropping. He was a spy. A repellent idea.

"Your wife will vouch for his qualities," said Kitty.

"Meaning?"

"Regarding the warrant, its suspension."

"I'm not going to drag her into this."

"Sir, she is a woman, she will understand what I am asking."

This answer was quick and smart and quite unexpected. He saw how intelligent Kitty was. He also noticed that his disappointment of a few moments before was ebbing. He felt a renewed sense of anticipation. He was going to enjoy this conversation, after all.

"What exactly do you mean by what you've just said?" he asked. "Are you saying that I don't understand you?"

"No, I didn't mean that, sir."

"I think you did but shall we see if I can understand?"

"I didn't say you couldn't, sir," said Kitty quickly.

She smelt of flour and soap and, faintly, of eau-de-Cologne. He imagined the bottle in the McKenna house, its precious contents eked out, not for months but for years.

"All right, go ahead, make me understand, then."

"I am not clever. I am a very stupid girl, or I have been. The summer before last I met Tim, and then last March, my parents discovered we were courting and told me to stop it. They said I was to break it off. They said he was poor, and I agreed, and I didn't listen to my heart. I went along with their wishes. So he swore in to the Ribbonmen then. In a fit of pique, frankly, and that was very stupid. At first I didn't care but as month followed month, I saw I was mistaken. I saw how much I did care. I saw that I loved him and I wanted him. Then he came and sought me out again. He still loved me, thank God. He said he wouldn't inform. He can't. But he wants out. He wants to go away. He wants to go away with me. Suspend that warrant. We'll get the boat and go to America. We'll never trouble you again."

"Let me get this right," said Thomas. He would enjoy the next part. "He's trying to kill me."

"Yes and no, sir. He's on probation. He's just the scout on your job. He doesn't do the business until the next job."

"He's helping those who want me out of the way – in my book that's trying to kill me – and you're asking me to help this man to go abroad?"

"With your help, this man will be my husband and we will go away from here for ever and never trouble you again. That is what I am asking."

"And if I don't help?" he asked.

"If Tim stays, it's death," she said, and looked straight at him. "As you know better than anyone."

He was puzzled. "What are you talking about?"

"You invented 'French's Law'."

Thomas laughed. "You will have to explain."

"If the Ribbonmen attack, Mr Laffin goes after them. He either shoots them or he catches and hangs them, even if this means you die. With those rules Tim'll end up dead one way or another – shot or hanged."

"Unless I suspend this warrant?"

"Yes," she said. She sounded hopeful. She sounded almost as if she thought he might agree. But he had no intention of agreeing.

He said, "In which case you two can go away without any trouble from the police and will never come back again?"

"Yes, sir."

"All right," he said, "but what do I get out of it?"

"One less Ribbonman."

"He's a criminal, for God's sake, and he's trying to kill me."

"He hasn't done anything yet. Just sworn in. It only gets serious the next time."

Her voice was quiet. Her argument was weak and she knew it.

"Oh! I'm letting him go in order that he doesn't murder in the future," said Thomas sarcastically.

"No, sir."

"Yes, I am. You're going to have to improve your argument."

"You're letting him go so we can marry and perhaps he'll be a father one day."

Thomas laughed. "Oh, that's another great reason for letting him go, that he might one day possibly become a father."

"I think it's the best reason in the world," she said firmly. Since she seemed to be unaffected by his humour, he decided to try a different line of enquiry.

"Tell me this," he said, "why does Tim hate me?"

"He doesn't hate you."

"Oh, really?"

"The Ribbonmen think that with you gone they might not have to pay any rent. But that's not the point. They'll pay if needs be."

"I'm glad to hear it."

"Your sin is changing the old custom."

The placing of sin and custom in the same sentence, now that was new.

"How have I sinned?"

"You've done away with the tenant right, you've put out old tenants, and you'll surely bring in new ones."

Normally, if a conversation got on to these matters, he was indifferent: there was a straightforward and, he thought, unanswerable justification for his actions – the tenants were behind with their rent, either because they were incompetent or irresponsible, and if you failed in business and could not pay your debts, then your assets were seized, those were the rules, that was the way of the world. In fact, in this case, he was being lenient and even indulgent, setting tenant right against arrears, letting the tenants keep their stock to sell, and paying the cost of shipping defaulting tenants with their entire families to America. His current policy, although no man was going to like getting a bit less tenant right than he thought was his proper due, was fantastically generous. That was what he had always believed; however, now, as he talked to Kitty McKenna, he felt anxious. He did not want her to think he had done wrong or that he was harsh. He wanted her good opinion.

"But the tenants all went voluntarily," he said smartly. "There were no evictions."

"You've still broken the rule and the law. Land belongs to the agreed tenants. However, you're moving them out and really you're . . ."

Kitty drew a finger across her throat and then put her hand down and looked at him. She was surprised by the brutality of her gesture.

Thomas felt annoyed at the idea that he was the villain. "I suppose," he said tartly, "when he's warmed with thoughts of old Ireland, your Timmy would kill a hundred agents, but really he's just kind and gentle."

"He's just kind and gentle, sir," she replied quietly, from the far side of the desk.

"Yet he believes it's for the good of Ireland to have me killed? But we're all Irish, me, you, whoever."

"The Ribbonmen think the landlords have no right to the land. They hope to frighten them off it."

She spoke in the neutral tone of a teacher. She was not expressing her own feelings, just explaining the way the world worked.

"Which they can't, of course," he said.

"Yes, so what they want to make certain is that the agreed tenants stay. But you help them leave and claw their farms back . . ."

"So they hate me," he said, "and I have to die."

"There are no feelings involved. They reserve all their hatred for the land-grabber," she said.

"The man who takes the lease on surrendered land!" he said. He could just about see why a man might baulk at taking land from which a tenant had been evicted, but if a man gave his farm back to the estate voluntarily, and was paid for it, what was wrong with someone else having it? Well, everything apparently, he thought sardonically, as he was no doubt going to discover when the time came to rent again the farms that he had got back over the last year. Of course, it was all ridiculous and he hoped this was how he sounded in his last remark.

But Kitty did not notice, or if she did she did not show it. "Yes, they only hate the man who takes land, and it doesn't matter if it was bought back or repossessed," she said.

He saw then that was no difference, at least in the eyes of those of whom she spoke, between forcing or buying someone out like he was. It amounted to the same thing. It separated a man and his family from the land that belonged to them. Of course it was quite wrong-headed to think like this and a tenant would have to ignore the fact that his policy was extraordinarily benign to think like this; however, setting these aside, he could see the logic of the position, at least as Kitty explained it.

"An uncle of mine," began Kitty, "he took three acres after they told him not to. So they beat him and put coals from the fire in my aunt's mouth. She got gangrene and died, and my uncle went away with the children to West Virginia. They can be very cruel."

Outwardly, her tone was calm and dispassionate. She was still trying to be the schoolteacher she had been a few moments before, but beneath the surface she was filled with fear and disgust. Now she was getting to her real feelings and he derived some satisfaction from the thought that her loyalties obviously did not lie with those who were against him. They had hurt her family as well.

"I suppose it's some comfort," he said, "knowing they're more cruel to their own than to ones like me. At least they intend just to kill me. No torture, and I do hate torture, you know."

He wondered what she would say next. Would she let her fear show more clearly? To his surprise she looked back steadily into his eyes.

"That's why Tim hates them, on account of the torture," she said, with surprising excitement; it was as if she was now really expressing what she felt. "That was an awful business with O'Duffy," she added.

Her words surprised him.

"O'Duffy didn't take any land," he said.

"Didn't he?" The words were out before she had time to think.

There was silence until at last Thomas said, "O'Duffy was a Ribbonman."

"Yes."

She was back in her neutral voice again. The advantage lay with him.

"But your Tim joined," he continued, dreamily, "when? March, I think you said, whereas that horrible business with O'Duffy was in January, two months before. I know, because it happened around exactly the time I came to Beatonboro'."

He'd caught her.

"Yes," she said. She looked at him for a moment or two longer, then looked down.

"Your Tim, he must have known about O'Duffy when he joined," continued Thomas. "In which case, how come it's taken him until now to grow a conscience?"

He heard her make a small whimper. He realised she had begun to cry.

"Because he was stupid then, and he didn't think," she shouted across at him. He regretted now the way he had just pressed his advantage. He had provoked her. It had not been fair. Or kind.

"And I was stupid then, and I didn't think," she continued. "And now we're in the most terrible trouble and nobody can help us except you. The future, if we stay, is that you'll hang him, or shoot him, or he'll go to jail and when he gets out the Ribbonmen will do for him, and that's no future for any of the three of us."

As soon as the words were out she put her hand over her mouth. Her eyes widened. The skin above and below her eyes went red. "What have I said?" she whispered. "Oh, my God!"

"Is it the truth?" he asked.

"Yes, sir. Oh, you must think me . . ."

"How far gone?" he asked, in his matter–of–fact voice.

"Not long, weeks," she said. But this detail did not interest her. It was his opinion that mattered. "What must you think of me?" she said.

"I have lived, you know. I know what men and women do."

264

She ran her finger along the edge of the desk. The wood here was carved with thistles, roses and shamrocks. "He's the only one, the only man I've been with, ever. Do you believe that?"

"Yes, I do," he said.

She wriggled. "I'm a fool," she said pathetically. "What a mess . . ."

"And money? What money have you?" They might as well talk about money, he thought. They'd talked about everything else. Kitty said nothing so he went on, "What am I thinking? Of course you don't have any money."

The room was silent. When she asked him at the start, he thought he would probably say no. Now he knew otherwise.

"I've hit the nail on the head, haven't I?" he said.

"Father has some," she said, "enough for a deposit on the tickets. But not enough for the full price."

She had not expected to discuss money but she decided to make the most of it. "He's going to borrow. We will borrow. God knows how, but we will. Of course, Tim hasn't anything. You see, we are totally and absolutely, the three of us, dependent on your charity."

There were the three of them again. The advantage had passed to Kitty. He knew it. He knew she knew it. She knew he knew it.

"I see it less as charity, more that I'm paying him a bribe not to kill me."

"You're paying so that we can go away and be a family," she replied firmly.

"Why should I do that?"

"Because I love him, sir, and he loves me."

There was nothing else left to say. Thomas looked across at the hearth and the basket of red coals glowing in the grate. He wanted to do what she asked but he had one worry. She was sensible in his presence, but how was she in Tim's? Perhaps her judgement was clouded when she was with his ex-gardener? Perhaps, because she was pregnant and in love, he had duped her? Perhaps Tim was lying to her but she did not see that?

"All right," he said, "once I'm certain of his real intentions, I'll hold back the warrant."

He saw her face pulling in two directions, towards happiness and disappointment.

"Can't you do it now? Don't you believe me?" She had cleared every fence, she thought, and now, suddenly, here was a new one. Her disappointment was huge. Thomas saw all this and he wanted to say yes. It would have been easy to say yes. It would have made her happy. It would have made him happy. But he knew that first he must make certain that Tim was genuine. One did not strike out a warrant lightly.

"I believe you," he explained. "I just don't know if I believe him. I must see him."

"He's hiding," she said hastily. "I could go and get him now. I could bring him here."

"I don't think that would be a good idea."

She smiled. "No, I suppose not."

"Do you know the old forge?"

She nodded. "Below, the new Union."

"Eight o'clock, tonight," continued Thomas, "and he'd better come alone."

She looked straight at him again. "You won't deal with us unfairly?"

"I have to trust you. You will have to trust me."

There was no answer to this. She knew the interview was over.

He walked her across the room and opened the door. In the outer office the lamps were lit. Their light was clear and white and clean. Micky was asleep in his chair, his chin resting on his chest.

"Lucky for some," said Thomas.

He opened the front door. He stared at Kitty's face as they said goodbye. Her eyelids looked paper thin, he thought, and the skin was stretched over the eyes. Her lower lip was thick, her upper lip was thin, with the teeth underneath showing through. Kitty smiled and went out into the street. He watched her walk away, and once she had disappeared from

266

sight, he went on looking into the street.

Then he closed the door and turned and looked at Micky. The bailiff was quite still and his breathing was quiet. Sleep was close to death, he thought.

For a moment Thomas toyed with the idea of waking Micky up and telling him what he had agreed, but then he decided he wouldn't. The simplest thing, it seemed to Thomas, was that no one should know, other than himself, Kitty and Tim. Of course, he knew that it was wrong not to tell Micky what he was going to do later. It went against what they had agreed. It was also wrong to talk to someone wanted by the police. But he also knew that he would not tell Micky, and that he would go to the old forge alone, because when the time came to suppress the warrant, as he suspected he would, it would be much easier and better if his bailiff didn't know.

Micky still had his pipe in his mouth. Thomas coaxed it out from between his teeth and laid it on the desk top.

The colza lamp on the desk began to smoke. For a couple of moments he watched the coils of thin, black, sooty vapour as they tumbled in the air above the glass chimney. Then he squinted at the burner. It appeared to be gummed up. It would have to be cleaned the next day. He made a note to speak to Micky about it. Then he turned the wheel and lowered the wick.

Thomas went home at six. He ate three slices of cold ham and a piece of cheese for supper. He did not feel hungry.

His eldest son, who was also a Thomas, had sent a letter from Dublin. The plates were cleared away and Helena read it out. Helena's speaking voice often sounded timid but when she read it was always clear and strong.

"I need to go upstairs. I need to wash and rest," he said, when she had finished. "Will you play cribbage later?"

"Are you tired?" asked Helena.

"Give me an hour," he said.

"I'll write back."

She pointed towards the room where she had her desk and

writing things. She stood up. He watched her cross the hall.
She went into the little parlour room and closed the door. He
could rely on her to stay in there. When she was writing,
Helena never moved. It was as if she was stuck to her chair.

He clumped up the stairs, banging his feet noisily on the
treads so that Helena would hear him. At the top, he went into
his bedroom and closed the door. He had put his guns in the
gun box by the bed when he had come in earlier; now he
took them out and checked them.

Then he took off his boots. He crept out on to the landing,
taking care to avoid the spot in the middle where the
floorboard creaked. He slipped down the back stairs. When he
reached the bottom he heard Maggie in the kitchen. It
sounded as if she was putting coal on the fire.

There was an old side door in the corridor between the
kitchen and the front part of the house. He had pulled the
bolts back earlier, found the key and opened the lock. No one
had noticed that he had done this. No one would. The door
was set in a recess where it was dark. Now, all he had to do,
after he put his boots on, was open it quietly and go out and
close it again. Then he would slip across the yard, collect the
lantern he had left in readiness in the tool shed, walk to town,
have ten minutes of talk in the old forge and come home. He
could do it in an hour, maximum.

Puck had been stopped by a policeman the week before
driving a cart that didn't have an owner's name written on the
side. This was against the law. All carts had to have the name of
the owner written on the side. The cart belonged to someone
else, Puck explained. Who? the policeman asked. Puck didn't
want to say the name but he had to. Isaac Marron, he said. The
policeman told Puck to tell Isaac Marron to get his name
written, in English, on the side of the cart, or he'd see both
men in court. Puck went back to Isaac and told him what had
happened. Then, a couple of days later, as Isaac had instructed
him to do, he took the cart to the sign-writer in Beatonboro'
and got Isaac's name and the name of his townland written on

the side. All that remained was to call in to the barracks and leave word for the officer who had stopped him on the road and who was called Cleary, that the work was done. When it came to the little things, Puck always had everything in order.

Rody walked with Puck along Beatonboro' main street as far as the door of the barracks but there he stopped and said, "I won't come in. I'll wait." It was evening, puddles everywhere, and a mist in the air that penetrated through every layer of clothing and froze the skin with its touch.

"Come on."

"No," said Rody. He did not think it a risk worth taking. What if someone had informed and the police had a description of them? Anyway, why let the peelers have a look at you? Out of sight, out of mind, that was Rody's motto.

Puck waved a hand, pushed the door and went in. The day room smelt of oil and woodsmoke. He walked across to the counter where a policeman sat reading a newspaper. There was printer's ink on the constable's finger-ends and when he reached up and stroked his moustache, a small amount of the ink transferred to the hair.

"Good evening," said Puck, cool and polite, and he saw that it was the same policeman who had stopped him, the one called Cleary. As the policeman turned to look at him, with an expression of supreme indifference, Puck felt excited. Here he was, unrecognised in the camp of the enemy. He had nothing to worry about. He was from another town, a dozen miles away and unknown in Beatonboro'. Confirmation of this came a moment later when, having said the cart now had Isaac's name on it, Puck gave his name and address and Cleary wrote them out without a second's hesitation. The policeman had never laid eyes on him before, other than when he stopped Puck the week before, and it gratified Puck that he aroused not even a hint of suspicion.

Puck left the barracks and found Rody shivering in a shop doorway with his collar pulled up.

"You should have come in. It was warm in there," said Puck.

They set off for the Union workhouse. They had an arrangement to play cards with the caretaker, an old fellow called Joe. When they finished, the caretaker would let them sleep in the kitchen, if they wanted.

They walked briskly and turned down the entry that connected the main street to the wasteland that lay between the back of the town and the workhouse. Neither man spoke. Their boots clanged on the cobbles. They heard someone splashing ahead of them in the puddles that lay on the ground.

"It's our man," said Rody suddenly.

The two men stopped. They could just make out a dark shape moving through the blackness lit up by a candle in a lantern.

"I think you're right," said Puck. The gait of the figure, it was unmistakably French.

"And no bloody Laffin."

"No," agreed Puck. "But what's he doing out here at this time?"

"He can't be going to the Union, there's no meeting there tonight."

The path forked but instead of taking the broader and more well-travelled route that swept towards the granite workhouse building half a mile away, their quarry took the other path, the one to the right, the one less trodden.

"He's going towards the old forge," said Rody.

"Why would he do that?"

The two men trotted forward, taking care to lift their feet. They were almost noiseless. Their quarry was walking fast and did not hear them following.

"There's someone inside the forge," said Rody.

"We have a chance."

"Indeed." Rody raised a hand. They stopped and watched French sweep on along the path. They agreed a plan in whispers.

Puck would go to Isaac's house. They had left the gun in a box at the back of the barn. Puck would load the gun and return as soon as he could. Rody, meanwhile, would stay and watch. The agent would have his chat. By the time he had finished, Puck would be back. Then they would get French as he returned along the path towards Beatonboro'.

"Nearly one year on this and, at long bloody last, here we go."

"Hallelujah," Rody agreed.

"Hallelujah, and Amen," said Puck, and he jogged away into the darkness.

Thomas followed the narrow path towards the forge, seeing his way by the pale light of the candle in his lantern.

The clock in the church tower in Beatonboro' began to chime. The sound of the bell was muffled by the fog. It was eight. If he got this over with quickly, he could walk home in twenty minutes. He could slip back upstairs, and then he could emerge with his hair wet and neatly combed as if nothing had happened.

He peered ahead. At the same time he remembered that it was on the broader path, the one he had left behind, that the man with the fake letter had tried to stop him when he was going to a meeting at the workhouse. It was possible, he thought, that Tim had been there that night. Not just possible – more than likely, surely?

Thomas stopped, slipped his hand under his coat and found the stock of the pistol that he kept on his left side, close to his heart. The handle felt smooth and warm.

He gripped the handle and went forward again. The forge was a black square with a dark, cloud-filled sky behind it. There were no stars, no moon. It was going to rain again, he thought. He stepped into a puddle that was deeper than he realised and he registered the wet almost immediately as the water soaked through his boot and his sock to his skin. He would have to stuff his boot with newspaper and dry it in front of the fire later. He could tell Helena he had got the boot wet while watering the pony. She would believe that. It was easy to lie to her and he could not possibly let her know that he was out. Never.

He could now see the door of the forge. He stopped. He puckered his lips and blew. Two clear notes sounded. He waited. Two clear notes sounded inside the stone square of the forge.

"Traynor?" he whispered.

"Yes."

"You're alone?"

"Oh, yes."

The unseen figure inside the tumbled forge was nervous. It was clear from his voice.

"I'm armed and I will not hesitate to use my guns," Thomas said.

"I understand."

"I'm coming in now."

He ducked through the door. Inside, the ruin smelt of rusted metal, nettle, and pee. Nothing moved at first, then Traynor came forward from a shadowy corner. With each step came a soughing noise as he trod through sticky mud.

"I'm not going to ask why you worked for me and spied at the same time. But I'm going to ask you some questions and you're going to answer them without any nonsense, understand?" This was brutal but Thomas had decided it was the only basis on which to proceed. "You've talked to Kitty McKenna?"

"Yes."

"What did she say about our conversation?"

"She told me she'd told you everything."

"Has she?" asked Thomas.

"That's what she told me," said Tim.

That wasn't the answer, thought Thomas. "But does she know everything?" he asked. "For all I know you have no intention of going to America and you're going to kill me now."

"No. I'm not."

"No?"

"I'm not." Tim pronounced the words without inflection.

What was this? wondered Thomas. Was Tim calculating that the truth did not need to be delivered in an exaggerated way because it spoke for itself? Or was Traynor acting the part of a man telling the truth? "Why should I believe you?" Thomas asked.

"Because Kitty does," said the younger man, without a second's hesitation.

"That's my proof, is it?" Tim's reply had impressed him but Thomas didn't let this show.

"Yes."

"But she loves you and I don't. Why wouldn't she believe you?"

The figure in the darkness stamped his feet and sighed. "I have two paths," he said.

"Tell me about them."

"I'm arrested on the warrant, I'm finished. Or I'm not arrested, I'm on for the next job, and I'm either shot, or I'm caught and I'm hanged."

"Either way, Traynor loses."

"But stop the warrant for a week, we get organised . . ."

"And you leave Ireland with Kitty for ever. Right?"

"Yes."

"Give me one good reason why I should agree?"

"She wants to marry me."

Thomas laughed. The boy swung between extremes. One minute he was adept, the next he was crass. "Oh, I'm doing this for Kitty? This is what she deserves, is it?"

"Yes," said Tim, his voice was hurt and faint.

"Why should I? I don't care about you. You've got yourself into this mess. Get yourself out of it."

"That's true. I did. I swore the oath." Tim spoke quietly, without emotion.

"It's all your own doing. Don't come whining to me about it."

"I had a stupid argument with Kitty. I joined because I was angry."

"You were like a child breaking a toy?"

"If you like."

Tim's candour impressed Thomas, but again he didn't let this show. Instead, he said, "More fool you."

"I know now what I did was wrong," said the younger man.

"Do you? Really?"

"Yes."

"No one made you join?"

"No, I chose, and now I'm choosing to get out . . ."

"You haven't told me why."

The dark figure, swathed in a coat, a hat pulled down over his face, and a scarf wrapped around his neck and chin, shrugged its shoulders.

"Kitty loves me."

When he heard these words, Thomas knew he should approve, he should help, he should agree to quash the warrant. Even if Tim was rash and weak, he was a nice fellow. He was lucky Kitty loved him. However, beneath what he knew was the right response, something else stirred in Thomas. A quite unexpected sense of protectiveness towards Kitty.

"But do you love Kitty?" he asked. In Thomas's experience, the callow and the immature, like Tim, often rejected the love they were offered.

"Listen," began Tim.

Thomas felt uneasy. He didn't want to discover that the eager girl he had met in his office, the girl who had talked with such conviction about Tim, had made a mistake, was wrong, was not cherished.

"After your talk, she came home. I was asleep. She woke me and she brought me over the fields to your house," continued Tim.

This was unexpected.

"We got over the gate at the back and made our way behind the bushes on the orchard side. From here we were able to see across the paddock. We saw into the parlour."

Thomas pictured the scene as they saw it – the wooden fence, the dark wet grass, the big, long windows of the house.

"You went to my house this evening?"

"Yes, and your wife, Mrs French, was sitting in there. She was playing the piano."

"What's the point of this?" Without his quite knowing how, they'd got away from the subject of Tim's feelings for Kitty and on to this. Thomas was prepared to hear what Tim had to say, but then he had every intention of steering the young fellow back to what he regarded as the only important question.

"Mrs French was wearing a blue dress," said Tim.

Thomas knew it well. It was a silk afternoon dress, with embroidered cambric collar and cuffs, worn with six or seven under-skirts, one of red flannel, a glimpse of which always excited him. It was what she had been wearing at supper.

"I bought that one for her. A favourite, with both of us," said Thomas.

"And Kitty said, 'Imagine her dressed in black – think of that!'"

"Which must have been easy for you – it being your life's work for the last while to make that happen."

"No, I'd never thought about that before, you see," said Tim.

"What's your point?"

"I don't want it now."

Thomas thought he knew where this came from. When they spoke in his office, Kitty had mentioned O'Duffy. The young man's terrible death disgusted Tim, she said. She had offered this as evidence that Tim was not a Ribbonman at heart. Thomas was not convinced. Now Tim was trying to build on that, wasn't he? He was trying to say to Thomas that he didn't want to take his life any more because he recognised it was wrong and it would cause Helena terrible pain. But what surprised Thomas, now that he had this assurance, was that it didn't seem all that important. All that really mattered now were Tim and Kitty's feelings towards one another.

"You still haven't told me if you love Kitty."

There was a very long silence.

Finally, Tim said, "Did she mention . . .?" and stopped.

Thomas kept his mouth closed. He would say nothing. Let the younger man answer the question.

The clock chimed the half-hour. Thirty minutes of talk

already. Why had he thought this would be quick? Ridiculous of him. Then he imagined Helena. He saw her finish her letter and climb the stairs. He saw her open their bedroom door and thrust a candle in. He saw the empty room as she might see it. Then he blinked and put the image out of his mind. If it was discovered he had slipped out there would be a row. But he could not think about that now. He must concentrate on this.

"You had a pretty frank conversation, didn't you?" said Tim.

"Get on with what you want to say, for God's sake."

"There is a . . . child . . . coming."

"You don't have to love someone to put a baby in their belly," said Thomas, "and you still haven't told me if you love her." He would chase this until he had an answer.

"Yes," said the younger man, speaking very quietly, "I love her, yes."

The younger man sounded sincere but Thomas wanted to be certain. He cocked his head sideways.

"I love her, yes," said Tim, a little more loudly, and finally, in his normal voice he said, "Yes, I love her."

They were there. Here was the answer.

"All right," said Thomas. "I'll cancel the warrant."

He felt Tim take his arm and shake his hand.

"A week's all you've got," said Thomas.

Tim turned and ducked through a small door at the back of the old forge. It opened into an old store with tumbled walls. Thomas heard Tim scramble over a wall in there, and then the clump of his boots as he made his way across the wasteland.

Thomas felt a strange combination of feelings. He was pleased. He had managed to get an answer out of Tim, and then he had made a decision. And not only that: he had made the decision he wanted to make. From the moment Kitty told him she was pregnant, Thomas had wanted to say yes. And from the moment he had watched her walk down the street, and then turned and looked at Micky and decided not to wake him and tell him what he was going to do, he had known that he probably was going to say yes. But he couldn't have said yes, not there and then, not just like that. He had to check that what Kitty had said about her fiancé was right. It was mad not to. And, happily, what she had said was correct. They loved one another and it was the right thing to help them.

He pulled out his pipe and tamped down the tobacco. He lit it and inhaled. He stood smoking for a long time. He felt a little sad at the thought of Kitty going away. In the distance, the clock chimed nine. Lost in his own thoughts, time had flown. His disappearance would have been noted by now, he realised. When he got home, Helen would ask him where he had been. What had he been doing? She would cry. She would wring her hands. He knew he had better go home now as quickly as his legs would carry him and try to make it up to her, yet still he did not move.

Puck and Rody squatted beside the bush at the side of the path.

The susurrus of talk in the forge had long since ended. Since when they had crouched on the ground and waited for French to come out. But French had not appeared. He had stayed in there. First he had just stood. Then he had lit his pipe. And still he had not emerged. It was mysterious. Perhaps he was waiting for someone else.

Puck suggested they go forward and fire through the door. No, said Rody. French would hear them creep up. He would get his pistols out and fire. Too risky. This was the best way. French had gone into the forge by this route, he would come out by this route. All they had to do was wait.

So they waited. The minutes ticked away. Then, finally, came the welcome sound of a stone scudding on the ground.

"Here we go," whispered Puck. He gripped the stock of the gun. A dark shape emerged from the doorway.

The path swept straight towards them, then veered away. They were about fifteen feet from the edge behind a tangle of old brambles and new ash saplings. They would have preferred to be snug at the side of the path but they had to take the best cover available, and besides, their weapon would easily do the job over the distance.

The dark figure of the agent moved slowly. He pulled on his pipe. The sound of spit bubbling in the stem was audible.

"Ready," said Rody, "aim . . ."

The agent was almost as close, almost, as he would ever come.

"Fire," whispered Rody.

As he squeezed the trigger, Puck tightened himself in anticipation of the explosion that would follow in a fraction of a second, the kick of the stock against his shoulder that would follow a fraction later still, and the agent's cry, as a wall of small but exceedingly sharp pieces of metal hit his face and body, that would follow a fraction of a second later again.

The hammer fell. There was a spark and then a desolate phut. The percussion cap had gone off but the powder in the breech had failed to ignite. A misfire.

"Run," cried Rody, and before Puck had time to think, he was on his feet, and Rody had his arm and was dragging him along. His legs began to move and he was running towards the workhouse. Any second now, he knew the agent must fire. But he must keep moving. He must put as much distance between himself and the agent as possible.

He heard the agent shout something incoherent, and then two shots.

"I'll get you," the agent shouted. Would he reload? Puck wondered. Or perhaps the agent had another set of pistols?

He hurt in his chest between his lungs. His arm was tired from the weight of the blunderbuss and the hand that gripped the stock was sweaty. He swapped the gun to his other hand.

They ran on. They ran to the workhouse, then along the side of the workhouse. Puck heard voices in the workhouse yard as they went past. These were the pauper helpers, he thought. Then they went down the hill behind the workhouse and into a wood, which grew there at the bottom.

It was dark among the trees and there was a smell of wet wood and leaf. The ground was soft and damp. They went some way into the wood. When they felt they were safe they stopped. Each man supported himself with an arm against a tree. Each man breathed deeply. The workhouse bell sounded behind, summoning the inmates to their dormitories.

"Damn, damn, damn," muttered Puck. "This was meant to be a simple job. That man is impossible to get at."

"Oh, we'd have got him all right, tonight, only you didn't prepare her properly, did you?"

Puck sat down on a fallen tree. He didn't like what he had just heard. He could load as well as the next man. He tamped down the wadding, the stocking of shot and the powder that was still in the breech. Then he took a percussion cap out of the patch-box and jammed it in place. He was reloaded. All he had to do was cock the hammer.

"This business was supposed to be a well-oiled clock," said Puck, grimly, snapping the lid on the patch-box shut. "Wind her up and off it was meant to go."

"We're biding our time," said Rody.

"It's in threes, of course, disaster always comes in threes," mused Puck, "and we've had three by the old forge. Disaster one – the letter wrongly addressed! Disaster two – we follow French tonight and it turns out the agent's not alone. There's someone in the forge. Disaster three, the gun misfires – the gun that I thought you cleaned today."

"Oh, shut up!"

"What did you do? Pee in the barrel?"

"You loaded her."

"And where is Tim, by the way?"

"I don't know," said Rody, in his matter-of-fact voice. Then he continued, "We've just been unlucky, you know. But when we line him up with that," Rody pointed at the gun, which lay across Puck's lap, "he dies."

"This is more than bad luck. This feels like Providence."

"Don't talk gibberish."

"What about that time the agent went out to that tenant – McAree, was it?" said Puck. He was determined to follow this line.

"McAree."

McAree was a tenant farmer who lived towards Shercock. The road to his house passed through a huge bog.

"The site was perfect," said Puck, "the best, until we went down that hole. That was Providence."

"God made that hole, did he? To catch us and protect French?"

"He didn't stop us falling into it," said Puck.

"Fact is, you said you knew that bog, but you didn't know that bog like you said you did, that's all."

"You were the one who fell into it first, actually," said Puck angrily.

"You were the one who scrambled out first and turned tail, actually."

"Meaning?"

"You'd wetted your new shoesies, hadn't you, dear?" said Rody, in a girlish lisp. "Had to get home and dry them."

"When I got out of that hole, all I was thinking about was the gun."

"Rubbish. You were thinking about your new brogues," said Rody coldly.

"Let me remind you what happened. You went in. I went in. I shouted –"

"Hold it. I had the gun," said Rody.

"No, you didn't."

"Yes, I did."

"No," said Puck angrily. "I had it. Then you asked for the gun. 'Give it to me,' you said. Then you screamed, 'Run!' "

"No, I didn't. We both fell in. Then you *threw* the gun at me. Then you got out and legged it and I had to follow. You were terrified." Rody folded his arms. This was what had happened and he knew the other man knew it.

The tips of Puck's ears reddened. He was caught out. "We ran together," he said.

"And you're wearing them now," said Rody.

"What?" said Puck.

"Those same damned brogues you were wearing that day you scuttled off."

"No, they're not."

"They're the same brown brogues," said Rody. "I remember looking at them this afternoon and thinking exactly that. Those are the shoes again that he wore when we fell in that bog hole."

"No, they're not."

"Yes, they damned well are."

"Ever since we started this operation, you have been telling me what to do. Go here! Go there! Watch! Wait! Load the gun! Unload the gun! Hide the gun! Get the gun! I've had it with you, Rody."

"I'm senior here!" said Rody.

"I am not taking orders from you any more."

"Without me, without my precautions, the peelers'd be straight on to you." Rody snapped his fingers in the darkness.

"All quiet for Rody Donohoe. The man the soldiers never caught. The man the peelers never got. The man who pissed in the barrel this afternoon when he cleaned this gun."

"Those are the same shoes, the ones you ran away in. I know it. They're identical."

"No, they're not."

"Yes, they are."

"Bastard."

Puck raised the blunderbuss. The O of the muzzle glimmered faintly in the darkness half a dozen paces from Rody's face. Puck had his finger on the trigger and his thumb on the hammer.

"Bastard," said Rody.

"Now, recite after me," said Puck. " 'These are not the shoes Puck had in the bog.' " Puck cocked the hammer. " 'These are not the shoes Puck had in the bog.' "

Rody stepped towards the gun. The muzzle was only a few feet away.

"If you don't say, 'These are not the shoes Puck had in the bog' – I'm going to blow your head off."

Rody came right up and rested his forehead against the muzzle.

" 'These are not the shoes . . .' " he said slowly.

"Go on."

" 'Puck had in the bog.' "

"Although they are very similar, of course."

Rody straightened and stepped back.

"Although they are very similar, of course," said Puck. "They are, in fact, the same shoe. I liked the first ones so much I bought another identical pair. They look the same but they're actually not the shoes I was wearing the day we fell into that bog hole."

Rody turned away and laughed quietly. "You bastard," he said, and Puck chuckled along with him in the darkness. "You bastard."

Puck released the hammer and laid the blunderbuss across his lap.

At half eight I went to our bedroom and found Thomas was not there. I thought he must have gone downstairs to the kitchen while I was writing away and I simply hadn't noticed him clumping across the hall. He likes to go and talk to Maggie in the evening.

So I went down to the kitchen myself. I found Maggie sitting by the fire but there was no sign of Thomas. Now I began to panic. I ran to the hall and called out. Maggie checked the offices. We searched the entire house. Thomas was nowhere. He had gone.

What did I do now? I had no idea. In one part of me I was absolutely sure there was a perfectly logical and innocent explanation for this. He'd gone off to see someone or to do something. He had probably even told me, I reasoned with myself, only I had forgotten. In another part of me, I was certain the worst had happened.

I decided to wait in the large parlour. Around nine thirty a sub-constable came to the back door and told me that my

husband was in the police station, he was making a statement, and he would be home shortly. My first sensation
was relief, the sweetest feeling in the world. No, Thomas
was not dead. The worst had not occurred. He was alive.
Unfortunately, this sensation was short-lived. For then I
began to think about what had happened. My husband had
said he was going upstairs but in fact he had gone out
secretly without telling me.

He came home around half ten. He came straight to me.
He saw by my expression that I was furious but in a cold
way. My heart had hardened in the hour since I had learned
from the policeman that he was safe.

"I owe you an apology," he said. He told me he had slipped
out to see Tim (who apparently is a Ribbonman – so much
for my judgement – I always thought he was a charming
young man). Thomas had gone to meet up with him because
he wanted to decide whether or not to help the young fool to
leave the country. Happily, he told me, the meeting was a
success and he had decided he was going to help Tim to leave.

"And then what happened?" I asked.

He coloured and said that after he had seen Tim, he was
fired on by a weapon that misfired – he had an idea it was a
blunderbuss. He returned fire but failed to hit his assailants.
The police, hearing shots, came out and he had to go back
to the station and make a statement.

I went to bed. My feet were cold but my heart seethed.
When Thomas came to bed I was still awake. His breath
smelt of brandy.

He squeezed my hand in the darkness and we both went
to sleep.

I wrote to Micky first thing the next morning and
Maggie dropped my letter off at the estate office on the
way to early Mass. I asked Micky to step down to the house.
He came at half ten. We had a few minutes in the little
room where I write. I told him what happened the night
before and he promised to speak to Thomas about it, but
without involving myself.

"How will you do that?" I asked.

"I'll find a way," said Micky, and he left with a glum expression.

Micky went out the back door and headed round the side of the agent's house towards the road. The wind roared and the branches of the copper beech waved against the grey sky behind. Further down the lane, there were trees on either side of the gravel. In one tree he noticed several birds' nests. They were dense black knots of twig that reminded him of burrs. There was a spray of bramble by the gate, brown thorns on stems that were damp and red.

He walked on quickly. It was Micky's nature, if something difficult had to be said, to say it and get it over with. His intention was to return to the office and say to Thomas that he had just been in the police station where Cleary had told him what had happened the night before. Then he would tell Thomas how furious he was with him.

When Micky got to the office a few minutes later, he found French's door firmly closed and voices coming from the other side.

Micky sat down at his desk grumpily and fiddled with his pen. He tried to work but couldn't. His mind was whirring. He got up and threw some turf on the fire. He spoke briefly to a tenant at the door about the delivery of some quicklime. He paced the floor. He stared at Thomas's door. Why couldn't the visitor hurry up? Micky wanted to get on with what he had to do; he wanted to say his bit and have it out with Thomas. How could the agent have gone out alone the night before and not told him? It not only went against the understanding they had – Thomas was never to go anywhere without Micky or someone else, ever – but look what had happened. Thomas had nearly been killed.

Micky heard the scraping of a chair leg in the inner office. He threw himself into his own chair, picked up his pen and dipped it in the ink-well. The door opened behind him. Micky looked up nonchalantly. To his surprise, he saw it was

Cleary, the constable. This was the last man he had expected to come out of Thomas's office, and then he saw this was to his advantage.

The constable closed the door behind himself and said, "Good morning."

Micky said, "Good morning. We're not in trouble, are we?"

Cleary smoothed his moustache. The policeman wanted to speak about something. Micky knew him well enough to know that all he needed was a little coaxing.

"What did he want?" said Micky quietly. Speaking at this level of volume, French could not possibly hear him.

The policeman bent forward. "Do you know Tim Traynor?" he whispered. "The one who whacked Croker Flanagan?"

Micky smiled as Cleary said this. "I get on with Haystacks, you know," said Micky. "He comes to the house as a rule, on a Sunday morning, and waits until they open up the chapel for first Mass. He's always early. He's a very religious man, did you know that?"

"He may be, but he's a terror and he got what he had coming to him," said the policeman grimly.

"Aye." Micky looked Cleary straight in the eye. Micky did this to remind Cleary his secret was safe with him. Micky did not gossip. He was sound.

"Well, he just asked me the strangest thing," continued Cleary, jerking his head in the direction of the door to Thomas's office. "The bench warrant for Traynor, I'm to drop it."

"Oh. Why would he want you to do that?" Micky's tone was cool, nonchalant, even.

"Tim Traynor wants to fly away and we're not to stop him. That's all Mr French told me."

"Didn't he give you any reason at all?"

"No, none. No reason given whatsoever except that there was a compelling personal purpose behind all this. But Mr French said he couldn't tell me about that. Not yet. I'd have to wait. He would in time. But he promised me this was the right thing to do and he asked me to trust him. Anyway, it's not as if this Traynor's done anything serious, I suppose," the policeman continued.

"No," agreed Micky.

"So I told him I'd oblige," and with that Cleary stamped out of the office.

The fire hissed. Micky waited. The door from the inner office opened a few minutes later and Thomas appeared.

"Cleary just told me you've suppressed the Traynor warrant," said Micky, while pretending to write.

"That's right."

"Why? Isn't he a bad boy?" Micky laid down his pen and sat back in his chair.

"Yes," said Thomas. The tone was faintly defensive.

"What are your reasons, may I ask?"

The clock ticked. Embers settled in the grate. From the street came the clatter of hoof on cobble, and a snatch of song. Micky saw how to play this. He had to act as if he was in the grip of a sudden brilliant intuition.

"Traynor's the tell-tale, isn't he? He's been telling them about your movements," he said, and stood up.

"Yes," said Thomas reluctantly.

"You saw him last night and now he's promised to go a long way away, and never, ever to come back?"

Thomas nodded slowly.

Micky saw that his questions had unnerved the other man. "America, I suppose."

"Yes," agreed the agent quietly.

"And you're paying?" A further nod from Thomas, smaller than before. Hah! Micky was no longer pretending to be prescient: now he genuinely was.

"What a brilliant swindle," said Micky. "Find someone, try to kill them, and then get them to pay for you to go to Boston."

"New York, actually," said Thomas, "with his girl."

"Who is, no doubt, having his child?" said Micky, with heavy irony.

"Yes." Thomas's mouth moved and the skin round his eyes twitched, a sure sign of embarrassment.

"I want us to cast our minds back," said Micky. "You made a rule. You would never go anywhere alone and there were to be no exceptional circumstances. We agreed that, didn't we?"

"Yes."

"We agreed that, and now, I'm telling you, don't you ever break that agreement again, like you did last night."

This was one of those rare but wonderful moments when Micky knew that every phrase and every gesture was absolutely true.

"Right now, as we speak, they're out there. Do you agree with that?"

"Yes," agreed Thomas.

"So, do we have an understanding? Never, never, never anywhere alone, never again."

"Yes."

Micky inclined his head as if he had not quite heard. "Sorry?"

"Yes."

Micky inclined his head further sideways.

"Yes," said Thomas louder still, and then louder again he said, "Yes," and Micky smiled.

That afternoon, Micky called up to the McKennas with enough money for the tickets, one way, Belfast to New York, as well as new clothes and new shoes for Tim and Kitty.

chapter thirteen

"So how do you explain what happened at the old forge?"

Puck looked at his feet and considered his answer. Then he looked up and said, "The powder was damp." This was the answer that he and Rody had agreed they would give.

"How did that happen?" asked Turk. He sat directly across from Puck, on the other side of the table, underneath a print of a sportsman firing a flintlock at a duck.

"It was a wet evening, like now."

Puck pointed at the open door. It was raining furiously outside.

"It wasn't raining last night," said Turk.

"It was going to rain," said Puck.

He felt anxious. He gazed through the door at the watery spears of rain that were hurling themselves at the ground. He did not like the tone of the questions. He did not like the mood of Isaac or Turk, Alex or Thady. He was glad they were in Dolly Walsh's pub and not in Isaac's house. A dog splashed by, its fur wet and matted.

"How long have you been at this?" asked Thady. There was the question Puck had dreaded.

"Some months," said Rody.

"A year nearly," replied Thady.

"All right," Rody agreed.

"And you've spent the monies we advanced, I see." Alex ducked his head down and looked under the table. When he sat up again he said, "Fine pair of shoes, Puck."

"The last were coming to bits," said Puck.

There was silence. The songbird in the cage on the pub counter knocked its beak against the bars.

"I am not happy," said Isaac unhappily.

"Nor are we," Rody agreed.

"They are beginning to laugh at us in Armagh," said Isaac. Although this was a lie, Turk, Thady and Alex shook their heads unhappily. Isaac had told them earlier he was going to tell this lie and they knew their roles.

"I'm sorry to hear that." It was Puck's impression that his apology sounded sincere.

"And Louth," added Turk.

"Haven't Ribbonmen always liked a bit of friendly rivalry?" countered Puck.

"I was recently described as the snail of Beatonboro'," said Isaac slowly. "I did not like that."

"No, you wouldn't," agreed Puck.

"Why don't you tell me what I want to hear?"

"Sorry."

"Sorry, that's right. Sorry, we have made a complete mess of everything."

"French is not easy," said Rody.

"Sheridan went like clockwork. That's why we brought you back."

"We were lucky there," said Rody.

"It wasn't luck. It was organisation."

"We gave you fifty at the beginning," said Alex grimly. "Then we gave you another sum of money. Has it occurred to you that with all this money spent and nothing to show, we might want it all back?"

"You can't," said Puck.

"Why? Because you're wearing it on your feet," said Turk. "Well, we may just have to cut those shoes off at your ankles."

"We will get him. We just need time and luck."

"You've had long enough," said Thady.

"He's never alone and he's let it be known Laffin fires on us, regardless of what happens to him," said Rody. "You know that. We have to be careful."

Isaac had waited patiently for this moment and now he formed his question. "Are you frightened?" he asked.

"No, we're sensible," said Rody. "We've got many more Sheridans and Frenches in us yet."

"I think you're frightened," said Isaac, "but we'll see."

He stood up. "Come and see me tomorrow in the evening, you two." Turk, Thady and Alex got up and went behind Isaac. The four men standing were an intimidating sight. "I've something I want you to do," continued Isaac. "And if you see Tim, remember O'Duffy to him."

Isaac pulled his hat over his head and walked out into the rain. Puck distinctly heard the sound of the rain as it hit the brim. The songbird began to warble in its cage. Turk, Thady and Alex filed out after Isaac.

"We're going to have to buck up," said Puck, when they were gone.

"Ah! they're all talk," said Rody. "Pay no heed to them."

The next evening Puck and Rody called at Isaac's house. Isaac brought them into the parlour. He did not invite them to sit down but he sat down himself. Then Isaac told them what he wanted them to do.

It was a minister of the Church of Ireland. His name was Barrett. He was an unpleasant man who obnoxiously tried to convert Catholics. He was an ardent Orangeman. He was a bigot. He was a nuisance. He always sided with the local landlord against evicted tenants. He was a man of many faults and made no effort to improve himself despite the numerous written warnings that had been nailed up on his church door.

Barrett was based in Cullaville but he had a second, smaller church in Crookedstone on the way to Crossmaglen. Every Monday morning he held a service in this small church. The following Monday would be no different. He would perform the service, and then he would leave the church and walk back to his house at midday. As it happened, there was a fair in Crossmaglen that following Monday. The road would be full of people going to the fair. Being the sort of man that he was, Barrett would talk to everyone on the road. And among those whom he would meet and talk with would be Puck and Rody. They were to shoot him and then melt into the crowds.

It was Sunday afternoon. Thomas said goodbye to Helena and went out to the yard where the car stood waiting for him in the rain. Micky was already aboard. He got in and took the reins. They were wet and slimy. He put his hand into his coat pocket and took out his gloves. They were leather, black, with close small stitches along the seams. They would get wet if he wore them now, he thought. Later, when he dried them, they would probably crinkle. Later still, Helena would discover the gloves. She would remind him that she had given them to him. She would complain. She would say he did not take care of what she gave him. He put the gloves back in his pocket and picked up the reins again.

"Walk on," he said. The pony started forward. The wheels turned on their axle. Rain slanted into his face. He narrowed his eyes. The eyelashes on his left side trapped a raindrop. He brushed it away with a thumb. He turned through the yard gate and on to the gravel. A crunching sound came from below the car.

Forty minutes later he saw the McKenna cottage. There was a pine tree behind a wall with a track opposite that he turned up and followed to the front of the house. He pulled on the reins and came to a halt. His fingers were cold and stiff. Along his shoulders, the rain had passed through his coat, his jacket, his shirt, his vest, right through to his skin. Yet the small of his back and his feet were snug and warm. The door opened back and he saw Kitty standing in the doorway.

"Good afternoon, Mr French, Mr Laffin," she called. "I see you've brought the good weather with you."

She told him to go round to the back. He would find a three-sided lean-to. He could put the pony and car in there, she said.

He went to the back as she told him. He felt cheerful. It was a miserable afternoon but he was glad that he had come. There was nothing like being in the company of the young to raise Thomas's spirits.

He put the pony and car away. When he came out from the lean-to, he saw that the back door of the cottage stood open. He saw Kitty waiting there. He ran straight across the yard towards her, splashing through the puddles as he went, Micky behind.

When he reached the door she stood aside and he went in. The cottage was dark and there was a crusie lamp hanging from the wall and a candle burning on the dresser. The room smelt of turf and flour, the fish oil that was burning in the lamp, and the wick of the candle. There were scones on the griddle. Two figures rose from beside the fire and came forward. Daniel McKenna welcomed Thomas and Micky to the house, while Bridie McKenna hung back and nodded sadly. Thomas wondered, in a vague way, if Bridie was cross with him because he was the one, after all, who had made everything possible. Once Kitty left, her parents would most probably never see her again. Perhaps it hadn't been such a good idea to come. But then he looked at Kitty's pale face and grey blue eyes, and heard her lovely smooth voice, and thought, no: for the pleasure of an hour in her company, he could easily put up with the grumpy mother.

Kitty took his coat and Micky's. He watched her hang them over a horse in front of the fire. She was a pleasure to watch because of the care with which she did this. Daniel invited him and Micky to sit and they did. Daniel began to ask about the price of butter. Tim appeared, his hair combed and wet, his face washed. Thomas's and Micky's coats began to steam. Everyone moved to the table and sat down. It was covered with a white cloth and the best cups and saucers had been laid out. The scones were moist and hot. The butter melted into yellow juice. Thomas asked the couple about their plans. Kitty told him they would walk to Belfast on Monday. They would sail on Wednesday. They would marry in New York in six weeks' time because they could not marry in Ireland. After the ceremony, said Daniel, they would have a daguerreotype taken of themselves in their wedding clothes, and then they would send this back. Bridie let out a huge sigh.

"It is a terrible shame you won't be able to attend, Bridie," ventured Thomas.

Bridie, who had said nothing so far and had spent the entire time staring at the tablecloth, now lifted her head and looked across at Thomas. "My heart is broken," she said, and she returned her gaze to the table again.

"We know that," said her husband, "but what else can we do? They have to go."

Thomas sensed a terrible silence looming. He knew these moments well. Everyone would stare at their plates, failing to find anything to say, willing someone else to say something. Finally, somebody would say something, usually an inanity. He decided he must have something prepared before the awful silence started. However, when he tried to think of something now, his mind was already a blank. The words had fled. He coughed. He heard Kitty say, "Tim, go in and put on the new suit, and let Mr French and Mr Laffin see." These were some of the clothes Thomas had sent up. He wanted to clap the girl on the back.

Tim went off. The kettle was boiled again. More tea was made. Bridie ate half a scone. The door of Kitty's bedroom opened and Tim came out. He took a couple of steps towards the table and stopped. Kitty told him to come right up to the table. He blushed and shuffled forward. He wore a dark brown tweed suit with a high waistcoat and a shirt underneath without its collar. He had new black boots on his feet which creaked as he moved. In his left hand he held a brown felt hat with a turned-up brim.

"Put on the hat," said Kitty, and Tim blushed again. "It's a fine suit, isn't it, Mr French, and we thank you for it," she added.

"Tim, it's a good suit," Thomas said. "I hope it gives you many, many years of service."

Kitty pulled the hat from Tim's hand. She tried to put it on his head, shouting, "Let Mr French see you with it on." Tim turned aside and wouldn't let her.

"All right, have it your way," she said, and she put it on her own head. "I rather like this hat, I might have it for myself," she said.

A small, sly smile stole across Bridie's face, the first Thomas had seen so far all that afternoon.

"Stop being such a fool," said Kitty's mother.

"You want to see what I have as well, I suppose, Mr Laffin, Mr French?" Kitty piped. She ran from the room before Thomas answered. When she came back a few minutes later, she didn't stand coyly in the shadow near the door: she marched straight back to the table and turned on the spot. She wore a brownish-pink taffeta walking dress with a plain white collar fastened with a brooch. She had lost Tim's hat and now she wore a bonnet, which tied under her chin with a bow.

"What are we losing?" said Thomas gallantly.

"You're not losing us," said Kitty. "We'll have only gone to another country. We'll write. We'll send money."

"We will," Tim agreed heartily.

Kitty and Tim began to speak of their new start in a new country. With their talk they hoped to drive away the sadness that filled the room. Daniel nodded in agreement, as he listened. Bridie said nothing. Thomas expressed agreement loudly and vigorously. Micky nodded. The young couple were about to embark on an extraordinary adventure and, he believed, they must be sent on their way with smiles, not tears.

Thomas felt a curious sense of pride as well. In some way this was his doing. He had paid for it. He had taken a gigantic risk when he had met Tim and confirmed Kitty's story. He had suppressed the warrant. Yes, it was a good deed he had done and he was glad he had.

Kitty took off her bonnet. Thomas stared at her across the table. She began to laugh. Her hand went to her neck. Her mouth opened wide. She was glorious, he thought.

Then he found himself imagining her as an older woman, perhaps twenty years in the future. He imagined her in America, in a city, in a house, in a room. He imagined her talking to a young fellow. This was her eldest son, conceived in Ireland, born in America. He imagined Kitty talking to this son and telling him about an old man in Ireland called Thomas, who had helped her at great risk to himself many years before.

And as the laughter swirled around him, Thomas imagined Kitty, in twenty years' time, looking back on her life and recalling for her son this precise moment in the McKennas' kitchen, this very instant, when her child was a tiny shape in her belly, and she was laughing, and it was her last evening in Ireland, and the man, Thomas, who had helped her, was sitting across the table from her.

It grew dark outside.

"We must leave," said Thomas, although he wanted to stay. Micky fetched in the lamps from the car. They were small and square with reflectors that threw the light of a candle into the darkness. Thomas took a reflector out of one of the lamps and began to polish it. This was unnecessary but he wanted to postpone the moment when he would have to say goodbye for ever.

Kitty came over and took the reflector and began to polish it. Tim was in the shed outside. The McKennas were at the table on the other side of the room. Thomas saw that he would never have another chance like this.

"Kitty," he said, "will you do something for me?"

"What?"

"It's a favour."

She looked alarmed.

"Will you include my name when you name your child?"

The back door banged open. It was Tim with a basket of logs.

"Yes," she said, and he heard Micky at his side snort faintly and mutter, "I knew it."

"It's still pouring," announced Tim. "I hope this doesn't keep up till tomorrow. We'll catch our death on the roads."

Tim closed the door behind him with a foot and hurried towards the fire.

Kitty woke Tim at four o'clock the next morning. He came down the ladder from his place under the thatch to find her pouring hot water from the sooty kettle into a bowl. He took the bowl into her room where there was a candle burning as well as three crusie lamps, which had been brought through from next door. He lathered his face and shaved carefully. He did not cut himself once.

After he finished, he cleaned the blobs of soapy foam out of his ears, then he went over to her bed. Kitty had laid out their new clothes, his suit and her dress side by side, and their boots on the floor in front. There were no wrinkles, he saw, in the material, and the cuffs were flat and the collars were straight. The boots were clean and polished. He was touched by the sight and suddenly he was overwhelmed by a great feeling of tenderness for Kitty, as well as a great feeling of joy at the thought that at last they were going away together and they could never come back.

Kitty knocked on the door and asked through the wood if he was decent.

"Come in," he said.

She opened the door. His eyes met hers. He pointed at their clothes and smiled and she smiled back at him.

"We might as well get this over with," said Bridie.

They rose together from their seats around the fire, the young couple and the old parents. Daniel opened the front door. Tim took the sack from the table. Inside it were their tickets, some clothes, and a few other possessions.

Daniel went outside. Kitty followed. The hem of her walking dress swung as she moved. Tim walked forward. The soles of his new boots were a little stiff as he moved. Oh, well, he would soon walk that out of them on the road.

He stopped at the door. He saw the old man on the path with his daughter behind. There was a hand pressing on his back. It was Bridie.

"Go on," said Bridie grumpily. "Don't be dawdling."

Tim went out the door and the old woman followed. Tim went down the path and the old woman followed. At the bottom he stepped on to the lane. Puddles lay everywhere like sheets of mirror. Bridie stopped beside her husband.

"Be off with you," she cried. "Go away." She was only just in control of herself.

"God bless you," said Daniel, in a monotone. His eyes were wet. He reached forward and touched his daughter on the fleshy place between the thumb and the first finger.

"Go on," Bridie urged again. "Be gone." Tim gazed at the older woman's face. Her eyes were small and dark and angry. The lines around her mouth were sharp and deep.

Kitty embraced her father, and then her mother. "Don't delay," said Bridie. She pushed away her daughter and wrapped her arms around Tim's shoulders. He had an impression of flesh, bulk and bust. Bridie smelt of flour, and lavender from her pillow, and very faintly of lamp oil. She pushed him away. She did this gently, not abruptly as he expected. Suddenly, he saw her small, heavy form as a bag full of tears. At any moment it would tear and then the contents spill out.

He felt Kitty's hand around his forearm. They did not turn but began to walk backwards along the road. They kept their eyes on the old couple and the old couple kept their eyes on them. He would never see Kitty's parents ever again, nor would they ever see himself or Kitty again. He saw the pine tree behind and remembered the hours he had stood underneath it. He would never see the pine tree again. Or the cottage. Or the well, which now appeared on his right.

Daniel raised a hand but his wife did not move. Tim saw the verge curve at his side. Soon, he and Kitty would come to the corner beyond the well. Once they were beyond the corner, they were gone.

He sensed Kitty turning, and at the same time she turned him. He saw the road bend to the left a few feet away. He turned and looked back over his shoulder. He saw Kitty's father standing in the middle of the lane with an arm raised, his hand in the air. He saw Kitty's mother standing with her arms hanging down.

Tim looked ahead again. The corner appeared to be flowing towards them, whereas in fact he knew it was they who were flowing towards it. They were like the cut-out puppets pulled by wires, which he had sometimes seen at the fair; the object was to knock down the cut-outs with scrunched-up balls of paper.

They rounded the corner. He and Kitty were out of sight now. From behind came a desperate, piercing cry, unmistakably female, followed by a rumble, low, guttural and male. He guessed the old couple had collapsed into each other's arms and were now holding each other where he had left them in the middle of the empty lane.

There was a pain in Tim's throat, faint as yet. His grief was hours away. He looked across the fields on either side of the lane. The grass was bright and unusually green. After rain, the land always looked newly washed like this.

The wind swirled and something sounded behind. Were they footsteps? He didn't imagine it was Kitty's parents. The only people he could imagine running up behind were the last people in the world he wanted to meet – Puck, Rody, Isaac.

His heart beat faster and he turned to look. Nothing. The lane was empty. It was drops of water, he realised, from the rowan tree under which they had just passed, splattering the lane. They made a sound just like footsteps.

He felt Kitty squeeze his arm. "There's no one behind us,"

she said. She kissed him on the back of his hand.

Their plan was to walk around Beatonboro' by a circuitous route and then go on to Newry where they would catch the train to Belfast and their ship.

Micky was just explaining to a boy that he wanted a parcel collected from Cullaville railway station, when the door of the estate office opened and Isaac Marron came in.

"I'm still waiting for my gates," said Isaac. "It's nearly a year, you know."

Micky lifted his hands. "Goodness, you're right," he said, "I'll get on to it straight away. I'll write to the foundry."

He scribbled a word on a piece of paper, exactly as a man would if he wanted to remind himself to do something.

Isaac appeared happy and left.

"What was that about?" called Thomas, from the door of his office. He had heard Isaac come in and then go out.

"Marron's looking for his gates," said Micky. "I must set them in motion."

Thomas remembered that Isaac Marron had been looking for some gates on the very day he arrived in Beatonboro'.

"I thought we'd done with that," said Thomas.

"No," said Micky dreamily, "it somehow completely slipped my mind. But I'll write this morning."

Thomas went back into his office, satisfied with this reply. What he did not know was that, months before, Micky had suspended the order for the gates until further notice.

After the boy left for the station, Micky sat down and wrote a letter to the foundry with instructions to proceed with the gates. He could have made the boy wait for this letter and put it on the train to Belfast, but Micky chose not to. After nine months, he decided, what was another day or two of delay?

Micky finished the letter and put it in an envelope. Thomas was whistling in his office next door.

"You're in a cheerful mood," Micky called.

Thomas came out of his office and came up to Micky's desk.

"I feel very alive today," he said.

"How's that?"

"I just am."

"What, with getting Tim away? Getting one over on the Ribbons?"

Thomas thought about this for a moment. Finally he said, "No. It's not that. It's something else."

Micky saw the agent looking at him carefully. He knew that look well. It advised him to listen and not to jump to conclusions.

"You see that tree?" Thomas pointed at the oak that grew outside the estate office, at the side of the road.

Through the window, Micky saw a section of the trunk and parts of the lower branches. "It was there in the time of my great-grandfather," he said. "He broke his collar-bone falling off it."

"What do you see?"

"Trunk, branches."

"That's all?"

"It's a tree and those are its parts. When spring comes there will be leaves on it."

"I see a wonderful bark, criss-crossed by fine veins, and this morning, in the winter sunshine, it has a faintly purple hue."

"A faintly purple hue?" said Micky carefully.

"Yes."

"You haven't been at the gin?"

"No."

"Laudanum?"

"No."

"Opium?"

"Nothing. It's because I might die that I'm seeing that tree, and you, and my wife, freshly, fully, as if for the first time in my life."

"I don't think you should be seeing me like Mrs French," said Micky, smiling.

"I feel as if this is the first time in my life I've been really awake."

"You must have taken something."

"Nothing. I'm just in an uncommonly good mood."

"If you want my tuppence worth," said Micky, who had decided to take the risk and say what he had been wanting to say ever since Thomas suppressed the warrant, "this is all because of Kitty."

The room went silent.

"Why do you say that?" said Thomas finally.

"She's turned your head."

"Well, there's some truth in that probably. But it's not so much that she's turned my head, my friend, as that I found her company just very, very pleasing, and that was, I think, because I'm getting old."

"Really."

"I just liked being near all that vitality and she was pretty. It cheered me. Yes, it did. That's all. There was nothing more."

"Really."

Thomas began to laugh. He laughed long and hard. When he finished, he looked at Micky and said, "You really do know me, don't you?"

Puck and Rody sat on a stone wall. The blunderbuss was in a sack on the ground between Rody's feet. That morning Rody had taken off the nipple with the wrench and cleaned the hole with a needle. Then the nipple went back on and Puck loaded the gun with extreme care. This time there would be no misfire.

A cart rumbled into view, heading towards Crookedstone. A group of girls sat in the back, all in bonnets. The driver wore a stove-pipe hat.

The cart passed. A girl waved. Puck waved back. The cart rumbled on. Puck and Rody peered ahead of the cart. They saw a couple of men, whom they presumed were heading for the fair in Crossmaglen, the town beyond Crookedstone. Presumably this was where the girls on the cart were heading as well. There was no sign of Mr Barrett, the minister, coming in the opposite direction.

Puck pulled a watch out of his waistcoat pocket and

released the lid. Normally his fob stayed at home but today he had worn it because he thought it made him look like a man on his way to a fair.

"Twenty minutes at least," said Puck.

The other man moaned.

While they waited, Puck and Rody watched the people who passed. They were all in a cheerful mood, because it was a fair day and they were going to the fair. There were many loud voices and much laughter. Every now and again the sun shone down from between gaps in the clouds, and the air grew warmer. The atmosphere was almost spring-like. After a while, Rody touched Puck with his elbow.

There was the minister, Mr Barrett. He was coming towards them, moving south and west and in the opposite direction to the flow of the people. He was a tall man, and he wore no hat. He was bald and even at this distance they saw his pate was red and pointed.

Rody and Puck stood up. They saw that the minister had seen them stand up. They saw the minister narrow his eyes. The minister did not know who they were. Then they saw the minister's expression change as he recognised their faces. They had twice been to his church in Cullaville the previous week. They had sat at the back of the church and stared at the minister, and Mr Barrett had noticed them during the sermon. Puck and Rody had slipped away just before the end of each service so that the minister did not get the opportunity to talk to them. He would get that opportunity today. That was the plan.

Puck raised a hand. The minister saw the wave and he waved back in the slightly lordly way that ministers had. At the same time he increased his pace and he smiled. He had noticed these two strangers in his church and now, here they were, standing by the roadside. He was eager to speak to them. He was always eager to speak to those who came into his church.

"Hello," called the minister. "Good morning, or is it good afternoon?"

Puck pulled out his fob and opened the lid.

"It's still good morning," said Puck.

"I noticed you gentlemen in my church," said the minister. He was moving very fast now. He was big, with arms that hung down and swung as he moved.

"Last week, that's right," said Puck innocently.

"I've never seen you before."

Mr Barrett was right up to them now, breathless, with beads of sweat on his upper lid. His eyes were bright and blue and excited.

Puck shook the minister's hand. At the same moment, Rody put his hand into the sack and pulled out the blunderbuss.

Another cart rumbled past. A boy stared from the front seat at the brass weapon in Rody's hands. Puck pointed a finger at the boy and wriggled it from side to side.

The sign was unmistakable: the boy shook the reins. The leather thwacked the back of the donkey and the cart moved away smartly.

At the same instant the minister's face changed. His look of anticipation – anticipation of a pleasurable conversation – gave way to alarm and terror. Puck had seen this look before on the faces of other men in exactly this same situation.

The next second the minister began to turn. While his brain tried to work out what was happening, his body had already decided what to do. A foot lifted from the road. At the same time the minister's arm came up, the one with the hand that held his walking stick. If he could knock the gun out of the hands of the man who was pointing it at him, then perhaps . . .

Rody squeezed the trigger. There was an explosion and a puff of smoke. The cart that had passed was still hurtling as fast as it could go away along the road.

The shot hit the minister's body. The force was so great it lifted the minister up and pushed him back a couple of feet. Then he dropped and fell to the ground. He let out a cry. There was a horrible mess all down the left side of the minister's chest: it was a mixture of blood, bone and vein, thread, wool and worsted. There were also pieces of metal glinting here and there inside the wound, and a fragment or two of button.

Rody pulled the catch and the bayonet, which lay along the top of the gun, flipped forward. He put the point of the bayonet in the soft, fleshy hollow at the bottom of the minister's neck. He pressed. The bayonet went in. The point passed through the minister's neck, passed out on the far side and went into the earth, which comprised the road.

Mr Barrett shuddered and pawed the air as he tried to reach for the blade. Then his arm flopped, his eyes closed, his body went still. Rody pulled the bayonet out of his neck. There was blood on the blade. It was dark, almost the colour of blackberry juice. Rody carefully wiped each side of the blade on the minister's trousers. He folded the bayonet back along the top of the barrel and fixed it in position. He put the blunderbuss in the sack.

"Let's go," said Puck.

He turned and began to move up the road in the direction of Beatonboro'. Rody swung the sack over his shoulder and went after him.

About a hundred yards along the road, the two men met a party of girls. Some of the girls had picked snowdrops and fixed them in their hair or in their shawls. The girls were laughing.

"There's a man up ahead on the road," said Puck, grimly. The girls stopped laughing. "Don't go near him. Don't touch him."

The girls went on their way, and Puck and Rody went on theirs. Everyone they met they told to ignore Mr Barrett.

After a mile, Puck and Rody came to a small copse of beech, ash and elm by the side of the road. They scrambled over the grassy bank and went into the middle of the trees. While Puck listened to people passing along the road, Rody reloaded the blunderbuss. It was a possibility, albeit remote, that they might meet the agent and he reloaded just in case. A few minutes later they returned to the road again and walked on. They hadn't gone a hundred yards when Puck saw a familiar figure moving along the road in their direction.

"Hey! Look who it is!" he said. "It must be our lucky day."

They ran back to the first gate, slipped into the field behind, and hid behind the hedge. They waited. After a minute or two, through a tangle of branch and stem, they saw Tim along with a good-looking woman who wore a coat and a walking dress. The woman held Tim by the arm. They guessed she was Kitty. Rody took the blunderbuss out of the sack. He stuffed the sack in his coat pocket.

Tim and Kitty walked past, oblivious of Puck and Rody. Kitty laughed. Rody and Puck sprinted to the gate, and climbed over it. They ran slowly after the couple, making very little noise, and at the last moment they sprinted around them and then they were where they wanted to be – they were in front of Tim and Kitty before the couple knew what was happening.

"Stop! Right there!" said Rody. He cocked the blunder-buss.

Tim and Kitty froze on the spot. The colour drained and their young faces went white.

"You must be Kitty," said Rody.

He watched the woman swallow. He realised she was too frightened to speak.

Tim dropped the sack and made as if to turn and run in the direction he had come from. Rody considered firing and, at the same time, out of the corner of his eye, he saw Puck dashing behind Tim and pulling something out of his pocket. A second later, as Tim completed his turn, he found himself facing Puck, and Puck, his arm outstretched, was holding a small knife with a black handle. Puck pointed the blade at Tim's throat. Tim turned back the other way. He put his arm around Kitty and Kitty pressed against his side.

Rody released the catch and the bayonet flicked forward. Rody pointed with the bayonet at the sack on the road.

"Pick it up," said Rody.

305

Tim bent down and picked up the sack.

The wheels of a cart rumbled in the distance. Puck glanced over his shoulder. Civilians, not peelers, as far as he could see.

"Walk," said Puck. "Back the way you came."

The four began to walk. Tim and Kitty went first. Rody and Puck followed behind. The cart Puck had seen came up from behind and drew level. Puck looked up at the driver and waved his knife. The driver shook the reins and hurried away.

They reached the wood where Rody had earlier reloaded.

"Go in," ordered Puck.

Tim and Kitty began to climb the small bank that separated the road from the trees. Because they were both in new shoes they slipped on the grass. Puck took Kitty's arm and helped her over. Tim sat on the bank and swung his legs across.

It was darker inside the copse than on the road. There were crows in the trees, cawing and flapping their wings. The ground was strewn with leaves and beech-nuts and fallen branches. As she made her way with Tim towards the middle of the trees, it seemed to Kitty that the four of them were making a tremendous racket, scuffing up leaves and breaking twigs underfoot. The crows heard the noise. They rose into the air in a great angry flock, circled around the trees – Kitty distinctly heard their wings beating through the air – and then flew away.

They came to the middle of the copse.

"Stop here," said Puck.

They stopped and turned. Kitty saw Rody with the blunderbuss and Puck with the knife. The muzzle, she saw, was a bright, round O. It was brassy gold. But at the other end of the barrel, where it narrowed, there in the darkness, lay powder and shot.

She stared at the two men. The man with the gun had a strong wiry body. His skin was poor, his cheeks were pock-marked. His eyes were very grey. He did not blink. The other man was smaller. His face was round and his eyes were round in the middle of his face. This man blinked. She felt more fearful of the one with the knife than the one with the gun.

These were the ones who were going after Mr French. They seemed rather ordinary, now they stood before her, which surprised her. They were just men. But they were men with a gun and a knife, while she and Tim had nothing.

There was silence. Why did no one speak? Why didn't Tim say something? Why didn't these ones say something? Why did they just stare? They were angry with Tim. She knew that. He'd run. They didn't tolerate running. But Tim hadn't informed. He had that in his favour. He'd had no contact with the police. When the speaking started, she would have to make that clear. Surely that would count for something. Or quite a lot. Tim had only run. Nothing else. To be with her. She was to have a baby. They were to marry. It wasn't such a terrible thing that they were doing, was it? It wasn't informing. Tim hadn't reported these ones to the peelers. They could go after Mr French, while Tim went with her. Once everything was explained, this could be straightened out. She was certain of it.

From the road came the murmur of two men talking as they walked by. Kitty wanted to cry out to them. Suddenly she wasn't so certain this could be straightened out. Except what good would it do to call out? Once the men on the road saw the blunderbuss and the knife, they would know this was business that did not concern them and they would go away. The driver of the cart that had passed them earlier on the road, he had done exactly that, hadn't he?

She felt her drawers were damp and cold between her legs. She had wet herself at some earlier point, she realised, but it was only now that she had noticed. Then she had a quite unexpected thought. Her body already knew the worst was coming; it was just that her mind didn't know this yet.

"I'll go," said Puck, mysteriously.

He put the knife in his pocket and left the wood.

Oliver Brennan, a farrier from Shercock, and his teenage sons, Dominic and Jonathan, drove slowly out of Crookedstone and along the road towards Beatonboro'. They carried a load of coal for Oliver's forge and because of the weight of the load they went slowly.

The road was filled with pedestrians and carts heading in the opposite direction. Oliver called out to those he met and they called back to them. Everyone he met that morning was in a good mood but his sons were silent. They had wanted to stay at the fair but he had said no. They had picked up the coal in Newry that morning, and now they must get home. Oliver Brennan could not allow the forge to stand idle for a whole day.

Oliver noticed something lying on the road ahead. Dominic noticed as well and pointed. His eldest son had a long white face with a tiny mouth in the middle, and thick black hair, which hung down in heavy curls.

"Someone's already had a good time at the fair," said his other son, Jonathan.

Oliver went, "Tut, tut." Oliver never touched drink. He had taken the pledge. His sons would not take the pledge. He suspected they took sly drinks behind his back. At fourteen and sixteen, he could only just still control them, and he knew that this would not last for much longer.

The cart drew closer. The body was on its back. It was a man, quite a big fellow, bald. The road was stained along one side of the body. The drunk was lying in his own sick, Oliver decided. Well, he would slow down and let his sons have a good look. They should see how men who were drunk disgraced themselves in public. The sight might help to concentrate their minds on temperance.

They were quite close now. It struck Oliver that the long black coat worn by the drunk looked decidedly ecclesiastical. Then he saw that the stain on the ground wasn't sick. It wasn't a mixture of brown beer and carrots and peas and cabbage, which was what every drunk he had ever seen always seemed to throw up; the stain was blood, and there was a great gaping wound in the man's chest.

He pulled on the reins and the brake and jumped down, his sons following. He looked at the body. There was a horrible wound on the throat. The man's eyes were open. Oliver saw him blink. Then he saw the chest of the wounded man rise and fall, almost imperceptibly.

"He's alive," Oliver exclaimed.

They flattened the coal down in the back of the cart, and then lifted Mr Barrett into the back on a plank.

"Crookedstone," said Oliver.

While his sons sat on the coal, held the body and stopped it rolling off, Oliver drove the car as fast as he could along the road. He heard the man groaning and he was aware of precious lumps of his coal flying over the side of the cart every time he went over a bump.

When he came into Crookedstone, Oliver saw all the shops were shut. Everyone had closed up and gone to the fair, he presumed. Only the Imperial Hotel was open. It was really a public house with a few rooms upstairs, but it would have to do.

Oliver and his sons carried the body on the plank into the bar. There were three men sitting on barrels around a fire and drinking porter. Oliver looked around. He expected to see tables and benches but the room was empty.

The three men, one of whom was the publican, got up and came over. The publican saw that Oliver did not know what to do with the injured man who was dripping blood on to the floor.

"You'd better put him on the bar," said the publican, pointing to the crude wooden counter, at the other end of the room.

As they went down, Barrett began to mumble. "Two," he whispered suddenly. "Blunderbuss. Men. Two."

"Will one of yous run down and fetch a peeler?" the publican called over to his drinking friends.

The three figures in the copse stood quite still and did not move. The crows returned. Kitty heard the scrape of their claws, the creak of their wings as they beat them through the air, the plop of their droppings as they hit the ground.

A long time passed. Then she heard footfalls. These came

not from the road but from the field behind the copse. The approaching figures came into the wood. The crows took off with a great deal of angry cawing and started to circle overhead again.

Puck appeared first, followed by four others. These others wore shifts decorated with ribbons and flour sacks over their heads. There were holes cut for eyes in the flour sacks. Kitty saw the ends of their trousers and their heavy working boots showing at the bottom of the shifts.

She and Tim were caught, she thought. Now it was time – what? – to be punished? To die? That was why these figures had come. It was time to die.

Then she remembered her baby. She tried to imagine what would happen if she threw herself on her knees and begged to be spared in order that the child would live? She heard Puck and the figures in the shifts moving closer, crashing through the undergrowth.

The figures formed a circle around herself and Tim. On the road, a child laughed.

"Sack," said a figure in a pointy hat.

"Sack," said Puck.

Tim threw the sack. It dropped at Puck's feet. Puck pulled out his knife and cut the drawstring. Then he tipped the sack and the contents poured out: two tin plates, two tin mugs, and two knives, forks and spoons tied together with string; a shirt; a woman's petticoat; a knitted tea cosy; a wooden tea caddy; a St Bridget's cross; a box of buttons, thread and needles; a map of Ireland with a picture of Hibernia playing the harp, Cupids above looking down from the clouds; two sheets and two pillow cases tied up with string, sprigs of lavender slipped under the string to scent the linen; a prayer book; a pen with a steel nib and a bottle of ink, the cork in the top sealed with a vein of red sealing wax; an illustration of Beatonboro' main street and three sentimental songs printed on heavy yellow paper, one of them called, "Oh, Carry Me Back to Lovely Beatonboro' "; a handkerchief with a rose embroidered in the corner; the horse-shoe that once hung on the door of the

McKennas' dairy; and two squares of folded paper with writing on them.

Puck bent down and unfolded the papers. He still held the knife in his right hand.

Kitty shook. Tim said, "Let me explain."

"Don't speak," said Rody. The raucous cry of a magpie drifted from above.

Puck stood up and showed the papers to Tim. "What's this?"

"Two sailing tickets for New York," whispered Tim.

"Return?"

"Single."

"Two sailing tickets for New York, one bloody way."

Puck showed Rody the tickets.

"Two sailing tickets for New York, one bloody way," repeated Puck. He spiked the tickets on to the end of the bayonet. "What was the oath?" he shouted.

There was silence and then one of the figures in a pointy hat spoke up: " 'I swear to attend when called upon; to observe the Ribbon laws; to cut or slaughter or hang or bury as directed; to keep our ways secret.' "

"How will you do any of this in New York, Tim?" asked Puck.

On the road, a farmer passed by. He drove a cow, and he urged it on in a low and serious voice. Kitty saw man and beast through the trees. She saw the farmer hit the animal on the haunches with an ash stick, and she heard the noise of the wood as it struck the pelvis of the beast. It was a flat sound that came out; it was always a flat sound because the body of a cow was so solid.

"Eat them," said the figure in the pointy hat, the one who had spoken before.

Rody stepped over to Tim and offered him the tickets. Tim reached forward. His hand shook. As he pulled away the tickets, Kitty heard the scrape of the paper along the blade.

"Eat them," ordered Rody.

Again Kitty wondered – What if she knelt on the ground?

What if she begged them to spare her child? She tried to imagine these figures saying yes but that was impossible.

At her side she heard Tim tear the tickets in two, in four, in eight.

She had the strangest sense that the ones in the pointy hats and shifts were something else other than men.

She heard Tim's mouth open. She heard him pass a strip of paper into his mouth. She heard his jaw move. She heard his teeth as he chewed. He chewed for a long time. Finally, she heard Tim swallow. The first strip of paper was gone. A second piece went into Tim's mouth.

These men had Tim and her, in a wood, near a road, with people passing on their way to the fair in Crossmaglen. She could glimpse the people passing by through the trees. She could hear their laughter and their talk. And the passers-by could glimpse the man with the blunderbuss and the other man with the knife and the four men in the pointy hats, and Tim and herself. They could see it all, if they wanted to. But would they come into the wood? Oh, no. They would get a glimpse and hurry on. They would know this was business that did not concern them. They would not involve themselves. Not even tell the peelers. She knew all this, and she knew that if it were her on the road, looking in, she would probably hurry on by as well.

Her thoughts skewed in a new direction. In a moment they were going to die. Or were they? If they were to die, wouldn't these ones have got on with that straight away, if that was their intention? But they hadn't. Instead, they were making Tim eat the tickets. Wasn't that a hopeful sign? She thought so. More like, these ones had settled on some less drastic punishment. After Tim had the tickets eaten, they would cut off their ears, or break their fingers, or shave their heads. Stood to reason. After all, what had Tim really done? Nothing so terrible. He hadn't informed. He hadn't taken land. He hadn't gone against the rule and the law. He'd run away, that's all, which surely wasn't that serious?

Tim coughed at her side and swallowed with terrible

difficulty. She wanted to take his hand but she dared not. These ones would mock the slightest sign of tenderness. Besides, she must avoid any movement that drew attention to herself. Or Tim. She must stay still. Absolutely frozen.

Tim would eat the ticket and then these ones would beat them, or shave them, or cut them, or do whatever they intended. Then they would go. They would struggle on to the road, she and Tim, and find some helpful pedestrian, and send word home.

Then her father would come with blankets and straw in the back of his cart. Her father would take them home. Her mother would nurse their bruises. The bone-setter would straighten their bones. The surgeon would sew up their wounds. They would recover. They would go back to kind Mr French. They would get more money. They would buy new tickets. They would leave again and go away to America and never come back to this place where the people loved nothing better than to hurt their own people.

"Why did you think you could leave without my permission, Tim? Didn't you think about that?"

It was the same muffled voice that had spoken already. It was hard to say how old the speaker was. Older than she. But his accent was unmistakable. His accent was her accent. It was a neighbour of some description. But how could this neighbour harm his neighbour? It was a mystery.

She noticed that each of the men in pointy hats carried a stick. She hadn't noticed this before. Yes, they were going to beat herself and Tim. Yes, that was what these ones did to those who annoyed them. And they had annoyed them, hadn't they, she and Tim? Oh, yes. Annoyed them by running. And now she and Tim would have to stand and take their beating.

"You could have come to us and told us you wanted to be off to America and we might have said yes," said Pointy Hat. "Or we might have said no – or I don't know what we might have said. Or we might have sent you to America, with our blessing, to do our work out there. But you didn't think about any of that. You thought only about yourself. Which is typical.

That's all you're capable of, isn't it? Thinking of yourself. Disgusting. You swan about with us for a few months, and then you meet this woman whom you knew from before, and you think, I'll go away to America with her. But we won't have that. We've been watching you. Watching your every move. Biding our time. We waited for today, the day you thought you were leaving. Our unit picked you up. As they were told to do. They brought you here. As they were told to do. And now you and her will be punished."

Kitty looked at the gun. She looked at the black-handled knife. She looked at the sticks. They were all three foot long, and knobbly. It was a beating. They'd already decided. That's what they'd come to do. That's why they had the sticks.

She thought about her teeth. She ran her tongue over the front of her top row. They were lovely, strong and white. When she smiled, she always opened her mouth wide and showed her teeth. Her teeth were lovely. Her mother and father always said so. Her parents had lost most of theirs but she had kept most of hers. And they filled her mouth, and they were good and white and clean.

What she feared now was that she would lose them. They would knock them out at the front and the side. They would leave her with bare naked gums. If she smiled the gums would show. If she closed her mouth, her chin would come forward, as lower and upper gum came together. Tim would not want to kiss her once she had no teeth. He would leave her, he would refuse to marry her.

The one with the knife came forward. He clamped the handle of the knife between his teeth and pulled the strings of the bonnet under her chin. The bow came undone. He gently pulled off her bonnet and threw it on the ground. What was this? Of course. They were going to cut off her hair. Better that than a beating. Oh, yes. She could spend a couple of years hidden under a bonnet. During that time her hair would grow. Then her hair would be back. Good as ever. A lot better to lose her hair than her teeth.

★

Isaac stood amid the trees and regarded Tim and Kitty through the holes in the flour bag pulled over his head. The flour sack smelt of flour. Funny that. No matter how often they were washed, a flour sack always smelt of flour. It just never went away. It was a smell that got into the material.

There was perspiration above his lip. And he was hot under the shift as well. That was the trouble with these disguises. It might be a cold January day, but when you had the things on over your everyday, outdoor clothes, you got hot. Very hot. He wanted to take it off. Let Kitty see him. What did he care? She knew him, of course, by sight at any rate. He had been out to the McKenna cottage a couple of times. He had bought a couple of goats once from her father. And he had got some pups off the old man another time.

Now Turk, of course, Turk she knew much better. He lived a few fields behind the McKennas. They saved their hay together sometimes, old man McKenna and Turk. They cleaned their common ditches together. They felled trees together.

If Kitty knew it was Turk hidden under the flour sack, that would certainly give her a shock. And what would old man McKenna make of it? And his wife?

Well, old man McKenna was never going to know, was he? That was best. If no one knew their identity, it gave them the edge. It kept everyone guessing as to who was really in the Lodge.

He coughed. Goodness, he was warm. He'd already told Puck what to do. And good old Puck, he'd gone to work. Got her bonnet off already. Not that she knew what was coming. Nor did that bastard runaway of a lover of hers. That's how Isaac liked it. He was keeping them guessing.

Tim was still chewing. A good idea that one. Isaac hadn't planned it. The idea had just popped into his head after Puck searched the bag and found them. It was a nice little extra. Tim tried to run. Tim was caught. Tim had to eat the tickets. It was a punishment that befitted the crime.

But not *the* punishment. That was coming. But not yet. They would wait until the last scrap was swallowed. Rody, of course, had the better blade. He would have to do the business with Tim. Isaac had already agreed all this with Puck, only he hadn't told Rody yet. He'd just waited and watched while Tim ate the tickets.

But the tickets were almost eaten. The last part of the last strip was in Tim's mouth. And once it went down, it would be time to do it.

Isaac looked across at Kitty. She was bareheaded. Her expression was startled. She was a pleasant-looking girl. Nice red cheeks, and lovely strong teeth if he remembered rightly, only he couldn't see them now, of course, because her mouth was firmly shut. Frightened. No doubt lovesick, as well, and mad about the boy. No doubt.

And they both disgusted him. Absolutely disgusted him. They were weak, degenerate, corrupt. It was their sort who ruined everything. It was their sort who botched arrangements, babbled to the priests, and ran to the peelers with information.

He loathed them, hated them. Well, their time was up. A pity he couldn't make their end more long and drawn-out. Rubbish like these ones deserved all the suffering they got. But they couldn't. No point tormenting himself about it. They'd just have to administer the punishment as best they could and that was it. It would be the talk of Beatonboro' for years to come.

Might as well get on with it, then. Puck knew what to do. And the others. Only Rody needed to be told. He had the better blade for the business. The bayonet. Puck's little knife, as Puck said, when they discussed this as they walked over, it was too stubby. He'd never get it in far enough. It was really for slashing and cutting. To go in a long way, something long and thin was required. The bayonet on the blunderbuss was the perfect tool for the job.

Isaac tapped Rody on the shoulder. Rody brought his ear to Isaac's mouth, and keeping Tim and Kitty in view, he listened carefully to the instructions Isaac whispered in his ear.

Rody understood and took a step towards Tim. Alex and

Thady each took one of Tim's arms. They moved Tim backwards quickly. Kitty heard this but saw nothing. This was happening behind, and she must not turn around and look, she thought. Keep still. Keep invisible.

She heard a sigh. An exhalation of air. That was Tim, she guessed, slammed against a tree. Now they would tie him there and then they would start. With the sticks, the beating. They beat you standing up. That was the form. If the one getting the beating was on the ground, the men couldn't get the sticks in. That's why they tied you to something. They got a better swing that way.

Strange. She knew this. Always had. It came presumably from her father and her mother. Doubtless she had heard them, mother and father, fulminating about some poor boy tied to a cart or a fence to receive his beating. Yet she had no idea when she had heard. It wasn't like, say, her alphabet. Or her numbers. She remembered learning these, Mr Murray at the front of the classroom, she on a bench, forming the letter A or the figure one on the slate in her hand. But this terrible piece of knowledge about beatings, it had always just been there, inside her head. For as long as she could remember.

Never discussed, of course. No. Never. Her parents only ever whispered about these things between themselves, and they never talked to her about them. Beatings and their administration belonged with those other matters that were never discussed: exactly what a man and a woman did when they were alone in their bed; the monthly bleeding of a woman; childbirth.

A hand was at her throat. Behind the holes cut in the flour sack she saw brown eyes. But they were not tawny brown like most eyes that were brown. These were almost black. Familiar also. Where had she seen them before?

The man undid the top button of her coat. And then the second and the third. The coat was black, made of heavy wool, waterproof. She and her mother had bought it together, in Long's the draper's, in Monaghan. Why were they taking her coat away, she wondered, and on this cold day?

She stared back at the eyes as the fingers continued to work

317

their way down her front. Oh, yes. These eyes. She knew these eyes and she knew who they belonged to now. It was their neighbour, Turk, wasn't it? Turk. Yes, it was Turk. And now this Turk was slipping her coat off her shoulders and laying it on the ground. Why did he do this? Oh, yes. Now she knew what they were going to do. He was undoing the buttons down the side of the walking dress. They were going to take her clothes and tie her to the tree. Leave her there to freeze. This was what they did to the girls. Tied them up in the woods and left them. This was another of those grubby facts about punishment, which she'd always known, yet which she'd never heard discussed.

Her mouth was dry. She wondered if she'd made a mistake. Maybe it wasn't Turk. Maybe it wasn't their neighbour. But no, she hadn't made a mistake. Yes, it was definitely him. He had bought her butterscotch from Newry once, when she was twelve. She could still remember the taste of one of the sweet squares melting on her tongue.

He gave her a kitten at fourteen. Called him Napper, she did. Had him four weeks. Then a horse trod Napper to death in the lane. They buried Napper behind the byre, in a box. Loved Napper, she did.

When she was sixteen, this Turk he gave her a set of ribbons. From Belfast. They were red, blue, green, black, yellow and white. She had them still. They were rolled up tight inside her sewing box, which was lying there on the ground. And now he was taking her dress off. This same man. Her neighbour.

And yet, although he was, he also wasn't her neighbour, Turk, just as these weren't really men or people. In his hat and shift dress this Turk was something else. Like a mummer. Something more than human. A May Boy. But which one? The May Queen? No. The one that was called the Captain. The one who wore a dress. A proper dress. Not an inside-out shift thing like this one. No, not that one either. Perhaps this one who was undressing her was the Treasurer. Also called the Fool. Yes, that was closer to the mark. That's right. This one,

318

undoing one boot-lace and then the other, and now pulling off her boots, he was the one with the money-box. Yes. The Fool. The one who barged through the crowds shouting for silence, dressed in a cloak made of many-coloured shreds and patches of cloth, rags tacked on, a huge brimless hat pulled down over his head, a goatskin for a face, two red circles for eyes, two rows of sticks for teeth, a beard of goat fur below, and fastened at the back, a dried hare's skin for hair, a woman's long hair. Her boots came off. She felt the wet of the ground through her stockings.

Strawboys, straw hats, straw masks, poured blood down chimneys, rolled wedding guests in dung, drank all the whiskey, feared, detested, spoiled the bride's day and night, yet had to come, bless the bride and groom, no Strawboys, no children, no increase, no multiplication, nothing. Her bodice came away. Same story with the Wren Boys with their blacked-up faces and lisping rhymes, and the mummers, and the May Queen and her May Boys, all had to be pacified, indulged, otherwise disputes, fights, arguments, very bad luck, no children, no harvest, no growth, no prosperity, no nothing. It was they who ensured the earth went on turning, the rain went on falling, the potatoes went on growing. They ensured day followed night followed day followed night. And these ones here, in the pointy hats, they were the same? Were. Weren't. Were. They made the rivers flow, the sun shine, the leaves on the trees fall and grow, fall and grow. Her drawers were down and gone suddenly. She was naked. She put a hand in front of her breasts and another in front of her legs.

Something rumbled on the road. She looked across. A cart. A few children in the back. Young girls. Coal-scuttle bonnets. They glimpsed her as surely as she glimpsed them. She imagined their faces were pale. Now they stared but did not want to stare, their expressions a mixture of fascination and disgust. Like she had stared at things seen like this, when she did not want to stare but could not help herself.

"Who's that passing there?" The one who spoke was the one with the knife with the black handle. His face was uncovered. He had a round, pale face, and small round eyes. He looked younger than he actually was. That's what she guessed now, anyway. "I'm sure I know those girls," he continued.

"It's the Coyles, isn't it?" It was the man with the gun who was behind her. He was guarding Tim, she presumed. Kitty couldn't see him. "They must be going to Crossmaglen fair," continued the one with the gun from behind.

The one with the knife waved at the cart and said, "Are you sure it's the Coyles? My eyesight's really gone downhill recently," he added.

Then he continued, waving his knife around and speaking over his shoulder to the one with the gun, "No, it isn't. That's that grocer's merchant, the one with all the daughters, what do you call him? Who's next door to the shoe-makers in Beaton. I should know. That's where I got my shoes. God, I can see his shop front with his name as if it were right here in front of me. Oh, God, if I don't remember this I'll be awake all night."

"McManus!" she heard the one with the gun exclaim.

"McManus, that's right, McManus."

The cart went on and then the road was empty. She saw no people through the trees.

"There's a lot of traffic going to the fair," she heard the one with the gun say.

"They won't bother us." This was from the one in the pointy hat, the one who spoke earlier, the one who was angry at Tim. The flour sack moved around his mouth as he breathed in and out. He scratched his cheek through the material. Fine fingers, clean nails.

"On your back," said the one with the knife to her. "Lie down."

She squatted on the ground, hugging her knees. So that was what they were going to do. This was worse than being tied to the tree and left to freeze. Much worse.

"Thank God I remembered that name," said the one with the knife. She watched him take off his coat and hang it on a branch. "A little thing like that can drive me mad and keep me awake all night."

The pointy hat who was in charge said, "Go on," to the one with the gun.

Kitty heard what happened next as a terrible scrabble and an appalled cry. This was Alex and Thady pushing Tim back against an ancient beech and gripping his head tight. If she could have turned she would have seen Tim staring ahead, through the trees and up to the sky.

In his last couple of seconds what Tim remembered was the letter. Obviously, he realised, he had deliberately written the wrong name, Tench, on the envelope, although at the time he didn't know that he had. And why had he done this? Because he hadn't wanted French to die, of course. But he had sealed his fate, and Kitty's fate, when he wrote the wrong name, hadn't he? Because from that moment then to this moment now, there was a direct line of connection. He saw this clearly and he knew then that he was beyond the help of God. He had brought this on himself.

Rody put the point of the bayonet in Tim's right eye and pushed. The point of the bayonet went through the brain, passed out through the skull and buried itself in the tree behind. Rody had to use both hands to pull the bayonet out of the wood again.

A little after midday, Cleary received a message from the Crookedstone sub-station. Mr Barrett, the Cullaville minister, had been shot and stabbed, and left for dead on the road outside Crookedstone. He was now in the Imperial Hotel, in Crookedstone, still breathing. Apparently, Mr Barrett had been attacked by two men with a blunderbuss.

As soon as he heard the news, Cleary went straight down to the estate office. Could the assailants be the same men as had been pursuing Mr French? If Mr Barrett could describe them, it might be very helpful.

The three men hurried by car to the railway line and

stopped the up train to Dundalk. The train made an unscheduled stop on the bridge above Crookedstone, a little before two o'clock. Thomas, Micky and Constable Cleary jumped from their carriage, scrambled down the bank, and walked into the Imperial Hotel ten minutes later.

They found Mr Barrett was still alive but unconscious. They waited in the bar in case Mr Barrett. regained consciousness but he did not. He died around three o'clock. Thomas described to Micky meeting the dead man on the train on the foggy day he came to Beatonboro' to start work as the agent. Towards four o'clock, Micky and Thomas left Crookedstone in a car provided by the police.

About a mile out of town, Thomas noticed a small crowd on the road ahead. They were standing on the edge of a copse. They appeared to be looking over a grassy bank into trees on the other side. As the car drew closer, Thomas saw a man at the back of the crowd looking round. The man saw the car, then detached himself from the crowd and ran towards them waving his arms. The movements were disturbing, as were his desperate but incoherent cries, and Thomas knew at once that there was something awful waiting for them.

Cleary pulled on the reins and slowed the car.

"It never rains but it pours," he said.

"Your honours, your honours." Thomas heard him distinctly. The man came up and took hold of the side of the car. The man was unshaven, and his eyes were grey as far as Thomas was able to see in the fading light. He realised suddenly that the awful signs of his own physical anxiety had begun to show. His stomach had gone tight and hard, while at the same time it was trembling. His thighs above the knees were trembling too. When Thomas was filled with desire they trembled in exactly the same way.

The man from the crowd was still shouting, while a few more had detached themselves from the crowd and run forward, and were now walking backwards, like him, holding on to the side of the car and talking up at them. The car had very nearly reached the point of the bank on the other side of which lay the terror.

"They're in the wood," shouted the man with grey eyes.

Thomas wondered who the word "they" referred to. The constable, Cleary, pulled on the reins and called out something to the pony. The car stopped. The brake went on. Those holding the rim of the car stepped back. Those standing by the bank turned and fell silent.

Micky flipped open the door at the back of the car and jumped down on to the road. Thomas jumped after him and Cleary followed.

"What is it?" asked Cleary.

The crows cawed in the trees overhead. Nobody spoke. A woman with red hair lifted a single finger and pointed back over her shoulder.

"In there," she said. "You'd better see for yourselves."

The crowd parted before them, like a crowd in a dream, and there was the bank, grassy except for one spot where the earth showed through, an obvious sign that booted feet had recently climbed backwards and forwards over it, and beyond the bank towered the trees with their dark trunks, and beyond the trees stretched the sky, white shading to grey, the exact colour of woodsmoke.

Thomas scrambled over the bank. There was something in the distance, in the middle of the wood. A shape, no, worse, two separate shapes, rising from the ground. The shapes were covered over. With leaves, was it? Probably. But not completely covered. And through the leaves the human outline showed through. Those were bodies on the ground. Two of them. Unmistakable at twenty yards.

He trod forward. The sound of the leaves under his feet was brittle and rough.

Now he was only ten yards from the shapes, the details were emerging. There were the heads, there were the torsos, there were the feet. Now he was five yards away. He saw a hand and two bare white feet.

And now he had reached the figures. They were very still.

And he knew who it was, oh, yes, although the leaves and the branches covered the faces and the bodies. Today was the day they left the cottage. They were walking to Newry. Along this road most probably. Catching the train. To Belfast. Today was the day. The two feet were Kitty's feet. One stuck up, the other lolled sideways. Oh, yes. And where were her shoes? He looked around. Oh, yes, there they were. On the ground over there. What looked like her clothes too. His legs trembled. And a sack. And what was that near the sack? It was a teapot. He distinctly saw the spout and the handle. He looked at the feet again. He saw blue veins on the soft white soles. Bare ankles, bare calves. Something on the leaves. Slippery and dark. Worse was to come. No escaping it. Had to face it. Had to. Had to. No point putting it off. None.

He heard his legs creaking as he folded down on to his haunches. Micky and Cleary on the other side, still standing. It couldn't be, he thought. Oh, yes, it is, the rooks cawed, oh, yes, it is. He reached forward and lifted away the branch that covered the head. Someone shouted from the crowd. An exhortation. Get on and get it over with. Until they knew who the dead were, there was always the possibility for everyone in the crowd that it was one of their loved ones. That was why the crowd wanted to know, and know now. But it wasn't one of theirs. Was it? No. Because he knew who it was, didn't he?

Thomas reached forward and began to clear the leaves from the chin, and around the mouth, and then the nose. He saw a mouth that was closed very tight, and the end of a nose that was blue. He saw there was blood on the skin between the nose and the mouth. And he knew who it was. It was Kitty. There was no point in going any further, was there? It was her? Unmistakably her. No point going any further.

Cleary and Micky, he saw, had lowered themselves on to their haunches. They faced him across the bodies. Cleary was reaching forward. He would do it, wouldn't he? Cleary took the branch from the other body, threw it behind. He swept the leaves away. Thomas saw Tim's mouth. The rest of the face was all blood. Two holes for eyes. Cleary reached over, repeated the action on Kitty. Once again, holes for eyes. Hair matted. Blood everywhere. It was her and somehow not her as well. Thomas touched the chin. Kitty was cold. Someone groaned in the crowd. He stood.

Thomas took off his coat and laid it over Kitty. The long black coat only reached as far as her ankles.

Another shout. This one was terrible. Now the crowd understood. Two dead. No more argument about it.

Micky took off his coat. He noticed the blood on the leaves around the bodies. It was red yet very dark. When a bottle of red wine was left open for a couple of days, the last glass went this colour, red but with black in it. Micky laid his coat over Tim.

"A bad business," he said.

"Yes," Thomas said. He noticed Kitty's feet sticking out from under the hem of his coat. One of her feet was pointing in the air, while the other flopped sideways. That wouldn't do, would it?

Now Micky watched as Thomas tenderly straightened Kitty's lolling foot, and got it pointing straight up like the other.

Thomas's face was white, and the skin was tight over the bones underneath; Thomas looked to Micky as if he had just at that moment shrunk to about three-quarters of his usual size. Death had that way of making the living smaller.

The policeman, Cleary, was scribbling in his notebook. Micky heard the pencil scratching on paper. The wind sighed in the branches overhead.

Thomas was staring at the shapes while Micky, in turn, was looking at Thomas's face. There was disgust and dismay there, of course. Micky knew the same feelings were probably there to be read on his own face. But there was also something else as well.

Over the last few days Thomas had been in better form than he'd been for ages. Micky had teased him and called it love but it wasn't. Kitty hadn't turned his head. Thomas was beyond that sort of behaviour. But Thomas had liked her enormously, enjoyed her presence, her liveliness, her vivacity. He'd even liked Tim in the end. And he had liked what he had done for them both, was delighted with himself for having suspended the warrant, for giving them clothes, for buying their tickets to New York. Helping the young couple had brought Thomas to life, no doubt partly because it was so different from the run-of-the-mill estate work, the daily grind, and partly because the young couple, and Kitty especially, had been so grateful. Thomas was usually a figure to whom people came to complain; how wonderful, therefore, to be the recipient for once of real heartfelt gratitude.

But now, all that Thomas had achieved with these two had been thrown down and trampled in the mud. The couple had been caught on the road, on the very day they were walking to the boat, to freedom, to a new life in America. Kitty'd been stripped and God knows what else had been done to her; in Micky's mind it was surely the worst that could be done to a woman, and then her eyes had been put out, and Tim had been butchered along with her.

So the dismal expression on the agent's face, that was no surprise, was it? Of course not. It wasn't just that he was appalled to find two people who'd been dispatched so cruelly. What Micky was seeing now was that baffled look of misery that mourners showed when they were burying their own children or their spouses or close family members. Because in that last few days, that's what they'd become, hadn't they? Family, or at least people about whom Thomas felt something not dissimilar from what he felt for his own children and his own wife. Tim and Kitty were weaker than Thomas was, but he'd looked after them and in the process of doing that he'd come to care about them intensely, Kitty especially. It was the closeness he felt to them that was the cause of the extra pain that now showed on his face.

As he stood watching Thomas, Micky saw all of this with great clarity and he saw these deaths were going to go very hard with the agent.

Cleary closed his notebook.

"Better go back to Crookedstone," said Cleary. "Tell them about this. Get some help. Shall we go?"

"I think we'll stay," said Micky quickly. "Won't we?"

He glanced at Thomas. He was right. The agent didn't want to leave any more than if the bodies were those of his sons or his own wife.

"All right," Cleary agreed.

The three men walked back to the road. They found the crowd standing in silence on the other side of the bank.

"Do you know them?" asked a voice.

"We do," said Cleary. "From Beatonboro'; Traynor and McKenna."

"Who'd do such a thing?" said another voice.

There were fifteen or twenty of them. Micky saw the women had their shawls pulled tightly around their shoulders, as much for comfort as to keep out the cold.

"Who found them?" asked Cleary.

"My son, sir."

A woman came forward with a young boy. He was eight or nine years old.

"He was running along in front of me," she explained. "He asked to go in the wood for a stick. I said yes. Then he bolted back over the bank with a terrible look on his face. He told me there was two people on the ground in there. I stopped a party of men and I asked them to go in, and they came back and they told me that my son was right. But they wouldn't look. They didn't want to. Then you came along."

"All right," said Cleary to the woman. "I'll take you and your son back to the police station in Crookedstone. Everyone else, go home, go on your way."

The people began to move off along the road. Cleary opened the door of the car and helped the boy and his mother to climb up.

"You really don't want to come? I'm sure we could all fit," said the policeman to Thomas.

"We'll wait," said Micky.

Cleary closed the car door. He took up the reins and set off along the road at a fast trot.

The car disappeared into the gloom. There was a short period of quiet and then there were footsteps and the low growl of male laughter. Micky looked up from his place on the bank where he was sitting. In the fading light he couldn't tell at first who was coming along the road towards them. It was only when they were really quite close that he saw who it was – Isaac Marron, Thady Burns, Alex Ward and Turk McEneaney, as well as two other men that Micky couldn't remember seeing before although there was something about their faces that did seem vaguely familiar. Perhaps he'd passed them on a road. He couldn't remember.

"Good evening, Mr French," called Isaac brightly.

Thomas stared at the ground. He did not look up.

"Well then, Mr Laffin," continued Isaac, in the same cheerful way. If the agent wouldn't talk to him then it would have to be the bailiff.

"What are you doing here?" demanded Micky angrily. Isaac and the others were intruding into their private grief. He wanted them to be on their way. He wanted silence for Thomas.

"Walking the roads," said Isaac. "That's not against the law, you know that, Micky."

"We're coming from the fair," Turk explained, in his best diplomatic manner. He was a bulky man with curly hair and staring eyes. He had trained himself never to blink in situations like this. With his eyes so dark and impenetrable, he believed this unblinking stare made him look less shifty, more trustworthy.

"That was bad news about Mr Barrett," said Alex.

"Oh, shocking," Thady agreed.

"What do you know about Mr Barrett?" asked Micky.

"He died in the public saloon in the Imperial Hotel some hours ago," said Thady.

"We heard the news coming along on the road," said Turk quickly. He spoke in the same diplomatic voice as before.

"Bad business that," agreed Alex.

Isaac looked over the bank and into the copse.

"And I heard it happened only a bit further down," said Isaac.

"What happened a bit further down?" said Micky.

"Mr Barrett was shot, a bit further down," said Isaac pedantically.

"Who says so? Your friends here, these two?" Micky pointed at the two strangers, one with pock-marked cheeks, the other, who was smaller, with round close-set eyes.

"No, the people said," interrupted Turk, quickly. "The people on the road. They saw this terrible deed and they were so frightened and they wanted to help and they didn't dare."

A cart came by. The driver sang, "Tour-a-lour-a-lou, tour-a-lour-a-lay." The cart went on.

"It's very fortunate we've met today," said Isaac. He added, "Sir," and the agent looked up from the ground.

"Why's that?" asked Thomas grimly.

"I'm in the fair earlier," said Isaac, "walking around, and what do I see? A beautiful pair of gates which a tinker man has for sale. I measure them up and I'm thinking to myself, They'd do very fine, they're just what I need, and then I think, What am I doing? Wasn't I promised gates? Your honour, I'm still waiting for my gates, but I know you won't forget me. Am'n't I right?"

"Gates?" said Thomas, grumpily. He wanted to sit in silence with his back to the copse and wait while night fell around him.

"On your very first day in Beatonboro'," Isaac went on, "we stood in your office and your bailiff said they were coming."

"Really?" Thomas wanted this man to go away and take his friends with him.

"And I was up this morning again, enquiring."

"Were you?" Thomas wanted to watch the landscape in front of him gradually slide into darkness. "My mind is elsewhere," he said. Thomas had not seen Isaac when he called that morning, just heard him, so it was easy therefore to feign ignorance now.

He saw Isaac raise his head and peer over the bank into the trees, as if considering what to say next. Then Thomas saw Isaac's face change and a look of alarm and anxiety start to show.

"Oh, my God!" he heard Isaac shout. "What's that?"

He was aware of movement as Isaac leaped up on to the bank and then jumped down on the far side. The other men, those three he knew and the two strangers, jumped up after Isaac. They were sprightly and powerful and agile and indecently hasty.

Thomas heard boots crash behind on the ground as the men jumped down.

"Don't go in," he shouted, but the men were already gone, rushing after Isaac towards the middle of the trees, where the bodies lay. Thomas looked over his shoulder and saw Isaac sweep away the leaves that covered Kitty's face. The white soles of her feet also showed clearly: they stuck up out of the leaves.

Each of the strangers said something. Thomas couldn't make it out: it sounded like an expression of despair. Then Isaac and the others formed a circle around the two bodies. Hands moved from face to chest, and from shoulder to shoulder, as each man blessed himself. There were snatches of prayer. Then the wood went quiet and each man stood with his head bowed. Every time Thomas had ever seen anyone in the presence of the dead, they stood in exactly the same way, just like this. Even children.

A pause. In the trees above Thomas heard the rooks caw, their call harsh and raw. Thomas turned and faced forward again.

Only a minute or so had passed, yet already, with the light fading fast, there was so much less to see. The hedgerows in the distance had merged into a composite hedgerow shape. The grass in the fields had lost its green and gone grey. The sheep in the fields had turned from white to dun. They reminded him of wood-lice.

"What was I doing talking about my gates?" he heard Isaac calling from behind.

Isaac slowly scaled the bank beside him and clambered down. Isaac's movements were subdued, like those of a weary man. His energy was gone. It was the same with the others who climbed slowly after him. They were tired and crushed. The men formed a sad huddle behind Isaac.

"The Lord have mercy on their souls," said Isaac, nodding back towards the bodies.

Heads shook and exclamations of disgust filled the air around Thomas.

"I hope so," said Thomas.

"He saw." This was spoken by Micky.

Micky pointed up at the sky.

"So, I see," said Isaac. "That's why He weeps."

Thomas saw the two men staring at one another. Isaac's expression was curious and watchful; Micky's expression was murderous and hateful. They reminded him of children, struggling to out-stare each other. It was Isaac who broke in the end.

"Good evening," he said, shaking his head sorrowfully.

Isaac turned and began to walk off. The others followed.

"Bastard," Micky shouted after him. Isaac was half a dozen paces away and he stopped to show he had heard. The others stopped as well. Thomas expected Isaac would now turn round and come back and an argument would start. The wood was still. But Isaac did not turn around. He started to walk on again. The other men walked after him. The group walked slowly, like men who were in no hurry. Thomas looked at Isaac's back and at the backs of the other men. He stared after them until they were swallowed up by the darkness.

"He didn't mean one word of what he said," said Micky firmly. "Everything we saw just now was pure pantomime."

"Probably," Thomas agreed mechanically but his mind was elsewhere. He hurt inside. His throat was sore. He was tender in his middle, as if he was bruised. He remembered these sensations from childhood. He always felt like this before he had to go back to school. Grief was not only a state of mind, it was physical; one felt it.

It was a big heavy feeling and it filled him up. He felt bloated, as if he had eaten too much. He wanted to lie down. He wanted to close his eyes. He wanted silence. He wanted no talking.

"He came here to gloat," he heard Micky saying.

"Yes," he agreed with Micky. It was all fake. Isaac was up to his neck in it. But Thomas couldn't think about that now. Anger, action against the culprits, retribution – all of this was impossible. The loss was so huge, it left no room for anything else. All that mattered now was the grief; all he could do, all he wanted to do, was to sit with it, and everything else would have to wait.

Down the road, Isaac came to a decision.

"I think it's time for Micky Laffin to go to the great place in the sky," he said. "And this time no notices on the chapel door."

It was later that same evening. The car pulled up in the yard of the agent's house and Micky opened the door at the back. Thomas got down and began to walk towards the back door. Micky called out something, which Thomas ignored. He felt as if he had not slept for days. It required all his willpower to move one foot in front of the other.

He reached the back door. Now it took all his strength, first to push the handle down, then to push the door back. Thomas wanted to collapse, there and then, on the mat, but he must keep going. He must get through the kitchen, and across the hall, up the stairs and into his bedroom. He saw his bed with his inner eye, with its polished wooden headboard, the bolster and pillows piled in front of it, the eiderdown, the blankets, the top sheet turned back over the blankets. He imagined he was beside the bed, dragging the covers back, and then tumbling forward on to the cold, white sheet.

Maggie was at the table in the middle of the kitchen. She was turning scones. She looked up. "Good evening!" she called. Then her expression changed. He knew at once that she had seen his face by the light of the lamp over the table and that his expression must be terrible. He raised an arm and waved. He was too tired. No speaking. Maggie bit her lip.

He staggered along the back hall, passed through the connecting door and into the front hall. Candle lamp burning on the table, candles guttering in the candelabra at the top of the stairs. He could carry the candle lamp up with him. No, too much effort.

He heard the sound of rustling skirts and hurrying feet. Helena darted from the front room, the big parlour. She was smiling; then she saw his face and her smile vanished.

She asked him what the matter was. Everything went quiet. Everyone and everything on earth was frozen at that instant except for him. This was to give him time to think. Then he knew that the only way was to deliver the facts. The world began to turn again.

Mr Barrett, he said, shot and stabbed that morning, taken to the Imperial Hotel, had died in the afternoon while stretched on the bar.

But it didn't end there, he continued, in a cold fury. Tim and Kitty, the ones he'd helped. Helena nodded. They'd been caught on the road to Crossmaglen, near where Barrett was attacked, wearing the clothes Thomas had given them, carrying the tickets Thomas had given them. On their way to catch the boat to America from Belfast they were, which now they'd never make. Taken into a wood. Kitty stripped, raped, he assumed, as well. Both of them stabbed, in the eyes, all over, and now very, very dead. What was more, Kitty was going to have a child. And the infant was going to be named after him, Thomas, if it was a boy. That was it. Nothing more to report. Now he would go to his bed, he said, his soft, safe bed, and he would fall asleep, and for a few hours he would escape what he knew. He would be oblivious to it all.

Thomas turned and put his hand out for the banister. He grasped the wood. He began to drag himself up the stairs. Helena followed behind. She was asking him questions. He shook his head and waved a hand. No talk. Bed, only bed, he said. If he could only get up the stairs and open the door, pull back the covers and sink on to the mattress.

He felt Helena taking his arm. She was helping him to climb the stairs. That was good. The flames of the candles on the landing were waving at him. And now, miracle of miracles, they were standing in front of his bedroom door and Helena was turning the handle. The door swung open, and there, lit by the fire burning in the grate, he saw the distinct outline of his bed.

He threw his coat and his holsters on the ground. Helena pulled the covers back and he tumbled forward, face down. The pillowcase smelt of hair and skin. Helena was unlacing a boot. She pulled it off. She unlaced the other and pulled it off. He rooted with his feet and found the space between the covers. Helena pulled the covers forward and a second later he felt their lovely weight all over his body.

His mind was empty and utterly still. The fatigue he felt was so vast, he imagined that he might now fall asleep and never wake up again. He would just close his eyes and drift off, for ever and ever . . .

Helena bent forward and put her mouth against the back of his neck. She heard his even breathing. Thomas was already asleep, she realised.

chapter fourteen

The first thing Cleary did the next morning was to write a letter about the events of the previous day to District Inspector Love in Monaghan, as was required by the *Standing Rules and Regulations*.

When he finished, Cleary sealed the letter in an envelope, wrote 'C' in the top left-hand corner, and arranged with the orderly for the letter to be sent on to Monaghan.

At ten o'clock, not long after Cleary had finished the letter, a man called Charlie Mohan walked into the Beatonboro' police station. Mohan looked sixty but was in fact forty-two. The skin on his face was brown and coarse with deep wrinkles in it. He had once been a small farmer up in the north of the county near Glaslough. He had lost his wife and three children in the Famine seven years earlier. Then he had lost his property. He had taken to the roads. He had walked them ever since, except for two short periods when he was in prison for drunken and disorderly behaviour.

"I saw who did Mr Barrett," said Charlie Mohan to Constable Cleary, who was sitting in his usual place on the stool behind the day-room counter.

Cleary stared back at the man on the other side of the counter. Charlie Mohan appeared sober and he looked relatively clean. His gaze was steady.

Perhaps he did see something, thought Cleary. It was worth listening, at least.

What Cleary could not know was that Mohan had spent the previous night drinking *poítin* in a shebeen. He had fallen asleep in the corner, talk of the three murders – and it was detailed talk – swirling around him, and in his dreams that followed, the truth had been revealed to him.

Charlie had woken at dawn, filled with a certainty and purposefulness he had not known for years, not since he was sober and he had his farm and his children and his wife. Charlie had stumbled outside and washed himself from head to toe in a freezing mountain stream. Then he had come straight to this place, the barracks, and now he was ready to say his piece to the policeman behind the desk. After years of despair, it was wonderful to feel useful at last.

"It was four boys in black," he said, "driving a cart with blue wheels."

Cleary told him to continue. Mohan explained that the day before he was on the road between Cullaville and Crookedstone, heading for the fair at Crossmaglen, when the call of nature obliged him to go into a field. This was true. He had been on the road and he had gone behind the hedge at one point.

While he squatted on the ground, Charlie continued, he heard shouting on the road. He turned and peered over.

On the other side, he saw four men in black. They had seized Mr Barrett and were attempting to manhandle him into the back of their cart. They were kidnappers. Mr Barrett resisted. A gun with a bayonet was produced. Mr Barrett was shot and stabbed. The four assailants then sped away, southwards, in their cart with blue wheels; Mohan hadn't seen the young couple but surely it was too much of a coincidence that there were two separate attacks on the same road at almost the same time. Surely, after Barrett, the men in black killed the young folk.

Mohan described the four assailants in considerable detail. He was also very clear about the cart – although unfortunately, being illiterate, Charlie hadn't been able to read the name that he said had been painted on the side – and the precision of Charlie's descriptions inclined Cleary to believe the fellow was telling the truth. As did Mohan's clean appearance and the fact he did not smell of drink.

The police were now in search of a cart with blue wheels driven by four young men who wore black. A few hours after Mohan gave his statement, a sub-constable met a cart with blue wheels driven by four men in black. They were brothers called Lamb, all of them extremely pious members of a Protestant sect, and they lived on the Castleblaney road.

At dawn, the next day, the police swooped on the Lamb house and the four brothers were arrested. "Why are you taking us?" they shouted, and the arresting sub-constable told them. "But we were in Enniskellen on fair day. We have witnesses," they shouted. Their protests were ignored and the four brothers were taken to Monaghan prison. Mohan, who had spent the previous night in the barracks rather than a ditch, was also taken to the prison. An identity parade was organised with some haste. All those in the line-up were prisoners wearing prison clothes, except for the Lamb brothers, who wore their own clothes. Mohan picked the Lamb brothers out of the line-up. They were the ones responsible for Mr Barrett's murder, he said.

Micky came with the car after lunch. We would all drive to the chapel together. We got into the car and drove off. The sky was pale and blue with thin patches of cloud, like gauze, laid over it.

We bowled along the little lanes in silence and arrived at St Patrick's chapel, beside Micky's cottage. The P P, Father

Smyth, had decided to hold the funeral out here on the advice of the police, who feared scenes of public disorder. A detachment of policemen were lined up along the chapel wall, their carbines slung over their shoulders.

We got down from the car and went into the chapel. The coffins were at the end, on trestles. The wood was pine, very yellow, but good wood. It was Thomas who paid for them.

Mr and Mrs McKenna, Kitty's parents, came in presently, and the other mourners in the chapel fell silent. The mother was veiled in black, and her face was hidden, but I knew she was crying because I saw her hand going under the veil to wipe her eyes every now and then. Her husband was a big man who moved stiffly. He had a big square of flour sack in his pocket, and he kept pulling it out and blowing his nose on it.

Father Smyth appeared and the service started. I found it extremely difficult to hear what he was saying. He spoke very quickly. He seemed to want to get the service over with and leave as soon as possible.

After the service we had the interment in the graveyard. Everything gabbled again. Then it was over and we got back into the car and started for home. Cloud was sweeping in from the west, chasing after us. I felt a couple of raindrops on my face; very cold and heavy they were – the advance party of the coming storm. It came a few seconds later in the form of a great cloud, which hovered about a hundred feet above the ground and squirted rain down on us like an unruly child pelting strangers from the window of a nursery.

That evening, after dinner, we went into the drawing room where a good fire was burning. I watched Thomas's face, just as I had watched the rain; I watched it darken and twist, shrink and contort; I have never seen him like this.

He talked in a disconnected way of his exhaustion. He said that even the simplest act, climbing the stairs to our bedroom, for instance, required every ounce of his energy. To him, the stairs were a mountain. He spoke of Sisyphus, condemned for eternity to push a stone to the top of a hill and watch it roll down. He said he felt a great affinity with this figure.

Micky sat at home in front of his fire. Since the funerals of Kitty and Tim he had found it hard to sleep, and most nights now he sat up smoking and staring at the embers.

He curled his tongue and pushed smoke out of his mouth. A ring floated in front of his face. He watched it quiver as it rose towards the ceiling. He thought he heard a noise outside. Then he dismissed the idea. If someone was out there, the dogs in the kennel would bark, and they weren't barking.

But no. There was someone. On the other side of the back wall, he heard what sounded like pebbles clinking together. And there it was again. Someone was out there.

He put down his pipe and stood up very slowly. He reached two pistols from the mantelpiece and cocked them, one after another. He crept across the flagstones towards the back. There were no windows here, just the door. There was a faint knocking coming through the wood. It was a tentative noise. Like a child might make.

"Who is it?"

"Croker Flannagan." This explained why the dogs hadn't barked. They knew Croker.

Micky took off the wooden bar and stepped back.

"Open the door, Croker."

The latch rose and the door swung forward. He saw Croker's familiar bulk in the darkness outside.

"You're a bit early for Mass," said Micky. "The doors don't open until six tomorrow."

Micky let out the hammers on the pistols as Croker slunk in. The visitor wore a cloak and a hat pulled down to his eyebrows. There was something wrong with his appearance.

"You can hang your wet things there," said Micky. He pointed at the hook on the back of the door.

Croker appeared not to hear this. He went over to the bench and sat down.

Micky put the guns down, put the bar back in place, picked the guns up again, then followed the visitor over.

"You can take it off, you know, the hat," he said, and he put the guns down.

"No."

The tone was flat, neutral; no offence taken, it implied, but the cloak and hat stayed on.

Micky settled in his chair.

"Pipe?" Micky asked. He pointed at the rack of pipes and the tobacco tin.

"No."

Croker glowered from under the brim of his hat. This was the moment Micky realised what was wrong. Croker's hair normally hung down in heavy brown coils, but tonight there was no hair.

"What can I do for you?" Micky asked quietly, and Croker told his story.

One morning, a couple of weeks after the murders, Croker came out of his cabin to find a warning had been nailed to his door some time during the night. Neither Croker nor his brothers could read, so Croker took the letter to Father Smyth to be read. It was a warning from the Lodge. It told Croker to keep his animals off his neighbours' lands, and that if he didn't he would be dealt with.

The Brady family were behind the warning. Croker was certain of that. But he didn't scare easy. He made a particular point of calling at the house every day and speaking to any numbers of the family who were unfortunate enough to be around. Croker also went on putting his animals wherever he wanted to put them.

A few days passed. One night, a man came to his house. He was small, with a round face and round eyes. Croker didn't know this man, but he had a vague idea he might have seen him in Beatonboro'. The man gave his name as Lucky Sullivan. He explained that he came from Clones and that he was organising a bare-knuckle fight. Would Croker consider participating? The opponent was a Roscommon man called

Masher Magee. If Croker won, he'd take a guinea home, and if he lost it would be fifteen shillings.

"I'll be taking the guinea home, then," said Croker, and the two men shook hands to confirm the agreement.

The next Saturday night, at the agreed time, Croker presented himself at the venue, a pub outside Shercock. Croker had Horace, his younger brother, with him. He always took Horace to these events in case there was a problem with the purse. Lucky led the Flanagan brothers to the yard at the back of the pub, pointed out the room where the fight would take place, and then he showed the two men into a meal store. Lucky said Croker could leave his clothes in there. He asked the Flanagan brothers to wait, and promised to return in a few minutes.

Lucky went off. Croker stripped to the waist and began to perform a series of stretching exercises. There didn't seem to be much noise coming from the pub, which was unusual before a fight. Croker sent Horace over to inspect the back room where the fight was to take place. Several minutes passed, his brother did not return and he began to grow alarmed.

He was just leaving to follow his brother over, when Lucky Sullivan appeared at the door on the other side of the yard.

"We're waiting for you," Lucky Sullivan called.

"Where's my brother?"

"He's in here."

"Why didn't he come back?"

"Why do you think? He's having a drink. He doesn't have to work tonight."

At that moment, a roar of laughter came from inside the room. The sound reassured Croker. He would show himself to the crowd and snarl a few words at the other man, Masher Magee. Bets would be taken. Then a space would be cleared, a line would be drawn on the floor, and they would start. The thing then was to come out fast and hit hard, and then to keep hitting this Masher Magee until he went down. Croker had fought six or seven of these contests; he had always used the same simple tactic; and he had never lost.

Croker began to walk across the cobbled yard towards Lucky Sullivan. The other man was smiling and waving him forward. Small fellow with a round face. It did seem familiar. There was a tarry smell but Croker thought nothing of it. Croker reached the door.

"Are you ready?" said Lucky. "My money's on you. You won't let me down?"

Croker smiled and shook his enormous head. "I won't let you down," he said to Lucky. He felt powerful, strong, confident. "Now let me at him."

Lucky Sullivan moved aside and Croker stepped through.

He found himself in a large room but there were only a few people inside. That surprised him. And what surprised him more, they were not people. They were mummer types, in pointy hats that were flour sacks, with holes cut for eyes, and inside-out shifts decorated with ribbons. The tarry smell of hot pitch was much stronger in here than it was in the yard. He heard a grunting. He saw a figure in the corner, doubled up and tied with ropes, a flour sack over his head. Judging by the grey woollen trousers and the heavy brown work boots, this figure trussed up in the corner was Horace. At that moment he realised this was not a fight. He had been lured here and something terrible was about to happen. He wondered whether to run across to his brother. Or did he turn and bolt out the door? His body was in advance of his thoughts. His body was already turning. He was going to flee. He would push Lucky Sullivan aside and rush out. If he could get across the yard, out the gate, and round to the pub at the front . . .

Croker felt a tremendous pain on the back of his head. His knees sagged. Lucky Sullivan had whacked him. As he hit the ground, Croker had a blurred impression of trousers and boots showing below the hems of the shift dresses. The boots were running towards him, across the earth floor, and there were ugly-looking cudgels swinging through the air.

He curled into a ball and the blows began to fall. He felt a rope tightening around his ankles. His arms were forced behind his back, another rope tied around his wrists.

He was dragged across the floor. He was set against something. A wall. He felt heat. He was by the fire at the far end of the room. He felt the heat from the embers. The tarry smell was really strong here. It was a bitter smell that was a taste as well. Hit him at the back of the throat.

A smart slap on the face and a voice that told him to open his eyes, pay attention. Heat all down his arm. Croker opened his eyes. All around him, boots, and trouser bottoms, and shift hems. Croker sensed watchfulness. They wanted to see. They also wanted him to know everything that happened.

Someone was talking. The one in charge, judging by the sound of his voice. Croker realised that this figure was talking to him. The figure told Croker that he was to leave his neighbours alone, and keep his animals off their land. He was to leave the Bradys alone, as well. And so that Croker would never forget these instructions, the figure said, he was now going to be taught a lesson he would never forget.

The bucket of hot pitch was shown to him. Croker saw the vapours rising from the dark black surface. When it was hot, pitch had a shine that it lost when it was cold. The tarry smell from the bucket was overwhelming. He felt sick. He knew now what they were going to do. Pitch head. The voice was still talking. Did he understand? said the voice. Did he understand that he was to keep his animals off his neighbours' land? And that he was to leave the Bradys alone? Did he? Did he really understand? And did he understand the consequences of any further infractions of the law? Next time Croker misbehaved, said the voice, they would kill him.

"Sit him up," said the voice again. His hair was tugged and he was manhandled away from the wall. He was straightened up. Someone was behind him. He felt the toes of their boots jammed against his bottom. He felt a hot scorching sensation on his shoulder as he was hit by the first blob of pitch. The bucket was tipped. He felt something heavy pressing on his hair. It was wide and solid, like two great hands weighting down on his cranium from above. Then he felt an intense burning heat, first on his ears and down the back of his neck, and then all over his scalp, as the pitch ran through his hair and reached the skin underneath. He let out a terrible scream. He felt the pitch running slowly down his forehead and over his eyebrows. It was burning hot but thick, almost toffee-like. He closed his eyes and squeezed them. He must keep the pitch out of his eyes. At all costs. He felt a great surge of angry strength.

Croker pushed back. If he found the wall behind, and got his legs under him, he could use the wall to stand up. And if he could only stand, there was a chance he could drag his head along the wall, and scrape off some of this burning, hot stuff.

Someone shouted something. He heard a clang. He guessed it was the bucket hitting the floor. They'd dropped it. Next he heard the sound of boots on the floor. He heard a door opening. He heard the sound of boots clanging on cobbles. A peal of laughter. Then he heard a hoarse cry from his brother.

Croker had found the wall now, and he had got his legs underneath himself. He wanted to stand up. But as he went to stand up, he felt his body going soft. He slid back down to the floor. He was floating away again, just as he had when they started hitting him with the cudgels. He keeled over sideways, smelt the earth of the floor for an instant, and passed out.

The owner of the pub had been warned not to go into the back room, but Croker's brother shouted for so long and so loudly the owner decided in the end that he must go and see. What the publican found was a huge man with pitch in his hair, unconscious in front of the fire, and another huge man trussed with ropes in the corner.

The publican untied the Flanagan brothers. He fetched Croker's shirt and coat from the meal store and Croker dressed himself. The pitch had set. It looked like a tight black hat without a brim. Croker borrowed a blanket to cover himself. He wanted no one to see him like this on the journey home.

They got back to their cabin in the middle of the night. Horace lit the crusie lamps and woke the older brother, Malachi. The two siblings set to work. They rubbed butter into the pitch and softened it. Then they began to cut and hack at the thick hair matted with pitch. By the following morning, Horace and Malachi had cleared the mess. Horace told Croker that he looked like a plucked chicken.

The story was over.

"That's terrible," said Micky.

Croker took off his hat and stared across at him. The hair, cropped down to the head, had the straight, raw look of a freshly cut hedge, while the scalp beneath looked like wet ground badly trodden by heavy cattle. It was a mess of blisters, black tarry smears and red skinless patches.

He looked into Croker's eyes. Was the big fellow angry, vengeful, fearful? But Croker chose not to meet Micky's gaze. Croker looked away before Micky was able to decide.

"Do you know who they were?" asked Micky. It was a pointless question but he had to ask it.

Croker shook his head.

"Why have you come?" asked Micky. It was the obvious question. Why had he come if he wasn't going to name names?

"Horace overheard something," said Croker. He put the hat back on his head and pulled it down to his eyes. "This was after they tied him up, and before I went across."

They had hurt and frightened Croker very badly, but he still wanted to get back at them. Even when there was no safe way to do so, no one ever lost that instinct.

"Whatever it is, I never heard it from you," said Micky. "Not even Mrs Laffin will know you were here and we were talking."

"They've switched from Mr French."

"Oh."

"They can't get him. It's taking too long. That's what they said."

Micky sucked on the woody stem of his pipe.

"It's you they've decided on. The next time they get a chance, you'll be done."

Croker drew a finger across his throat.

After Croker left, Micky went to bed and lay in the darkness staring at the ceiling. His mind worked slowly. Micky smiled in the darkness. He would go and talk to his old friend Constable James Cleary.

Micky knew they'd switched to him, but *they* didn't know he knew. Now he knew this, there was a good chance he could catch them while they were waiting for him. Of course, any arrangements he made with the police would have to be discreet. He couldn't go marching around the countryside with a detachment of peelers at his heels. Just himself and one man would do, and he didn't doubt James Cleary would be up for it.

Thomas was woken by Helena shaking his shoulder. He opened his eyes to find the bedroom dark and a night-light burning on the bedside table.

"You have to get up," he heard Helena saying in her tender, coaxing voice. Since the afternoon in the wood, it was the only voice she ever seemed to use with him.

He watched Helena open the shutters. It was not yet dawn outside. He thought he could just make out the faintest glimmer of light on the eastern edge of the sky, the first fingers of light from the sun trying to edge over the horizon. The day was coming, but he didn't want to get up. He wanted to pull the covers over his face and wriggle down the bed. But he couldn't stay in bed. Today, no matter how tired he felt, no matter how dismal his feelings, he would have to get up, he would have to shave, he would have to dress, and he would have to go to Monaghan. He had to go. Micky had a plan. If he didn't go, it wouldn't work.

Yet at the same time as he knew this was what he had to do, he also did not believe he could manage any of it. Everything that had made him what he once was had gone. He simply dragged himself from one moment to the next moment, sustained entirely by a dumb capacity to endure. It was irrational, unthinking, but thank God, for this ability to plod on like a beast.

"Come on," Helena coaxed. He felt her take his arm. He felt her tugging him out of bed. He threw back the covers and swung his feet to the floor. Helena went on pulling and he stood up now. He let her pull him into the dressing room. All the candles were lit and he saw steam rising from the washing bowl. He realised that Helena had got up, lit the candles and got the hot water while he was asleep.

Thomas shaved, then Helena dabbed cologne on to his face. It made his skin sting. Then she led him over to the chair where his clothes were laid out. She helped him to dress. When he was finished, she tied his boots and combed his hair.

They went downstairs to the kitchen together. There was a fire burning in the hearth and the table was laid, cutlery and plates and saucers and cups and jam pot and egg cups. Helena told Thomas to sit. He sat.

Helena topped an egg, dug out some egg white and egg yolk, spread both on a piece of toast, and lifted the toast up to the edge of his mouth.

"Big day," she said. "You must eat."

Today was a big day. Yes. He was for the courthouse in Monaghan and the magisterial inquiry, and Micky was staying behind. Micky had a plan, didn't he? And he had to go, didn't he? Otherwise the plan wouldn't work. And would it work? Micky thought so, and if Micky thought so, that was fine with him. Whatever Micky said.

"Come on," he heard his wife murmur. "Just a mouthful."

She wormed the toast through his lips and past his teeth and he felt the warm coarse hot toast on his tongue, and the egg against the roof of his mouth.

"It'll do you good, make you strong," he heard his wife saying, talking at him as if he was a boy.

He was on a rocky path, he thought, in total darkness, save for a candle. He held this in one hand, while sheltering the guttering flame with the other. The wind was blowing and threatening to blow out the flame. If that happened he would not be able to light the candle again. He would be in total darkness then. He would lose his way. He would be finished.

Yes, eat, he thought, he must. Four men were to be examined by the resident magistrate, Willcocks, in Monaghan courthouse. He had to go, he had to be there, he had to watch. Yes. Must eat.

He closed his mouth and began to chew. He swallowed and his mouth was empty. Helena smiled. "Well done," she said.

Thomas left Beatonboro' under police escort, a little after first light. As the car went up the street, he saw Jeremiah Farrell, the local chimney-sweep, coming down the street on foot. Jeremiah carried his brushes in a sack on his back. Thomas knew Jeremiah. Jeremiah cleaned the chimneys in the estate office and at his home.

"Good morning, Mr French," the sweep called out to him. "And good luck."

"That was a strange thing to say," he said to the police driver, as the car rattled out of the village and into the countryside. "Why would he wish me luck?"

"A figure of speech, Mr French," said the driver carefully.

Thomas looked at the fields that flashed past, at the stands of trees that stood here and there between the fields, and at the grey and brown and black leafless branches of the trees, with the pale and gradually brightening sky behind them.

He was on his way to a magisterial inquiry under police escort, wasn't he? Later that day he would listen to the magistrate examine the four Lamb boys who were up for the charge. The funny thing was, he didn't think they'd done it. Why would four extremely religious young men kill Mr Barrett? Or Tim and Kitty, for that matter? He couldn't see them posting the two warnings on Barrett's church door. He couldn't see them shooting the old fellow. Or taking Tim and Kitty into the wood and doing what they did. Not four extremely religious young men like these ones.

Still, the Crown had a witness: this old fellow Mohan who had picked the Lamb brothers out of an identity parade in Monaghan jail. But at this parade the Lamb brothers had worn their own clothes while everyone else had worn prison clothes, so it wasn't so surprising the brothers were picked out by the witness. As many people in Beatonboro' had said, Micky included, it was not just highly irregular, it was a sign of desperation. The authorities didn't care about right or wrong, guilt or innocence, just as long as someone went to prison for these crimes.

His thoughts trickled on like this for a moment or two then stopped, and his mind went empty again.

Later that same morning, Micky stood outside the estate office smoking his pipe. He told everyone who passed that as Thomas was away at the magisterial enquiry in Monaghan, he intended to take off, after lunch. He woud walk home then by himself. If the weather held, he would fish. Turk McEneaney was one of those whom Micky spoke to. Turk went straight to Isaac's farm. He found Isaac in the byre, forking yellow, buttery-coloured hay to his cows. Turk told Isaac what he had heard.

"Good," said Isaac.

"Are you going to do Laffin today?" asked Turk.

Isaac went on working. He liked Turk but he trusted no one. "Go home," said Isaac.

Turk left. Isaac went and found his farm-boy, Joseph. He told Joseph to dig the garden. He went back to the house, put on his pea-green coat, and walked to Mellontown, two rows of terraced houses in the middle of the countryside.

Isaac found Rody in the street with Geraldine's three children. Rody was rolling a hoop along the ground, his stepsons chasing after him and laughing.

As soon as he saw Isaac, Rody rolled the hoop back to the children, and walked over to the older man.

"Where's Puck?" Isaac asked.

Rody nodded at the house. "Top room," he said.

Isaac went up to the top room and opened the door. He found Puck fast asleep. Isaac shook him by the shoulder.

Puck opened his eyes and said, "You've just woken me from a wonderful encounter."

"What with?"

"The Queen of Egypt. If I'm turning down Cleopatra, the news had better be good," continued Puck.

Puck and Isaac went down to the kitchen. Rody closed the shutters behind the front window and took the gun from the bottom of the turf box where he kept it hidden. Rody began to load the gun, watched by Isaac and Puck. There were no patches in the patch-box. Puck reached into the pocket of his coat that was hanging on the door, pulled out a handkerchief, and tore squares from opposite corners. He was careful, when he finished, to put the handkerchief on the table and not back in his coat pocket.

When the blunderbuss was loaded, Rody put it in a sack, muzzle upwards, so that nothing would fall out of the barrel. Geraldine came in from the pump with two buckets of water, her boys running behind. The boys saw the men pulling on scarves. They knew the men were getting ready to leave. Where were they going and when would they be back? the children wanted to know.

Rody told the children that he and Puck and Isaac were going off to rescue a cow that had fallen into a well. The place where they were going was dangerous and so they couldn't bring the children with them, he added.

As Rody was talking, the oldest boy noticed Puck's handkerchief on the table. He liked Puck and now, he realised, here was an opportunity to do something for the older man that would make the older man like him.

The boy ran to the table and picked up the handkerchief. At the very same moment, Isaac, promising each of the boys a coin, put his hand into his pocket, pulled out all his change, and began to search for three farthings. The two younger boys began to jump and clamour for their money. The room was filled with childish shrieks and adult laughter. No one noticed as the oldest of Geraldine's sons slipped Puck's handkerchief with the patches torn from the corners into the pocket of Puck's coat. The boy then ran to Isaac for his coin.

"Can I have money?" he asked.

"Of course you can." Isaac laid the last bown farthing on the hand stretched up towards him. At the same moment, Puck took his coat from the hook on the back of the door and pulled it on.

"Well, goodbye," said Rody. He kissed Geraldine on the forehead.

"I love you," she whispered.

"I love you too." He said this loudly. He wanted the others to hear and he wanted her to know that they had heard. Geraldine's face went red with pleasure and embarrassment.

The three men went out by the back door. It was February, cold and dry. The sky was covered with a thin white cloud, and the sun in the middle of the sky was round and very white, like the globe of an oil lamp.

The men walked to the end of the garden and went into the field at the back of Rody's house. The journey they were about to make would have to be across country. They couldn't go by road in case they met a police patrol and were searched and the gun was found. Since the deaths of Barrett, Kitty and Tim, the barony was proclaimed: it was prison or transportation if they were caught with the blunderbuss.

After walking for an hour, the three men arrived at the place where they planned to lay their ambush: it was a hairpin bend where the road swung around Malarkey's rock and doubled back on itself. This was the way Micky went home.

Puck and Rody got behind Malarkey's rock. It was ten foot high and covered with mould and liverworts. According to one local story, it had been fired from the catapult of a giant in county Kerry, and this was where it had landed. Isaac climbed to the top of the narrow spit of land between the two parallel stretches of road linked by the bend. Rody and Puck were a few yards below him.

"I see Laffin," Isaac called. "I whistle and duck. Then it's up to you two. Do you know what to do?"

Puck said, "We let him come along the road, we let him go around the bend. When he comes out on the far side, Rody shoots him from behind. I go down and cut his throat." Puck waved his knife. "Where will you be?"

"I'll be here," said Isaac. He had climbed into the deep crease that ran along the top of the high ground. No one on the road, whether coming from Beatonboro' or the other direction, would ever spot him up here lying down in this slit in the ground.

From his place at the rock below, Puck looked back up. He could just make out Isaac's head sticking up from the trench amid the ferns that grew everywhere.

"Did you clean her?" This was Puck again. "No, you didn't. Look at that barrel."

"That's dirt from the rock," said Rody patiently. "The rock we're sitting against." It was true. Green mould from Malarkey's rock had got on to the rim of the barrel.

"It's your day to keep her clean." Puck was unstoppable today.

"And you're a nagging old woman," replied Rody.

"Nah-nah-nah-nah-nah!" Puck sang back.

"Do you two always carry on like this?" said Isaac. He genuinely wanted to know.

"Yes." This was Rody.

"Don't you get tired?"

"Of each other?" said Puck.

"Never," Rody shouted theatrically.

"He's coming," hissed Isaac.

Isaac squeezed down into the crease in the ground. He could see Micky standing alone about fifty yards away. Isaac thought the bailiff might just have caught a glimpse of him, but Laffin couldn't see him now. Impossible. When they'd reconnoitred this spot the previous week, he'd got Puck to lie in the crease, exactly where he was lying now, and gone down to the road to see for himself. Isaac hadn't seen a thing then, so Micky couldn't see a thing now. So long as nothing aroused Laffin's suspicions, the bailiff would eventually start to walk again. He would walk along the road, and when he got to the corner, Rody and Puck would be waiting.

In their place behind the rock, Rody cocked the blunderbuss, and Puck spat on the handle of his knife and then gripped it hard.

"You hear that noise?" Puck whispered to the other man. " 'Tis the God Hercules, whom Antony loved, Now leaves him." He had learnt these and other lines from Shakespeare a long time ago from some travelling actors.

"Be quiet," ordered Isaac, and the two men at the rock fell silent.

Fifty yards away, Micky stood in the middle of the road. With his eye he followed the road to the hairpin bend where it swung around Malarkey's rock and disappeared. Cleary, meanwhile, hidden from Isaac's view, was crouched behind a gorse bush half a dozen paces behind Micky.

"What did you see?" asked the policeman.

"I thought I saw someone on the higher ground above the road," said Micky.

"Anyone there now?"

Micky could have sworn something had moved up there, but all he could see were ferns swaying in the wind, and the white sky behind.

"No one that I can see," Micky answered the policeman.

"This is what we'll do," Constable Cleary whispered. "The road doubles back on itself here. I'll sneak across to the other stretch and work my way back to Malarkey's rock. They won't be expecting that. If anyone's hiding round there, I'll get them from behind. Meanwhile, you stay here and give them something to look at. You're not to move unless I call you."

The policeman crept across the countryside to the parallel stretch of road. He looked up at the spit of land. This was obviously the place to put a look-out but he couldn't see anybody up there.

Cleary crawled slowly along the verge, keeping close to the

stone wall. A couple of minutes later, he passed directly below Isaac. Neither man saw the other.

When he got near the bend and Malarkey's rock, Cleary peered cautiously over the wall. His heart quickened. He saw two men waiting by the rock, both staring in Micky's direction. One man had a gun.

Cleary stood up quietly and pointed his carbine across the wall.

"Drop the weapon," Cleary shouted.

As soon as he heard the strange voice, Rody's first thought was to get the weapon as far from himself as he was able. He threw the gun into the air. It somersaulted twice, rebounded off the rock, and landed amid ferns with a dull thud.

"Hands up," said Cleary.

Rody put his hands up. Puck dropped the knife and put his hands up. Nobody moved.

"Micky," Cleary bellowed, "I've got 'em."

As soon as he heard the policeman, Micky hurried along the road. He appeared below Malarkey's rock a few moments later. He had his pistols drawn.

"What have we got here?" Micky called up.

Rody turned and smiled down at Micky.

"Move," said Cleary.

Puck and Rody stepped away from Malarkey's rock and jumped down on to the road. Constable Cleary picked up the blunderbuss and Puck's knife, and then jumped down after them on to the road.

The two prisoners stood back to back. Micky circled around them. He stared first at one face, and then at the other. These faces seemed incredibly familiar to him but he couldn't remember where he had seen them before.

"Walk," said the policeman to the prisoners. He gestured with his rifle in the direction of Beatonboro'.

Micky stepped sideways as Puck and Rody moved forward.

"Do you know these ones?" asked the policeman.

"Yes, but I can't remember from where," said Micky. Then

he said, "Oh, yes, I do. On the Crookedstone road, with Isaac and his friends."

"You do. Well, then," said the policeman, "maybe these are the ones who've been chasing Mr French."

In his hiding place, in the crease on the hill, Isaac lay quite still as he listened, first to these words and then to the footfalls of the four men as they walked away along the road.

The courthouse smelt of paint and lime. Thomas noticed these smells when he sat down. The bench he sat on was cold and slippery.

Mr Willcocks, the magistrate, ordered that the Lamb brothers be brought in. A bulky man came forward. Thomas heard the man introduce himself as Mr Lanesborough. He was not local. Belfast accent, by the sound of it. Counsel for the accused.

"Where is Mr Mohan?" asked Mr Willcocks. A lot of shuffling and muttering. Eventually it was explained Mohan had disappeared.

Willcocks demanded facts. Since the identity parade, a policeman explained, Mohan had lodged at Monaghan police station. Slept in a cell. All was well until the previous morning when Mohan had become agitated. He had walked out of the station in the middle of the morning. He had not been seen since.

Willcocks was annoyed. Couldn't some way have been found of keeping Mr Mohan? A police sergeant explained Mohan couldn't be kept locked up. He hadn't done anything wrong.

Mr Lanesborough was at the bench. Another man came forward. Thomas didn't catch the name. Farmer. Watery blue eyes. On the day in question, said the farmer, he had had the four Lamb brothers working on his farm. They'd rebuilt an old dry-stone wall. Done a good job, he added. An account book was produced where the Lambs' pay was listed. And suddenly that was that. It was over. The Lamb brothers and Mr Lanesborough were sweeping out.

Thomas left the court, and went and sat on another bench

in the hall. He had spent an entire day waiting around for absolutely nothing.

The police driver appeard and said, "Mr French."

He followed the man outside and got into the car beside two other policemen; each of these men held a carbine, stock on the floor, muzzle towards the sky.

"Beatonboro'," said the driver.

There wasn't anywhere else they were going but Thomas said, "Yes," anyway.

Familiar trees and fields flashed by; these signalled to him that they were nearly at the village. "Take me home," said Thomas. Then he heard the driver saying, "Oh, hello, what's this?" and he looked up.

The gate of his house was about fifty yards ahead and there was a sub-constable standing by one of the piers. As the car drew closer, the sub-constable put his hand up so there could be no misunderstanding: this was the car he was waiting on. When the car was five yards from the gate, the driver hauled on the reins and it came to a complete stop.

"What is it?" the driver called down to the policeman, who was hurrying forward.

"Message for Mr French," said the sub-constable, with a huge smirk on his face. "Mr Laffin and Mr Cleary send their compliments." The young sub-constable looked up at him. "They caught two fellows loitering on Mr Laffin's road this afternoon. And they recovered a weapon. A blunderbuss." Now the smirk turned into a gigantic smile.

"They'll have to be remanded into custody. You're wanted down the barracks as quick as you can."

Extract from Constable Cleary's confidential Patrol Diary, Tuesday 18 February
PUCK GARRETT. I know nothing about anything.
MR FRENCH. Simply sitting in the country, were you, smoking?
PUCK GARRETT. (*Pointing at Constable Cleary*).Yes, minding

my own business when that peeler came.

MR FRENCH. Favoured smoking spot, is it, Malarkey's rock?

PUCK GARRETT. Indeed.

MR FRENCH. It's in the middle of nowhere.

PUCK GARRETT. Go there all the time. Lovely sheltered place.

MR FRENCH. Where are the pipes? You don't have any on you.

PUCK GARRETT. Must have dropped them when we were arrested.

MR FRENCH. Really?

PUCK GARRETT. Yes.

MR FRENCH (*Points at blunderbuss on the table*). And you never saw the blunderbuss before?

PUCK GARRETT. Oh. So, that's a blunderbuss, is it? No, I've never seen one before.

MR FRENCH. It's not yours?

PUCK GARRETT. No. (*Turns to Rody Donohoe*) Look at the barrel, Rody. What a shine on it. So that's a blunderbuss. Well, you learn something every day, don't you?

MR FRENCH. The constable has sworn you were taken with this gun.

PUCK GARRETT. No.

MR FRENCH. He did say so. I heard him.

PUCK GARRETT. No, first he found him and me. Then he found the blunderbuss.

MICKY LAFFIN. Which you'd thrown away!

PUCK GARRETT. No, I didn't. Never saw it until now.

MICKY LAFFIN. It just happened to be beside you, I suppose, quite by chance?

PUCK GARRETT. That's what I said.

MR FRENCH. In which case (*holds up a handkerchief with its corners torn out*) how come the gun contained two patches torn out of this handkerchief which Constable Cleary found in your pocket?

PUCK GARRETT. Exactly.

MR FRENCH. Exactly, what?

PUCK GARRETT. Exactly as I would expect.

MR FRENCH. What? These pieces of material tore themselves from the handkerchief, flew to the gun and inserted themselves in the barrel?

RODY DONOHOE. Go on, tell him, Puck.

PUCK GARRETT. It was him – the policeman.

RODY DONOHOE. He tore out the squares . . .

PUCK GARRETT. And stuffed them in.

RODY DONOHOE. Your man, Mr Laffin, he saw it all, didn't you, Micky?

MR FRENCH. Take them away, take them away.

PUCK GARRETT. It's been a pleasure, Mr French, a real pleasure.

(Charged with possession of an unlicensed weapon in a proclaimed district, the prisoners were remanded into custody on the instructions of Mr French and removed to the cells.)

They were in the porch. As Micky stepped through the front door, Thomas noticed the chalky smell of geraniums. He sniffed the air. It was a smell he loved.

"Come on," Micky called from outside. Thomas stepped through the front door of the police station, and into the main street of Beatonboro'. It was balmy outside in the dark street and the smell of woodsmoke hung in the air.

"Do we think it's them? Those two were the same ones who followed me."

"Those two? Yes. Has to be," said Micky. "Or my name isn't Micky Laffin."

"What about the rest of it? Did they do it, do you think? I do."

Micky clamped his teeth shut and pursed his lips as he did when he thought. "Barrett and Tim and Kitty?" he said finally. "Who knows? Maybe. Probably. And if they didn't do it, then they certainly know who did, I'd say. But they're never going to tell us. Never. We could talk to those two for a month of Sundays and we'd never get the truth out of them." Micky shrugged his shoulders philosophically. "It's a disappointment, but there it is."

"So, if they're the ones who were after me, that's over now, and I can go home, alone."

Micky was silent for a moment as he pondered this. "I suppose," he said finally.

"They'll have to organise themselves again. That'll take a while. I'll be quite safe tonight, I'm certain of it. And I'll enjoy it. I haven't had a carefree walk for nearly a year."

The two men said good night. Micky went off to Martin Quigley's house, where he could hire a car to take him home at a very reasonable rate, and Thomas went the other way towards home.

When he came to his own gate he noticed a cluster of snowdrops growing around the bottom of the pier. He crouched down and squeezed one of the blooms. There was nothing fragile or delicate about the flesh. Like so many things in the natural world, it combined beautiful softness with fantastic solidity.

It was always going, the earth, it occurred to him now, like an unstoppable engine. First it forced growth; then it brought on winter and killed everything off; then it started growth again. Year after year after year, on and on it went.

A minute later he found Helena in the front room staring at the fire.

"Come and see something," said Thomas.

He marched her to the gate, wheeled her about and pointed at the clump of snowdrops in the shadow of the pier.

"Yes," she said.

"Aren't they beautiful?"

At that moment footsteps sounded in the darkness. Helena squeezed his arm anxiously, fearfully.

"It's all right," he said, "that's over. It's finished. I walked home alone this evening, in the dark."

In the darkness he saw the splayed, spiky outline of a chimney-brush sticking up behind the approaching figure and he realised who it was. "Good evening, Jeremiah," he called out to the sooty figure.

"Good evening," said the sweep. Jeremiah Farrell passed on.

"Badger," said Thomas, without any conscious thought.

"What?" went Helena.

"Badger. Black face, bright eyes, Jeremiah Farrell the sweep," he said. "Badger."

Her hand suddenly slid up and down his arm in a rush of real affection.

chapter fifteen

From the *Monaghan Bugle*, 19 April 1855, 2nd edition:

At the Courthouse

Yesterday, your reporter observed the trial of Puck Garrett and Rody Donohoe before Judge Leahy-Blood. Both men were found guilty of the crime of carrying arms in a proclaimed district, and both were sentenced to the utmost penalty the law allows for this offence – two years' imprisonment with hard labour. Neither man showed any emotion as he was led from the dock to start his sentence.

A few days after he received his sentence, Puck Garrett asked to see Thomas French and Micky Laffin. The two men went to see the prisoner in his cell in Monaghan jail. Puck explained that he could not serve his sentence. He confessed that he and Rody had conspired together to kill Thomas and Micky. He said he was willing to testify against Rody Donohoe in return for a new life, a new name, a new home.

From the *Monaghan Bugle*, 15 June 1855, 1st edition:

Unexceptional Scenes at the Courthouse

Rody Donohoe, who appeared in this newspaper only two months ago in the "At the Courthouse" column, in connection with his possession, along with one Puck Garrett, of a weapon without a licence in a proclaimed district, is once again in the public eye, this time on the far more serious charge of the attempted murder of the well-known and popular Beatonboro' agent Thomas French Esq. and his bailiff, Michael Laffin.

Perhaps the most interesting aspect of the case is that the chief witness for the Crown is none other than Rody Donohoe's erstwhile accomplice, Puck Garrett. Scenes of outrage and excitement, with each man denouncing the other, were expected by the authorities; this is usually the case when one man in a conspiracy turns approver. However, the behaviour of the parties during the hearing was exceptionally equable and even good-tempered, with the chief witness for the Crown doing all the speaking and the accused remaining calm. The exchange, which we reproduce in full below, represents the tenor of proceedings, as well as being the nub of the Crown's case against Mr Donohoe:

MR JOYCE (*for the prosecution*). Your name is Puck Garrett?
PUCK GARRETT. Yes.
MR JOYCE. Were you involved in a conspiracy to murder Mr French?
PUCK GARRETT. Yes.
MR JOYCE. Would you like to tell the court with whom you acted.

PUCK GARRETT. I can only identify one party to the conspiracy.

MR JOYCE. Go ahead.

PUCK GARRETT. Rody Donohoe.

MR JOYCE. Is he in this court?

PUCK GARRETT. He's sitting over there.

MR JOYCE. When did you meet Mr Donohoe?

PUCK GARRETT. Some time in March, last year.

MR JOYCE. Under what circumstances?

PUCK GARRETT. At a Ribbon court before a Ribbon judge.

MR JOYCE. Could you tell the court what happened on that occasion?

PUCK GARRETT. We were brought into a room. The Ribbonmen were masked then, as they always were. They told us Mr French was sentenced to death. We were offered fifty pounds as a start to put him away and more to come. We spent a year pursuing Mr French but we were never able to get him.

MR JOYCE. Surely you must have had a chance to shoot him at some point?

PUCK GARRETT. We had many chances to shoot him, yes, but he always had someone with him, usually Mr Laffin, his bailiff, and we knew Mr Laffin had been instructed to ignore Mr French, in the event of his being shot, and to pursue us. So, although we could have shot Mr French, there was never a moment when we believed we could both shoot Mr French *and* get away.

MR JOYCE. What happened then?

PUCK GARRETT. By the start of this year, we had received a hundred pounds from the Ribbonmen and still we had not once been able to come at Mr French. So we decided we would shoot his bailiff, Mr Laffin, instead. In February of this year, as we were waiting for Mr Laffin on the road he takes to his house – we were apprehended by Constable James Cleary. I received a sentence of two years with hard labour for possession of a weapon, the one with which we intended to kill Mr French. During the weeks of my confinement that followed, I had ample opportunity to reflect on my behaviour and I decided, in the interests of justice, and because of my thirst for a clear conscience, and a wish to make my peace with God, I would make known to the authorities our part in the conspiracy to kill Mr French and Mr Laffin.

Mr Donohoe offered no evidence in his defence to the court. The jury retired for forty minutes and when they returned gave a guilty verdict on the charge of conspiracy to murder. Lord Cantwell donned his black cap and sentenced Rody Donohoe to be hanged by the neck until he was dead. The prisoner made no reaction and was led away to his cell.

The day after Rody Donohoe was sentenced, Puck Garrett asked to see Thomas and Micky again. The two went to see the prisoner, this time in Monaghan police station where Puck was now held for his own protection. Since he turned approver, several prisoners in the jail had threatened to kill him. It was his last day in Ireland; the next day he was going to Canada, with a new name, to start a new life.

At this meeting Puck told the agent and his bailiff that he suspected Rody Donohoe knew the name of every Ribbonman in the country. Puck suggested to Thomas that he make Rody an offer: names in return for a pardon. Thomas went to see Rody. The prisoner was tempted at first by the offer but, in the end, he decided he preferred not to name names; he preferred death.

From the *Monaghan Bugle*, 14 July 1855, 1st edition.

Public Execution Ends with Bizarre Scene

Throughout the early part of yesterday morning, crowds of visitors began to drift into Monaghan town. Public houses reported a brisk trade but the atmosphere was far from joyful; our visitors had not come to socialise or enjoy themselves, but to witness one of the most melancholy spectacles known to man: a public execution – in this case that of Rody Donohoe, who was last month sentenced to hang on the unusual charge of conspiracy to murder the land agent on the Beaton estate, Thomas French, and the bailiff, Michael Laffin.

As the morning wore on, the crowds left the pubs and moved to the square in front of the jail. All eyes were focused on the iron balcony fixed to the outside of the jail wall. The rope with the noose on the end was plainly in view for all to see. It hung down from a metal bar that jutted out from the wall above the balcony. The mood of the people, as judged by your correspondent who stood among them, was a mixture of the sombre and curious. They had come to see a man die; many had brought their wives and children with them; presumably they believed the experience would be educational. They knew what to expect but they were also frightened by it.

Towards midday, a door opened and several figures stepped out on to the iron balcony; these included members of the prison staff, the county sheriff, a clergyman, and the prisoner, Rody Donohoe. The crowd fell immediately silent. The priest and the prisoner shared a few quiet words. The prisoner was pale but showed no other sign of fear. He did not speak. The rope was adjusted around his neck; but even then he did not falter nor flinch in the least, yet neither was there any appearance of defiance or braggadocio in his manner. The prisoner stood like a brave, firm man, whose mind was made up, calmly awaiting his death.

Next, a cap, usual on such occasions to conceal the distortions of the countenance, was placed over the prisoner's face. At that moment a single wild whoop was heard among the crowd, answered not long after by a shrill whistle. For a moment, your correspondent was left wondering whether a desperate and reckless attempt to mount a rescue was about to commence. The prisoner was known to associate with members of the Ribbon conspiracy in Beatonboro' and there had been much wild talk in the preceding weeks of springing him. But whether these strange sounds were intended to signal the start of a rescue attempt which then never materialised, or whether they were an expression of solidarity with the accused, or whether they were simply an expression of anguished feeling, your correspondent will never know; because a few seconds after these mysterious noises, the death signal was given by the sheriff, the iron bolt which holds the trap shut was withdrawn (this is managed from inside the jail), the trap door opened, and the prisoner dropped through the balcony, and hung suspended in the air. He scarcely struggled at all, dying almost at once, his neck (I am reliably informed) having been broken by the force of the fall.

The crowd now began to disperse. Your correspondent watched them leave, and was about to leave himself, when a car came into the square at speed, containing three passengers and a driver. The car drove straight to the front wall of the jail and stopped directly below the balcony. Acrobat style, one of the passengers climbed on to the shoulders of another and was then hoisted upwards towards the body. The legs of the dead man were now within the acrobat's grasp. To the surprise of your correspondent, and those few people left in the square, the acrobat then grasped the dead man's legs and swung from the body in what looked – as far as I could judge – like a determined attempt to see if the accused really was dead, and, if he wasn't, to make certain that he soon would be. In all my years on the *Monaghan Bugle,* I have never seen anything like this in my life. Nor had those who remained in the square. Shouts and jeers went up. A party of constables, who were standing near the corner of the jail, heard the commotion and rushed forward. The driver of the car saw the police coming and, after shouting to his colleague to let go the body, he shook the reins. But the acrobat was oblivious to the driver's cry. The car sped off and he was left holding on to the dead man's legs. The car, however, did not get far. The police stopped it and arrested the occupants. They also arrested the dangling man hanging on to the corpse.

Your correspondent now made haste to the area of the balcony in front of the jail, where the four perpetrators of the bizarre spectacle just described were being held by the police. I asked the now handcuffed acrobat to explain why he had done what he had done. In reply, he told me that as no man had ever hung for conspiracy in Ireland before, he sniffed a conspiracy himself. Believing the execution could have been a charade, a cruel deception on the part of the unscrupulous authorities to make the good people of Ireland believe someone had been hung when in fact they weren't hung, he had come to check for himself that the death sentence had been carried out. "I just wanted to be sure the fellow was truly dead," he concluded.

His name, as you may wish to avoid this man, was Isaac Marron, and tomorrow, along with his three associates, Alex Ward, Thady Burns and Turk McEneaney, Mr Marron will be explaining his behaviour to the magistrate in court, and your correspondent, for one, will certainly want to be there to hear what he has to say.

After he read the article in the *Monaghan Bugle,* Thomas asked Micky to invite Isaac to come to the office to discuss the terms of his tenancy agreement.

Isaac came on a Thursday morning. There was an exchange of pleasantries. The three men filed into Thomas's office. Thomas sat behind his desk. Micky stood at the side of the desk. Isaac was invited to sit in the chair on the other side of the desk. There were flowers in a jug on the table.

"How long have I been here?" asked Thomas.

"I wouldn't know," said Isaac carefully.

"A year and a half?"

"Seems right."

"I came here in January eighteen fifty-four, on the twenty-fourth of January, to be precise. Now that's a day I don't forget," said Thomas.

"So I was right," said Isaac. "You've been here eighteen months, more or less." Isaac was puzzled by the line of Thomas's questions but he didn't let it show.

"You were at the hanging?" said Thomas abruptly.

Ah, so that was what this was about, thought Isaac. "What of it?" he said coolly.

"Nothing – just, you were at the hanging, that's all," replied Thomas, mildly. "I'm just saying, I read about you in the newspaper and what you did to the body."

"You did."

"Did you enjoy doing what you did?"

"No."

"Why did you do it, then?" said Thomas, in the same mild voice.

"I don't have to answer that question."

"You knew Rody Donohoe, I presume?" The voice sounded a little harder now to Isaac's ears.

"Never clapped eyes on him until the hanging."

"Oh," said Thomas, disbelieving.

"I thought I was here to talk about my tenancy agreement but since I'm not, is there anything else you want to ask? Or can I be excused?"

"No, hold on. How's your farm doing?" said Thomas.

"Fine."

"How are the crops?"

"Good barley expected, potatoes coming along, the pigs are blooming."

"Do you need anything?"

"A hundred acres would do me nicely."

"I'll ask Mrs Beaton," said Thomas, smiling, "but in the meantime, have you everything you need to keep it neat and tidy just now?"

"Some lime would be nice."

"Some lime. Write that down, Mr Laffin. How much?"

"A couple of barrels."

"What about some gates?" said Thomas suddenly, and quite nastily.

"Gates!" They had been ordered but still not delivered.

"Yes, gates. Two nice new iron gates. I promised them a long, long time ago. I promised them, in fact, on my very first day, in this very office."

"That's right, I never did get them," said Isaac cautiously.

"I know you mentioned them to Micky, but why have you never come and spoken to me about them, then? Other than that day we met on the road outside Crookedstone."

"Oh, that was a terrible day. Those poor creatures, God rest their souls," said Isaac. He sounded genuinely sorry, to his own ears at least.

"But why did you never come and speak to me about these gates that you were so insistent on having?"

"They must have gone out of my mind, I suppose."

"Oh, surely not, surely not out of your mind."

"They must have. I can't think why else I forgot about them."

"But you didn't forget, or are you now forgetting that you didn't forget?"

"You've lost me there," said Isaac. He looked across the desk at Thomas, his face quite blank. "What was that you said?"

"You don't remember what you said?"

"I don't know what you're talking about."

"Is it not a fact that you once said to Mr Donohoe, 'Don't shoot French until I have my gates.' Now that sounds to me like a man with gates very much on his mind."

"I haven't a notion what you're saying."

"I'm only going on hearsay, of course. I wasn't there. But Rody Donohoe was there and that's what he told me you said."

"I don't know how you got that. I never saw Rody Donohoe in my life, alive. I only ever saw him dead."

"You never saw or talked to Rody Donohoe while he was alive?"

"No," said Isaac.

"That's not what he says."

"You mean, that's not what he said. You can't say 'says' of a dead man. You have to say 'said'. They're past tense, the dead."

"You're quite right. Anyway, that's what he said."

"It's his word – that of a dead man ..."

"Against yours – a living man, that's very true."

"Have you finished?" said Isaac.

"Well, do you still want the gates?"

"The gates."

"Really, that's all I wanted to know."

"I don't know."

"You seemed very anxious to have them on the day I arrived. And I know you spoke to Mr Laffin once about them since."

"That's true."

"So what happened? How come you don't need the gates any more? Animals not straying?"

"The cow and the pigs wander, they range around, and now I think their master might range as well," said Isaac slowly.

"Really."

"I think he will."

"Where?"

"Boston."

"Oh."

"The usual conditions, of course. My arrears waived, passage paid. I want the same terms as anyone who voluntarily gives up their lease," said Isaac bluntly.

"Of course, Mr Marron. And identical terms for Mr Ward, Mr Burns and Mr Turk McEneaney. Will you pass that message on to them?"

Isaac nodded as he stood. He would pass the message on to them. He went to leave, then turned and looked back at the desk. "I don't hate you, Mr French," he said. "You can't help your nature or what you are. But I hate you, Mr Laffin."

"The world isn't ever going to be the way you think it ought to be," said Micky, "with all of us stacked up on the right side, your side."

"One day it will. Goodbye, Mr French."

"Goodbye, Mr Marron."

Once the ping of the doorbell told him that Isaac had left the office and gone out into the street, Micky turned to Thomas and said, "You just told a lie."

"I did?"

"Rody never told us anything. You made it up, all that stuff about the gates."

Thomas smiled and said "Yes. It was an intuition. With my inner eye, I suddenly saw Isaac standing in his Ribbon outfit, and with my inner ear I heard him say, 'Don't shoot French until I have my gates.' "

Micky laughed when he heard this, long and hard.

Micky and Thomas were still wearing the guns they had put on eighteen months earlier. At the end of the day they took the guns out of their holsters and unloaded them. Then they took off their holsters. Then they sat at the table in Thomas's office and began to clean the guns carefully.

"There's a man I know," said Micky suddenly, "called Mixty Maguire. Do you know Mixty? Got a twenty-acre farm. Owns it outright. Not a tenant."

"I know who he is," said Thomas, rodding the barrel of a pistol with a rag and a piece of cane. As always, the gun oil made his nose itch.

"He was in the pub the other night, crying into his beer, 'Oh, they took my land, they took my land.' I hear this and think, What's this? Has he gambled it away? How's he lost it? So I says, 'When did you lose it?' and Mixty says, 'Recently.' So I says, 'Well, how long ago is recently? When was this?' And do you know what he says?"

"No."

"Mixty says, 'When Colonel John Beaton came from Scotland.' "

"Which was 1612, or thereabouts."

"You have to go very deep but there's the core. There was the start of what we had to endure."

When they had finished cleaning their weapons, Micky locked everything away in the gun cabinet. "This last year and a half, it's been a dirty business," he said, staring out of the window at their yard, bathed in late-afternoon sunlight. There was something about this time of year that he found melancholy. Perhaps it was the knowledge that the days were already getting shorter, and although it was imperceptible, the slow descent into winter had already begun. "We're Irishmen," said Micky, "but they'd have killed us, no bother."

"And then expected our children to live happily with theirs."

Suddenly Thomas looked at the older man and asked, "How many dead that we know of?"

Micky thought for a moment and then began: "Hugh McGuinness, poor old Sheridan, Mr Barrett, Rody Donohoe, I suppose we have to count him, Tim Traynor, Kitty McKenna – six." He held up six fingers.

"And O'Duffy," exclaimed Thomas.

"And O'Duffy," echoed Micky, lifting a seventh finger. "That's a lot of blood but it's not enough to turn the Mills of Louth. There's never enough for that."

"No, it's eight," exclaimed Thomas suddenly. "We've forgotten. Kitty's unborn."

"Right enough, Kitty's unborn . . ." Micky looked at the eight fingers of his hand. "Oh, it's a dirty business, all right," he said. Then he smiled. "Yet we keep on moving, don't we? We just look up and keep climbing the hill, pushing a rock in front of us as we go. There's no other way."

Thomas said nothing. He gazed at the empty fireplace while Micky went on staring into the yard. Outside, the sun slipped towards the horizon and the long shadows of evening began to stretch across the ground.

"Shall we go, then?" asked Thomas finally. He really must rouse himself, he thought, and go home.

"Why not indeed?" said Micky, but neither man made a move. They stayed in the room as it gradually grew darker and darker, each lost in his own thoughts.